Paul Stuart Kemp was born in C... ...in 1972. As an Engl... ...st the mainstream ... ...s popular fiction, a... ... British cities such ...

Paul Stuart Kemp ...

## by Paul Stuart Kemp

### <u>Novels</u>

Eden
The Unholy
Bloodgod
Ascension

### <u>Short Story Collections</u>

The Business Of Fear

# The Business Of Fear

## Paul Stuart Kemp

decapita

Published in Great Britain in 2003 by
Decapita Publishing
PO BOX 3802
Bracknell RG12 7XT

Email: mail@paulstuartkemp.com
Website: www.paulstuartkemp.com

Cover artwork by Giovanni Di Natale
Illustrations by Paul Stuart Kemp

Photograph of author by Jeanette Kemp

The Author asserts the moral right to be
identified as the author of this work

ISBN 0 9538215 5 2

Set in Meridien

Printed and bound in Great Britain by
Cox & Wyman
Reading, Berkshire

# The Business Of Fear

# CONTENTS

# Introduction

My name is Paul Stuart Kemp, I write horror stories, and this is my first collection of short fiction. I have published this collection myself, something which I have done for my previous four novels, and before we go any further I'd just like to say a few words about the business of self-publishing.

There are a few people in this world, usually critics, who demean and dismiss this perfectly valid form of publishing out of hand. They see it as cheating, as not really publishing at all, and if the work was any good, they say, then 'proper' publishers would snap it up like hot cakes. But what is publishing really? That's the real question. I write stories because I want you to read them, and if nobody else is going to publish them for me, then I know I'm sure as hell going to do it myself.

Publishers have a responsibility to make money for their shareholders, which is their perfect right, but the general trend today seems to be publishing for money rather than content. Now this might seem like sour grapes, and to a degree it is, but there are a lot of excellent writers not being given the opportunity to be published because of bullshit celebrity biographies and flavour-of-the-month TV tie-ins. So what I want to say to you now, my friend, is that my intention is not to mislead or to cheat you or anyone else by publishing my own work myself. I am not doing anything devious or underhanded because my fiction is not being published by a mainstream publisher with big offices in big cities. I write because I want my work to be read. And that is the bottom line.

Let me also tell you that I'm not doing this for the

money either, shamelessly scribbling twenty-odd shoddy stories and putting them quickly into book format just so I can sell them. So I'd like to make things perfectly clear, in a guarantee just between the two of us (and before you hear any tawdry gossip or defamatory rumours from anyone else), that I do this because I love writing and I want you to read my stories. That's it.

Okay, I feel a lot better for that, and I'd like to thank you for putting up with my rant, especially at the beginning of your new book.

So, the title of this collection is The Business Of Fear, and apart from being the title of the lead story, what does that actually mean?

Well, writing is a business in every sense of the word. There's training involved for a start, but that does not necessarily mean formal training. Writing is a craft, an ongoing learning experience, and writers need to work hard at it if they are to continue to get better. It has both investment and returns, profit and loss. I invest a lot of time and energy in creating my fiction, and I do it to the best of my ability in order to produce something that is both original and saleable. I am, after all, putting my name on everything I do. My name is my trademark, my personal guarantee, and my investment to you, my shareholders, because without you and your support, I am just some strange fucked-up guy throwing words into an indifferent and bemused cosmos.

My profits and returns are the letters and emails I receive from readers, and let me tell you that I am utterly thankful and grateful for them all. That is the reason why I continue to write, for the positive responses from those who buy and read my books. I also obviously receive royalties generated from book sales, which is something else I also enjoy (I'm not going to lie and tell you otherwise). But I still work for a living, just like everyone else.

Which brings us to the fear part of the title. This is what motivates me more than anything else, trying to scare you witless, trying to manipulate your emotions and hoping you might leave the light on for longer than you did the night before, constructing stories that might just make you check inside your wardrobe before you go to sleep at night.

If I can make you look behind you when you're out walking your dog in the woods; if I can make you look under your bed before you slip beneath the covers; if I can make you think twice about venturing out into the night because of what might be lurking hidden in the darkness, then I've done my job. I want you to be afraid, believing everything I whisper in your ear, believing that it might just all be true.

Now let's get down to business. It's time for you to turn the page. It's dark in there and you're going in alone. But if you get too scared, don't worry, I won't be too far away. Just pray that the hand that takes hold of your's belongs to me, and not to something that might lead you into even greater peril.

11th February 2003
England

# Death Of A Child

I see her eyes even now,
Staring back at me,
Cold and black and yearning.
She was dead when she was found,
In a makeshift grave of cruel black earth,
A husk of a body that was once so alive.

It was in the silent black woods,
At the back of the house where I live,
That someone came upon her body.
I don't know her name,
But she must have had one,
Spoken softly by someone who once had loved her.

I sit here now in the house,
At the front of those woods where I live,
Shivering and seeing her still.
I cannot conjure her a name,
For if I do she will come here and stay,
To live alone with me in my thoughts and dreams forever.

I cannot shake away those deathly black eyes,
I have to be cold in how I view her.
The television shows death as a matter of fact,
And it hurts me with relentless images of her.

I wish I had not seen those silent black woods,
or that makeshift grave of cruel black soil,
or that angelic face staring back at me so lifelessly
like a cold china doll.
But I did.
And she is dead.
And there is nothing I can do now but try and forget her.

Let me tell you something, my friend. Let me tell you a tale about the business of fear, for it is a business, an industry that constructs horror, manufactures chills, produces sights and feelings designed to scare. I've been that man, the constructor and the manufacturer, and it's brought me to where I am now.

I've lost everything. No, not lost, that's not right. I handed it all away, everything I had. I can remember clearly how it all went too, how the darkness that I had created thrust me deeper into a hell more terrible than my own imagination could ever conjure. But let me first begin at the beginning. My name is Kingsley Stevens. I am a horror writer. And this is my tale.

It is dark outside. Ironically, midnight has already come and gone, but the graveyard shift is still in full flow, and the fire that burns in the lonely grate warms only my outer skin. My bones feel numb, my teeth aching in a skull that feels like ballast, and my innards churn with bitter acid.

The house is empty, as quiet as a morgue, and my stomach aches with both memories and hunger. But do I really want to appease either? Do I deserve that after what I have done? Perhaps I should start somewhere after the beginning, perhaps that will make more sense. Very well, but I will be brief.

The clock on the mantle will chime at six, and I have set a bottle of pills next to it. I have given this night to think things through, given myself the graveyard hours to judge my own actions. I believe myself guilty already. What paltry defence I possess stands in the wings, uncertain, wary. What arguments can be made? What surprise witnesses can there be that have not already been called and cross-examined into insanity? The clock reads one fifteen. There is not much time. Let us begin.

It was a perfect blue-sky day when it started, and I sat staring out through the window of my study at nothing in particular. The sun was hot, the sky cloudless, and the trees that lined the edge of my garden drifted like verdant green sheets beneath the gentle cooling breeze. It had gone ten thirty and I remember that I'd made love to my wife less than two hours previous and showered and changed into the expensive silk shirt she'd bought for me last birthday. My new manuscript was plotting out really well, and my first feature film was to premiere at the end of the week. The world was sailing on high seas, and I was standing right on top of it. Nothing could have brought me down. Or at least that's what I thought. You see, that was when the phone rang. That was when I was first told that the deaths had started.

I'd had the second handset installed in my study after my first novel had been published, an act of self-indulgence I'll admit, but the advance of fifty thousand pounds had set me on my way to becoming a professional full-time writer, something I'd always dreamed of being, so I'd figured to flesh out the job as I imagined it would be. The book was called Butcher's Block, and my publisher had been excited about it from the beginning, a grisly murder story set to follow on from where Hannibal Lector had trespassed. Throats were slashed with razors and beheadings were commonplace, and all of them took place in urban tenements and kiddie's playgrounds. That was the beauty of Butcher's Block, to bring the blood and guts horror out of Vienna or Transylvania and right into people's front rooms. Where could you hide from a monster if your home was his hunting ground? The film rights were sold swiftly to an up and coming production company with a lot of money, who were just as eager to paint the cinema screens red. My life stepped up another gear, and on the rollercoaster went.

"I thought I should be the one to tell you, Kingsley," it was my agent, Dave Cuttlebauer, on the phone, "you know, before you read about it in tomorrow's paper."

"Read about what?"

Two squirrels were chasing each other across my manicured lawn towards the trees, their tails bobbing madly behind them. They reminded me of the two cartoon chipmunks on TV, Chip and Dale.

"It's about Silver Moon..."

Silver Moon was the name of the film. They changed it from Butcher's Block, which I preferred because it had ramifications about the murderer and the grisly deaths that took place, but Dave Cuttlebauer agreed with the film company and said that the public would never go for it, and so it became Silver Moon.

"What about it? The premiere's still going ahead, isn't it?"

"Oh yeah, don't worry about that. The thing is, one of the senior editors was going over the film, and she kind of... well..."

"What?" I wanted to know.

"Well, she kind of died."

My breath froze when he told me that. Even the squirrels stopped chasing each other as though they'd overheard the conversation.

"The paramedics seem to think that she had a heart

attack."

The line went silent for a few moments after that, and then Dave Cuttlebauer went on:

"And if that ain't the biggest promotional sensation of the year then I don't know what is."

I was dumbfounded. A little sickened too about what he'd said, and a long way queasy, but his shallowness just kicked me like a crazy mule. I should have known then but it was all too late. I was in the business then, my name had been printed on book jackets and on film posters just like I'd always dreamed of, and there was no going back. Not then.

"Listen to me, Kingsley. The paper's are going to get hold of this and go ape-shit - New horror film scares woman to death. I tell you, there ain't no budget in the world that could buy you publicity like that, especially for a horror film. Not even all that Blair Witch hype comes close."

I still couldn't find any words to say to him. What the hell was there to say? My head was going crazy, trying to work out just what I'd been told, sifting through the metaphors and Dave Cuttlebauer's newest plan to take the movie-going public by storm.

"So she was scared to death?" I finally managed to say to him.

"Fuck, who knows, she'd probably been diagnosed with a condition for years. But that's not the point, though, is it? She saw Silver Moon and it killed her. That's the only headline you need to worry about. We're hitting the box offices hard this weekend, my man, I can tell you."

"I guess so."

"Look, don't worry about it. I just wanted to call you to give you the head's up before you pick up whatever paper you're going to be reading in the morning. The film didn't kill her, that's just stupid, and it's sad that she's gone, but the fact remains that it'll boost ticket sales phenomenally. Have a good day, Kingsley, and I'll see you Friday night for the big kick off."

"Yeah, thanks. See you Friday."

The line clicked dead and I replaced the receiver with slightly numb hands. Dave Cuttlebauer was right, it was good publicity and it would help my career no end, or at least that's what I thought at the time. Yet it didn't exactly seem like something I'd be proud to put on my business cards.

Kingsley Stevens
He'll Scare You To Death
Literally

After that call, I just couldn't get my head round the new manuscript sitting on my desk in front of me. I had a title roaming about in my head, Whorefrost, and I'd had it for some time and liked the double meaning. But I was having problems making it stick to any kind of a good idea. It was going well before, and I'd roughly plotted a tale about a woman who becomes cursed by an ice goddess before taking sexual vengeance on a family staying in a cabin built over her resting place. It had seemed good before, but after that phone call I thought it just stank. A fucking ice goddess, what the hell was I thinking? I tore the text off the writing pad, leaving only the title sitting at the top of the page, and threw it in the bin. Then I pushed myself away from my desk, deciding to leave the whole thing for a while, and went downstairs to find Catrina.

She was outside, busying herself with her herb garden out on the patio. She looked up as I stepped onto the stones but returned to her patch of coriander and rosemary.

"Silver Moon's killed somebody," I told her bluntly.

"Has it?" she replied, without looking up.

"Someone died while they were watching it."

Cat turned her head this time, but her gardening gloves continued weeding, continued turning over the dark earth.

"What are you talking about?"

I walked round so that I stood right in front of her.

"Silver Moon. One of the editors was doing some work to it and she had a heart attack."

Catrina looked confused but resolute in her answer.

"That's not your film, love, she probably had a heart problem."

"I know, I know. But Dave Cuttlebauer said it would be great publicity, you know, a horror film that scares people to death."

Cat smiled at this, and I could see all the headlines of the publicity myself, so I felt kind of stupid acting like I was. This was like the best thing that could have happened, and yet somebody was dead - really dead, not just horror film dead.

"He's probably right," she said, but she could see the concern on my face. "Look, people have heart attacks all the time, especially in that industry with all the stress and everything. It's sad that she died but you can't beat yourself up over it, it's not your fault."

"I know," I said again, and wandered away to inspect the lawn, leaving her to get back to her herbs.

I knew the truth of it, of course, but it was just the way Dave Cuttlebauer had blurted it out - your film's killed someone - it was like a prosecutor pointing the finger. And Catrina was right, I knew that too, these film people must be riddled with ulcers caused by stress, and a heart attack was just the final straw. What was I getting so worried about, that was their question, and at that point they were right. Who could've known what would happen? No, everyone expected the paper would come out the following morning and my film would get a mention between pages three and six, a small but handy scandal to increase box office ticket sales, and that would be that.

As it turned out, the following day's newspaper ran a disrespectfully short piece - article was too big a word for it - and I had to search for it to find it just before the centre pages. Editor dies in cutting room, was all the brief headline said, and then there were just three paragraphs following. No photograph of any kind, neither myself nor the film poster, not even the late editor. Whatever publicity might have been gleaned was gone. And it suddenly felt to me like she had died for nothing.

By Friday the whole incident had pretty much gone from my thoughts. It was the night of the premiere, and Catrina and I were picked up in a limo that Dave Cuttlebauer had arranged, to take us into London. I guess I had been kind of fooling myself about what the premiere would entail. I mean, I'd seen all the pomp on TV surrounding premieres for films like Titanic and Reservoir Dogs, crowds of people flocking to see the stars as they arrive. Silver Moon had no stars, at least no Hollywood A-list stars, so the limo pulled up at a kerb devoid of anyone except passers-by. We were both wearing full evening wear, and even though that was my film up on the billboard outside, and my film about to play for the first time inside, I still felt kind of stupid crossing the pavement to step inside a cinema with strangers watching, their expressions confused and wondering why they didn't recognise us.

Dave Cuttlebauer met us in the foyer as we entered and shook my hand enthusiastically.

"See, I told you I'd get us all here one day, didn't I?"

"That you promised," I said to him with an uneasy smile.

He ushered us through to a box overlooking the main auditorium, and there we sat, just the three of us. The film went well in general, I thought - a bit laboured in some places, some of the more important characterisation brushed over - but Dave Cuttlebauer reminded me that when they have to cram 160,000 words down into 90 minutes of celluloid, sacrifices have to be made. But my characters were mostly up on screen, speaking mostly dialogue I had penned myself, and my name rolled at the end. So it was pretty much a kind of deja-vu bliss for me for that hour and a half. The after-show party, however, was to be held in one of the distributor's residences in Kensington, but as we left the cinema and started for the limo that was waiting at the kerb, I noticed a woman standing less than twenty yards from the door. She was dressed in a glittering evening gown, so I assumed that she had been part of the premiere's audience. But she was not as joyful as I, in fact her face was one of distress. Her eyes were wide inside a mask of pale skin, her bottom lip trembling as if tears were close. I didn't break my stride as our eyes connected - Catrina was holding onto my right arm, and Dave Cuttlebauer was talking briskly into my left ear - but my heart lurched as I caught sight of something glinting in her right hand.

We could only have been half a dozen more steps away from the car when it happened, but I couldn't help my cry when it slipped, as the woman raised the knife to her throat and pulled it swiftly across.

I felt someone take hold of me as my legs buckled, but so suddenly did the strength drain out of me that neither of them could have saved me from falling to my knees. I hit the pavement hard. I remember hearing my knees crack on the concrete as I watched the torrent of blood spill from her neck, washing down over her glittering evening gown like a red sea. She stood upright for a few moments, teetering on her heels, her eyes stark and wide and intent upon me. Her lips parted and closed as though she was trying to speak, but what words she wanted me to hear I neither heard nor understood. She toppled suddenly, her head sagging back upon its severed stalk, her knees buckling, as she fell vertically downward in one swift motion.

Catrina and Dave Cuttlebauer were still clasping me with wide hands, keeping me upright, and checking me over with open palms. They hadn't seen her, hadn't seen what I had seen, what this woman had wanted me to witness. I didn't know that woman but she had wanted me to know how my film had affected her. She had seen Silver Moon and been terrified by it. Something had disturbed her, to the point where to take her own life was easier than to live another moment in a world where the horrific murders of Silver Moon could be possible. I had brought a sick and brutal murderer into her world, I had made that possible, and she had seen the reality of what could be. The thoughts that had turned inside my head, the thoughts that had made my serial killer, had claimed another life.

That was the second death and it was already two too many. The ambulance came and went, and the police asked all the questions that they could ask, Catrina and Dave Cuttlebauer repeatedly telling me how insane it was to blame myself. But who else was there? Something had come from my own imagination, from some dark pit inside my head, that had caused two women to make a choice, involuntarily or not. What the hell did that make me? What lurked inside me that could cause something like that? It was a question that I had to ask myself, and the more I asked it, the more I risked every sane notion I had.

It would have been easy to argue metaphysics and religion all that night - had freewill created Butcher's Block, was the devil playing out some cruel scheme, or was I simply capable of dreaming up the most horrific of possible nightmares? How does that make me any different to a real serial killer, except that I kill with words - the deeds are still there, the intent, the pleasure and the desire to see blood flow by my hand? What was I doing every time I went to my study to write a little bit more of that book? Was it murder, slow but deliberate? I didn't know then, and if I'm honest I still don't know now.

It's nearly two o'clock. The pill bottle sits beside the clock like a brown time-bomb. Is it that that's ticking, or is it the clock itself? It's getting difficult to tell anything apart anymore. My head hurts with questions, my eyes too from searching the wretched darkness of this room, but you never saw that woman, you never saw her neck open like a knife through an overripe melon. You know shit about it, and I pray to

24

God that you never do.

I never saw that first woman die, but I've seen it in my head a thousand times; the convulsions, the thrashing fit, her mouth awash with spraying foam. With my eyes closed her agony is vivid, with them open the heartache of what I have done forces my eyes clenched with grief. I want my body numb, my twisted innards to be gone, but the pain remains.

You might think that that would be all, but you'd be wrong, my friend, so very wrong. Silver Moon was to go on general release the following week, and things were about to get a whole lot worse. I think you know what's coming, but there was nothing I could do about it. Companies had invested big, and they wanted their return. Perhaps it's a good thing that horror films attract smaller audiences than most of the trash that the industry generates, but the body count still rose. It didn't take the article that was printed in the papers the day after the premiere to bring in the crowds, but once they started coming to see what the 'suicide movie' was all about, the death toll just steadily grew. Sixteen people died that first week, all by their own hand, and a lot of families began asking questions, demanding answers from the filmmakers and from me. Dave Cuttlebauer told me to keep a low profile, just to be on the safe side, and to keep out of the line of fire until things quietened down. But things didn't quieten down. And by the end of the second week a further twenty seven people had committed suicide.

Cinemas across the country finally pulled the film shortly after that, and the police stepped in to investigate. They interviewed everyone - the producers, the director, myself and my wife - but there were simply no grounds to take the investigation further, and so the case was abandoned.

The film itself was shelved rather than destroyed, but I was glad that at least it was gone from public sight. But then word got around that illegal copies had found their way onto websites, and what becomes banned soon becomes hot property. Lawyers did their best to halt access to these sites, but it was too late. Downloads were skyrocketing and deaths soon began to be reported internationally, copies of the film found on every one of the deceased's computers.

Eventually even those website hosts found some moralistic viewpoint, with pretty much all of them pulling the plug on their copies of Silver Moon. The damage had been done, however, but it seemed certain that the death toll had pretty much ceased. My name, of course, was associated with every death and suicide, and far from being praised as having done my job well, I was being branded a murderer and worthy of either imprisonment or the death penalty.

It's now two twenty-five, and I can't see any other way out than to swallow the contents of that brown pill bottle. What defence has there been so far; that I was only doing my job as a writer? That just doesn't swing it. You could say that by definition I'm probably the most successful horror writer ever - I've scared dozens of people to death, what horror writer has ever done more?

But that didn't lead me to where I am now, sitting alone in an empty house, oh no. I still had my money and my possessions, I still had my wife beside me telling me everything would be okay; I even had royalties coming in from the film for Christ's sake. No, I've told you about the beginning of my tale, or rather somewhere after the beginning. Let me tell you now what happened after all the suicides from the initial film screenings.

The hate mail was inevitable, after all the anger and loss that came about in the wake of the deaths, and at first all the letters came to me via my publisher. Book sales were up after the cancellation of the film, the public thinking that this was a safe way to find out what all the fuss was about. But my publisher chose to take Butcher's Block off the shelves, thinking it bad taste to continue, and not something they wanted their company to be associated with either. Not only that, but they wanted their fifty thousand pound advance back too, in exchange for returning the publishing rights.

I was at an all-time low, and even Catrina began to despair. But when hate mail started coming direct to the house, packages too, of dog shit and dead animals in boxes tied up with string, things spiralled downwards at colossal speed. Cat and I both began to get scared then, both began to think that maybe things wouldn't get better, that maybe this would haunt us for the rest of our lives. Our home address was out in the world of the crazy and the furious, probably on those same websites that had made Silver Moon so readily downloadable. It was only a matter of time before someone arrived on our doorstep with a knife or a gun, so Catrina gave word to Dave Cuttlebauer of what was going on and then we split. Needless to say we didn't tell him where we were going; partly because we didn't know ourselves, and partly because to admit that was to invite insanity.

It was six weeks after Silver Moon had premiered and I didn't want to think how many people were in the ground because of me. Catrina, although much quieter and more withdrawn than her usual self in the wake of the aftermath, seemed largely unaffected by the film itself, for which I was glad. She'd read everything I'd ever written, all my short stories and unfinished novellas, including all six drafts of Butcher's Block, so perhaps that explained why she hadn't been disturbed by the film. She knew what went on inside my head, perhaps more than me, and knew it was all fictional - or at least that's what she consistently claimed - so that was some small comfort. It had crossed my mind so many times since that premiere that that was it with my writing, it was over, no more would I write another horrific or grisly story. And yet there I was, sitting in a hotel room with my wife, two hundred miles from our home, the threads of my life spinning themselves out in a plot inside my head. I couldn't help it. Parts were already becoming fictionalised, new characters being introduced at a furious pace where ones needed to be: a flirtatious assistant for Dave Cuttlebauer, a shell-shocked sister for Catrina. I tried to stop but it just kept coming. Should the death toll increase? Would that heighten the horror? Would the hotel manager get a knife across his throat for disclosing the horror writer's whereabouts to a website host?

The ideas continued to flow, my own mind condemning me deeper and deeper into a hellish void of my own making. I sickened myself, but I kept thinking - you're a writer, this is what you do. Even as I sit here recounting my tale to you, I cannot honestly say whether some part or other is fabrication. Is everything accurate? I no longer know. Did events happen as I have said?

The facts have slipped and contorted into a better

way of telling, but do not pity me, for the main story ultimately remains the same. I have killed people, with words and with ideas - the embellishments merely colour the narrative.

I have suddenly become my own main character, struggling to overcome forces that have reared up to claim me. Will I overcome them? Will I survive to face the final page? Does it even matter, for that in itself is an embellishment?

Lies, all of them. The fire in the grate has guttered into cloudy grey embers, filaments of orange glowing dully between them. I can only hang my head and think out loud. But that is the problem, isn't it? When I think, I write things down, I manoeuvre them, change them, distort them into something hideous and malformed, and all in the name of fear. My thoughts do not stop, even now, but just keep on coming, distorting my own life, my own fears, in order to make them worse and therefore more terrible. The clock is approaching three. But why wait to take the pills, why wait to kill myself and have it all over and done with? What contribution can I make that can possibly make amends for what I've done?

I reach over and take hold of the brown pill bottle. It is light in my hand. Strange that something so small and so insignificant can take a man's life. Turning it in my hands feels unworldly. Is this all it takes to deliver me into oblivion and end all this hurt and pain. But who am I kidding? It's not hurting, and it's not pain. It's guilt, that's all, pure and simple. I can't live with this guilt, and I'm taking the chicken shit way out. I can see all the tiny white pills inside, coloured pale brown by the plastic of the bottle, and I am mesmerised by them.

I jerk in my chair as the rumble of thunder shudders the night air outside, reverberating through the roof and the walls of this house. I half look up, my ears now acute to the sound of the world outside. The leaves are moving in the trees, and somewhere they have found one of the windows, tapping against the pane.

Returning my attention to the pill bottle, I am surprised at how easy the cap turns in my hand. Suddenly the bottle is open and tiny white pills spill out onto my open palm. I glance up at the clock. It has just turned three. This was my life; that's all I can think now as I begin to place the pills on the back of my tongue and swallow.

I'd thought that when the time came, I would simply throw back my head and swallow the lot in one swift motion. Now that the deed has begun, I cannot go through with it so quickly, cannot end my life so fleetingly. Surely there should be some gesture, something to note the passing.

I place another on my tongue and swallow. What do I think will happen? That someone will rush in to save me in the nick of time? Nobody knows I'm here. There will be no saving of Kingsley Stevens, not now that I've started my own suicide.

Thunder growls around the room again, rumbling overhead in the rafters, shaking the foundations beneath my feet. I swallow a third pill, my fingers shaking as I do so. What will death be like? Will it hurt? Will I fall into a stupor like a drunk and know nothing?

A fourth slips down and a flash of lightning illuminates the entire room with a flickering blinding starkness. Perhaps this isn't such a smart idea. Perhaps something good will come from the whole incident after all. My fingers feel numb, but they are learning the motion now, picking up a pill and bringing it to my lips. My mouth too has learned well, manoeuvring my tongue to accept it, swallowing it down swiftly into an empty stomach.

The thunder claps loudly again, rocketing the room as if to shake it to pieces. The wind too has picked up as the storm grows nearer, harrying the trees outside, shaking the leaves hard against the glass in some other room of the house.

I continue to feed pills into my body, not knowing whether my light-headedness is my imagination or the bridge to some lethal state. Is it already too late? Could I still turn back?

My head jolts suddenly. Pain sears through my neck, my eyes wide, as lightning once again lights up the room. Are those ghosts staring back at me from the flickering shadows, their talons waiting to scratch deep into my flesh. I see that my hand is empty, the pills all gone, the brown plastic bottle somewhere at my feet; but a blanket of darkness sweeps almost immediately down over my vision, stealing the sight from me, as I feel death tugging my body mercilessly towards it.

I have lost all feeling in my hands and feet, and my limbs are like lead. A burning pain has gripped my abdomen and festers like a small fire. Somewhere outside my head I hear the booming rumble of the storm as it continues to shake the building, and the window that had struggled to keep out the tempest suddenly blows inward in a jangling of glass as the bough finally smashes its way into the house.

I am sucked into a void away from that, my body bustled and battered like a tiny boat caught up in the vast tides of a tumultuous ocean. Snatches of livid colour slash the blackness all around me, burning the air, searing what was once my flesh. Vicious screams now cut the air like the cries of harpies, the ghosts that had watched me from the shadows of my room, and I see their talons unfurl, ready to tear me apart.

Other forms loom in the swirling madness, shapes and figures, all of them screaming. I see faces torn with anguish, slashed to ribbons or burned to ash, necks opened, wrists slashed, skulls gouged and cracked. And then I see the face of the woman who chose to open her own throat in front of me outside the cinema, I see it clearly amongst all the horror that is still descending swiftly around me, and then I understand. I've delivered myself into the hellish limbo reserved for the suicide, halfway between heaven and hell but never to see either, and granted them one last fit of revenge.

Their teeth are growing, their claws unfurling, and I shut my eyes as I wait for what I deserve.

But do not pray for me.

Never ever pray for me.

# Bad Kitty

Lys eased open the shiny brass letterbox and peered into the dark hallway, the familiar jingles of the radio noticeable by their absence. She called out her grandmother's name, and then listened hard as her words failed to penetrate the stillness. She tried knocking on the front door again, but it seemed certain that Irene was not at home.

Turning round to study the front lawn, as well as the quiet street on which the house sat, Lys tried to find some clue that might be waiting there for her. Yet she discovered nothing but the attentions of a small ginger cat surveying her from the wall of the house on the opposite side of the street. She looked back at the front of her grandmother's house. Two milk bottles sat beside the doorstep in front of the tiny cellar window. Why wouldn't Irene have taken them inside, she wondered?

Unable to think straight, she went to the front window and gazed into the living room, putting her hands either side of her face to shield the daylight. Everything seemed to be in its place, but there was still no sign of her grandmother. Before continuing round to the back of the house, she glanced back over her shoulder. The small ginger cat had disappeared from its spot on the wall. Off to catch a mouse or two, she mused.

The back garden, when she reached it, was a little overgrown if anything, but nothing else. The washing line was bare, the bird table nearby littered with scraps. Lys frowned as she approached the back door. Everything seemed fine, she thought, and yet something gnawed at the pit of her stomach to the contrary. She knocked lightly before trying the handle. It turned, and slowly she pushed the door open. As she went to step inside, however, she noticed a movement from the corner of her eye. Glancing down, she caught sight of the ginger cat sitting in the shade beneath the hedge. She half-smiled at its interest in her, enough to cause it to follow her from across the street. And yet now that the cat was closer, it seemed so much larger than before. It held her gaze briefly, studying her, its eyes glittering, before she turned away and stepped across the threshold.

Once inside, she stepped across the linoleum towards the counter. She tried her hand near the kettle but it was cold. Her mind began to play perverse games with her as she saw a number of cat hairs on the surface of the counter and also across the floor, and she wondered just how the cat from outside could have found his way in. But then she recalled Irene's own cat, Caesar, a slim black creature with bright yellow eyes, and her fears diminished. The thought of him made her glance down at the floor, where in the corner of the room sat Caesar's food and water bowls. Both were empty. Strange that her grandmother should forget about her beloved Caesar. Lys stepped across the kitchen and went down on her haunches in front of the two bowls. Both were completely dry. They had obviously not been filled in days.

Lys pushed herself to her feet with a slight shake of her head and wandered through into the hallway, calling Irene's name as she went. Again there was no answer. Lys was starting to panic now. Irene had not answered any calls she had made all week, which was most odd, and now it seemed as though she was not even in the house. With her heart beginning to beat faster, she quickly ascended the stairs, hurrying through into the main bedroom. The bed was neatly made, and the blankets had been turned down. Everything was in its place on her small bedside table, including the pill bottles she always kept with her. Even the next of kin card with Lys's own details on was in place. She frowned as she stared perplexed at the bed.

Slowly she crossed the room to the window and gazed down into the street. Where could she be, she wanted to know? She could barely go outside on her own, and she spoke to her on the phone at least three times a week. She would have told her if she was going somewhere. It just didn't make any sense. Her gaze dropped down into the street again and came to rest upon a large grey cat on the pavement, its thick bushy tail curled up around its feet. It licked one of its extended paws a number of times before it stopped to look up at her. Its gaze suddenly seemed impenetrable, and after only a few moments Lys forced herself to look away, her heart suddenly beating more quickly. When she finally chanced a second look back at the street again, the grey cat had gone.

With her head still in a daze, she wandered back to her grandmother's bed and perched on the edge of it. A number of cat hairs littering the sheets caught her attention - Caesar's, no doubt - and carefully she brushed them away. Speaking of which, she thought, just where was Irene's cat? She'd not so much as seen his tail since she'd set foot in the house. Unless he'd run out in search of a full food bowl.

Lys pushed herself to her feet and stepped back out onto the landing. At the top of the stairs she called

Caesar's name. She waited a few moments but there was nothing. Finally she doubled back and poked her head around the bathroom door, just to make sure Irene had not stumbled and fallen, before she headed back downstairs.

The door beneath the stairs that led down to the cellar stood slightly ajar, and Lys felt sure that it had been closed before she had gone upstairs, although she wasn't certain. Slowly she crossed the hallway towards it, her eyes fixed on the sliver of darkness visible between the door and the jamb. The metal of the handle was cold as she put her hand to it, and as she gently pulled, she listened intently to the darkness in the cellar beneath the house.

It sounded unlikely as she listened, but she thought she could hear a low breathing, plus a scrabbling sound that came in fits, yet she couldn't be sure that it wasn't coming from the street outside. It might also have been the wind, she reasoned, whistling in through a gap somewhere. Lys eased the door open a little wider, pushing her face close to the widening gap, her eyes straining against the gloom. She had only been in her grandmother's cellar twice before, and although she could vaguely recall the layout, she failed to find the light cord when she reached her other arm into the darkness for it.

Lys took a breath and chanced her head through the door, gazing quickly down the unlit steps in the hope of finding Irene there. Echoes of light from the sunlit world swirled before her vision for a few uneasy moments, disorienting and startling herself as she fought to see through them. Her hand swept blindly out for the light cord again. She missed and stumbled forward a step, catching her balance just in time as something brushed against her shin. She let out a scream of panic and pushed herself back out into the hallway, staggering weak-legged until she hit the wall on the other side. She stood there panting, clutching herself, her eyes forced wide and gazing down in disbelief as the slim black shape of Irene's cat, Caesar.

He stood in the doorway to the kitchen, completely unabashed, and watched her with dispassionate and unrepentant yellow eyes, his head cocked slightly as if to regard this most pathetic of intruders. Her hands were still shaking, but she managed a small smile for this ownerless creature, and went towards him, scooping him up off the floor and carrying him through into the kitchen.

"You bad kitty," she scolded him playfully, stroking his head. "You gave me the most awful fright."

Caesar raised his head indifferently to her, seemingly ignoring her attention, and let her take him towards the counter.

"If you haven't been out, you must be very hungry," Lys said to him, setting him down before searching the cupboards for a tin of catfood.

She glanced back at him when she found a tin of chicken. He was standing exactly where she had left him, and he was still regarding her somewhat suspiciously. She tried to smile at him again, but couldn't. Pulling open one of the drawers, she took out the tin-opener and set to opening the chicken. Still the cat surveyed her with his unblinking yellow eyes, even as she slopped the meat and jelly out of the tin and into his food bowl. She held open the bin with her foot and dropped the empty tin into it before stooping to fill his water bowl from the tap. As she set it back down on the floor next to the untouched food bowl, she glanced up to see that Caesar had not moved an inch. He was still watching her, and it was beginning to feel a bit creepy.

"What?" she yelled at him, taking a step towards him, but then stopping. "You've been here for God knows how long with no food. Why aren't you eating?"

Caesar blinked sleepily at her and then ran his small pink tongue up across his lips in a yawn. Lys watched as he then dropped down from the counter onto the floor and then meandered out of the kitchen and back into the hallway. Lys shook her head as she watched him go, but then took off after him.

"Where's Irene?" she called, but he was suddenly nowhere to be seen.

The door beneath the stairs was still open and she went cautiously to it, peering down into the darkness in the hope of seeing his tail disappear, but there was no sign of him down there. She heard a scuffling sound coming from the living room, and closing the door after her, retreated back along the hallway and into the living room. She scanned the room quickly for him, and found him sat on the window sill, watching the street outside. She smiled compassionately as she went to him.

"You miss her, don't you, you sweet old thing?" she said, stroking the top of his head gently.

Caesar chose either to silently agree with her or else ignore her entirely, and continued to watch the world through the glass. Lys followed his gaze, and smiled to see that the ginger cat from across the street had returned. It was no longer on its owner's wall, however, but sat in the middle of Irene's front lawn, cleaning itself. Lys rubbed Caesar's silky black ears some more and then turned to take a seat on the sofa while she wondered what best to do.

She supposed that she ought to contact the police. She hadn't spoken to Irene for over a week, which was very odd for a virtually housebound old woman. All the signs she had seen so far, however, indicated that she had probably just popped out for a while; the made bed, the sight of everything in its place, washing on the line; but what contradicted these things was what was making her anxious. She hadn't answered any calls for over seven days, Caesar's food bowls had been dry and empty, and the house was unlocked at the back door. Lys fretted as she decided to make herself a cup of tea while she waited some more. Caesar was still perched on the window sill, his tail hanging straight down, as he continued to watch the garden. Lys smiled at him as she passed, and only slowed her step as she saw that the grey cat she had seen from the upstairs window, had joined the ginger cat. Both were now staring at the house, Caesar staring back at them. Lys swallowed as she watched the four unfeeling eyes gaze unblinking back at her. It was definitely getting creepy now. Slowly she edged away from the window, and left the living room with a shiver. Perhaps the three cats were just staring each other out in a territorial fashion, she reasoned. Perhaps as soon as Caesar got outside, there would be a huge fight between them for the role of dominant male. That was probably the answer.

Lys felt slightly better about it all when she finally swallowed the first sip of Darjeeling. Leaning back against the counter, she raised the mug to her lips again as she gazed idly out into the back garden. The tea was hot, and it was already beginning to settle her edgy nerves, which was good. A sparrow was sat on the bird table outside, pecking at the scraps Irene had left for them, and Lys watched it for a while, the sight of it relaxing. A movement in the hedge caught her eye, and unbeknown to the sparrow, a dark coloured cat stalked from its tangled depths and stood to watch it. For a moment, Lys had the urge to go to the kitchen window and frighten the tiny bird to safety, but a second later the cat continued on its way, striding beneath the bird table itself.

There were a lot of cats in this neighbourhood, she thought to herself, and remembering the deserted streets she had walked to get here, let herself imagine more cats than people. She smiled to herself at the notion, and pushed herself from the counter and took her tea back with her into the living room.

Caesar was still sat on the window sill. He hadn't moved. Lys set her mug down on the coffee table and picked up the handset of the telephone, calling through to the local police station. They told her that there had been no emergency calls from the house over the past week, and they had no details of anyone fitting Irene's description. They suggested waiting it out until the following day, and if she still hadn't appeared, then yes she should report it officially. Lys was less than satisfied as she replaced the receiver, but what choice did she have? She couldn't very well force them to search the streets. She reclaimed her tea and then sat back on the sofa, sipping frequently as she thought. Caesar suddenly mewed from the sill, and Lys glanced over at him. Perhaps Irene had come back, she thought, and he could see her walking down the path. Lys got to her feet and went to the window. Her grandmother was nowhere to be seen, although the dark coloured cat from the back garden had joined the other two cats still sitting on the grass. The house was a cat cinema, it seemed. All three of them were just sitting and watching. She wanted to shoo them away, but then didn't.

Her watch read five thirty. It would getting dark in a few hours. It would take her a while to walk back to the station if she wanted to go home, or else she could stay here a while and see if Irene did indeed return. She weighed these options in her mind, and decided that she had to know one way or another.


It was nearly ten o'clock when she opened her eyes. She must have nodded off for a bit in front of the television and not noticed the time. The sky was black outside, of course, and the streetlamps doused everything with a pallid yellow light. Her lower back was stiff and it ached as she got to her feet. Putting a hand to it, she went to the window and pulled the curtains closed. Caesar had gone and was nowhere to be seen, and Lys stood there for a while taking in the silence of the house, only the television burbling to itself.

She went back and turned the set off and then wandered into the hallway, calling Irene's name to see if she had returned and chosen not to wake her. Her call went unanswered. The door beneath the stairs stood ajar, and she wracked her brains to try and remember if she had closed it or not. She recalled Caesar appearing from its shadows and frightening the life out of her, but she wasn't she sure if she had pushed it shut after that. She went to it and began to close it. That same scratching noise from before drifted up the stairs and her hand froze on the door handle.

She listened intently, inclining her head a little further towards the gap. There seemed to be no low breathing like there had been before, although the wind could've died down from earlier in the afternoon, but the scratch-scratch was definitely the same. She called Caesar's name and waited for him to appear, watching the darkness in the hope that his bright yellow eyes would gleam as he ascended the wooden steps. She waited a few moments, called his name again, and then opened the door wider, taking a step into the darkness.

Her hand found the light cord more easily this time, and the bright bulb above her head gleamed as she pulled on it, illuminating the stairs below. A second later, and Caesar's head appeared around the corner at the bottom, his tiny pink tongue lapping up over his lips.

"Come on, you daft old cat," Lys said to him, waving for him to climb the steps towards her. "You probably shouldn't be down there, scratching your claws against Irene's things. Come on upstairs."

Caesar looked back behind him at whatever he was scratching and then trotted forward and up the steps, skirting past Lys's ankles and then back out into the hallway. Lys made sure the door was closed this time, and rattled it in its jamb just to make sure. Bending to scoop up Caesar, who was still stood on the hall floor looking up at her, she carried him through into the kitchen. She noticed straight away that his food bowls were still untouched. She frowned to herself as she set him down in front of them, but he only gave them a momentary glance and a sniff and then trotted away, back into the hallway. Lys shook her head as she reached to draw the kitchen curtains. How could he possibly not be hungry? It had surely been all day that he'd gone without food. She shrugged. If he wanted to go hungry, then so be it.

The thought of the cat's stomach reminded her of her own. It was growling suddenly, and she put a hand to it before opening the refrigerator to find something to fill it. She could smell the catfood from where she stood but it didn't put her off taking out some bread and ham to make a sandwich. With another cup of tea made, she took both it and the sandwich upstairs to eat before going to sleep in Irene's bed. If she did return from wherever it was she'd been, then at least she'd find her straight away, and wake her with answers to her whereabouts.

Sunlight woke her through curtains she had forgotten to draw. The day was bright and sunny and she blinked at it as she looked up. Picking up her watch from the bedside table, Lys discovered that it was not much past seven, and it was fairly obvious already that Irene still had not returned.

She rolled over and gazed up at the ceiling as she wondered how best to tackle the day. Where could her grandmother have gone? Lys was trying hard not to worry too much, but there was only so far reason could go. She was virtually housebound, and yet she was not in the house, and hadn't been, she supposed, all week. She must certainly have left of her own accord, the lack of any forced entry told her that much. Although she would undoubtedly have opened the door to a stranger should he have knocked with a half-reasonable excuse. Lys sat up suddenly. Perhaps that was the case, she thought, putting her hand to her forehead and sweeping her hair back from her face. Perhaps somebody had come to the house and taken her. She shook the thought away quickly. Why would anyone want to kidnap her? If it was money they wanted, they would've just ransacked the house in their search. Lys slipped her legs from beneath the covers and got to her feet. Dressing quickly, she realised that she could at least call the police again, and report her missing. It was not what she deemed the best thing to do, but it was the most sensible. Let the professionals take care of the situation. They knew best.

There was a terrible smell in the hallway as she descended the stairs. It was slightly sickly but with a prickly tang somewhere in it. She curled her nose as she went through into the kitchen. The chicken flavour catfood was still untouched in the bowl, and she stooped to pick it up before setting it quickly down outside the back door. She left the back door open to let some fresh air, and hoped that if Caesar was feeling peckish by now, then he could find his own way to it and eat it outside.

The stench put her off finding anything for breakfast, but she boiled the kettle anyway, taking a cup of tea out into the back garden for some fresh air herself. The morning was bright and crisp, the air like cool diamonds as she breathed it in deeply. She stood there beside the bird table, gazing up into the clear blue sky, squinting against the brilliant sunshine, and sipped at her tea. She was glad that she stayed the night after all. A jingle of metal caught her attention behind her and she turned to see a ginger cat, presumably the same one from yesterday, stepping in through the back door.

"Shoo, shoo, out of there," she cried, giving chase, but as she reached the back door lost sight of him. She wandered into the kitchen looking for it, but it had gone. Damn, she thought. She must have frightened it further into the house.

Lys wandered back through into the hallway, scouring the corners for any sign of the ginger cat, but there was none. She stuck her head around the living room door but again there was no sign. As she went to leave, however, she noticed the window sill, Caesar's favourite haunt, and wandered towards it to see if his adversaries were still awaiting their bout. What she saw, however, when she looked through the glass, made her jaw drop with disbelief.

Outside on the front lawn sat maybe two dozen cats; grey, black, ginger, tabby, they were all there. On the pavement sat another couple. On the wall of the house on the other side of the street, two tabbies and an albino. Her gaze dropped to the front lawn beneath the window sill once more. Two black cats emerged into view from beneath it as if they were leaving the house. It was then, of course, that she remembered the tiny window that opened from the top of one of the cellar walls.

A sweat broke on her brow, her throat suddenly dry and tight so that she couldn't swallow. Slowly she stepped back away from the window, back through the living room door and out into the hallway. For some reason, she glanced over her shoulder at the door beneath the stairs. It stood ajar once again.

She went to it, slowly at first, but then covering ground with speed to view the scene in the cellar. Lys tugged on the light cord and descended quickly, her breath suddenly ragged in her throat, her hands out to the wall either side of her for support on the narrow staircase. As she stepped out onto the dusty cellar floor, a furore of squeals and cries rose up, as if she'd raised the souls of a thousand banshees, and a veritable multitude of cats streamed past her shins as though the very floor itself was alive with bodies. Lys let out a cry of her own as she struggled to keep her balance, she sheer weight of flying fur and claws disorienting her as they rammed against her. Her vision drifted up towards the tiny cellar window as she put a hand out to the nearest wall for support, and she saw there too a stream of cats fighting their way to escape.

Silence finally descended on the cellar as the last of them scrabbled to freedom. Lys stood panting with shock and exhaustion as she surveyed the state in which the cats had left it in. Boxes had been overturned, jars upended, their contents scattered and partially devoured, newspapers lay torn, and the stench of cat faeces pricked the musty air. As her eyes became more accustomed to the half-light, so she began to step through the debris. That same smell of stale catfood that she had noticed earlier was down here too, only much stronger, and the combination of that and the excrement was enough to make her put her hand over her nose and mouth. The gesture served another purpose, however, for as she continued to search amongst the mess, she caught sight of a small figure half-hidden by torn magazines and broken boxes, and her hand caught the sob when it came. She had found Irene.

Her hands began to tremble as she knelt down beside the old woman, and lifting the torn paper and cardboard from her body saw the extent of her defacement. Across her grandmother's face and arms,

46

scraps of meat had been torn leaving dark raw tracks where the cats had gnawed at her with their tiny needle teeth. Her dress had been ripped in several places where they had fought for their food, and her blood had soaked through most of them, the stains now black and encrusted. Her tears came freely now, and her shoulders hunched as she let them come. How could Caesar have done this? How could the other cats from the neighbourhood have come in and eaten bits of her? Through her tear-washed vision, she looked down at the dusty floor and at the marks scratched there. Lys sniffed as she followed their trail across the floor in broad sweeps. Strange the cats to have done this, she thought to herself, as she wiped the gel of snot and tears from her face with the back of her hand. She sat back on her heels now and stared at them. They were pointless and yet they suddenly confounded her, inextricably capturing her thoughts. Lys was still sniffing when she noticed Irene's hands; more precisely her fingertips, and the dirt built up beneath her nails.

From behind her, she suddenly had the sense of being watched. She moved her head, a little at first, and then fully, until she could see the bottom of the stairs. Caesar stood there, motionless, watching, his bright yellow eyes piercing the half-light of the cellar. For a moment, they just stared at each other, his tiny pink tongue flicking up and over his lips. It was then that anger suddenly welled swiftly inside her and she reached blindly for the nearest thing to her. It was cold and hard, a glass jar, and she hurled it at the black cat as hard as she could. Her accuracy was not even close, and the jar shattered some yards from Caesar. It did the job, however, and Caesar bolted for the top of the stairs as shards of glass skipped across the hard floor.

Lys exhaled heavily as she looked back at the fingernails and the marks in the dirt. Her attention flicked from one to the other, her thoughts defying cohesion, until a feeling of dread suddenly broke over her, and with the revelation, a shiver that ran down her back. Irene hadn't fallen unconscious. She had lain here and struggled. Perhaps even as the cats began to bite into her. The shaking returned to her hands and she now began to panic. She had to call the police, she knew, but the thought could suddenly not put strength into her limbs. She just sat there staring at the marks in the dirt and the state of Irene's fingernails. Then the dread built into a kind of sickness, her stomach turning over on itself until she thought she was going to throw up. That was the source of the scratching she had heard the previous night, and my god, this morning as well. Irene had been alive. She had been alive yesterday and through the night while she watched television and slept in her bed. The feeling of sickness convulsed with a sudden jolt and she doubled in half as she vomited. The police had to be here, she thought, as another weight of puke came up into her mouth. The police had to be here now.

She forced herself onto her hands and knees, her fingers slipping in the wet slap on curdled tea and bile, and then hauled herself to her feet. Quickly she staggered as best she could to the bottom of the stairs before dragging herself up them with the aid of the banisters.

There was a telephone in the living room, but she steered clear of that as she recalled the sight of Caesar's favourite resting place - he was the last thing she wanted to see right now - in favour of the one in

Irene's bedroom. She slammed shut the door behind her, and after checking that the windows were closed, even though they were on the first floor, she collapsed onto the bed sobbing. Lys pushed the hair from her face as she reached to pick up the handset. She almost expected the line to be dead, like they usually are in horror movies, but the tone was clear and she dialled back through to the local police station she had called the previous day.

The line connected through to an answering service, informing her that her call would be connected shortly. She tapped the handset nervously as she gazed out through the window at the clear blue of the sky. It was still a perfect day, too perfect somehow, almost as if it had chosen to ignore the death of her grandmother downstairs in the cellar. She shook herself into check quickly, and cursed the tardiness of the police station under her breath.

As she heard the line connect in the earpiece and a human voice ask after her enquiry, she heard a low creak behind her with the other ear. For a moment she was confounded by the two sounds, but as she glanced over her shoulder, she dropped the handset altogether as she saw Caesar standing in the now open doorway. She swallowed hard, her eyes forced wide, her breathing halted, as she stared back at the black cat with the bright yellow eyes, the muffled sound of the desk sergeant now a vague distraction in some other place else entirely. Lys rolled off the bed away from Caesar. Slowly she backed away towards the far wall, and watched as Caesar came after her, his steps matching hers. His tiny pink tongue flicked out again, rasping quickly across his lips, and then he sprang effortlessly up onto the bed where she had been laying.

A motion to her right caught her attention, and as much as she loathed to take her eyes from the cat, the movement demanded it, and she turned her head to see another cat, a mottled grey tabby, perched on the window sill in front of the now open window.

The wall came cold and hard at her back now, and she spread her palms out to either side of her as though she could press herself through it and out the other side. It resisted her efforts, offering her no chance of escape. Caesar was now no more than five feet from her, his paws on the edge of the bed as he inclined his lithe body towards her. Even the tabby had approached some distance across the floor and waited, its bright eyes cold and alert. The thought of escape came into her head once more, but as she looked from the tabby to the bedroom door behind Caesar, her heart sank as she saw that three more cats had appeared to seal off the route.

Caesar sat on the ruffled sheet and watched her. It seemed he was not ready to devour her just yet, but what of the tabby? What of the three other cats waiting at the threshold? What of the rest of the multitude that had occupied the front lawn and swarmed from the cellar?

Lys drew a shuddering breath as her eyes drifted once more to the open window. It was one of the large windows, possibly three or four feet in height. She could feel the breeze coming through it now on her face, and it almost seemed to invite her to it. Caesar got to his feet once more, she could see the motion without turning her head. His strike could only be seconds away, and then she would feel his needle claws and teeth sink into her. She knew it would be no other way.

The window would of course be her quickest means of escape, but at what cost? Broken bones, undoubtedly, and if not that then an attack by the cats already outside. Better to chance the open bedroom door with its sentries, she reasoned quickly, and then make for the stairs. Lys chose her moment. With a cry she started for the door, hurling herself past the bed before tumbling out over the threshold. She felt only a small scratch of pain, presumably the tabby leaping at her as she passed him, perhaps even Caesar himself or the three guards, but the next thing she was aware of was the sight of a dozen more cats waiting for her out on the landing.

Blindly she stumbled through them, crying out in alarm as she felt them leap up at her, their bodies climbing and clawing at her legs as they sank their teeth deep into her. She caught the edge of the banister with one hand and hauled herself towards the top of the stairs. More cats were ascending, the steps alive with crawling bodies and opening jaws. Piercing needles raked the back of her hand, bringing pain of the same ferocity as the claws still pulling at the backs of her legs. Still she urged herself forward, her feet already descending, one step, two steps. Her foot landed awkwardly on something soft that gave and crackled beneath her weight. Her ankle twisted as her balance went, and her hands shot forward to grasp some kind of purchase, but there was simply none to be had.

Lys tumbled and hit the floor at the bottom hard. She heard a loud dull thud somewhere inside her head, and had the vaguest sensation that she had broken something. Blackness came swiftly to claim this notion, and all thoughts of injury went with it.

The sound of shallow breathing inches from her face came to her before her sight returned. Her head ached with no little ferocity and a knot of sickness tugged inside her stomach. Her hands were shaking violently and she became away of her teeth chattering, and biting down on something like grit in her mouth. Her eyes still would not open, and she suddenly began to feel very afraid that she had done some serious harm to herself. The breathing near her face continued, and on it she could now smell something sickly and rank, which did nothing to help her own feelings of nausea. Suddenly her sight returned, and her eyes flickered open to see the face of a large ginger cat sniffing at her. Their gazes connected, and instantly the moggie reached its snout forward to inquire more intimately. Lys tried to force herself back away from it, but she could move no more than a few inches, painfully little as a second cat trotted into her peripheral vision to take an overly keen interest.

Lys gasped out loud as she felt something touch her lower leg. It was the cats, she knew it, and she tried again to move, to even sit up, but her body simply would not obey her. A trace of something wet and rasping drew across her leg now, they were tasting her, teeth or claws or both surely only moments away. All sensation in her body suddenly went, and a dark shape came into view behind the ginger cat. It was Caesar. Slowly he stepped past the first cat on the scene, and proceeded to sniff her face very closely. Lys tried to shout at it to get it the hell away from her, but even that comfort was beyond her. She breathed raggedly as she lay helpless beneath his authority. She was at his mercy. She was at the mercy of a small bastard cat. She seethed inside, somewhere beyond all the pain and the aches of broken bones.

Caesar looked, it seemed in an almost blithe manner, towards the other cats surrounding her - and judging by the cacophony of mews that suddenly rose up all around her, their numbers had swelled dramatically in the last few minutes. It was then that she felt the first stabs of biting pain as they sank their teeth through her clothes and into her flesh once more.

Her body convulsed and a barely-registered scream loosed her throat. Her eyes closed to a blanket of darkness, her hands shaking violently, as she waited for something inevitable to happen. This was the end, was all she could keep thinking, as they took it in turns to tug scraps of meat from her body, and feed on the blood drawn from the opening wounds. This was the end, to die at the mercy of a small bastard cat, and the straying moggies of an elderly woman's neighbourhood.

# The Garages

We all knew Bob. He lived at number seventeen, he played golf regularly, and he parked his Toyota at the front of his house when he could. He always had a nice word for me whenever I passed him because I'd never had reason to fall out with him, unlike some of the other miserable sods who seem to take pride in ignoring their neighbours.

Bob was in his sixties, at least he looked it, and his wife looked twenty years younger. Either she was doing well, or he was doing bad, or else there really was a twenty year span between them. I didn't know Bob well enough to ask in the first year of living in The Grove, and after the first year it just seemed like the kind of thing that you're meant to know. Still, Bob was a decent sort of guy. He'd chased the local kids away from the street years before we moved in to number nineteen, so it always seemed kind of quiet, especially given the reputation of the area. But house prices were cheap, it was all we could afford, but thanks to Bob, the no-good punks had gone elsewhere.

But the problems started for Bob when the letters started coming from the council. The Grove is a cul-de-sac, and a small one at that. Parking is ridiculous, especially weekends and evenings, and it's kind of the only real issue to bitch about. The guy at the end thinks he owns the whole damn street and doesn't give a shit about who he blocks in with his two cars. But the point of the letters concerned the garages, or rather the lack of use of them.

Now, every house has its own garage situated in the block. Twenty four houses, twenty four garages. Not a problem you would think. In fact it wouldn't be, except that only four out of the twenty four garages contain cars. The rest of them are full of shit that the owners won't store in the house or take to the tip. Everyone has a problem with the parking, but why only four people - myself included - are intelligent enough to realise that there wouldn't be a problem if everyone used them for cars is beyond me.

Still, for the purposes of my explaining what happened to Bob at number seventeen this is irrelevant; except for the fact that Bob was one of the twenty. I knew this, but I didn't really give a shit too much about any of it because we had just the one car, and we only had a problem when we had someone come visit us and couldn't find a spot.

We'd played golf a couple of times, Bob and me, a handful of awkward rounds where we were not quite pally enough to relax, but pally enough to swap stories and gripes. We went in his Toyota the second time, and returning to the garage block where we unloaded the car, I got to see just how much shit he'd managed to store in there in his eighteen years of living in The Grove.

He had crates and packing boxes filled with his kid's (now grown up) toys, old books, records, hand tools, garden tools, two ladders, a table and chairs covered with a filthy white sheet, a dresser and wardrobe, a wine cooler heaped with old car parts, and shelves stacked with jam jars crammed with nails and screws. I mean, you name it, it was in there somewhere in a box, covered in dust, and threaded with spider's webs. His golf clubs he tucked just inside the door, along with his trolley and shoes, but how he managed to get to anything at the back if he ever wanted it without the use of climbing gear and a miner's lamp was beyond me. But I guess that's what the other nineteen of his kind were doing; just adding to whatever was in there, stacking a new line of shit in front of the old, and avoiding sorting it out.

But I'm digressing. It was the letters that led to Bob's arrest, and it took a series of them to actually have any effect on anything.

Residents had complained to the council, blaming everyone else for the parking problem instead of themselves, and with each of their official letters that went ignored, and with the council becoming tired of the growing complaints and pleas, they decided to force the people of The Grove to use their garages. They had to be emptied, residents were told, and used only for cars. Fines would be imposed if necessary, and regular unannounced checks made. Residents were furious, despite the knowledge that this was what they had been demanding all along, but the order went ahead.

Now, if Bob had set to emptying his garage alone then he might have gotten away with it. But the owners of number twelve and number eight were hauling out old mattresses and offcuts of carpet when Bob's wardrobe tumbled out of his garage and onto the concrete hardstanding.

The doors flew open because the lock had been broken, and the body that was inside flew out like it was spring-loaded. Steve Williams from number twelve and Allan Mackenzie from number eight both saw it. There was little Bob could do. It was Steve that phoned the police. And it was Allan that watched Bob until they came.

Two squad cars came roaring round the ring road

with sirens blaring, and proceeded to block the entire street by parking diagonally across it. Doors opened all down The Grove, white nets twitching, as faces appeared to see what was going on. Poor old Bob stood there as four uniformed officers questioned him and stared down at the body of the dead kid, his hands outstretched in defence of his innocence, as everyone in the street watched him.

Within twenty minutes a white van arrived to take the body away, two men in see-through overalls loading it onto a gurney before leaving slower than they came. Two more police cars arrived too, come to inspect the garage and the inside of Bob's house at number seventeen. It was bad to see Bob's face, bad to see his wife's too, even worse to have everyone in the street watching it all through their windows.

But eventually, though, they took old Bob away.

I saw him go, his face looking back over his shoulder at his wife clutching herself with grief. It was a bad day, I'll tell you that.

There was some gossip around The Grove after that, over-the-fence stuff mostly, but nothing malicious. Most people knew Bob, but not all, and even though the general feeling was that he hadn't done it, nobody was sure. Word began to go round about how he'd been seen taking his wheelie bin down to the curb late at night, later than was natural; about how he'd taken to digging in his garden, vegetables allegedly, and with more gusto than was right; about the car that he drove; about the smell coming from his shed; but mostly about the bodies that he kept stashed in his garage.

But I liked Bob, and I refused to add to the slander. Bob helped me fix the window in the kitchen when it got broken. He even drove me down to Angel's

Glaziers on the Southern Industrial to get the glass because my girlfriend had taken the car that day. He was a gent, that guy, and I wouldn't listen to a bad word said about him. Which was probably why I felt kind of bad about Bob getting arrested for murder, because it was me that killed that kid.

Some punk with no respect for nobody, he'd gotten into my house through the kitchen window, and I'd come downstairs and caught him with his hands on my CD player. To this day I can still remember his face. He wasn't the least bit scared that I had caught him. In fact he started shouting abuse at me, threatening me, but what he didn't know was that I wasn't about to take shit from some mouthy little motherfucker like him.

I beat him some before I hauled him back into the kitchen. I would have left it at that except for the fact that he kept mouthing off. He was going to get the police, he said, and I'd get done for GBH, for assault, and for God knows what else. Fuckers like him don't deserve rights, and I wasn't about to let him have the chance. I was going to teach him good.

I pulled out one the knives from the knife block on the worktop beside the sink and stuck it in him. It went in clean, neater than I thought it would, and it went in quiet too. That punk kid just stared at me like I was really in trouble now, but then his eyes suddenly widened like a fish (I think the pain came then), and he pissed himself all over my fucking floor, so I stuck it in him again.

He'd been holding onto me up until then, but his fingers went limp suddenly and I dropped him onto the floor. He wasn't getting out of my house alive, not after what he'd done, not after what he'd said to me. I was going to dump his body where no one would find it, in the woods or something, that's what I thought at the time, but then my mind began to work out just what would actually be involved, and the whole idea started to change.

I would have to carry the body from my front door to the garage, a route which was effectively visible from every house. Even disguised inside a roll of carpet or inside the wheelie bin, I would still need to haul it out the other end and dig a deep hole before anyone saw. I tried to imagine how long it would take to dig a six by six foot hole, and realised that it would be hours, and that's if I didn't come across any tree roots or rocks.

That was when I remembered Bob's wardrobe, tucked at the back of his garage that hadn't seen daylight in eighteen years.

I took the kid's body round in the wheelie bin at three in the morning. Bob's garage was locked, so I went back for my big screwdriver and my mallet, and broke the barrel. It was a haul dragging that dead weight across the shit Bob kept heaped in there, but I managed to get him to the wardrobe, and managed to force that lock too.

Once I'd pulled the garage door down, however, I realised just how obvious that broken lock looked. So heaving that door back up, I took his golf clubs and trolley, and dumped them in the boot of my car on the other side of the block.

I left the garage door up, just to complete the picture, and that was as far as Bob looked. I spoke to him a few days later and he told me all about the thieving bastards in the area. I nodded to him, remembering the kid holding my CD player, and how that was one less bastard to worry about. Bob was insured though, so he got a new set of clubs out of it; a more secure lock on his garage too.

Bob's trial comes up soon. I'll have to go down to the courts to see what happens. I'm sure he'll be fine, the evidence is purely circumstantial anyway. And me? They've got nothing on me. I'm just the average guy who works nine to five, pays his taxes and keeps his mouth shut.

# Otherworld

People disappear all the time, that's the simple truth of it - some run away from home, others into the arms of another lover; some are murdered, others simply lost - but it's usually something people do alone, a solitary recourse for an insecurity or a feeling that something better than what they've got just has to be around the next corner. It's a frequent occurrence for individuals who yearn for something more, or for those vulnerable to the predators of our society, and it is heartbreaking for those who are left behind who have to find some way to fill that person-shaped gap. But it's rare for a whole family to disappear.

A family consists of a group of individuals, all with their own hopes and dreams as individual as their faces, so for each one of them to disappear either at the same time or within the span of a few days of each other, you would think, would be close to impossible. If this is what you think, then let me tell you a story about one such family, because their disappearance had nothing to do with poor home life or indifferent partners, serial killers or voyages abroad. They were a family that lived in the London green belt, in a suburban home in the heart of a populated area, but like most families their problems came not from an outside source, but from within, down in the dark depths where few people have ever stepped. But this is not a tale of social relations or of household feuds, but something else entirely.

Let me tell you the story, but not from the beginning - no good stories begin at the beginning anyway. Let me start you off from a moment of crisis, with the young boy alone in his room. And let me start it in the middle of the night too. That's when horror stories are meant to begin.

i

Sebastian sat upright in bed. The door to his wardrobe stood ajar, and from inside he could just make out the distant echo of horses' hooves thundering across dry dirt as it faded into silence. He blinked into the darkness of his room, his heart still hammering in his ten year old chest, as the remnants of his nightmare ticked over on the other side of his eyes. It was a recurring nightmare, of men covered with blood, of death, and of corpses rotting beneath a heavy sky. His skin prickled with cold as the cool air found his sweat-soaked pyjamas, but his eyes would not leave the wardrobe door that still stood partially open.

It had been closed when his father had kissed him goodnight, Sebastian had made sure of asking him to double-check it, and yet here it was again, standing ajar with the sound of heavy horses receding once more into the black silence. He wanted to call out to his parents, but the sound of his voice shrill in the bedroom was more than he could bear. It would be oppressive, his voice, pressing against the dark that hung in his room, that seemed somehow to deaden at night. His lungs tensed instinctively, but he held his scream in his throat. He did not want to scream, he was a big boy now, but no sooner had he let the air slip from his lungs than they drew a second bigger breath. It held at the back of his throat like the first, but it was painful this time, and as his chest began to hurt with

62

the pressure, so he let it slowly out through his nose, quietly into the quiet dark room.

His eyes would not leave the blackness of his wardrobe, the blackness blacker than the rest of the room, and very slowly he pushed his duvet aside and slid his legs out from beneath it. He could feel every coarse fibre of the carpet beneath his bare feet as he stood up, and with his eyes still fixed utterly upon the void behind the door, he began very slowly towards it. All he needed to do was push the door closed again. The catch would click (he had heard it so many times in the frail light of his nightlight as his father had seen to it) and then The Otherworld would be gone once again. He could do it, he knew that he could. It didn't seem impossible when his father did it, so why should he worry now?

His hand reached out in front of him like a oversized marrow, a quintet of numb swollen fingers sprouting from them, oblivious to his control. Somewhere beyond his touch he could make out the metal of the handle, and then the door shakily began to close. His heart skipped wildly as the marrow slipped from the handle, and he lost his balance and teetered in the darkness as though he might actually stumble forward and into the void inside the wardrobe, into the realm of the bloodied men and forced deaths, but somehow his weight found part of the door and it slammed shut with a loud thud.

Sebastian reeled back into the middle of the room disoriented, his heart hammering painfully in his chest, before spinning back in the direction of his bed, sliding swiftly back beneath the duvet, and hauling it over his head like a shield.

The room remained silent, but the echoes of his

heavy breaths and the thud of the door reverberated loudly inside his head. Tears began to well and he tried his hardest to keep them back. Even with no one else in the room to see, he did not want to give himself over to them. Sniffing hard, and with his throat coarse and scratching, he lifted his head back above the top of the duvet and looked once more back towards the wardrobe door. Through the murk of the room he could see that it was still closed, but his chest would not slow its ragged pace. It was still dark outside, the middle of the night: he had a lot of hours left to wait out.

It was probably only ten minutes before the weight of sleep began to leaden his eyelids, however, and as Sebastian began to drift once more into dreams, so the sound of horses' hooves thundering over dry dirt returned, pounding on the other side of the wardrobe door once again.

But sleep had already claimed him, and the ghosts wanted him to see some more before the sun's first rays found their way in through his curtained window: his eyes flickered open over the top of the duvet to see the wardrobe door swinging slowly open; his breath froze in his throat as the sound of human cries pierced the air; the stench of blood and open wounds soured the air on a dry heat-filled wind that suddenly circled around his bedroom; and Sebastian could only clench his eyes shut and his hands into fists, and endure the sickening ordeal.

ii

Rafaela poured herself a glass of orange juice and put the carton back in the refrigerator. She half turned as she drank and looked at her husband sitting at the kitchen table, a fork of scrambled eggs in one hand, the morning's paper in the other.

"Did you hear him again last night?" she asked.

David Summers finished his sentence before looking up at her.

"He's fine," he said. "All kids have nightmares. We've been through this."

"But he keeps having the same nightmare, over and over again. A horrible nightmare."

"It's just a phase, it'll pass," David said dismissively, returning to his paper.

Rafaela turned to look out through the window, leaning against the counter as she drank her orange juice. It was a little after seven thirty, and four workmen had already set up their equipment further along the street to repair the potholes in the road. One of them, she could see, presumably the foreman, was stood a little way away from the others and looking about; at the moment he was looking in her direction, but from such a distance he surely couldn't see her watching what they were doing.

She would have to wake Sebastian soon for school, she knew, but after another night with not enough sleep she did not have the heart to deprive him of what few decent hours he did get. The sun was already above the rooftops, rising into a June sky, cloudless and bright. It was going to be a hot day, twenty five at least, and she'd dressed for it in a sleeveless white sweater and light blue peddle-pushers. She glanced over her shoulder again at her husband, but she knew that he had done all he was going to do: reassure his son as best he could and close his wardrobe door every night to keep the monsters out. Fine if you were following the instructions of a child-psychology book, but this was their son goddamn it; she just couldn't bypass Sebastian's fears so easily.

"I'm just going to wake him," she said, putting her glass down in the sink and making for the door.

"Don't coddle him," David warned, lifting his eyes above the top of the paper. "They're just dreams."

"Our son is hurting and you don't care enough to listen to him."

"I've listened," he retaliated, raising his voice for the first time, "but they're dreams, pure and simple. All kids dream of monsters in the closet, it's classic -"

"Don't spout psychology at me, I know damn well what metaphors mean. This is about our son and his health. He's not sleeping, David, and it's affecting him. It seems sometimes like he's too scared to even close his eyes. I want to take him back to see Doctor Wendell."

"Not him again."

"Yes, him again. Sebastian needs help, and I'm going to make an appointment for him after school."

iii

Sebastian swung his feet beneath his chair as he gazed around the waiting room at all the brightly-coloured posters: talking lumps of cholesterol, young men holding smoking cigarettes, charts of fruit and veg, ways to avoid the flu, and the importance of injections. Some of the posters he didn't like, because they were dark and made him feel uncomfortable, something about the way the people in them looked back at him; but others were of cartoon potatoes and rabbits holding carrots, and he liked those very much.

Although his mother had brought him back to the doctors again, she kept trying to tell him that there was nothing wrong with him, nothing really wrong, and that Doctor Wendell was the best person to help get rid of the nightmares he kept having.

Sebastian wondered whether Doctor Wendell had a gun, whether he was going to sit in his bedroom at night and keep watch on the wardrobe door, and if any of the wailing monsters that lived in The Otherworld pushed their decaying heads through the gap - wham! - the doctor would blow them off. He suspected that this wasn't going to be the case, but he sat there wondering about all the different weapons he might have hidden away in the big grey cabinet in his office to pass the time, as he sat and stared at the posters.

His mother sat beside him, reading one of the glossy magazines that sat in a pile on the low wooden table in front of them. He didn't want to look through any of them. They all had pictures of women on the covers, grinning up at him in such false ways that they made him uncomfortable. There was one that had a car on the front, he could see a wheel and a bumper tucked away halfway down the pile, but he didn't want to reach out and pull at it in case people looked at him if it sent all the others sliding to the ground. It was busy in the waiting room, busy and yet somehow suffocatingly quiet. He felt that just to sneeze would break the quiet like a china plate, and then he would be in trouble. Better to sit quietly, he considered, and just look at the posters on the walls.

His mother turned a page and he glanced at her. She was absorbed by her magazine, and didn't see that he was looking at her. Turning back, he noticed that someone had taken a seat opposite them, a middle-aged man with pale skin. Sebastian noticed that he didn't have one of the glossy magazines either, wasn't even interested in picking one up either, and they sat looking at each other for a while. Finally Sebastian looked away. He heard his mother murmur quietly near his ear as she leaned over towards him, telling him that they were going to be next, and her words seemed louder than they did at home, clearer and somehow solid.

He looked back to where the man was sitting and saw that he was still looking at him. His skin was very pale, almost bleached and dry looking, like old paper scrolls that he had seen in museums. His eyes were dark, black even, and seemed very large. His hair, ruffled and uneven as it was, seemed dirty or dusty, and as his lips parted to take a breath, his teeth quivered and moved around as if of their own accord.

"You don't need to be in this place," the man suddenly said to him, his voice, rather than echoing loudly like the receptionist's, travelled across the space between them flat and without resonance.

Sebastian looked at him. His skin now seemed to be shifting about his face like his teeth, sliding like picture tiles in one of his puzzles to reveal parts of bone-white skull in the gaps beneath. His hands began to tremble, his heart fluttering, but still the man went on:

"No, there's nothing wrong with you that this place can fix. What you need's a good shovel, boy, and plenty of hard graft."

"What are you talking about?" Sebastian said, grasping the edge of his seat with clammy fingers.

The man grinned back at him with his yellow dancing teeth.

He felt his mother lean over next to him.

"What's wrong?" she asked.

Sebastian shot a look at her, but kept quiet. When his mother returned to her magazine, he looked back at the man but discovered that his dusty hair had sprouted since he had looked away, and now hung long and bedraggled across his eyes like thin grey string. His huge black eyes now swung in their hollow dark sockets like two hanged bodies on the end of a hangman's noose. And that grin still remained, a cackling laugh rocking behind it, skittling like a marble in a wire cage.

Sebastian cried out again, and pulled his hands up over his eyes. He felt someone take hold of his arm and he screamed, imagining a skeletal claw dragging him down into the burning depths of hell. But then his mother's voice came, cutting through it all, and it was close beside him, insistent and anxious:

"What's wrong?" she wanted to know. "Don't cry, we're going in next."

Sebastian could only point at the man as he wailed.

She tried to quieten him, kissing his forehead as she stroked his head gently.

"We have to go in to see the doctor, honey. It's for the best."

"The man," Sebastian managed to cry now, his eyes still clenched and behind his balled fists.

"What man?"

"Over there."

"There's no one over there, Sebastian."

His hands dropped away in front of him and he stared through the blur of tears at the chairs sitting in a line opposite them. They were empty.

Of course they were empty. Only he could see the monsters.

He stared back at his mother who was wearing such a pained expression that it hurt him to see it. He could feel his own tears still skipping down over his cheeks, but he wiped them away now as he looked at her. She asked him what he had seen, but he shook his head now. He couldn't speak anymore, didn't want to speak about the ghastly visitor that he'd seen.

When the receptionist finally called out his name, his mother got to her feet and held her hand out for him to take. He took it gladly and stood up, but as he walked beside her towards the wooden door that led through towards Doctor Wendell's surgery, he noticed that every eye in the waiting room watched them go, and everyone of them regarded him in the same way: there's something wrong with that kid, those eyes seemed to say, something wrong in the head.

Sebastian wanted to cry out to every one of them, and explain that it wasn't him, wasn't his fault at all. But then he noticed someone else standing at the back of the waiting room, the middle-aged man with long dusty hair and black swinging eyes. He hadn't left at all, he'd just gone to stand at the back in the corner. But now their eyes had met once again, he was grinning back at him once more, his teeth dancing in his white-bone skull like marionettes on jerking strings.

Just as his mother opened the door and stepped through, pulling Sebastian's hand after her, the middle-aged man tipped him a wink as if to say 'I'll be seeing you real soon, kid'. Sebastian's legs buckled, and he swung from his mother's hand like a pendulum, hitting the floor at her feet and knocking his consciousness out of his head with a dull heavy thud.

He opened his eyes to Doctor Wendell's face. His head ached, and he felt sick, and a dull thump seemed to be punching his thoughts. His mother suddenly appeared behind the doctor and he threw his arms out towards her, but blackness suddenly swam across his eyes and he lost control of his senses momentarily and fell back onto the couch.

"Take it easy there," he heard the doctor say, his voice drowning out his mother's distressed gasp. He opened his eyes again, but slowly this time, and put a hand tentatively to his head. It was pounding painfully, and for a moment he wondered whether his head had been opened somewhere, his brains being pumped out onto the pillow. That was what it felt like anyway.

"I've treated him for the bump," he heard the doctor telling his mother, " but keep an eye on him for the next few days. He may not want to eat tonight but try and get something light inside him."

"Yes, doctor," he heard her say.

"Now then," Doctor Wendell said, turning back to look at him, "what was the problem you came here with?"

The doctor was perched on the edge of the couch beside him. Sebastian could see his silver stethoscope hanging round his neck and wondered if he'd placed it on his head to listen to what was going on inside it. If he had, he wouldn't have needed to ask.

"Mum said I needed to come, for my own good."

She was standing behind the doctor, and he saw her smile at him now, but he knew there was little comfort in it for her, and certainly no humour. She knew he was crazy, just like all the other people in the waiting room had known it in one single outburst: her crazy little kid.

"Still the nightmares?" the doctor asked him.

His mother's smile faltered behind him. Yes, of course it was still the nightmares. Except the nightmares had begun to creep into the daytime too. Sebastian nodded.

"Well there's little I can do about bad dreams," Doctor Wendell said. "I don't really want to prescribe any sleeping pills, but I may give you something mild, just for when things get a bit much. But warm milk is probably best, just before you go to bed."

He turned round towards his mother then and began speaking to her in quieter tones. Sebastian heard him say that he was going to refer him to one of his colleagues at a hospital somewhere, and a look of anguish washed over her face. She shot him a glance afterwards, and Sebastian could see that she was trying to disguise her grief, but he couldn't help but feel guilty for making her feel so bad; he had done this to her, him and his death-filled head.

Even when they left Doctor Wendell's surgery, Sebastian could tell that something was not right; but his mother would say little about it, even in the car on the way home. Sebastian didn't know what was going on, but there was something about the phrase 'one of my colleagues' that unsettled him. It sounded serious, more scary, as though Doctor Wendell was ill-equipped to help him and a new approach was needed. Perhaps it was a mental doctor, he thought to himself. Yes, a mental doctor to sort out Mrs Summers' crazy little kid, to flush the monsters out of his head and leave it fresh and clean inside, just like all the other normal little kids.

It turned out that Mrs Deeder was really nice. A plump woman several years older than his mother, she reminded him a lot of his maths teacher Mrs Day; she was really nice too, had a lot of time to listen, and smiled pretty much all the time. She called her office her 'soft room', and it was more like somebody's living room than a doctor's surgery. There were no stethoscopes to be seen, no needles, and no boxes of shining metal instruments. There were also no posters, just a few framed certificates hanging on the wall behind her desk. There was a large black chair that reclined with the use of a remote control, and it whirred almost flat. It was very comfortable and Sebastian liked it immensely. If this was how crazy people were treated then it seemed okay by him.

His mother sat in a chair behind him where he couldn't see her, and Mrs Deeder sat beside him, a notepad in her hand, and she smiled as she operated the chair into its horizontal position. Sebastian wanted to have a go, but he didn't want to ask, not on his first appointment.

"Tell me a little about these dreams of yours," Mrs Deeder began. "What are they about?"

"Just stuff mainly," Sebastian said shrugging, not sure of how to start. The whirring of the chair's motor had stopped and he wanted to make it go upright again.

"Try and explain for me."

Sebastian pursed his lips. His forehead rumpled. He didn't know how to begin, nor where to start.

"Your mother said something about monsters."

"Kind of," Sebastian said, squirming a little in his

chair. "But I don't so much see them as hear them."

"Go on."

"I hear them in my wardrobe. I hear horses galloping, and people shouting, and crying."

"From inside the wardrobe?"

"It opens by itself, as if they're trying to get out, but sometimes I get out of bed and close it."

Mrs Deeder scribbled something in her notepad.

"Do you see them?"

The image of the man in the waiting room flashed back into his head: his dancing teeth, his long straggly hair, his eyes hanging like dead men.

"Sebastian?"

"I never used to see them."

"But you do now?"

Sebastian turned his body to try and look for his mother but she was sitting out of sight.

"She's still there," Mrs Deeder told him, her smile as warm as it was wide. "Do you see these people?"

"I saw one while we were waiting to see Doctor Wendell."

"In the daytime?"

"Yes."

Mrs Deeder scribbled something else in her notepad.

"And what did he look like?"

Sebastian tried to swallow but his throat felt as though he had been eating dirt. Mrs Deeder had offered him a glass of water when they'd first arrived and he'd said no. Now he was wishing that he'd said yes.

"I didn't like him. I could see his bones through his skin."

"Did your mother see him?"

Sebastian waited for his mother to answer but it seemed as though she wasn't allowed to and so he shook his head.

"Why do you think that was?" Mrs Deeder asked him.

"Because I'm crazy?"

Mrs Deeder smiled again.

"You're not here because you're crazy, Sebastian. You're here because you have a problem that Doctor Wendell doesn't think he can help you with. But I can. I need to find out what you're dreaming about and then try and help you to stop dreaming about it. That's what you want, isn't it?"

He nodded, and she smiled again.

"Do you often see them in the daytime?"

He shook his head. He wanted to look round for his mother again but he fought the urge. He wondered what the time was, and how much longer this might go on for. He hadn't asked, and his mum hadn't told him.

"When is it worst?"

"Nightimes mostly. I'm fine when dad tucks me in, he makes sure the wardrobe door is closed, and I'm fine when I do my homework. But when the light is out and I'm lying there in the dark..."

"That's when the noises start?"

Sebastian could feel himself trembling, his fingers turning numb and swelling like balloons. If he closed his eyes he would be there - back in his bedroom with the thundering hooves and the cries of men and the stench of blood on a hot dusty wind - and he didn't want that, and it hurt to keep them from blinking.

"Sebastian? Are you okay?"

"Yes, Mrs Deeder."

"Would you like a break?"

"No, it's fine," he said, pushing his hands up across his face.

Mrs Deeder waited for a few seconds before continuing.

"Tell me about the noises," she said.

"It starts off quietly," Sebastian began, "once the house is silent and mum and dad are asleep. Horses start to gallop. I can hear them snorting with fatigue and pain, as though they've been ridden hard. Men start to cry out in agony, some of them shouting that they'll kill me."

He caught Mrs Deeder's glance towards his mother and stopped. Something was going on, he knew it. What weren't they telling him? He'd answered her questions, why wouldn't they tell him if he was crazy or not?

"What else do you hear?"

Sebastian scowled at her, his lips clamped shut. She smiled but he simply stared at her. He wouldn't tell her any more, not until they told him what he was, not until they told him what he had become.

Mrs Deeder glanced at his mother once again and then closed her notepad and set it down on her big wooden desk beside her.

"It's okay, Sebastian, we can take a break now. I understand that it's difficult for you to go through all this, but we'll get there together, I promise."

He saw her take up the remote control, and he sat motionless as the chair whirred into life. But there was no pleasure in it now for him, except for the hope that this was all over, that he would soon be going home. The chair reached its normal position and Sebastian pushed himself out of it, looking for his mum almost immediately and going to her outstretched arms. She hugged him hard and kissed his forehead, and for a moment he thought that he was going to cry. But he didn't want her to see his tears, and certainly didn't want Mrs Deeder to see them. What would she make of that?

"I can see you again next Wednesday if you like," he heard Mrs Deeder saying to his mother. He spun round to look at her, and saw her pen poised over a big black book. He looked up at his mother with horror and saw her nodding.

"Same time?"

She nodded again.

His head was literally spinning as he was ushered out of Mrs Deeder's soft room and back through the secretarial office that led out to a long corridor. His mum didn't say a word as they made their way back through the hospital, but only once they were outside and about to get into the car, did Sebastian break the uncomfortable silence between them:

"Mum, am I crazy?" was all he said.

She shot him a very focussed look, and told him that no, he wasn't crazy, he was just a troubled little boy with a lot of problems on his mind. But as they pulled out of the parking space and headed out of the hospital car park, he saw her wipe something from the corner of her eye, muttering something about dust in the air.

v

The workmen were still there when they got back. The foreman was standing perhaps fifty yards away from the other three workers, who were busy

77

pounding fresh black tarmac into holes with a huge noisy jackhammer, and he watched them as they drove past. Rafaela thought he was going to wave or flag them down or something, the way he was scrutinising them, but he just stood and stared. He didn't wear a yellow reflective waistcoat like the others, just dark clothes, but then she reasoned that he wasn't doing any work to require a yellow coat.

David was not home yet and Sebastian went outside to play in the back garden. After putting her handbag down on the kitchen counter and checking the weight of the kettle (finding it empty she filled it from the sink and then switched it on), she went through into the dining room to watch him. She wasn't sure what she expected to see. She'd kept an eye on him before, of course she had, but after the visit to the psychiatrist everything just seemed to be on its head. Her son was seeing a psychiatrist for Christ's sake, what the hell kind of parent did that make her?

Rafaela wiped away a tear that had found its way onto her cheek as she watched Sebastian sit on his swing. He pushed his weight back into it but didn't swing, just sat there looking down the long garden. She wanted to go to him, but what could she say? What did he want her to say? He wanted reassurance but she just didn't have any, not anymore. The truth was that she suspected what he was saying was true, but she couldn't give in to that, could never give in to that, at least not out loud. Mrs Deeder could help him, she had to believe that, and hopefully come next week she would get another chance.

The kettle was boiling in the kitchen, she heard it click off, and she lingered momentarily at her vigil before walking back in. Pulling a mug down from the cupboard beside the window, she spooned in a measure of coffee from one of the silver containers they had received as a moving-in gift last year. She wondered what had happened to them of late, how the move down south had promised both a boost to David's career as well as the family's welfare as a whole. The reality had proved dubious on both points, and although neither of them had openly discussed it, she had thought it was certain that they both regretted the move.

Rafaela spooned in two sugars and poured in milk from the refrigerator and stared idly through the kitchen window as she stirred her coffee. The foreman was still there, looking her way again as his workmen packed shovels into the back of the rusty white truck. Is that where the crazy kid lives? she could almost hear him saying. The one that sees dead men?

She shuddered inside and moved away from the window, taking her coffee through to the dining room, back to where she had stood concealed behind the dark velvet curtains. Sebastian was no longer sitting on the swing but had moved further down the garden. He seemed to be looking at the flowers she'd planted down there, either that or the fishpond. A family of frogs had appeared and she hoped he was watching them jump and swim, some healthy inquisitiveness to take all this horror away. That was all they seemed to talk about lately, the horror and the death, and that surely couldn't help: keep dragging up what has happened, keep dragging up the filth. What they needed was a break, a holiday, even if it was for only a week. David had said that he was having problems at work and couldn't even take a day off at the moment, let alone a whole week. But perhaps she could go away, just her and Sebastian. It wasn't ideal, separating the family unit, but anything that might get him away from the source of his nightmares would be a godsend. Sebastian was backing away from the pond, and Rafaela nearly dropped her coffee as she saw him stumble down onto the grass onto his back. Something in her head told her to wait: the last thing Sebastian needed now was a hysterical mother. Kids fall, that's what they do, the voice told her. And sure enough, he rolled round onto his hands and knees and pushed himself back up onto his feet. Her heart was still yammering as she watched him stand there, looking back at the pond once again. Perhaps one of the frogs had leapt his way, perhaps there was something about them that he didn't like either. She didn't particularly like frogs, at least not up close. She could look at them from a distance, but there was something about their little slimy bodies that made her flesh creep. She'd almost stood on one of them on the patio a few weeks ago and nearly died. It had just sat there looking at her with its beady little black eyes, and in the end she had gone back inside the house to get away from it. Shameful to admit, she knew, but true. But a phobia was better than hallucinations of dead people, and so she left him to explore in the garden some more as she went upstairs to run herself bath.

vi

Sebastian had wanted to cry all the way home. He had been glad when his mum had suggested playing in the garden, glad that he wouldn't have to see her hide her tears for her disappointment of a son, glad that she wouldn't see his tears if they came (which he still wasn't sure whether they would or not) but glad mostly just to get away from her scrutiny. He knew that she watched him, just as he knew that she suspected his cracked mind. Normal people didn't hear the dead in their wardrobes, or see them in doctors' waiting rooms.

He sat on the swing and looked at his feet. She was probably watching him right now, standing behind the curtains somewhere where she thought he couldn't see her. But he'd seen her many times, and he knew the weight of her eyes to the point where he didn't even have to look.

His dad had hardly spoken to him the previous night, just a handful of grunts and barely raised glances over the top of his paper. Sebastian didn't like that, didn't like the silence of his father, hated himself for what he had done to him. He wanted to be a good son, wanted to be normal for him, but sometimes it was too much not to cry out in the middle of the night when the sounds of the dead rocked his wardrobe, rattling the doors, wanting to get out, because he knew it would stop as soon as his dad opened his bedroom door and switched on the light. His father used to be gentle and comforting, sitting with him for a while or fetching him a glass of water, but the more Sebastian called out the more irritable his father had become. Sometimes his father would scowl round the door, other times he would not come at all. He knew his father had a pressured job, and he tried not to call out for him, but sometimes it was just too scary.

Sebastian got up from his swing and mooched down the garden with his hands in his pockets, his eyes still cast at his feet. The frogs were at the pond. Two were sat just on the edge and he could see a third one swimming around the lily pads. Sebastian stood on the edge of the pond, his feet beside the two frogs (who seemed to be regarding him closely) and gazed down into the murky water. It was only shallow but he wondered how difficult or how easy it might be to just fall in and drown. He looked at his own reflection in the gently-rippling surface, water boatmen skipping across his skin, snails hiding behind his eyes. How easy. The pull was hypnotic and he swayed suddenly and had to catch his balance. A ripple passed across the surface of the pond and he jerked as the face in the water changed, what was once his now changing into something else: skin began to fall away to reveal bleached and battered bone, eyes rolled backwards into the head leaving two gaping sockets, and gleaming teeth suddenly grinned out at him, the lower jaw cracking open as though it wanted a good yack.

His knees buckled, as they had done in the doctor's surgery, and he fell away from the edge; but Sebastian managed to keep his balance somehow. He staggered back to the pond to where the skull was still jawing slowly in the motion of the water. But something else was moving in the dark murky water behind it, something he could barely glimpse in the sludge. Then he saw a tail, something striped, flick over the top of the skull, and his heart skipped over in his chest. He could feel himself shaking, could feel his voice rise up into his throat. But he wouldn't cry out, he wouldn't. The creature in the pond swished the black sludge into a billowing cloud suddenly, covering the skull like a veil, and for a moment the water was like a turbulent thunderstorm. Then the surface suddenly broke as this thing splashed out, its claws clasping his jumper, its furious snarl just inches from his face; its weight was slight, but it was its momentum that carried them both over onto Sebastian's back.

He hit the ground hard. He felt his head and back thump against the grass and for a moment he had no breath. His eyes flickered with uncertainty, flashing intermittently with black semi-consciousness and striped flicks of a tail. His hands, however, went instinctually to his chest, his fingers finding the writhing creature but sinking deep into the mud-like meat of its foul body. Lifting his head to get a better look at this thing, his fingers suddenly clenched thin air: there was nothing there at all to hold on to.

He lay there for a few moments just staring down at himself. His jumper was intact despite how the creature had torn at him, his hands clean even though he had felt them sink deep into whatever soft muck had made its body. But there was now no proof, no evidence that anything had happened at all. His heart still yammered as he rolled over and pushed himself to his feet, but he knew that he had to take one more look into the pond. He knew what he was going to see before he even peered over the lip: nothing but clear water and his own reflection. The two frogs still sat on the edge of the pond, although one of them had hopped further away, and although he could not see the third frog, the water remained wholly undisturbed. He put his hand to his head as tears finally came. He didn't want to, but when he turned to face the back of the house his eyes scanned the windows; and although he could not see his mother anywhere, he was sure that she had seen it all.

His father spoke little to him again that evening but at least he kissed him goodnight when he tucked him in at nine thirty.

"You sleep well tonight," he said to him, after he'd kissed his forehead.

Sebastian could see dark patches beneath his father's eyes, could see tiny red veins stark against the whites of them too. He also had the dirty smell of alcohol around him, something which he'd noticed becoming stronger over the past few months. His hair stood up at the back and his shirt was soiled around the collar. He thought how daddy needed a good sleep too.

"I'll try," was all Sebastian said.

His father attempted a smile, he could see how he tried, but he seemed so exhausted, so desperately tired, and Sebastian suspected that the alcohol he drank of an evening probably wasn't helping. But he wasn't going to say that out loud either.

His father got up from the edge of Sebastian's bed and turned to leave. He paused at the wardrobe and checked that the door was firmly shut before giving his son another smile over his shoulder. Then he stepped through the bedroom door, said goodnight to Sebastian once more, turned off the light, and then closed the door after him.

For a moment everything seemed fine: Sebastian lay in bed in the darkness listening to the sound of his father's footsteps on the hall landing, and then descending downstairs. There was a moment of silence after that, and then he could hear the soft drone of the television. He lifted his head and looked at the wardrobe, holding his breath as he strained his ears, listening for any movement from within. But it was quiet, as was the whole house (apart from the television downstairs) and he lay back down and closed his eyes.

He must have drifted off quickly, because when he heard something that sounded like fingernails scratching on wood, the clock on his bedside cabinet read two thirty. His eyes were wide, and he lifted his head slowly to look at the wardrobe, keeping his body as motionless as he could, and saw that the door was slightly ajar. The sound continued, like a corpse trying to drag itself up out of a grave with only one hand, and was joined now by ragged breathing, in and out, in and out.

Sebastian froze as he stared at the dark void behind the wardrobe door. There was nothing there to see, nothing but the impenetrable darkness inside, but his eyes began to play cruel tricks, visualising horrors, skulls and hollow eyes, rotten grinning teeth and daggers running rich with blood. His breath rose in his throat as a scream threatened, but then he remembered his father's weary face, remembered how he too needed sleep. The scream held, blocking all air in and out of his lungs.

The scratching heightened, sounding as if the corpse was ready to claw its way through. His eye caught the flash of yellow-white bones in the uncertain blackness and the scream forced its way out as his muscles jerked with terror. The scratching halted, the graveyard corpse slunk back into the murk at the bottom of his wardrobe, and the echoes of his scream became replaced by footsteps padding hard along the hall landing.

His bedroom door opened and the light from the

hall flooded in, silhouetting the shape of his father as he reached for the bedroom lightswitch. Sebastian rubbed his eyes at the bright light when it came, and saw the bulk of his father looming towards him out of the halo.

"Shut your fucking row," he hissed, jabbing a finger into Sebastian's face. His face looked worse than it had at nine thirty, but now it was creased inside a sleep-deprived rage. "If I have to come back in here one more time…"

Sebastian saw his dad's finger retreat into the ball of his hand, his whole fist clenching suddenly as though he was going to punch him hard.

The words were already on Sebastian's lips - I heard the dead people in my wardrobe - but he managed to hold them. In fact he remained silent as he dad stood back up straight and just glared down at him, his chest puffing hard. Sebastian could see his jaws clench too, could see his teeth locked as his thin lips parted. All he could do was stare up at him and regret what he had done.

"Fucking kid," his dad muttered, as he turned and started back for the door. He turned with his hand on the lightswitch, his eyes piercing, as he offered one final hushed threat. "You get your fucking head sorted, you hear? Or I'm gonna shift you off to some fucking nuthouse before you can shit."

viii

David got back into bed still fuming. His head ached and his neck ached, and the space behind his eyes prickled as though there were rusty needles there. Rafaela was thankfully still asleep. God knows how she managed to sleep through all this, but he didn't need her to have restless nights either. At least she kept the kid out of his way when he got in from work. Things were bad enough at ECO Electronics without making his home-life hell as well.

He closed his eyes and listened to his blood thumping inside his head. He knew men who'd had strokes from stress, and sometimes in the worst bouts of his own stress he imagined what it might be like to have one. It was morbid, he knew, but deep in his gut he knew one was coming. He couldn't carry on like he was. Fucking up in conferences, losing files, missing appointments with customers from around the world. Mix all that with a son who was fucked in the head and man, you got yourself a stroke!

He took a deep breath and tried to let it out easy. But it went in stinking of stale brandy and came out ragged like a flogged horse. His hands were still shaking, that was the problem, and they hurt from where he had made fists. Shit, he shouldn't have done that, that was wrong. But every fucking night, waking up screaming, talking about dead people in his bedroom - that was fucked up. He'd seen stuff like that on TV and he'd even found it funny - in other people's kids. But fuck, this was his own kid; his own kid had lost it. He didn't want to think how things would progress from here - mental hospitals or asylums or whatever they were called - and Rafaela had already taken him to a psychiatrist. His hands were still shaking, his head still thudding as though all of his millions of thoughts were punching the inside of skull one after the other.

Shortly after that was when the tapping started again.

His eyes flashed open, then flickered towards the archway that led to their en-suite bathroom. It wasn't there, he told himself, no fucking way man. There was no fucking animated corpse in his bathroom. It was the kid: his words had gotten inside his own fucking head and were messing with him.

But the tapping went on, tap-tap-tap, cutting through the darkness of their bedroom like an icy knife. The sound got inside his head, deep into his sinuses, it even got into his bladder so that he had to get up and take a piss.

He glanced across at his wife, but her head was still buried in her pillow, her mouth open slightly, as her deep sleep carried heavy breaths in and out of it, her chest rising and falling softly. She was beautiful, deeply beautiful, but he couldn't even take pleasure in that lately. They loved each other greatly, but that wasn't the problem. His mind just wouldn't disengage and let his heart take control.

His bladder twisted painfully and he recoiled beneath the duvet, relenting and sliding back out of bed before hurrying through into the bathroom. He pulled on the light cord, the three low-watt recessed bulbs illuminating the room with a gentle glow, and pissed a steady thick stream down into the bowl. The pain subsided instantly, but as he finished and pulled the handle to flush, the tapping grew louder behind him. He spun on his heel, searching for the source of the sound, but there was nothing there. He checked the taps in the basin and in the bath but none of them were leaking. He glanced under the sink but the downpipe and trap were fine. But the sound was not coming from there anyway. He stood for a moment just listening to it, tap-tap-tap, and then his eyes fell upon the mirrored medicine cabinet that hung on the wall. Slowly he reached his hand out to it, took hold of the door, and pulled it towards him. The brown pill bottles and jars of creams were all still in place, but his eyes went instantly to the finger that was sitting in there. It was just an ordinary finger, except for the fact that it did not belong to any hand, and it just sat there, idly tapping at the side of a bottle of calamine lotion, tap-tap-tap.

Something snapped inside David's head then, he felt it go, but later he would remember standing there for a few seconds simply staring at a disembodied finger tapping against the side of a bottle inside his medicine cabinet. And then his consciousness slipped away from him altogether, and he collapsed straight down onto the floor.

ix

His eyes opened through a throbbing scarlet haze and found Rafaela's beautiful face bearing down upon him like an angel. It brought agony to keep his eyes both upon her and focussed, but to not have her in his vision he knew would hurt more. He reached out a hand to her and realised that she was cradling him in her arms. He could see her lips moving but could not hear her gentle voice, could hear nothing but the thumping of his own blood inside his head. Her brow was knotted with anxiety, and she leaned closer to him and he saw her lips move again. He tried to lip read but she was speaking too many words way too quickly. A whine came in his right ear, and his hearing returned like a hand-slap against his head.

"- have you been like this?" she said.

He caught only the last of Rafaela's sentence but it felt like he had been sucked back into the real world again. An image of the tapping finger flashed before his eyes, but he pushed it away as he tried to sit up.

"Don't try to move," Rafaela instructed him. "It's okay, I've got you."

"How long have I been here?"

"It's gone seven."

David looked down and saw her satin night-gown, saw himself in his pyjama bottoms, his chest bare. He was still in the bathroom.

"I've got to get to work."

"No, honey," she insisted, putting her soft hand upon his chest. "We should get you to the A&E and get you checked out first."

"I can't miss work, I have to go."

David pushed himself past her hand and rolled over onto his hands and knees. As he lifted his head, however, the bathroom flooded with blackness and his senses slipped. He felt his head drop, felt his neck snap it back a heartbeat later, and remained where he was for a few seconds as he sucked in hard air.

"You can't go, not today," he heard Rafaela saying behind him.

He knew it was crazy to go. Hell, he'd probably crash the goddamn car before he was even three streets away if he stayed like this. But Venkner would fire him for sure, today of all days.

"I don't have any choice," he said to her, easing himself slowly back onto his feet and then steadying himself with a hand against the toilet. "It's either that or we lose the house."

"David…"

"It's true, love. It's a mixed-up market at the

moment, and, well... nobody's expendable."

"But I thought things were fine."

"Fine like a horse's head on the pillow."

Rafaela stared at him. Her silence was both painful and upsetting, and he glanced up at her apologetically.

"I didn't want to worry you -"

"So you waited until you collapsed before you worried me?"

"This has got nothing to do with anything. I probably just had one brandy too many last night."

"You can't just shake this off."

"I got pissed, alright?" David raised his voice for the first time, regretting it immediately. He lifted his eyes and found the hurt on Rafaela's face straight away. He pursed his lips and tried to smile. "I'm sorry. Everything's going to be alright, okay?" He winked at her and she half seemed to believe him. "Come on, help a drunk get to his feet and give him a hand to get dressed."

He'd met her in Rome twelve years ago. He'd been travelling through Europe on a year out from university and she'd served him coffee in a street café. He'd been with two other guys from uni, Matt and Dervish, and they'd ribbed him about how he'd sat and stared at this young waitress as she'd waited on all the other tables. She'd still never confessed to him whether she'd been aware of his constant attention as she'd worked, but he'd asked her out for a drink that evening, and she'd smiled the prettiest smile he had ever seen and politely said yes. She'd not known too much English, but their first evening had perhaps been all the better for that: learning each other's language, the English word for love, the Italian word for kiss.

He, Matt and Dervish had made plans to only stay

in Rome for three nights, and he had seen her on each of those three. They'd never made love, which was something he'd adored about her, but they had kissed in some of the most romantic settings the city had to offer. He professed his love to her and gave her his address and telephone number and begged her to contact him in November when he returned home. The train took him away from her on the fourth day, and she even took a lengthy break from the cafe to wave him goodbye, but for the remaining two months he could do nothing but think about her and the small café in which she worked. In some ways it ruined the rest of his exploration around Europe, constantly thinking about her, constantly wanting the journey to be over so that he could go home and make plans to see this beautiful young woman called Rafaela.

But come November he received neither a letter nor a phone call. He wrote to her with no reply, and felt sicker than he'd ever thought was possible. He toyed with booking a flight to Rome just to see her, but Dervish told him that if she wanted to know, she'd contact him; why fly out to see her like a stalker when the signs were so clear. December the fourth she wrote him a long letter, telling him that she'd been in Ravenna looking after her mother and had only just got his letters. He bought her a ticket to England where they spent their first Christmas together. Six months later they were married and Rafaela came to live with him in Nottingham as a British citizen.

"Tell me you're alright to go and I'll make you some breakfast," Rafaela said to him, snatching away his fondest memories of her as she fetched his socks from the drawer.

"I'm alright," he said to her.

"Cross your heart?"

David checked his heart with two fingers and smiled at her. She returned his smile but it came uneasily. He could see how concerned she was but David already had his balls in a vice. If he called in sick he would be fired for sure. Donny Miyaki was flying in from Japan later that day with talks of a merger. Venkner wanted it dusted by close of business so he could suck up big to the boss man, and if any one element was likely to fuck it up, lately that element would be David Summers without a doubt in anyone's mind, including his own.

"Eggs?" Rafaela asked at the door.

David was going to say 'Just coffee' but decided better of it and nodded.

"Poached, scrambled or fried?"

"Poached. I haven't had that for ages."

"Poached it is then," she said, and mouthed a kiss before disappearing from sight.

David continued to dress as he tried to ignore the dull ache still throbbing inside his head. A couple of aspirin would clear that, he thought; just a hangover from one brandy too many last night.

He pulled his jacket from its hanger and slipped it on, straightening his tie in the dress mirror beside the wardrobe. He had to impress today, that was all there was to it. A good breakfast and a couple of aspirin and he'd be set for the rest of the day.

He turned, admiring his look in his charcoal-coloured Armani suit, but as he went for the door he caught a flash of something ghastly behind him in the reflection, a grinning corpse with hanging flesh, a blood-blackened hand clutching a long rusted knife. The sight was fleeting as he moved, and he spun awkwardly as he searched the room for this apparition. But the room was empty, the air suddenly cold and damp, and he stood for a few moments with his pulse racing as he stared at the blank walls. But he dared not look back in the mirror, not if that creature was going to be in there waiting for him. He turned and ran out through the bedroom door and across the landing and down the stairs, his feet hammering like falling brimstone.

Rafaela was standing over the cooker when he stepped into the kitchen, busy with a pan of eggs. She glanced round at him, still smiling sweetly, for which he was glad, and he went to her and placed a kiss upon her cheek.

"I love you," he whispered.

"I love you too, David. Now sit down, it's nearly ready."

X

David didn't crash by the third street, but drove steadily and without incident through the heavy outer London traffic to Stockley Park. The two aspirin had done their job and, although his body still felt a little groggy and awkward from half the night spent doubled-up on the bathroom floor, he was now in good spirits. He waved at the security guard at the gate who looked only at the car pass on his windscreen and not at him. The clock on the dashboard read eight twenty but the car park was already filling up. He parked two thirds away from the main building, but with one hand on the ignition, ready to turn off the engine, he suddenly stopped: the presentation he'd updated the previous night was still at home, he'd never picked it up from the living room, the laptop either.

"Fuck," he said aloud, restraining himself from punching the steering wheel in case the airbag popped. His mind raced. Thirty minutes home, thirty minutes back. But it wouldn't be thirty minutes, though, would it? It was already nearly half past eight. Most of Uxbridge was already at a standstill as it was. By nine o'clock the traffic would be impossible, which would mean he'd be walking into the office after ten. Venkner would fry him. But then he'd fry him if he didn't have Miyaki's presentation either.

Then a thought came: Rafaela could email him the file from home. She didn't really know about computers, or how they worked, but he could talk her through it. A measure of hope came, doused almost immediately by the knowledge that she would almost certainly be on the school run by now. She'd probably be back by ten past nine at the earliest, and that was if she wasn't continuing on somewhere afterwards.

David dug his mobile out of his briefcase and dialled home. He thrummed the top of the steering wheel with the fingers of his left hand as he listened, but it just rang unanswered. He glared at the clock on the dashboard again. Fuck, he thought, knowing that he had little choice but to return home.

Putting the car in reverse, he pulled wildly out of the space and drove back out the car park, past the security guard who frowned at him, and out of Stockley Park. The flow of traffic into the business park was a boon, given that everyone was going into work and not out, but the moment he hit the main road, the traffic snarled, and he was forced to join the queue.

It was nine fifteen when he pulled into his

driveway. Rafaela's car was gone but that was irrelevant now. He forced the key into the front door and dashed through the house into the living room but the laptop wasn't on the side where he'd left it. It wasn't on the coffee table either. David searched the room frantically for it, searching his memory too in case he'd left it somewhere else, but it was certain that it wasn't in the living room. He put his head round the dining room door but they hadn't set foot in there since his birthday. It was not in the kitchen either and all he could do was clamp his hands to his head in despair.

Valuable minutes were ticking by, he was already late, and now it was for no reason. And then doubts began to spring into the chaos already circling his head: had he even brought the laptop home? Was it still on his desk at work? He tried to think but his thoughts just wouldn't come clearly. He could visualise the laptop on his desk, could see pages of Miyaki's presentation on the screen, but what day was that? What day?

David tugged at his hair until it hurt. What the fuck was wrong with him? He'd been damn good at The Marketing Suite in Nottingham, but the money had been shite and London had loomed like a dream. The reality had turned out better than he'd expected, surprising given the stories he'd heard. His salary had doubled, they'd given him a classy car to drive around in, and he'd been able to afford a house for his family instead of the one bedroom flat he and Rafaela had bought after getting married. But he was fucking it up for all of them, and he just couldn't get his head around why. Did Londoners play a different kind of hardball that a northerner couldn't cope with? Was marketing different down in the south? Or was he just an ignorant office boy who'd had an easy portfolio and was now struggling with the real game?

He couldn't move them back up to Nottingham, not to the life that they'd lived before. Here they had so many opportunities, so many nice things, and he wouldn't say to Rafaela that he couldn't cut it and that the ride was over. And what made things worse was the fact that he couldn't just go and get another job. He'd only worked for ECO since the move and Venkner wasn't about to give him a glowing recommendation, and any new employer would want to know just what he'd been doing since he'd come down to London.

"Fuck," he shouted at the top of his voice, and spun in a circle in the kitchen, taking everything in that his doubled salary had helped pay for.

He wandered back into the living room in a kind of half-crazed delirium. He poured himself a measure of brandy from the decanter and suddenly thought: a decanter, what the fuck am I doing with a decanter? He could just imagine his friends back home: what's wrong with pouring a drink from the fucking bottle it came in, posh-boy? But fuck them, he was doing better for himself and his family, he was just under pressure from the merger with Miyaki's corporation.

He took a sip from the tumbler and felt it warm his throat. His fingers were shaking but he just gripped the tumbler tighter and drained the last of the brandy. He turned, his eyes half-lidded, and saw the laptop sitting on the floor under the side table, just where he'd left it the previous night. He stared at it for a few moments, unsure of whether it was really there or not. He even poured himself another quick measure of brandy, downed it, and then crossed the room to scoop it up. It was nine forty when he got back in the car, and with the laptop safely on the passenger seat beside him, he reversed quickly out of the driveway, and headed off once again.

With the exception of white vans and courier bikes the roads were virtually dead. He tore across the roundabouts, keeping his speed, as the haze of brandy warmed his insides. A delivery truck blared its horn at him as he rounded a forty mile an hour bend at a little over sixty, his tyres stepping over the white line into the oncoming traffic, but he pulled it back as the truck swerved up onto the pavement, and continued on his way.

Stockley Park was like a ghost town when he got there. Every car park for every business was full but there was no living soul in sight. The only things that moved were the tall thin trees that lined the boulevards and the Canada geese that walked around the water features. The barrier was down as he got to ECO's building, and the same security guard that he had seen earlier walked over to him, his hand raised to stop him. David went to explain how he'd had to go home for his laptop but the guard wasn't interested, he just leaned in towards the window.

"The car park's full," he said. "You'll have to use the overflow and get the shuttle bus back."

"But I'm already late. I have an important presentation."

"The car park's full," the security guard repeated. His walkie-talkie crackled and he lifted it from his belt. Standing upright as he looked around, he spoke into it, but David couldn't hear what he was saying. He waited patiently until the guard finished, but all the guard did was look back at him and say:

"You'll have to use the overflow. There are only spaces for visitors."

David glanced at his staff car pass as the idea came but he knew it was no good. Putting the car into reverse, he pulled back onto the main roadway and tore off round to the overflow. It wasn't the biggest diversion in the world, but to walk back took about the same time as the shuttle bus. It was only ten minutes extra, but it pushed him way past a ten o'clock entrance.

Venkner wasn't there, which was a blessing, but his secretary gave him a long look when he sat down at his desk. She said nothing, but he could imagine her writing a secret note to Venkner, her pen scratching across expensive paper, the time neatly underlined. But never mind, David thought, he was here now and he had the laptop, and that was all that mattered.

xi

His stomach was fluttering even before he was called to say that Mr Miyaki had arrived in reception. He must have checked over his damn presentation every half hour, looking for something he might have overlooked, some oversight, some discrepancy that the big boys might kill him for. But it seemed perfect to him, details of the merger set out neatly and clearly; he only hoped he could get through the meeting intact.

David got up from his desk and gathered all of his materials together, and carried them through to the large meeting room that looked out over one of Stockley Park's lakes. The projector was already set up, and he struggled to connect the laptop to it with fingers that seemed to have lost all knowledge of how to work. He was relieved, however, when he turned both the projector and the laptop on, and found both to be working fine, and he clicked through each of the twenty seven presentation slides without a glitch. He clicked the presentation back to the first slide and then switched off the projector.

As he poured himself a glass of water from one of the bottles that had already been set out, the meeting room doors opened and Venkner appeared with Michael Stamford and three Chinese men in a volley of cheerful banter. David stood upright and smiled awkwardly at them. Venkner cast him a glance that seemed to say 'Don't you dare fuck this up', and then guided the three visitors round to the side of the table opposite the display wall. David loitered beside the projector as they settled themselves, Venkner remaining on his feet, Stamford, ECO's financial director, sitting beside the Chinese.

"We'll do some quick introductions," Venkner announced to his guests, and showed an open palm to David, but kept his eyes away. "This is David Summers, our marketing man. He's set up all the details of the merger, so if you have any questions feel free to direct them his way." He looked at David this time as he showed his other open palm towards the three visitors in turn: "David, this is Mr Miyaki, and Mr Hawasito, and Mr Hoi."

Venkner then nodded for him to begin and stepped out of the way, taking his vantage point in front of the windows overlooking the lake.

"I'd like to thank you for coming here first of all," David began. "The presentation should last about an hour. There are refreshments on the table, please feel free to take them as you wish, and as Mr Venkner pointed out, if you have any questions, just stop me."

Turning back to the projector, David switched it on and the first slide from the laptop shone up onto the display. The rudimentary details of the merger were shown with text, and David illustrated each point, elaborating on the key points he'd spent so many hours clarifying. Occasionally he'd glance at Venkner, and was glad to see that his scowl lessened the more he talked. He knew he was doing well, better than he thought he'd do. The Chinese nodded thoughtfully as he progressed, and as he went on to each successive slide with growing confidence, he barely noticed the fluttering in his stomach.

By slide eight he was in full flow. The financial data was all up on the wall and he was glad to see that Stamford had not interjected to point out that any of his information might be incorrect. David went through all the projected savings in detail, but as he glanced at Mr Miyaki he noticed that another visitor had taken a seat beside him. He'd not noticed anyone else enter the room or heard any apologies for a late entrance, and it caught him off guard for a moment, pausing mid-sentence. Venkner caught his eye, rolling his hands over as if to say 'get on with it' and David duly returned to the wall, picking up his stream of reduced costs.

But the new arrival nagged at him, urging his attention away from the slide shone up onto the wall of the large meeting room. He had to have another look, and finishing his sentence he glanced round. The stranger was indeed still sitting next to Mr Miyaki. David stared at him for a moment, mesmerised, his brain straining for recognition. Then the man tipped him a wink, raised his hand to scratch his head, and then slipped his entire scalp off the back of his skull like a greased hat.

David jerked with shock, his stomach turning over as if he was going to throw up, and he staggered back a step. He felt everyone else's eyes close in upon him and he took them all in in turn. Venkner's scowl had returned, Stamford was frowning with confusion; the three Chinese were exchanging glances.

David's eyes went back to the stranger. His hands were both up in front of his face and pulling away scraps of flesh from his face, revealing blood-red bone and cracked teeth. But he was still grinning, still tipping him that wink, even as he pushed his hand through the blood that coated his skull, wiping it away like a tennis player wiping away sweat.

"Who the fuck are you?" David demanded to know.

Venkner had taken a step towards him, but it was clear that even he didn't know quite what to do.

"Get the fuck out of here, you hear me? Get the fuck out."

"Summers," Venkner cried now. "I think it should be you who gets out of here."

David stared at him speechless.

"Outside, now," Venkner hissed.

David started away towards the door, his eyes back on the hideous shape that had stretched an arm around Mr Miyaki, hanging across his shoulders like they were old buddies discussing their college days. At the doorway, Venkner took hold of him and hauled him out into the corridor so hard that he nearly fell.

"Get your fucking shit and get out of here." Venkner was right in his face now, seething and flushed. "You're so sacked it's not even funny. If this deal is blown you can expect legal action too."

But all David could do was stare at him. He probably didn't even register what Venkner was saying, not really; all he could think about was the apparition that was even now probably swapping phone numbers with the executive from the Far East.

Venkner had told him to collect his things but he didn't even bother going back to his desk. The last thing he needed to see was Venkner's secretary glaring at him across her desk. She wouldn't know he'd just been sacked but he didn't want her to see the state he was in and mistake it for dejection at being fired. So he simply walked out of the building, realised he was not even parked in the main parking area, and turned and walked in a kind of daze along the narrow path out towards the overflow. His company car was no longer his to drive, but he figured that he had to get home somehow; they could come get their own damn car when they realised he still had it. He had other things to think about: like how he was going to support his family now, how his son's nightmares had gotten into his head so much that he was seeing them at work, and whether his psychiatrist offered family discounts.

xii

David didn't say a word over dinner. There was very little he could say. In a couple of days someone would come for the car and then Rafaela would know. He could say he was sick until that time came, he couldn't go into work, and that Rafaela had been right about taking some time off until he felt better. It would give him a chance to take a breath and make some decisions.

He didn't have a drink after dinner, but he did sit and watch TV with Sebastian while Rafaela read quietly in her armchair. He hadn't seen much of any programme in a while and it seemed like he'd lost track with current trends. There used to be a lot of game shows, but now they'd been replaced by dramas, endless dramas filled with miserable-looking people with poor speaking voices. He watched Sebastian more than the set, and saw how attentive he was to it all. It didn't seem to matter what was on, he just sat cross-legged on the floor with his eyes transfixed.

At nine thirty he coaxed Sebastian up to bed. His son gave his usual plea about staying up a little longer, and David realised that it was probably the first time that he'd actually seen his son say it in months. Normally David wouldn't even look up from his paper. 'Time for bed', he'd say, and then he'd hear Sebastian begin to argue, and then he'd reiterate it, all without looking up.

As he looked at his round wide-eyed face he couldn't help but think that he wasn't such a bad kid. Okay, so he had nightmares, so did every kid, and he'd had them plenty when he was one. Some of them recurred with frightening regularity: he remembered one in particular that would have him crying out loud - it had only one single paisley shape in it, that was all, but it came to him so huge and so suffocating that it scared him beyond measure. He never confided the content of his dream, only that it was terrifying, and his parents had never pushed. Maybe if they had, he would've been carted off to a shrink just like they were doing to Sebastian.

He watched Sebastian trudge out of the living room with a kind of quiet pride. He did as he was told, he didn't mouth off, and he was doing good in school. Things could be a lot worse, and he knew it. So he'd lost his job, so what? He had a good kid, a beautiful wife, and a fine home. There was minimal unemployment in the south, and he knew that he'd soon get himself another job, maybe something different, something other than marketing where every other suit and tie was an arsehole desperate for attention and promotion.

"I'll be up in a minute to tuck you in," David called out after him.

"Okay, dad," he heard Sebastian call back happily.

David smiled to himself, and then glanced up to find Rafaela smiling at him, one of her eyebrows raised in that sexy way of hers he loved so much.

"What?" he wanted to know.

"Just you," she said.

David grinned and then settled back to watch the TV for a few more minutes. He glanced back at Rafaela a moment later, but her head was back down again and reading, the smile still on her lips.


Sebastian was climbing into bed when David entered his bedroom. He went over and sat on the edge, tucking the duvet around his son's chin.

"We haven't had a chat for a while, have we?" David asked him.

Sebastian shook his head, his brow twitching with confusion.

"We should, though, shouldn't we?" David went on. "Chat about things."

Sebastian nodded.

"Like school - that's going okay, isn't it?"

"Yes, I suppose so. I don't like maths, though."

"I didn't like maths. I suppose you got that from me. But you still need to learn it all, it's very important."

"I know."

"Any others you don't like?"

"Sciences I'm not good at. Especially chemistry. None of it makes any sense."

"Have you spoken to your teacher about it?"

"I can't really understand what he says. He's got a big moustache that gets in the way."

David laughed. He'd met Mr Hansen and he did have a big moustache. He had a very strong regional accent too, Yorkshire perhaps.

"I like art, though."

"Do you?"

"Miss Simmons says I'm really good. She gave me a special project to do. Still life. No one else is doing that in my class."

"That's great Sebastian. I'll look forward to seeing what you've done."

Sebastian looked genuinely thrilled at this and his teeth appeared all along the top of the duvet.

Then something tapped behind them. David heard it but he didn't look, but Sebastian rolled his head to one side and looked past his father. His grin went in a second. David saw his son's face change, and then he followed his gaze, turning his head to look behind him now. A tall figure stood in front of the wardrobe, the same figure from his presentation, scraps of stained cloth and skin hanging from his skeletal body. His face was one of pure evil, his sunken eyes fierce, his grin of mostly missing teeth bared into a snarl, as he stood with a long rusted sword in one bloodied hand.

David felt his skin turn to ice. His breath froze in his throat. Then this thing lunged at him, swinging its sword down and cleaving the bed in two as David pushed himself away from the lethal blow, tumbling down onto the floor. His head struck something hard, but he fought to look up to locate this monster as he heard Sebastian scream. His hands found the edge of the bed, now frayed and separated with springs coming away beneath his fingers, and as he hauled himself up onto his knees he saw that his hands were covered in blood. Sebastian was nowhere to be seen, the monster too was gone, and David watched helplessly as the wardrobe door swung idly on its hinges, as his son's screams echoed hopelessly into a fading decaying silence.

David scrambled across the floor towards the wardrobe, his mind racing with the insanity of what he had just seen, and hauled open the door. But there were no monsters inside, no passageways down into hell, and no sign of his son. He couldn't even hear him screaming any more, and all David could do was stand there listening to nothing but his own raggedly-drawn breaths, as he stared into the wardrobe that stood devoid of everything but Sebastian's clothes. His son was gone.

xiii

Rafaela had heard the screams and come running. She appeared in the doorway and found her husband slumped on his knees sobbing. He glanced up at her as she entered, tears running down his face, but he was too distraught to speak clearly.

"Why... why didn't I... why couldn't I save him?"

"What happened?" Rafaela wanted to know, rushing to his side. But David didn't want to be helped, he wanted to stay in front of Sebastian's wardrobe and clasp the wooden door in his hands.

"They took him," he stammered.

"Took who? What are you talking about?"

"Sebastian. They've taken him."

Rafaela stared at him open-mouthed. Her heart was racing, and now her fingers began to shake. She glanced at the wardrobe David was sitting in front of and then back at him again. She hoped he wasn't inferring what she thought he was.

"Sebastian?" she cried out, turning in a circle in the bedroom. "Where are you?"

"I told you... they've taken him"

"Sebastian?" she screamed now.

David reached out and took hold of her wrist, but she pulled it sharply away from him.

"I'm going to call the police. Someone's taken my baby."

"Not someone, some thing. I saw it. The police can't do anything."

But Rafaela left him to his madness and hurried downstairs, dialling 999 and demanding the police, giving what scarce details she could to the woman on the other end of the line.

It was a long wait, sitting in the kitchen alone. Occasionally she'd get up and pull back the curtain when she heard a car outside in the street, but it was nearly three quarters of an hour before she heard a knock at the door.

David had not come back downstairs. She could imagine him still sitting there, staring at Sebastian's clothes, and for the first time she wondered whether

David had shown signs of insanity before now, and whether she had failed to notice. Perhaps Sebastian had inherited it from him? Perhaps David's family was strung through with mental disorders?

Her head was spinning as she opened the door. Two uniformed officers stood on the doorstep, and Rafaela duly let them in.

"You've reported a kidnapping?" the dark-haired officer asked her.

Rafaela nodded. This was crazy, like a bad dream.

They went through into the kitchen where they proceeded to fill in a form on a clipboard, asking her all sorts of pedantic questions - her age, her telephone number, her address (the same address they'd just turned up at!) - instead of looking for her son.

"What makes you think he's been kidnapped?" the dark-haired officer asked her.

"My husband said somebody took him. He saw it upstairs."

"Did you see it happen?"

"No, I was downstairs. My husband, David, he was up in our son's bedroom with him, and then I heard screaming."

"You heard your son screaming?"

"Yes. Then I rushed upstairs. Sebastian was gone and my husband was..."

"Your husband was what?"

Rafaela paused. Now she was talking out loud, she could hear what all this sounded like. She didn't need to hear these two policemen offer their opinion, she could see it in the glances they suddenly exchanged.

"My husband doesn't beat my son," she said defiantly, but her words were fading. What did she know about him anyway?

"If we can look around please, madam," the dark-haired officer said. "Then we'll need to take a statement from both you and your husband."

"But what about my son? He's still missing."

"We'll get a description from you, but try not to panic. He's probably not gone far. Is there a tree house in the garden, or a place he goes to when he's scared?"

Rafaela stared at them. Why hadn't she seen this coming? Sebastian was scared everywhere he went, he saw monsters in his day dreams. Or was the monster still in the house? She glanced over her shoulder, imagining David in her son's room. Was he the monster? Did he...

"Mrs Summers?" the officer prompted.

"I don't know," she stammered, pushing her hands through her hair. "There's no tree house, but he's safe here in the house. Why would he run away?"

"We need to ask, madam, there's no accusation at the moment."

"No, of course. Look around, though, please. My... my husband's still upstairs. Second door on the right."

She watched them go, and saw the light-haired officer put one hand on his night-stick. She staggered to one of the kitchen stools and sat down, glad to have the weight off her feet. She was light-headed and felt sick. Her fingers were trembling as she looked at them, reminding her of old people's hands shortly before they die. Rafaela pushed her hair back away from her face and took a long but painful breath. She could hear voices coming from upstairs now, her husband explaining Sebastian's mysterious disappearance. She could feel bile rising in her throat, anger beginning to set in upon her terror. But there was no evidence, except for David's insane story about Sebastian's dreams coming to life to get him. But Sebastian hadn't been asleep. David had been in there with him. Alone. Always tucking him up in bed alone. She felt vomit lurch up out of her stomach but she managed to hold it. Not now, she thought desperately to herself. There was no evidence.

She pushed herself to her feet and went with uncertain steps to the kettle. She should make some tea for them all, she thought, that was what happened in circumstances like these: let the police do their job, while the mother makes the tea. The kettle trembled in her hands as she tried to fill it from the tap, water spilling down both sides, skipping out and over onto the counter top, and she felt its weight go as it slipped out of her fingers and into the sink.

Rafaela clutched her mouth as tears came, silencing her sobs so that nobody would hear. The street was dark through the undrawn curtains. No movement, no one driving home, no sign of any kidnappers. She would have heard a struggle, though, wouldn't she? David would have fought them if there'd been any, and yet there was no sign of his being beaten by anyone, no bruises or cuts to his face.

Then she heard the sound of all three men descending the stairs, and she hovered in the middle of the kitchen until they appeared. David stood between them, his hands behind his back; his face was creased in two, but he didn't say a word, didn't even look at her. Rafaela took a step forward, so many questions already on her lips, but the dark-haired officer stepped forward to intercept her as the light-haired officer walked past with her husband. It was then that she saw he was wearing handcuffs.

"What's going on?" Rafaela demanded to know.

"It will be easier to ask our questions down at the station, that's all."

"What are you doing?"

"Please," the officer said, holding his hands up. "Another car will be over to look outside for your son, he won't have gone far. We've looked through the house but it's clear that he's not inside. If you'd like a counsellor to come and speak to you, I can arrange that for you."

Rafaela stared at him, and then shook her head as the craziness sneaked behind her sanity and got in.

"Everything's going to be alright," the officer went on. "We'll find your boy and have him back to you in no time. But in the meantime, have a hot drink, and have a seat somewhere comfortable. I'll wait here until the CID arrive. They'll be here soon."

"But why has the other one taken my husband away?"

"He's going to wait with your husband in the car. We want to ask him a few questions, that's all."

"Is he under arrest?"

The officer took a breath and lifted a hand again as if to placate her, ready in case flew off the handle at him.

"Under the circumstances presented to us, we are arresting your husband on suspicion of murder. He says he witnessed the kidnapping, but there are a lot of things that we don't like concerning what he says he did and what he says he didn't see. That's what we need to discuss with him."

Rafaela turned away then, her hands gripping the edge of the sink.

"Oh, and one more thing," the officer called after her. "Please don't go into your son's room until the CID get here."

Rafaela tried to sit patiently in the living room and wait for the other officers to arrive but something about the dark-haired policeman's last words just wouldn't sit right in her head. She attempted to reason the likelihood that in order to investigate her son's disappearance, the police would not want anything disturbed in Sebastian's room, and a worried mother was almost certain to go in and tidy important evidence away. No, she told herself, they needed to check for fingerprints and any objects left behind, and a fretful mother needed to be told how it was.

But the words just wouldn't sit right.

Rafaela went through into the kitchen to where the dark-haired officer was still sitting on one of the stools, his elbows on the breakfast bar. He had a mug in front of him, and he looked up as she entered. She saw that he'd taken the kettle out of the sink and replaced it back on its stand. He told her it wasn't going to be too much longer. His radio crackled, and badly-distorted words spewed out, but Rafaela couldn't distinguish any of them. It clearly wasn't for him because he ignored it.

"Can I make you a cuppa?" he asked her.

"No," she rasped as she shook her head, her voice almost gone.

The officer turned the mug in his fingers, his eyes still on her.

"I know this is a difficult time for you Mrs Summers," he began, "but can I ask at what point you knew your son was missing?"

"I heard him scream, and then I ran upstairs."

"So you were downstairs?"

"Yes, I was reading in the living room."

"So what happened then?"

"Well, I heard Sebastian scream and then I ran upstairs to his room. David was kneeling on the floor crying."

"And Sebastian was nowhere to be seen?"

"I didn't see him. David said he was gone. I called him but David insisted he wasn't there anymore."

"And there was no one else in the room?"

Rafaela stared at him, her face set in a grimace of confusion.

"There were no kidnappers in the room with him," the officer went on.

"No, just my husband."

"Did it look like he'd been struggling with anyone? Was he out of breath? Was he sweating?"

"No, he was kneeling in front of the wardrobe, just crying."

"I see."

He said nothing after that, and Rafaela could feel him confirming his own suspicions inside his head. She wanted to tell him that David wasn't like that, but she'd had those same suspicions herself so many times in the last half hour, aggravated by memories of his stress, his anger, and his increased consummation of alcohol. How could she not think the worst after running those exact same events through her head, over and over again? The facts all seemed to point to it. There seemed to be something else the officer wanted to say, but he just wasn't saying it. Rafaela stared at him but it was clear that he was not going to offer another word. It was then that his former words returned to her: Don't go in your son's room until we've said it's okay.

"Do you need to check for more evidence?" she asked him.

"When the other unit checks the area around the house I'm sure we'll find him."

"That's not what I asked."

The dark-haired officer returned her stare this time. His lips were tight and his eyes had gotten bigger.

"What are you not telling me?" she wanted to know.

"Please," he said, "The CID need to investigate and the forensic officer and photographer need the room just as it is."

"What's going on?" she demanded now, but he didn't say a word. "What don't you want me to see in Sebastian's room?"

"Please, don't go in there until they've cleaned up."

Those last words hit her in the head like a boxer's glove. She reeled across the kitchen, her hands finding the edge of the counter top and keeping her balance. She saw the officer get up from his seat, but she was already running for the stairs.

She heard him call after her but she wasn't going to stop, not until she saw whatever it was she had missed and they had found. At the turn of the stairs she saw him below her, but she raced on, dashing along the landing and putting her weight against her son's bedroom door. It swung open and she stumbled in, her eyes scanning the mess that it had been left in. But she saw it now, saw what she had missed when she had seen only her husband sprawled on the floor. Sebastian's bed was stained almost black with a single wide slash of blood. It was still drying into a hardening crust, but the fan of blood was unmistakable. Her hand went to her mouth as she felt her legs weaken, but she kept herself upright, even as the officer stumbled through the door after her and took hold of her shoulders.

"Please," she heard him say close to her ear. "You shouldn't see this."

Rafaela wanted to say that this wasn't her son's blood, wasn't her husband that had killed him, but no words would find their way out of her mouth. Her throat had dried up, and her eyes refused to leave that sickening spray of blackened blood. Why weren't the officers more distressed than they were? Could they not see the blood? Was it all an illusion, all a part of the same grim nightmare that only her family could see?

Slowly she let the police officer guide her back out of the room, but the tears tracked down her cheeks as the sobs came, and she allowed him to take her through into the bedroom where she fell onto the bed. She heard him say something as he left, and heard the bedroom door click closed as he went back out onto the landing.

Just what had gone on in her house, she wanted to know? Her family had gone, been destroyed by something that belonged in the fictional world of television or horror films. She'd never known anyone who'd been murdered before, or even known a relative or friend of anyone who'd been murdered; she could feel herself becoming a statistic, a headline of news that would be forgotten the following day.

Her body shook as she wept into her pillow, her body curled up tight into a foetal ball, as the officer outside her bedroom door waited for a better equipped team to come and clean up the last visible remains of her son. Would they even find his body, she couldn't help thinking, if they hadn't been able to find it in the house? But there were no answers to be had, at least not tonight, lying alone in a darkened house with a policeman who couldn't help her. All she could do was cry, without her husband and without her son, alone in an unlit room.

When Rafaela woke, the room was half-lit by daybreak. She glanced at the clock on the bedside cabinet and saw that it was six thirty. She'd slept soundly and now lay there wide awake. Pushing herself out of bed she went through into the bathroom to pee and to splash some water onto her face, and then came back into the bedroom to change, slipping on an old grey sweater and jeans. Stepping out of her bedroom, she was startled to find a female officer asleep on one of the chairs she'd brought up from the dining room. Her head was sagged forward, her mouth hanging open, and a gentle rhythmic snoring rasped around her like an engine. She looked at her for a moment, realising that she had obviously been sent to watch over her during the night, and then wandered along the hall to Sebastian's room.

The door had been pulled to, and Rafaela hesitated for a moment, her hand poised over the handle. But with a determined breath, she turned it and walked in, steeling herself for the sight that had shaken her the night before.

The duvet, sheets and pillow were gone, taken, presumably, by the CID either as evidence or just as a matter of sanitation. Rafaela stood staring at the ragged naked mattress for a long time, unable to grasp the weirdness of seeing it both torn and undressed. The wardrobe door still stood open, and she wondered if the police had been through Sebastian's things, perhaps taking some of his clothes. She walked towards the wardrobe now, the source of all his nightmares, but she was only halfway there when something scuttled across the floor past her feet, a long black tail trailing after it, and scurried into the wardrobe. Rafaela gasped with surprise, and faltered momentarily before yanking open the wardrobe door to see what it was and where it had gone. But there was nothing inside but Sebastian's clothes on hangers, and his shoes piled up on the floor. But it was dark in there, unbelievably dark, and whatever creature had run inside could easily be hiding in there.

She went back across the room and took up Sebastian's cricket bat, returning to the wardrobe where she began pushing the shoes around with it. But nothing stirred, nothing living anyway, and she began to wonder whether she had really seen anything running across Sebastian's floor. But she still felt as though something was in there, she could feel it looking back out at her, watching her, and it chilled her skin just to stand there, in case this thing was part of Sebastian's nightmare made flesh too.

Tentatively she put the cricket bat down on the floor and took a step back as she heard her name being called out in the hallway, but the feeling of being watched wouldn't leave her. Rafaela was glad of the excuse to leave Sebastian's room, realising that the female officer had woken to find her room empty.

"I didn't know where you were," the female officer explained.

"It's alright, I wasn't going to kill myself," Rafaela said, walking past her towards the stairs.

"We didn't think you should stay in the house on your own."

"I appreciate the gesture, but I'd really rather be on my own right now."

The female police officer stood at the top of the stairs and watched her descend. Rafaela looked up at her as she reached the half-landing.

"Go home," Rafaela said to her. "Get some proper sleep. I'll be fine."

The officer pursed her lips.

"If you're sure. I can always -"

"Go," Rafaela said again, and continued on down the stairs.

The officer appeared in the kitchen doorway as Rafaela was filling the kettle.

"I've put the chair back where I found it," she explained. "I'm sorry to have disturbed you so early."

"Would you like a cup of tea before you go?" Rafaela asked her, thinking that she had been unnecessarily brusque with her.

"No, I think I'll just head off," she said, and went towards the front door.

Rafaela stopped her before she'd gotten halfway.

"Look, I'm glad you stayed, it was really nice of you."

The officer smiled.

"It's no problem," she said. "I just wish I could of done more. I'm sure your boy will turn up sooner or later. He's probably just run round to a friend's."

"I wish I could believe that," Rafaela said, and went back to making herself some tea.

"Try to stay calm," the officer said as she opened the front door, "and let us do our job. Everything will work out, you'll see."

Rafaela wasn't so sure but she tried to take her mind off it all, studying the back of the cornflakes box as she took it down from the cupboard, the proteins per 100g, the riboflavin. But it was only a couple of minutes before the female officer knocked on her door once again.

She put the box down and went to the front door, but it wasn't the female officer standing on the front step, but a man. She didn't know him but he looked strangely familiar. She wondered, in a brief flash of hope, if he was a neighbour come to say that her son had stayed the night at their house. But as he opened his mouth and began to talk gravely to her, she realised her error: this was not one of her neighbours, but some nut off the street who'd come looking to scare her.

"I've been watching your house," he said to her. "There are problems here."

"Go away," Rafaela demanded, closing the door on him. But his hand was quicker than hers and he took hold of the door, jamming his foot in the gap.

"You need my help, Mrs Summers. More than you think."

"Let go of the door. The police will be back any minute."

"I had to wait until they left, so I know they won't be back for a while. You need me. The spirits of the dead have taken your son."

Her skin froze, and gooseflesh raced across her body. Her skull felt like it had been gripped by two huge icy hands, and all she could do was stare at this madman. Her hold went on the door and she realised how easily he could force his way in if he wanted. But he did not take a single step into the house, but just stood on the threshold looking at her. He even retrieved his foot from the gap in the door.

"I can get your son back for you, but you must take me to the source of the disturbances."

"How do you know..?"

"I've been watching you and your son -"

"The workmen," she declared. "You were with them."

"No, I was just standing near them, watching. I can feel the ghosts, Mrs Summers. I can feel their malevolence and I know what they've been doing to your boy."

"How?"

"I can see their energies, and I can sometimes see their forms. The police can do nothing to help you. Please, let me come in and I'll do all I can to help get your son back to where he belongs."

Rafaela knew the insanity of it even as she stepped back and allowed this stranger into her home. The man was in his fifties, about the same height as her, but about twice the heft. Once the front door closed behind him, if he'd chosen to do anything other than what he'd promised, she knew she would be powerless against him. But all he wanted was to know where the disturbances were their greatest, and Rafaela duly showed him upstairs to Sebastian's bedroom.

The man stood in the doorway and stared at everything in turn, running his hands through his thinning grey hair. He had the smell of stale sweat about him, and his suit, which was old and brown, looked dirty, as though he'd been sleeping rough. He held a black leather bag in his left hand, the kind that doctor's used to carry on house-calls, that opened up to reveal stethoscopes and surgical instruments, but Rafaela had no doubts that his bag contained nothing like that.

"This room feels horrible," he gasped, turning to look at her with distress. She was standing behind him, wringing her hands. It seemed like he was almost ready to cry. "Have you never felt this hatred before?"

Rafaela looked past him into the room, and shook her head.

"I can feel a furious anger in here, raging around this room like a vortex. Can't you feel anything?"

"No," Rafaela said, staring around Sebastian's bedroom. "Nothing."

They both stepped back out of the room, the stranger closing the door behind him.

"I will need to separate all the spirits that are in there and find the one that took your boy."

"There's more than one?"

"There's a lot of malevolence in there, and although they're directed in similar ways, making it seem like one entity, I can hear many voices. This is going to take time."

Rafaela stared hard at him.

"Who are you?"

"My name is Vincent Barnum", he said to her, "and I belong to the Order of Constantine."

They stared at each other for a few moments after that. Rafaela did not know what to make of this man, but he seemed to know more about what had taken Sebastian than the police, and, more importantly, how to get him back. He asked to be left alone in the room, and that it would be safer for her to wait downstairs; she didn't like how everyone kept asking her to wait downstairs, and wondered whether she would be better asking them to move her bed down into the living room and have done with it. But she left him alone in her son's room and closed the door after her, putting her ear to it to listen to what he was doing. She heard the click of his bag opening, and various articles being taken out. She heard some of Sebastian's furniture being moved, and then heard Vincent speaking in a low voice, obviously not to her. Rafaela lingered at the door for a few minutes, uncertain of what to do, but eventually she did as he had instructed her and left him alone to do whatever it was he had planned.

An hour passed during which she could do nothing but pace from room to room downstairs. No sounds came from the room, and the whole house was filled with a silence that seemed almost solid. At two o'clock, Rafaela went through into the kitchen to put something in her stomach. She'd not eaten anything since the day before, and although her belly ached more with sickness than hunger, she knew she had to eat something. Cooking was out of the question, and pulling open the fridge door, began to pick at whatever she could find on the shelves.

She started as a huge crash shattered the silence. Rafaela hurried to the bottom of the stairs and looked up, waiting for either the priest to appear or for him to at least shout something down. She waited for what seemed like a long time but nothing came, no shout and no further sounds.

The minutes ticked by and Rafaela eventually returned to the kitchen, perching on the edge of one of the stools and staring into middle distance. Three o'clock came and went, and still there were no further sounds from upstairs. She began to wonder whether Vincent was still in the house or not, so quiet was it, and wondered also why the police had not called back. Perhaps what Vincent had told her was true - the police could do nothing to help her, and they knew it. Rafaela had fallen asleep when the second crash came, her head against her arms folded on the countertop: it sounded like pottery smashing against a wall, maybe Sebastian's bedside lamp, and she stumbled to her feet, again uncertain of what to do. She hovered in the hallway, wringing her hands, his skin crawling with feelings of ineptitude. Then Rafaela warily ascended the stairs, holding onto the banister rail as she went. Another crash came, followed by the sound of something cracking and splintering. At the landing she could hear Vincent's voice, his words interspersed with gasps of pain. She hurried to the door, wanting to help him, but held back. What was he doing in there? What else was in there with him? She could hear him struggling to speak aloud now, the language he was using foreign to her, as a heavy drone guttered the air on the other side of the door. Rafaela hesitated, her fingers on the handle, but as a fourth crash came she found herself turning the handle, but the door would only open a few inches; it was jammed against something heavy, and she had to put all her weight against it, pushing her way in until the gap was wide enough to squeeze through.

The sight on the other side almost made her sink to her knees: Sebastian's bed was overturned and lying against the door, the floor was littered with debris, part of the ceiling had come done to reveal gaping rafters, and the walls were cracked like parched earth, and bleeding real blood. But amongst it all, kneeling amid the carnage and chaos, was Vincent Barnum, and towering over him stood a barely-fleshed skeleton with a wide-bladed short sword clasped in its raw and bloodied hand. The skeleton turned its grinning skull towards her, but Vincent's gaze did not falter from the black book in his hands from which he was still struggling to read. Then as Rafaela watched, the skeleton returned its attention to the man kneeling prostrate in front of it, took hold of his head with its bony left hand, and ran him through with its filthy blade.

Rafaela screamed as she watched Vincent convulse around the sword that had so easily penetrated his body. Blood pulsed up out of his mouth before it came from the wound, she saw it spurt out like a livid fountain. But as the skeleton rammed its sword in even harder, all the way to its soiled black hilt, Rafaela wept aloud as she saw Vincent lurch violently forward, his head snapping back before hanging lifeless from a neck that seemed too weak to hold it up.

Rafaela struggled to stagger back out through the door as the skeleton turned to look at her once again. It still had its hand on its sword, and she reasoned that it would take a few seconds to tug its weapon back out of the dead man from which it was still impaled, giving her at least a short head start, before it came after her. But as she tumbled backwards out of the doorway, she fell and landed hard on her back in the narrow hallway, wasting what slim advantage she had. Scrabbling to her feet, she ran headlong and blinded with tears as she heard more furniture cracking and splintering behind her. Her hands barely grasped the handrail as she threw herself down the stairs, her feet sliding without proper purchase across the carpeted steps, until she tumbled to the floor at the bottom. Her eyes lifted to what might be coming after her as pain came stabbing at her shins, her breath like lead weights in her lungs, but there was nothing else on the stairs, no monsters come running after her to slice her clean in two. She listened for the thudding footfalls of the creature that had killed Vincent Barnum, but there was no sound at all, neither from his room nor from the rest of the house.

Rafaela lay in the hallway, her back against the wall, struggling to breathe as she waited for the inevitable, but there was nothing, just a chilling hollow silence that suffocated an already empty house. Slowly and painfully she managed to get to her feet once more. Her shins throbbed more than ever, but now she realised that she'd hurt her right forearm and elbow in the fall as well. Nothing was broken, she suspected, but the pain was sharp and stinging. They were sore to touch through her sweater, but there was no blood seeping though, which was something. She stood upright and looked up at the landing through the banisters. It was still empty, still eerily quiet, and for a crazy moment her thoughts even entertained the notion of going back up there. She had to run, that was the logic of the situation, to get out of the house and to get help. But what logic was there anymore, and what help was there to get? The police? And what if Vincent was still alive? She'd seen him run through, but what if there was still some breath left in him, some tiny shred of a pulse left in unopened veins? If she left now without checking, that frail breath might expire altogether, his pulse extinguished without her ever knowing. And to leave the man that would save her family to die when she could so easily save him in return, she knew, would haunt her for the rest of her life.

Once more she climbed, her hand guiding her up stairs she did not want to climb ever again, as images of that skeletal murderer harried the air in front of her like a sickening vision. If it killed her too, her mind crazily informed her, then she would have no one to blame but herself. Fate had given her her escape and she had chosen not to take it. Fate would surely only shrug a second time.

The hallway seemed a mile long, and every footfall offered another chance for the skeleton to leap from a doorway and slice open her belly. The door to Sebastian's room still stood ajar, and as she stood with her back against the opposite wall, Rafaela peered slowly in through the breach left open. Sebastian's bed still lay overturned on the other side, and she could see lengthy shards of broken timber laying against the far wall, itself cracked open like a mountain fissure. Taking a step closer, she could make out that everything on Sebastian's bedside cabinet had been knocked off, and then as she took another step and could see over the edge of the bed, saw his lamp on the floor, smashed and lying amid yet more debris.

Rafaela pushed on the door until the bed halted its progress. Hesitantly she eased her head round until she could see the whole room. It had remained silent since she had landed at the bottom of the stairs, and now she confirmed that the monster that had slain Vincent Barnum had indeed vanished. She tried to look for where he had fallen but she could not make him out, and so stepping fully into the room, Rafaela trod across the debris of smashed furniture and broken toys to where she had seen him fall, but he was nowhere to be seen. She turned in a circle looking for him but there was simply no corner for him in which to hide. Whether alive or dead, he had simply vanished along with his killer.

Her eyes went to what was left of Sebastian's wardrobe, the place where he had seen his nightmares made real, the place in front of which Vincent had attempted to perform his exorcism. The sides had been smashed and lay strewn in splintered pieces across the floor, along with shreds of Sebastian's clothes. The base was still mostly intact, and some of Sebastian's shoes still sat on top of it. She stooped down as if to pick one of them up but halted, sensing the futility of the action. But then her eye was caught by something black and half-hidden amongst a mess of plaster knocked down from the ceiling. It was the bag Vincent had carried and she went to it now, if only to see just what exactly he had brought into her home. There were a number of small mostly hand-written books, some in languages she did not recognise, others in English but explaining strange acts and rituals. There were few pictures to illustrate the contents of the books, but it seemed clear what their purpose intended to achieve. A day ago and she would have dismissed them all out of hand, but now she was not so sure. She didn't really know what she had seen in Sebastian's bedroom, or what had happened to her son or husband, but here she was, on the edge of believing anything was possible.

At the bottom of the black bag were tools and instruments - a hammer and chisel, a knife and a crucifix, a medallion and a ring both inscribed with the same archaic symbol, a mirror and a candle - all looking like they had been collected over time and thrown into the bag never knowing whether they would ever be used or not. But Vincent Barnum was dead now, dragged away by the unholy thing that had murdered him, and his collected weapons or aids would be of no use to him now. She packed everything neatly back into the bag and closed it, picking it up and taking it with her as she left Sebastian's bedroom. Once out in the hallway, she closed the door after her. If there had been a lock on the door she would have turned it, knowing that she had no reason ever to go back in there again. Something final had happened, a chapter had been finished without her consent, and somewhere inside her head Rafaela knew it would not be revisited.

She went downstairs, taking the black bag with her, and went into the living room. She stood at the window looking down the length of the garden. It had only been the day before when she had stood in the exact same spot and watched Sebastian studying the frogs in the pond. The garden was empty and looked lonely without anyone in it. The house was silent all around her and tears suddenly threatened. Her chest ached and her body still hurt from her tumble down the stairs, but she would not give in to it all. She owed it to Sebastian, wherever he was, not to give in.

She turned and saw the door to the dining room, and wandered through still carrying Vincent's bag of archaic wizardry. One of the chairs stood out from the others, presumably the one the female police officer had not put back straight. Rafaela went over to it and nudged it back under the table so that it matched the others and then set the bag down on the polished surface of the table. Closing her eyes, she tried to feel the spirits in the house just as Vincent had done. She listened and tried to hear them, tried to hear their malevolence and rage. But she could make out nothing in the silence, nothing but the muted rumble of a car passing by in the street.

Taking a breath, she looked around the dining room, the only room in the house that they rarely used. It was pristine and new, hardly ventured into since they had decorated it, and she realised as she stood there that it was directly beneath Sebastian's bedroom.

The deep red carpet caught her eye, and she found herself staring at it, mesmerised by its flawless pile, its unspoilt colour. Her hand wandered to the black bag, her mind unsure of quite what she was going to do as her fingers undid it and retrieved the knife from inside. Kneeling down, she opened up the blade and put its keen edge into the carpet, forcing it towards her in jagged movements as it struggled to cut through the thick weave. Her mind distantly exclaimed how David would be furious when the police brought him home, but another part of her mind wanted to see just what was under this new carpet. Slicing a V-shape, Rafaela pulled back the wedge of reveal the concrete floor beneath. She recalled the grey concrete when David had pulled up the existing green carpet before laying the new red, and yet she continued to hack away at it, slicing awkward chunks of new carpet away and placing them behind her in a pile. Only when she had cleared a circle of about a metre across did she stop, and then she pushed herself to her feet and looked down at her work.

Her husband was going to kill her, that was the first thought that entered her head. The carpet had been expensive, and she had cut a huge hole in it for no apparently reason, and yet something still nagged inside head. She reached round and took out the hammer and chisel from Vincent's black bag and knelt down once more, aiming the chisel squarely in the middle of the circle and pounding it hard with the hammer. The harsh ring of metal upon metal echoed around the silent room, paining her ears, but she aimed the chisel a second time and pounded it again. A tiny shard of concrete skipped across the floor, leaving an almost imperceptible mark, and she looked at it with an almost detached curiosity for a few moments. Then she lined the chisel up again and began to pound it over and over again until sweat began to run down into her eyes, dripping onto the grey concrete dust that was slowly accumulating inside the circle of ragged carpet.

It was madness, she knew, but she couldn't help herself, couldn't help the work her hands wanted to do. They continued to pound the hard concrete floor until her arms could no longer hold the tools, the hammer and chisel slipping from her fingers as Rafaela fell back onto her heels, her lungs puffing hard, her sweat soaking the back of her thin sweater. The hole was possibly two inches deep at its lowest point, and she knew that it was not enough, although consciously she still had no idea what she was hoping to achieve. And yet when she pushed herself back up onto her feet, instead of going into the living room to sit down or into the kitchen to quench her thirst of find something to eat, she went out into the garage to where David kept his bigger gardening tools and returned to the dining room with a full length pickaxe and a shovel.

The concrete came away in big jagged lumps, tiny shards (of the size of her former efforts with the hammer and chisel) ricocheting off the fireplace and immaculately-papered walls, as she swung down at the floor with all her strength. When the hole became over a foot and a half in depth, Rafaela set to work on widening the hole in the carpet, hacking away at it with the knife and piling the pieces up in the corner of the room. Then she continued to pound at the floor, breaking away lumps of concrete and shovelling them out of her hole, piling the rubble up in a mound next to the carpet.

The deeper and wider the hole became, the more awkward it became to work in such a confined space. After an hour, Rafaela put down the pickaxe and began taking the table and chairs out of the dining room and into the living room, stacking them in the space in front of the window. With the dining room cleared, Rafaela widened the hole in the carpet another few feet with the knife, and then set to work once again with the pickaxe.

It was dark when she finally slumped against the wall with exhaustion. Her shoulders and arms ached furiously, and her lower back felt as though someone had driven over it. Her knees struggled to bear her up and threatened to give way, and as she leant the pickaxe and shovel against the fireplace, she staggered backwards to examine just what she had done through the course of the afternoon and evening.

The hole was more impressive than the hammer and chisel had achieved. She'd cut virtually all the carpet out of the middle of the room, and had needed to lengthen the hole in order to climb down into it and operate the shovel. At its deepest point she stood waist high with the dining room floor. The hardest part had been cutting through the metal wires that crossed through the concrete in a grid. She'd needed to return to the garage for David's hacksaw for that, and it had proved time-consuming to clear the sides of the hole just to get access to each line of wire. But she'd managed it and now there was a bloody great hole in the middle of her dining room.

She'd hardly eaten a thing all day, and although her

stomach growled, she was not as hungry as she thought she would have been. Forcing her legs to carry her through into the kitchen, she opened the refrigerator door and studied its contents. There was enough food to satisfy the various wants of a family, and she gazed at it all with mild confusion for a few moments as though her labours had caused her to momentarily forget just who she was, and that she was not a woman living alone in a silent house. Still standing in front of the open refrigerator door, she pulled out a pack of ham and began to push slices of it into her mouth; taking hold of the cheese box (which she opened on the shelf), she took hold of a lump of Cheddar and began biting chunks off it; there was some leftover salad in a bowl and she took up handfuls of shredded lettuce and onion to her mouth. Rafaela ate contentedly enough in this way until she felt nourished, and then she took out the container of milk from the door before closing it, and carried it through into the living room. She didn't remember doing it, but she'd somehow managed to haul the sideboard through into the living room as well. The glasses and china which had sat on it were stacked in the corner, which she couldn't remember doing either, along with the hostess trolley, making the living room difficult to navigate easily. Squeezing past the sideboard, Rafaela slumped onto the sofa and curled her aching legs up under her. Opening the milk, she drank until rivulets spilled over her lips and ran down onto her filthy sweater.

She drained the carton and then sat for a moment just staring into space, weary and cataloguing the aches in her body. Her mind was heavy, and now that she'd sat down, her eyes threatened to close. Putting the empty milk carton down on the floor, Rafaela stretched out on the sofa, if only to close her eyes for an hour or so before continuing her labours in the dining room. When she next opened her eyes, daylight was flooding in through the open curtains of the living room, and the clock on the mantelpiece read eleven fifteen.

XV

They'd told him that he'd been arrested under suspicion of murder. They'd stripped him of all his clothes and given him a white paper suit. They'd scraped under his fingernails. They'd taken a sample of his blood. And then they'd taken him down to the cells, along a corridor of heavy steel doors, and walked him inside. He had no watch, but it had taken hours, and he could only guess that it had all finished at something like four in the morning.

The cell was small and square. The walls were light blue, the ceiling high with lights built into it. The floor was covered with a kind of gritty linoleum that curved up at the edges of the walls. There were no bars on the window, just square glass bricks that he couldn't see through. There was no metal-framed bed, as he'd seen in films, just a big step three feet high and three feet wide with a thick hardwood top upon which lay a thin mattress.

He sat down on the edge of what passed for a bed. It was covered in a kind of thick plasticky nylon, the pillow too, and he wondered, as he stared at them, just how many greasy faces and bodies had been pressed against them in their lifetime, how much blood and spit and semen had been washed off of them, if at all.

On the other side of the cell near the corner was a chrome toilet. A single toilet roll sat next to it, and there was a chrome push-button flush instead of a handle. He looked back at the door and realised that it had opened outwards, realising too that it had probably been designed that way to prevent prisoners from barring it. Not as though there was anything in the cell in which to do so: there was no bed to rip out, just the step built into the wall, and there was nothing else in the cell besides the toilet. It would even be difficult to harm oneself: there were no light cords hanging, he'd had all his clothes taken, and David now saw that there wasn't even a single object from which to hang anyway. Even the toilet had no handle.

He lay down on the thin mattress, his back finding the hardwood board underneath, and pressed his head into the filthy crackling pillow. His mind reeled with so many thoughts, but like looking through the glass bricks of the cell window, he couldn't see any of them clearly. It felt as though his brain was numb, as though he was trying to get inside to where his thoughts were with huge boxing gloves strapped to his hands. His bones ached and his fingers felt like they didn't belong to him, but when his eyes slid closed, they didn't open again until the clanking of the metal door later that morning.

David lifted his head. Daylight came in through the window, sterile and bright. He blinked in the direction of the door but there was no one there. Then he saw the tray lying on the floor: his breakfast.

He had no idea what time it was when the door opened again, there was no clock in the cell, and he could make out no passage of time through the window, only whether it was day or night. Two men entered the cell, both wearing suits instead of black and white uniforms, and they stared at him as he sat on the edge of the bed. They introduced themselves as Detective Sergeant Harrow and Detective Constable Booth, and asked him to go with them to an interview room. David dutifully got to his feet and stepped out of the cell, the air of the corridor cold on his skin through his paper suit, walking between them along the corridor the way he had come earlier that morning.

He hadn't noticed it before - his mind had been too clogged - but every door they came to was locked, every single one, and the man who had called himself Detective Constable Booth unlocked them from a long string of keys.

The interview room was a square bland room with walls painted the same light blue as his cell. Detective Sergeant Harrow guided him to a chair before sitting down opposite him, and then he switched on a tape recorder that sat on the table between them. Detective Constable Booth stood behind Harrow, as Harrow began to speak, giving details of himself and the DC into the tape recorder, as well as the date and time and David's name and details. David sat watching it all as though it was a movie, as though any minute now there would be an intermission and he could get up and go to the toilet. But there was no intermission, and no trip to the toilet, and DS Harrow looked at him with a stern expression, and then began the interview.

"You declined the presence of a solicitor when you were asked last night, Mr Summers, is that correct?"

David couldn't remember what he'd said last night, the whole thing was still a mess inside his head, but he nodded nevertheless. As soon as he got through all their questions he'd be able to go home, go home to Rafaela, go home and try and find his son.

"What were you doing in your son's bedroom last night between nine thirty and ten o'clock, Mr Summers?"

David stared at him. What did he think he'd be doing in there?

"I was tucking him in," he said.

"Is it normal for you to be in there?"

"Yes, of course it is."

"Were you alone?"

"Yes."

"There was no one else in the room?"

"No."

"There were no neighbours or friends in the bedroom?"

"No."

"It was definitely you?"

"Yes."

"What made Sebastian scream?"

David stiffened in his chair. The face of the monster flashed through his head.

"Mr Summers? What made your son scream?"

"He was scared…"

"Of what? Of you?"

"No, no. It was…"

"Mrs Summers said she heard him scream. She would know the sound of her own son's scream, would she not?"

"Yes, of course she would -"

"So what made Sebastian scream?"

David felt his lips dry up, and he ran his tongue across them.

"Why are you avoiding my question, Mr Summers?"

"I'm not, I'm trying to answer it, but it's complicated."

David ran a hand through his hair.

"Did you kill your son, Mr Summers?"

"No, I did not fucking kill my son, what kind of fucking sick question is that?"

"Sit down, Mr Summers, and answer my questions. What happened in your son's bedroom between nine thirty and ten o'clock last night?"

David sat back down in his chair. DC Booth hadn't said a word since the interview had started, but he'd kept a watchful eye on him throughout. David knew what all this looked like, and cursed Rafaela for calling them. There was nothing they could do to find his son. He'd seen what had taken him, and no lawman in the world could do anything about it.

DS Harrow glanced round at DC Booth and whispered something into his ear as DC Booth leant over towards him. What was exchanged David couldn't hear, but then DS Harrow looked back at him, and then spoke into the tape recorder:

"Interview is suspended at -" he glanced at his watch, "ten thirty seven am."

David watched as DS Harrow switched off the tape recorder and then got to his feet.

He was led back through the station the way they had come, where he was placed back in his cell. He expected either the Detective Sergeant or the Detective Constable to say something to him, but neither of them did; they simply closed the door after him and locked it.

David perched on the edge of the bed and stared up

at the window. Daylight streamed in but he could see nothing of the world outside. They were going to lock him up for life for killing his son. He knew how everything sounded, he heard it the same way they did. But he hadn't killed him, he hadn't.

He tried to pass the time but it was agony. Locked up in his tiny cell he was powerless to help his son. He didn't know what he was going to do, but at least if he was at home it would be a start. He could look for him, search the neighbourhood, ask people if they'd seen...

He clenched his eyes shut and wrung his hair in his fists. He'd seen a fucking monster take his son, a real flesh-dripping monster, kidnap his boy in his own fucking house. He wanted to kill himself just to step out of this nightmare, just to ease the punching hurt that was killing his insides. But he wanted to kill whatever had stolen him first, wanted to find it and rip it apart, the way it had found him in the dining room and in the garden and in the bathroom and in the boardroom meeting with Miyaki. Tears began to run down his cheeks. He folded his arms up over his head and let the sobs come, his paper suit crumpling as he rolled over onto his side, and slowly he rocked there as his pain consumed him.

The only things that marked the passage of time were the meal trays that carried his lunch and evening meal, and the gradually-diminishing light through the glass blocks of the window. It was dark when his cell door opened and a uniformed officer came to collect him. He was led back through the station to the booking room where his clothes and possessions were returned and he was allowed to change out of the paper suit that had felt so harsh and cold against his body. He was given a copy of a form, a computer-generated bail sheet, which the officer went through with him, but all of it seemed to roll past him without any meaning.

"We are releasing you on bail pending further enquiries," the officer said to him. "Come back in four weeks time at ten am. If you don't, you can be arrested and fined or imprisoned or both, for failing to answer bail. Do you understand?"

David nodded as he murmured that yes, he understood.

The officer then escorted him out into another room where two more uniformed officers led him outside to where there were police cars parked. It was night, the sky overhead black and clear. One of the officers opened the back door of one of the cars and David climbed inside, where he sat in silence as they drove him home.

He felt every curtain in the street twitch as he walked to the front door of his house, but he kept his eyes forward. Only once he was over the threshold with the door closed firmly behind him did he dare breathe a sigh of relief.

He wanted to call out to Rafaela, to let her know that he was back and safe, but it felt too much to have his voice loud in the quiet house. The light still burned in the living room, and he went through to stand in the doorway, hoping to find her still up and awake. The smile fell from his lips as he saw all the dining room furniture piled up in the room, the table and chairs in front of the window, the china in the corner. Rafaela was nowhere to be seen, and he began calling her name now as he staggered through into the dining room, wondering just what the hell was going on. He expected the room to be empty, of course, but he did not expect the new carpet to have been shredded. A huge hole gaped from the middle of the room, in front of which he now stood, his hands on his head. He called Rafaela again, shouting her name into the silent house. But there was no reply, either from upstairs or down.

David stepped closer to the hole and stared down into it. A shovel lay at the bottom amongst the wet mud and muck that lay beneath the concrete foundation of the house, most of which was piled high in the corner of the room behind him. He shouted Rafaela's name again, but then he saw something down at the bottom of the hole, something curved and coated with black filth.

He clambered down into the hole, his hands against the rough sides to steady himself over the uneven ground, and lifted the shovel out of the way. The muck at the bottom of the hole was cold on his hands as he dug it away from the object he had seen, but he knew it was a skull even before he had gouged the congealed mud from one of its eye sockets. His heel skipped over the slick ground as he staggered back a step, but he managed to keep his balance as he stared at it. For a grisly moment he thought that it was Sebastian's skull, or even Rafaela's skull, his mind conjuring horrific images of something rising up to claim them, but it was apparent that this skull had been buried beneath the house for a very long time. And then a grim reality swept over him, bringing with it a question that he couldn't answer: the remains of a body was here, Rafaela was not - what had happened to her?

He opened his mouth to scream her name, but as he inhaled, something black rose up at him out of the filthy grave. It was swift and swirling, and tendril-like hands shot up over his legs and torso, grasping at him and pushing themselves into his mouth and down his throat. They stifled his screams before they were even formed, and David flailed only briefly before they tightened around his arms and chest and began to haul him down into the opening muck.

He tried to struggle but the battle was already lost. He felt the coldness of the desecrated soil against his face, the coarseness of the grit between his teeth as he was pulled through it. He was aware of pain, of things moving beneath his skin, of being invaded by something that desired his flesh more than he. He remembered the skull, the mud-filled sockets staring at him. All this flashed through his head in the seconds that he was dragged through the filthy black soil beneath his house. Images pounded his thoughts - of Rafaela, of Sebastian, of rats gnawing and ripping at bloodied carcasses - but they were not his own thoughts, but sights seen by another's eyes, forced into his own skull. The light from the room above him was gone, he was beneath the surface of the soil now, and all he could feel was the mud against his flesh as he was tugged through it, down and down into his sordid grave, furious black hands holding him so tight that he knew they would never let go.


And never let go they did.

People disappear all the time, that's what I told you, and not every disappearance can be explained. I don't know who was buried underneath the Summers' house, I have no name or face to give you, their bones were put there long before my time.

Nobody knows what their house is built upon, or

what secrets are buried in the black soil beneath us while we're safely tucked up in bed. England has a lot of history, a lot of death and blood in the earth. It doesn't just go away.

The police called at the house a few days later to check up on Rafaela Summers, and to ask if her son had returned from a friend's or a neighbour's house. It was those two officers who looked in through the dining room window too.

The hole was examined, as was the empty house, but they found only one skeleton inside. It was bagged and sent to forensics for examination, but it would prove to belong to neither David nor Rafaela Summers, and far too small for young Sebastian, and would ultimately be dated and sent to a museum (as I said, it was a very old collection of bones).

In time, the hole was concreted over and likewise repaired, a new carpet laid in the dining room, and the house sold. I hear that another family has moved in, a young family with a boy of similar age to Sebastian. I don't know how they're faring because I don't know if the ground was ever blessed. England has a lot of history. Who knows if there are more bodies under the house, left to rot in unhallowed ground.

## What Came In The Floodwater

The autumn had been particularly severe. Great grey clouds had hung from the skies like soaked sheets from as early as the first week of September, dropping rain that drowned the earth like a vast squeezed sponge. After decades of annual floods, the local authority had finally invested in a flood relief system, spending something like twenty eight million pounds on huge drainage ditches and deep troughs for the Thames to spill over into. But these had been full by the middle of October. By November, the road at the front of the house wouldn't drain. By December the carpets in the front room were wet.

It was now March and the waters were an uncomfortable memory.

Ernie Hansen woke to a scratching sound. His eyes flickered dumbly in the darkened room, blurred and still half-asleep, until they settled on the clock radio beside the bed and made sense of the glowing red numbers. Twelve seventeen. Just after midnight. Dorothy wouldn't have come home in the middle of the night surely. He lay awake for a few moments, ears straining for the sound to come again, but it wouldn't. Had it been her key in the front door? Had he even heard it? Then the scratching came again, from somewhere out in the hallway, against the door, a familiar scratching.

"Shut up, Milton," Ernie growled roughly over his shoulder.

The scratching stopped.

Damn cat.

Ernie closed his eyes and went back to sleep.

The phone rang over breakfast. It was Dorothy. Her sister's flu was still no better, temperature still up, appetite still down. She'd have to stay a few more days at least, keep the household in order.

"How's things with you?" she asked. "Got to grips with the oven yet?"

"Funny, Dot, very funny. Actually things are running like clockwork."

"That's good to hear, Ernie. I had visions of the house falling to ruin."

"Thanks for your vote of confidence."

"How's Milton? Is he eating again?"

"Just as pain in the ass as ever. Woke me up last night too. Scratching. Wanting to come into the bedroom."

"You should put him out. He doesn't like it in the house at night."

"Well he doesn't seem to like it outside either. I'm going to take out that damn catflap so he'll have to stay out."

"Don't you dare."

"Yeah, well. Why can't he behave like a normal cat?"

"There's no such thing. They're independent. Free spirits."

"Not in the middle of the night they shouldn't be."

"You're just grumpy because you had a short night - hang on a minute, love." She covered the receiver with one hand. Ernie could hear a short muffled conversation. She came back on the other end. "I've got to go now, Ern, Barbs wants some soup."

"She's got you running round after her like a slave again. You know that, don't you?"

"Says you," Dorothy cried with a laugh. "Every

little sniffle you have and you're tucked away in bed, asking me for everything under the sun."

Ernie didn't reply. He knew it was true.

"Anyway, got to love you and leave you," she said, and smacked a kiss into the phone.

"Yeah, you too, hon," he said.

Ernie replaced the receiver in the cradle. Glancing down, he saw Milton staring expectantly up at him from between his feet. The long-haired tabby cocked his head to one side and ran his tongue neatly across his lips.

"I suppose you want feeding, do you?"

The cat stared up at him.

Ernie shook his head and then pushed himself muttering to his feet, taking the bag of dry cat food out of the high cupboard before shaking a small measure into Milton's bowl by the back door. He watched as the cat then padded slowly across the white tiled floor, offer a cursory but disinterested nose at the meal, and then pad slowly away and out through the catflap.

Damn ungrateful cat. You'll get no more later, just you wait and see.


It was late in the afternoon when Ernie got up from the snooker on BBC2 and caught sight of Milton out in the back garden. He was playing with something, pawing it, and by the time Ernie got outside to see what it was, found that Milton had already eaten half of it. Whether it had once been a mouse or a bird was now too late to tell, but it almost seemed as if he'd managed to turn the thing inside out, so ragged and red raw was it. A tuft of what could have been either feathers or fur stuck out from one end of it like a shuttlecock, and Ernie gazed down in disgust at it for a moment, before shooing the cat away from it, watching as he pelted off back towards the house. He picked the remains up at arms length with a tissue from his pocket, and going to the dustbin at the side of the house deposited it neatly inside.

What the hell did people keep cats for anyway? They weren't any use for anything, and they were forever catching small animals and depositing chewed lumps of them around the house and garden for you to find at a later date.

The sight and the smell of whatever he had caught went from his mind as he settled back in front of the television. Stephen Hendry was now five frames up. No surprises there. His opponent seemed to think so too, and stared glumly into middle distance, occasionally sipping water, occasionally shifting weight on his ass cheeks.

The tension on-screen was beginning to mount. Hendry seemed on for a possible one-four-seven. He'd already potted eight reds and eight blacks, the commentators whispering incessantly about past histories and Cliff Thorburn's legendary break, and it was then that Ernie jumped with a start, as the scratching he'd heard the previous night started up right over his head. He shot a glance up at the ceiling, as if he might be able to see right through the floor and see Milton clawing away at their wooden bedroom floor. He cursed the thing as he scrambled out of his chair, images of the tabby leaving deep grooves across the stripped boards flashing in his head like an old black and white cinema flick.

When I get my hands on you, you little bastard, you won't be clawing anything for a week.

Ernie flung the bedroom door open, and if there had been a cartoon speech bubble above his head it would have said gotcha, and sure enough there was Milton, going at the floor as though he was trying to dig a hole. Ernie stormed at him shouting. The cat darted swiftly under the bed, eluding his kick, and then bolted for the door in a blur of grey, claws skittering for purchase, leaving Ernie to gaze at his floor in dismay.

Dorothy phoned later that evening and Ernie relayed the events of their cat's busy day. It was her cat, he said. It only seemed to misbehave when she wasn't around to see it. Nonsense, she'd said. Milton's fine.

Fine, my ass. One more trick and he's gone. A car got him. That would be the excuse. Just you wait and see.

It was twelve fifty six when the cat woke him.

Ernie glared at the clock radio's glowing red numbers as his teeth clenched in his head. It was louder than it had been the night before, which meant that Milton was clawing somewhere close, maybe even inside the room. He inclined his head a little and gazed at the door. It was indeed open a few inches. He'd got in.

Ernie lay still in the darkness for a few moments as he tried to pinpoint just where he was, scratching and clawing at the wooden floorboards. This was going to cost a small fortune to have the damaged boards pulled up and replaced. And for what? For an ungrateful brat of a cat, that's what.

He leant slowly over the side of the bed and lifted the duvet in the hope of seeing the long-haired tabby, hoping he might get a chance to grab one of his slippers and hurl it, catch him a good 'un before he went running. But he looked up and down in the darkness, past his slippers and the attachments for the vacuum cleaner tucked away under the bed, but there was simply no sign of him. He leant over even further, putting his hand down to the floor to prevent himself from falling, twisting his neck so that he could see under the whole bed, even under the wardrobe and Dorothy's dressing table on the other side of the room, but of the cat there was simply no trace.

Ernie clambered back into bed with a frown, pulling the duvet back over himself. Perhaps he wasn't in the bedroom after all. It occurred to him then that the scratching had let up for a few moments as he'd straightened the covers, sending the room back into silence, but now it started up again, scritch-scratching across the floorboards like he was trying to burrow through the damn thing.

That cat's gonna have to sleep outside. That's where cats go after dark anyway. Outside. Dorothy pampers him too much. He'll get none of that from me. No sir. As he closed his eyes and tried to return to sleep, his head became filled with illustrations of the scratching sound. Not of cat's claws or Milton running over floorboards, but images of children's hands clawing at walls, scratching feverishly until their fingers wore down to bloodied knuckle joints. The images were disturbing and out of place. It was a cat, a damn stupid cat, so why did his mind have to conjure anything so horrible. Perhaps it was the sight of the bloody raw thing Milton had killed earlier. It had been horrible. The images continued, however, despite the quiet of the darkness, and they continued into his dreams when they came, too, festering like yellow bruises into scenes of animals trapped in sewers, clawing to get out, eating each other in blind fits, rats, alligators, vermin, all trapped inside a sickening stench.

At six o'clock he woke with a thumping headache that clamped his skull like a tourniquet. The toast made him feel nauseous, the tea made his head swim. And the images of tiny skinless fingers and half-eaten rats would not leave him.

Dorothy phoned at eight thirty. Barbs was better, eating well, and she would hopefully be back tomorrow evening. Ernie listened only enough to murmur noncommittal agreements, one hand holding the receiver, the other his head.

"We're going to have to get Milton trained or something," he muttered eventually.

"You can't train cats," Dorothy said, not noticing the subject change. "They're free creatures. They do as they please."

"Well I think ours is perhaps just a little too free. He wouldn't come when I called him last night."

"When was this?"

"Last night. In bed. I was asleep, and he bloody woke me up again."

"What did you want him for anyway?"

"He was scratching about again in the bedroom. It's going to cost a fortune."

"You should've put him out into the hallway."

"That's just it, Dot, I couldn't find him. I thought he was under the bed, but I couldn't see him anywhere."

"Well, you can't train him. You're just wasting your time if you try."

After Ernie had hung up, he took up a couple of Anadin for his headache, swallowing them straight down with a mouthful of hot tea. He was in pain from a terrible night's sleep, and all because of their damn stupid cat and his incessant scratching.

You'll be out in the garden tonight, cat, that's for sure.

Eleven PM. Milton crept stealthily across the lawn, as cats are known to do, illuminated by the light of the moon, and Ernie watched him from the bedroom window with a contented grin on his face. Pulling the curtains closed, he climbed into bed and switched off the light. The night was warm, his bed warmer, and he snuggled down with the hope of reclaiming what sleep he'd been deprived of, now that the cat was out of the house for the night. He'd pushed Milton out with a satisfying shove, moved the bin against the door of the small plastic catflap, and then watched Milton's bewildered gaze through the kitchen window before putting out the light and leaving him to it.

It was then that the scratching started again.

His eyes flickered open, hovering in an unfocussed limbo of darkness, and a barb of unease scrawled itself across the nape of his neck like a pencil as he listened to the sound, sharp little claws scrabbling across the wooden floorboards like rats playing football. Only now it sounded different to how it had sounded before. He could imagine tiny snaggle teeth burrowing into the boards as well as tiny claws, gnawing and nibbling, splintering the timber. His brow slowly furrowed, and a feeling like damp knotted towels crept into the pit of his stomach.

If the scratching wasn't the cat, then the question occurred, what the hell was it?

Ernie swallowed the ball of fear that had stuff in his throat and leant slowly over the edge of the bed. He went as far as he dared, squinting into the dusty murk, but there was nothing there that shouldn't have been there, just his slippers and the vacuum cleaner attachments. He turned his head to look under the wardrobe and the dressing table on the other side of the room, but they too were both still clear.

He realised now, as he looked for whatever had found its way into the room with them, that the scratching had stopped as soon as he had leant over the edge of the bed, as though whatever had been making the noises had suddenly noticed his scrutiny. The silence was coldly clammy after the former warmth of the room, and it felt like being watched from between the stones of a graveyard, and it sent an irregular twitch of unease across his body. But then it started up again, scritch-scritch-scratching across the wooden floorboards like tiny little teeth and tiny little claws, eager to be out from its hiding place, eager to get to him.

It was then that he realised that his head was only inches from the floor.

The chill of fear gripped him instantly, and he hauled himself back into bed, tugging the duvet up around his chin like a five year old scared of the dark. His eyes scanned the darkest shadows of the bedroom again, between the furniture, at the corners of the room, until the unnerving realisation suddenly came. The scratching wasn't coming from above the floorboards, but from underneath them. Something wasn't trying to get out. Or even trying to get in.

Whatever vermin had found its way under the floor, and it could surely only be a mouse or God forbid a rat, it seemed to be chewing and scrabbling at the wood, desperate to find its freedom. Perhaps it had even been making a nest for itself, his trembling imagination conjured for itself, breeding a plague of filthy grey creatures down there that would soon be clawing for his eyes. The ghastly image knotted his stomach.

Ernie shook himself back to sanity, and leant over and smacked his hand against the wood, hoping to disturb it, to chase the mouse - for that was what it must be, it must be - from both the floor and his head at the same time. It was childish, he knew, but it had the desired effect. The scratching halted, and his head felt lighter, more secure. Even so, Ernie moved a little further away from the floor, and a little further towards the middle of the bed. The warmth was reassuring, better than the air of the room that now seemed unclean.

Wasn't the cat supposed to be keeping the house clear of mice?

Just his luck that he'd put him outside tonight too.

You'll be in here tomorrow night though, cat, that's for sure.


The following evening, Ernie set about taking up a couple of the floorboards in the bedroom, jimmying them with a crowbar and pushing some traps in that he kept in the garage. He peered into the darkness between the joists before he replaced the boards, peering through the dust and grime for the little bastard that had decided to set up home under his bed and keep him up at night. He had half a mind to shove Milton down into the gaps to flush the critter out where he could take a whack at it, make the tabby work for a living, make him chase up and down the skirting boards like they did in cartoons.

With the planks replaced - he didn't want to nail them down because he'd only have to take out the traps and the dead mouse sooner or later anyway - he went through into the bathroom to wash up, wondering as he did so just how long the mouse might take to stumble blindly onto one of the deadly traps. He tried to keep an ear out for any more scratching, or even a muffled spring-loaded snap, but the bedroom remained silent, and so after he'd dried his hands, he left it alone and went downstairs to watch television.

Later on in bed, he lay awake for a while just listening for the sound of one of the traps, when suddenly he leapt up with a start as one of them suddenly did snap shut. He realised as he sat up just how quickly his pulse was racing. The mouse was dead, he knew by the sound of the muffled snap, could almost see it tiny furred body broken in two by the metal bar, blood seeping from the wound. He settled back into his bed with a satisfied smile. He'd take up the boards in the morning and dump its carcass in the bin, but for now he just wanted the bliss of silence.

The scratching started up again.

His eyes gagged open with a start, and for some reason they moved across the room to the dressing table. In the reflection from the mirror, he could just make out the shape of Milton in the darkness, his back arched in agitation as he gazed down into the shadows beneath the bed. Ernie wanted to get up and lift the boards there and then, lift them up and let the cat go in and get the persistent little fucker, and yet something held him back. He suddenly didn't want to get out of bed, didn't want to put his bare feet down on the floor. A chill of fear passed over him, despite the warmth of the duvet, and slowly he eased himself over the edge of the bed, lowering his head down towards the floor.

The scratching continued, despite his proximity and scrutiny, only now it sounded as though the teeth had got bigger and more insistent and were chomping out great lumps of wood. From the other side of the room, Milton now began to hiss with terror, and as Ernie's eyes scanned the floor, so he could make out the shape of the cat more clearly, concertinaed up with his hackles raised, hissing at the darkness under the bed.

Ernie could still see very little, but as his eyes strained against the murk, and with there still being no sign of any mouse, he could make out the floorboards that he had removed earlier begin to shake, rattling the vacuum cleaner attachments that lay next to them like aftershocks from an earthquake. He suddenly regretted not nailing the boards down, regretted it as much as if he'd buried a coffin with the lid open and now had to gaze down at its waking rotting occupant.

The boards began to buck and lift now as though whatever was beneath them had now chosen this moment to get out. The gnawing heightened and quickened, and for a few dumb moments, Ernie struggled to realise just what was going on.

And then it came to him.

The space between the loose boards was not big enough for this thing to get through. Whatever it was that was down there, it was too large to get out.

He was shaking now, his own hairs raised as high as those on the back of the cat on the other side of the room. He shot another glance across at Milton, and could see that it had backed off all the way to the closed bedroom door. Suddenly one of the boards popped up out of the floor, clattering across the floor as though it had been shot out of a cannon. Ernie reeled in terror, as the flank of something black and furry forced itself upward. A scarlet eye opened in the middle of that dark mass, sharp and unblinking, and it seemed to rove about the room until it finally fixed itself upon Ernie, fixed itself upon him with a hateful and insolent contempt.

So it was you that smacked the floor above my head, it seemed to say. It was you that put these traps down here to snap my fur and clamp my tail.

A row of grey jagged teeth suddenly emerged over the edge of the wooden boards, teeth that now began to chomp down on the wood, splintering it and increasing the size of that horrible hole. He tried to cry out, but his throat had suddenly dried to a desert dune and wouldn't carry a single word let alone a scream. All he could do was sit and stare at this thing as it chewed and clawed at the wood, forcing its ragged mass through the ever widening breach.

From the other side of the room, a second assault started up, scratching and clawing at the wooden floor. Ernie shot a white-eyed glance in its direction, only to find Milton, not attempting to flee this thing, but clawing at a second hole in the bedroom floor. A black clump of hair was already half exposed, a vicious talon swiping at the cat who even now was slashing back with a swirling fury. Ernie watched in horror as a third hole splintered behind the cat, another mass of black hair burst through to land a deadly blow to his cat. Milton's flank was opened like a purse, spilling looped innards like glistening red change. He let out a yelp of agony, and as he turned to protect himself, caught a second blow that slashed his face open to the bone. Ernie watched with absolute dread as Milton staggered sideways a half step before collapsing in a bloody tangle. Ernie's breath sank out of him as he watched him die, and it was only a shower of dust that fell across his face like powdered cobwebs that shook him out of his daze.

His eyes flickered uncertainly up towards the ceiling, his vision swirling, his consciousness staggering. The white paint was broken in a patch above his head, and even as he struggled to make sense of why the black hole should be there, something tumbled out through it, down and into his lap.

He cried out in both alarm and pain as the thing bit into his thigh. Instinctively he grabbed hold of it, its hair damp and thick, and hurled it away from him. The bed itself suddenly rocked as the mother broke free from the loose boards in the floor and out into the room, and Ernie almost tumbled back off the bed so quickly did he shove himself backwards.

It appeared now, black against the blackness of the room, hunched over the edge of the bed, its scarlet eyes glittering with hunger, its jaws now parting to show two rows of evil sharp teeth. It hissed, a long steam-like hiss, that threatened to strip his flesh. So intense was its gaze that he barely noticed its children sink their teeth into his feet and draw blood. He stumbled back another step, his eyes only dimly aware of yet more ragged creatures forcing their bodies out of more openings in the floor, more gaps in the ceiling, and even the breach beneath the bedroom door.

His back hit the window sill hard, but the impact forced breath into his lungs and a scream slipped easily from his throat. He stood and screamed at the rat-creatures that scurried across the wooden floor towards him like a rancid thick tide, eager to devour him, tear at him, while all the time their mother stayed on the other side of the bed to watch them take the first feed. Ernie turned in a fit of desperation, knowing that he would never make it to the door, but perhaps might survive a fall from an upstairs window.

His hands fumbled with the latch even as tiny jagged teeth clamped around his calves and pulled. Pain penetrated his upper legs as they began to scrabble up him, using their brethren as a living writhing ladder, to sink their blood-stained teeth deep into his meat. The window suddenly opened and he felt the cool of the night air crisp on his face and neck. He clasped the frame with two weak hands, but even as he pulled himself towards the cold air of the night outside, he felt a spasm of burning agony in his lower back as the mother took hold of his spine in her jaws, twisted her head, snapping his vertebrae, before his head went black, his knees buckled uselessly, and he tumbled back into the room of crawling fur.

His sight flickered open briefly only once more, to see the jaws of the mother grin proudly as she waited over her children, watching them feed without interruption, before she would bend down and satisfy her own overdue hunger.

# The Man Beneath The Carpet

In time, maybe I will forget, the sights and sounds of what I had believed to have been a man beneath my carpet. Even as I sit here now in my North London home, the mere mention of him sounds preposterous. Had I lived through it at all, I still wonder to myself? Yes. I have the nightmares of him to remind me.

I say 'him' as if I had seen his face, but I had not. I say that he lived beneath my carpet, but that too is not entirely the truth. There is so much that I feel I should unburden, even if they are just words on a page, but perhaps if I can at least put the past few years into some sort of cohesion, then it might not seem so terrible.

The clock on the wall tells me it's getting close to midnight - what was once the carpet man's favourite time - but I am glad to see that my hands are not shaking. There used to be a time when every night I would begin to shake just at the thought of his imminent arrival. I wonder if those times are over now. I haven't seen him for a while.

Perhaps I should explain a little about myself first. I am twenty five years old now, and alone, but when I first started seeing the carpet man, I was not much older than twelve, I think. There would only have been fleeting glimpses then, a slippery shadow cast across the floor or an unexpected shifting movement, and only if I were to wake during the night. I'm not sure what I thought of those early glimpses, or whether I even registered them as real, but as time went on and I began to realise that there was something there, I realised also that this was some kind of secret never to be told. There was nothing I could tell my parents, of course, I knew that much at least. I was certain that it would be dismissed as a child's attention-grabber, because I was a child, after all. So it became something of a solitary event over those first few months, a spectacle of something extraordinary that I could not tell another living person, not even as those glimpses became more and more frequent, and the sight of him changed from perplexing to ghastly.

I've just moved my chair closer to the window so that I can write more easily by the light coming in from the streetlamps outside. My back is towards the wall just behind me as always though. My fear of something creeping behind me is an old but rational one, and it's just something that I've had to live with. Anyway, I can see through the window and down into the street below, which is quiet at the moment, but it will be buzzing with traffic come the morning. I like North London. It distracts me. There is plenty of noise and plenty of people, and plenty of hard surfaces to walk on. I always thought it strange that he didn't like hard floors. I guessed that he just couldn't get beneath them. It had been an amusing thought, in a way. I liked it.

I think I may have turned thirteen when the appearances began to increase. I'm still not sure to this day whether he used to wake me in the night or not, but I do know that I always used to open my eyes to the sight of him. Between my bed and the bedroom door he used to stay, just his head and shoulders forcing the carpet up. It wasn't that he stretched the carpet up in any way, or tugged it away from the walls, but it just seemed to form some neat little package around him. Not so neat that I could ever see his features, but neat enough to show me that he was there and watching.

Was his mood ever malevolent? I don't know, but there were countless times when I was scared and I seemed to think so. Cruel, evil, spiteful; all words that I used over the years to describe his encounters with me. He would rise several nights in a row, sometimes, roving beneath my bedroom carpet. Round and round the room he'd go, for no reason but to torment me, to keep me awake. He sometimes made no noise at all, and sometimes he'd make a scratching sound. I used to feel unbalanced, as though I might topple inside, and I would cry, and pull at my hair to make him stop, but he would not, and he would only disappear when he felt like it. For years I could do nothing but lie in bed beneath his mercy. I wanted to scream out to my parents sleeping in the next room to tell them of the man that kept me from my own sleep, but I knew that I mustn't. The man beneath the carpet was for me to see, and nobody else. I knew that he would disappear back to wherever he came from the moment anyone took a step outside my room, or laid their hand upon my door. It wasn't until I put faith in my own bravery, however, that I realised just what lengths the carpet man was prepared to go to, just to frighten me.

I must have put up with helplessness for at least a year or more before I finally tried to leave my room. I'd only just begun to sleep with the door open, so that the light from the landing could spill into my room. I don't know why I thought that would help. Perhaps I reasoned somewhere in my head that my parents might glance in one night while the carpet man was there and catch him. I never stopped to think what they might have done about it. But this one night, though, the night when I managed to muster all my courage and make a run for the open door, was the night that seemed, in hindsight, almost a turning point in my life with him, and it turned out to be a turning point for the worse.

I remember that I woke to the sound of him scratching across the floorboards. At first I couldn't see him, but then he appeared from behind the corner of the bed as he moved across the room, the carpet shifting evenly and smoothly as he glided beneath it. He came to halt in his usual place and stopped to look at me. As I've already said, he had no eyes that I could see, but there was no mistaking that he had them, and that he had them on me. My hands were already shaking, which made easing my bed covers down more difficult, but I didn't want him to know what I was about to do.

I took a breath as I tensed all the muscles in my body, and then started to count down my escape; three, two, one. I reached zero and then froze. I couldn't do it. I thought that he would suddenly grow arms from the depths of the carpet, arms that I had never even seen him possess for over a year, and grab hold of me and pull me down. At that age, and even at my present age now, I still don't know what kind of logic could've made me believe that my bed was the safest place to have been, and that if he'd have wanted to grab hold of me he could have done so long before. However, after that count to zero, I took another breath, held it, tensed my muscles afresh, but still couldn't manage to make that dash from my bed. There was no catalyst, no single moment to instigate my flight. The house was silent, the carpet man had ceased his scratching, and the only sound I could hear was the heavy thumping of my own heart. I tried the countdown once more, the numbers descending this time with the pounding in my head and chest. When I reached zero a third time, I forced myself up onto my elbows. The movement was small, but it was enough to give me momentum. With the covers already eased back I urged my legs out from under them, thrusting my feet down towards the floor. I was quick, but the man beneath the carpet was quicker.

My foot touched not the floor at all but the carpet over his head. I remember looking down at the sight of him there and holding a scream in my throat. I had been seeing this man for over a year, but never once had I made any kind of physical contact with him. Here I was, though, upright and standing on top of him. I lurched forward awkwardly in a kind of half-stumble, but he was there to catch my second footfall. I stepped back, and again he moved so that he was beneath me. I tried making for the open door, but each time I put my foot down towards the floor, his head and shoulders would shift beneath the carpet to be there waiting for me.

Within a few strides it seemed obvious that I couldn't make it at all, and I stumbled back towards my bed, his faceless head there beneath me with each step to bear me up. I lay back crying for much of the night after that, shaking and huddled with my arms around my head. You cannot begin to understand how frightening all of this was for me, to have a creature come into my room every night and for me not be able to do anything or tell anyone about it. There was no excuse I could think of in order for me to even sleep in any room but my own. As things transpired, however, it seemed that any kind of escape such as that would have been futile anyway, for it turned out that he was not restricted just to my bedroom.

I think it must have been either my fourteenth or fifteenth birthday when he came beneath a carpet in a room of the house that was not my bedroom. I'd had some friends from school round for a party and we'd just finished eating. Wandering through into the living room, I waited on the sofa while they went to collect the presents that they'd left in the hallway on their arrival. Eagerly anticipating their return, it was just seconds before they came back through the doorway that I caught sight of him. A movement behind the television was enough to catch my attention, and even with the sound of their footsteps growing louder along the hallway, I couldn't stop myself gazing into the darkness there. The carpet was raised, of course, and I could see the outline of his head and shoulders, motionless as he watched me.

My joy drained out of me in an instant. I still recall the sight of my friends tumbling through into the living room, and their expressions of glee dropping in a matter of seconds as they saw me. My face must have been disturbing for them to look at, so shocked and afraid was I by the sudden and unexpected sight of the carpet man's presence in the living room. They didn't stay long after that. The air of happiness had gone, drained like water down the hole in a sink.

He used to appear frequently after that, all over the house, but never so that anyone else could see him; when someone had just left the room, when my mother had turned her back for a moment, when my father was dozing. These were his favourite times, when I could not shout "There he is, the carpet man is over there, don't you see him?" I hated him for that more than anything, I think. He would not let me share him. I had him all to myself, whether I wanted him or not. That was the deal, I think, too. That I had no say, no will.

I'm drifting. I don't want to get back into all that negative stuff. It's taken far too long to get as far as I have, without giving him the satisfaction of going through it all again. Where had I got to? Oh yes, my birthday, and how he had managed to make even that day his own.

I can't say that I began to get used to seeing him everywhere whenever he felt like it, because I didn't. Nightime had been bad enough, but then he started to appear during the day as well. There wasn't a time when I was in that house that I could honestly not expect him to appear. In the morning while I was in the bathroom, he would push up the carpet and watch me in the shower. If I was eating in the kitchen, I would see or hear him beneath the carpet in the hallway. Even climbing the stairs, I would glance behind me to see him at the bottom, only to have him appear and waiting in front of me on the landing and trail after me like a dog from one room to the other. Only when I was not alone, could I be sure he would not show himself. But even in that I could not relax. He'd shown me so many surprises over the span of seven years that I deemed him capable of anything.

A car has pulled up down in the street, a blue one, the blonde girl and her boyfriend who live across the street. I can see them moving about inside, but not so much that I can see what they doing. I'm two storeys up. My view is expansive, but not good for spying through car windows. She's getting out and waiting for him to get out also so that she can lock it. He does now, and the yellow indicators flash as she points her keys at it. They ascend the steps leading up to the front door. He's got his arms around her waist and is kissing her neck as she tries to find the lock with her key. It's her place, I think, but he stays a few nights a week. I've seen them making love a few times when they've left the curtains undrawn. They seem quite passionate. Tonight will be another one of those nights, I guess.

I was older and dating when the carpet man threw yet another of his surprises at me. I was at college, and seeing someone from my English class. We were at a pub in Kilburn, I think it was, with a few of our other friends from the college, when I saw him. Since the years of his appearing throughout my parent's house, it seemed that he had picked up a few new skills along the way. The pub was crowded, a welcome distraction from my home life, but that seemed not to bother him. It was as I sat at one of the tables, talking and laughing with my friends, that I saw him. I glanced across at one of the white plastered walls, and saw his head and shoulders rippling beneath it. I was so stunned by the sudden sight of him that I dropped my drink. The glass hit the wooden table with a loud thud, spilling its contents before tumbling into my lap and onto the floor. This brought hysterics from my friends, and to a certain degree dispelled the shock of seeing the carpet man again. Not wanting to leave the group, but realising I had to, I made my excuses and reluctantly got up from the table to go back to the bar and get myself another drink.

The shaking in my hands returned there and then, and I feared that I would drop my drink a second time as soon as I got served. I remained at the bar, however, shivering and perspiring, while the din from the crowded pub echoed in my ears. The cigarette smoke seemed to sting my eyes and sinuses, my head was pounding, and I could only barely concentrate on standing upright.

Although the pub was extremely busy, a movement in my peripheral vision caught my attention enough for me to glance round at it. It was the carpet man, and he was roving beneath the plastered walls across the room towards where I was standing. I watched as he suddenly changed course and veered up and across the ceiling and then down behind the bar. The bottles of spirits rattled in their mountings as he moved behind the wall to which they were attached, but somehow nobody else noticed. Lines of glasses chinked as he forced them from their stationary places, shuddering on their shelves as though in the grip of an earthquake, but still no one glanced his way.

My hands were trembling so much that I thought I might drop the money I was holding onto the ground and not have enough sanity to stoop to pick it up. I could feel the sweat on my brow cooling as a draft blew through the bar, beads of it breaking away to track down into my eyes. I wiped them away swiftly so that I could keep my sight fixed on the carpet man. He had come to rest beside the till, his head and shoulders raising one of the beer towels up off the bar, it's rectangular cloth forming neat folds around him. I felt like screaming, but knew that I could not in such a place. I glanced back towards my friends to see if they were ready to leave, but they were talking boisterously, throwing their heads back now with fits of laughter. What could I do?

167

I became aware of somebody talking beside me. I turned dumbly in his direction and realised that he was talking to me. Did I know him? I had no idea. I still don't know to this day if it was someone I knew, or whether it was some innocent stranger. I thought perhaps he was asking if I was waiting to be served, but cohesion came swiftly and I realised, somewhat foolishly, that he was trying to chat me up, asking if he could buy me a drink. My thoughts were racing uncontrollably and for some reason I must have said yes. I was glad to be able to step away from the bar for a few seconds so that I could catch my breath, but as soon as the man turned around and held my drink out for me, I panicked and fled.

I never returned to that pub in Kilburn. In fact shortly after that I dropped out of college altogether. My friends quizzed me frequently about what had happened. I couldn't answer them, and to be honest, I couldn't face looking at or even talking to them at all after that. I couldn't return home either, not to the house where the carpet man had lived with me for so long. So I found myself travelling north, and to a small one bedroom flat in Manchester, where I lived fairly reasonably for a while. I got myself a job doing menial work in an office. I went out most Saturday nights. I started seeing someone from work. Then one night at a club, the outline of a head glided effortlessly across the dance floor, it's slippery shifting shape startling beneath the white flashes of a strobe light. What else can I say? I ran.

From Manchester I went further north to Liverpool, and again tried to make things work. I lasted over a year until the carpet man tore beneath the pavement in front of me, lifting slabs up to the left and right. I stood there just standing and staring at him. Passers-by grunted and cursed as they were forced to walk around me, but I could simply not deal with the sight of seeing him once again.

Eventually I left Liverpool, of course, and travelled further north and across the border into Scotland. I found a small rural community, but the quietness of the place just unsettled me, reminding me of the quietness of my parent's own home. Edinburgh was much more to my liking, but again the carpet man found me. This went on for a few years, an endless circle of travelling and settling, the days of imminent flight constantly unnerving. I can not begin to tell you the depression and loneliness of those years, not being able to tell another living being. I might perhaps have tried with some of the people I grew relatively close to over that period, but after the experience back in that pub in Kilburn, where nobody else had witnessed what I had seen, I knew that this was something personal and terrifying for me and me alone.

I can see the moon over the roofs of the buildings opposite now that the clouds have cleared, and it is large and white and beautiful. I can see a number of stars also in the breach of cumulus, twinkling brightly. They, too, are alone, I guess. Millions of miles separate them, but from here, they all seem like part of one wonderful connected family, glittering together and blessing us with the ability to watch them.

I've been here in North London for only a few months, and Kilburn is not that far away. I've been thinking of returning there and perhaps trying to find that pub again. Don't ask me why. I don't think I could tell you even if I wanted to. The street outside is quiet again, and it echoes the silence of this room. I can sit here without moving, and without listening to the scratch of my pen across this paper, the silence is unnerving. Are those shadows moving? There, by the wall. I look but I can see nothing now. Perhaps it was my imagination. Daybreak will come in a few hours and I can return to my new job in the city. There are a lot of people in the city, and where there are a lot of people, there is also a lot of noise. It's something that I've grown to love, noise. It helps stop my hands from shaking. Hell, it stops my whole body from shaking. Those shadows, they are moving. I sit up a little straighter and stare at them, but there seems to be nothing in them now. I reach for my cigarette lighter and hold the flame to the stub of the joint which I can barely hold in my fingers. As the blue smoke curls lightly into the air, I inhale gratefully as I press my head against the cold glass of the window and gaze down into the street below. My car is parked at the kerb just outside the entrance to my flat. I like to know that it's handy.

## The Ghost Behind Me

Trying to convince someone that it actually exists, that's been the hardest part, and I'm still not sure I've cracked it. Trying to prove to someone that my head isn't fucked, and that there is something that lurks behind me, a veil, a shadow, a ghost.

How best to describe it, this thing that floats behind me? It's a reflection, that's what my doctor keeps telling me, or a blot on my retina or some other such shit, but I know the truth. He keeps saying that I'll be fine. But fine from what? I know the ghost's there, he doesn't. What is there to keep me locked up in here for anyway? It's not as though I'm trying to kill anyone or anything.

It's there now, I can see it hovering behind me as I look in the glass of the door to my room, a shifting grey mass that sits there doing nothing. My doctor keeps trying to convince me, but I know different. There he is now, Dr Lenten, strutting across the corridor like he's some fucking god or something. I'd like to stick that clipboard of his so far up his ass... but maybe that's just the anger he says I've got. Hell, I never had anger like this before he dragged me into this place.

It's moving, this ghost of mine, roving about behind me almost enough so that I might actually get a proper look at it, but I know I never will. I know as soon as I turn my head it's going to disappear, but it's taunting me, goading me into looking anyway. Perhaps if I'm quick this time I'll catch a glimpse of its face. Does it even have a face? Not that I've ever seen. In all the years it's been haunting me, I've seen only that same grey reflection behind me. It's still moving.

I'll catch sight of you one of these days you bastard, just you wait and see, then we'll see what the doctors make of you. I'm going to see you and then I'm going to prove that you exist, and then I'm going to get your sorry ass exorcised.

But enough already. I don't want to get angry again. It seems that I've been getting angry too much lately. It's not doing my heart much good, and I'm sure not going to let that fucker be the end of me. It knows that I see it. It just wants to fuck with me, whatever it is, play around and see if I'll bite. I just want to tell my story here while I can, before it makes me do something I don't want to do. I don't like it being there. I don't want it there. It hangs around me and it disturbs me and I just want it to go away. Oh God, why can't it just leave me alone.

If I close my eyes it disappears from the reflection in the glass. I can't shut my ears, but then I've never heard it make a single sound, even though I can almost feel it breathing right against my neck, perched by my shoulder, looking down at me, grinning and cruel. Perhaps you have one too, a ghost by your shoulder, what do I know? Perhaps the world is full of them, a whole world full of floating grey ghosts, hovering and devouring...

My eyes snap open. I can't stand it. I want this to end, oh please God, I want this to end.

I take a deep breath and try to block out the moment, session one, and try instead to concentrate on the past. If I think hard enough I can shut him out, session two.

I'm not sure when I first started seeing him, but I think it was shortly after my thirty-first birthday. I can dimly recall looking into the bathroom mirror one morning as I was shaving. That's when I noticed something moving about behind me.

I was alone in the house, my wife had already left earlier, when I felt a strange clammy shudder pass over me, almost as though someone was stroking my back. I hurriedly snatched up a towel to dry my face, to clear the water from my eyes, spinning round as I did so. The bathroom was empty, just as it had been before I'd entered, but it was the strangest and most shocking experience I think I'd ever felt up until that point; the realisation of something new, something extraordinary, paranormal. Only once I was back in my bedroom and changed did it pass from my mind, slipping from my memory with all the ease of a midnight dream.

It wasn't until the next morning when I was brushing my teeth, that the same thing happened to me again, a grim dark shape floating behind my back. I fell to the floor, with my back hard up against the wall, my body shaking furiously as though someone had jumped back and forth all over my chest. My heart was pounding and wouldn't slow, and my eyes could settle on nothing, but instead flickered without focussing from one part of the bathroom to another, searching for this barely glimpsed entity.

I must have sat there for the best part of an hour, sitting and staring, fretting and shaking, unnerved by this thing that had touched me in my own bathroom, almost reached inside me physically. I felt as though I'd been violated somehow, alone in the bathroom as I was. I thought I was safe even in my own house, but as my roving eyes settled momentarily on the shower opposite me, I saw my own reflection cast in its mirrored tiles, and there behind me, hovering in a gap that was not even there, I found the great grey shape of the ghost.

I bolted from the room, my chest literally stricken as I ran choking from the house. I clambered into my car and drove like a lunatic at ridiculous speeds, not knowing where I was even headed until I found myself on my way to my wife's office. I screeched to a halt just outside her building, but I thank God that I went no further. I sat there panting and sweating, staring out at the busy street as the engine idled, my fingers slick against the cream leather of the steering wheel, while the sight of me staggering into her office and jabbering about dull grey masses rocketed through my head. It was enough to snatch me back to reality. I turned the car round slowly and returned home, calmly and with measured breaths, marking the speed limits perhaps too accurately as I went, and for a while at least that was the last that I saw of the dark grey ghost.

There's a nurse staring at me, squinting over the top of her clipboard. What the fuck does she think she's doing? Shit, she's writing something down about me; I hope I wasn't talking out loud to myself again. They don't go much on that in here. Fucking bitch. What the fuck does she know about me? I'd shout at her if I thought it would do any good, but you can't hear shit through this door. I could be screaming and they wouldn't hear me. Oh, I guess that's the point, isn't it? Lock the poor fuckers up until they kill themselves. One less crazy to worry about.

She's trundling away now, probably going to check on the poor freak next door, make sure he hasn't swallowed his own tongue or something. Why doesn't she find something better to do instead of making shitty little notes about guys like me who need some real help?

Deep breaths, that's what I need. I can feel myself getting uptight again. My chest feels as though it's wrapped up in parcel tape, bound and gagged tighter than a fishtank in the mail. This ain't no way to continue. Deep breaths. Deep breaths. Okay, now where was I?

Things seemed fine for a while after that second glimpse. A few months went by and I completely forgot about the thing that I thought I'd seen. I hadn't told my wife anything about the encounter, but for the first few nights afterwards I so desperately wanted to. But what would she have said? You're imagining things. It's probably just a mid-life crisis. But as the days passed, and I fell back into my own mundane routine, I became more and more unsure about whether I had actually seen anything at all.

So my memory kindly erased both incidents, and I got back to my day to day shit, until one day I was driving to pick up some stuff for the house, I forget now what it was, when I suddenly get this eerie feeling like I'm being followed. I check in the rear view mirror and there are a few cars in the lane behind me, but nothing unusual. But this feeling keeps on, nagging at me, unnerving me as I'm driving. And then, just as I'm checking harder in the mirror, my eyes pick up the outline of a dull grey mass, floating right behind me as though it's sitting right there on the back seat like a fucking passenger. The memory of it hurtled back into my head like a bullet, and I'll tell you now, I was fucking freaked. I cried out in alarm, and swerved across both lanes as I craned my neck over my shoulder. But I saw nothing after that until a few hours later when I slowly opened my eyes to a paramedic hunched over me.

"You're going to be alright," I remember her saying to me through the shattered side window, the face of the second paramedic contradicting her words as I saw him cast horrific glances at the bottom half of my body. I'd swerved right off the road in my panic, hit a parked car, and managed to trap both my legs under the dashboard, breaking one of them in the process. It hurt like hell, but at the time I was just more concerned about that shifting grey mass that had hovered behind me, taunting me into what would later be called a suicide trip by one of the ward nurses. The paramedic must have injected me with something heavy because I can't recall being particularly anxious about the crash, only that I was aware of the ghost still being there, watching me, malevolent and smug from the safety of the back seat.

I was in the regular hospital for about a week, I think, before this guy turned up at my bedside to ask me a few questions about the accident. I forget now whether he was from the police, or the insurance company, or even some quack sent in to investigate the dreams I'd been having, but what I told him - and don't forget that I was on some serious medication, and my tongue was perhaps looser than it might otherwise have been - brought me quicker into this room that I'd have ever thought possible.

The ghost was a fairly regular visitor to my room. I had a semi-private room in the Godolphin Wing of Wexham Park Hospital, just one other bed next to mine, and that was only occupied for three weeks out of the six that I was in for, an elderly gentleman in for a knee operation. Jim Beeson or something, I think his name was. Anyway, there was a mirror on the wall opposite, and I could see myself whenever I was sitting up, meal-times and suchlike. It would hover there, in the space that wasn't there between my back and the upright pillows, hovering like a blurred pencil smudge, grey and shifting. Not always a visitor, and never when anyone human was present.

The drugs in my bloodstream made a lot of my time there seem just as blurred, just as distant and uncertain. It's slippery to latch onto any particular instance of its being there, or even of any malicious acts it may have performed when we were alone. But I was always aware of its presence, I could feel it like a strip of Velcro stretched across my skin, crawling across it. The air would feel thicker too, damp even, almost like a heavy soup. I don't know, it's difficult to explain. It was just unnerving to have that thing in there with me, and not have anyone else see it or feel it, not even old Jim Beeson.

The notes that must have been made at the time - and I'll tell you I made myself heard about it more times than I can remember - must have made it into a few filing cabinets around the country. My GP even quizzed me about it on a routine check-up a few months later. I'd not seen the ghost for a while, and I had to think back. Yes, I told Dr Lewis, I had been seeing things, or at least I thought I had. I was back to that stage of not being sure after a brief period of not seeing it. Dr Lewis cast me a few disparaging looks over the top of his bifocals as he jotted down some scrawled notes in my file. An uneasy sweat covered my body in his surgery, pasting my shirt to my back with a humid vile glue. That scrawl did not look good.

It was during that check-up that the eye-test was first mentioned. Only I had ever seen this grey mass, and Dr Lewis was the first to think it might have something to do with my vision. An appointment was made with the optician in the high street and I promptly attended one afternoon after work. My sight was fine, he told me; edging towards long-sightedness perhaps, but nothing that needed correcting, and certainly no sign of retinal damage. I was surprised at how good-humoured I was upon leaving. I strode back to my car as though I'd been cured, as though my body had been given a clean bill of health and I was free. Only once I was back behind the wheel and waiting to pull out of the parking space did I see it again, sitting on the back seat, watching smugly as I attempted to pull out and back onto the road.

My hands clenched to white-knuckled fists as I caught sight of it from the corner of my eye, my skin running with a clammy sweat, my heart shuddering erratically. It seemed to be hovering over the back seat, roiling like an impending storm cloud, its fury held threateningly at bay. I couldn't quite get a look at it, always shifting and just out of reach, slippery, elusive. I must have sat there for some considerable time, because I remember someone honking at me, shaking me out of my stupor, my eyes flashing out of the windscreen to find another driver gesturing at me angrily to come out of the space if I was coming. I rolled forward slowly, my touch on the controls distant, my feet numb against the pedals, back on to the main road. I was honked several more times on the short journey home, but only when I had pulled up in the driveway did my unholy passenger depart. I got out of the vehicle alone, and went to the front door unheeded.

That bitch nurse is back. I've got half a mind to tell

her to go fuck herself, to take that clipboard of hers and shove it. Hey, that's not a bad joke; half a mind. She'd like that, I'm sure. Come here, bitch, and I'll tell it to you. Oh, fuck off then, carry on with your duties. I'll see you later, I'm sure.

I think it was few months after that that I first received a call from Dr Lenten. He called me at my office, explaining who he was and how Dr Lewis had referred the case to him. I wasn't sure about a psychiatrist listening to the incidents I'd been having, or even if I was a 'case' or not, but at the time I think I was just glad to have anybody listen without a look of amusement or disbelief.

I began a few sessions with him, once a month for a little over a year. The ghost returned just a handful of times over this period, for which I was at least glad. Dr Lenten did nothing to help me get rid of it, but I managed to remain relatively calm whenever it did appear, and I managed to keep a tap on that restrictive feeling around my chest.

My blood pressure was soaring, you see. I was heading towards something bad, angina perhaps, or, God forbid, even a heart attack. Dr Lenten at least gave me support with that. Now I don't know what he's up to. My blood pressure must be through the roof again, now that they're keeping me in here like this. He sees me more regularly now, once a week usually, only now I'm not even allowed home. I haven't been home for two months, haven't seen my wife for six weeks. What's going on? What am I even doing here?

Calm down. Take deep breaths. That was session one, way back when. It works sometimes, but other times it just makes me worse and makes me want to scream. It's not me that's the problem, it's this thing that hovers behind me. It's hovering there now, just behind my left shoulder, peering out through the glass at that nurse who claims not to be able to see it either. If I try and turn stealthily enough... Shit, it's fucking gone again, back into the place where I can't see it at the small of my back. I keep trying and trying to gaze down there, but I just can't manage it.

I feel sometimes like those crazy mutts that chase their tails round and round. I used to stare at them and wonder why they did it. Now I guess I know the reason. I've become one of those crazy mutts myself. Perhaps I should start barking too. I wonder how that dumb nurse would like that? Wouldn't that look outstanding on her daily report? Room ten; observed patient talking to himself; observed patient spinning round; observed patient barking like a crazy fuck.

God my head hurts, all this shit whirling round and round like a drain filled with mud. I don't know how much more I can stand. Why don't they just let me go home? A decent night's sleep and I'll be fine, I'm sure of it. Shit, that nurse is talking to Dr Lenten. She's showing him her clipboard. Now they're looking across the hall at me. He's nodding at something she said. Jesus, it's going to be the straps again. Not session fourteen. Not again.

# Man In A Red Suit

It was Christmas Eve, and Johnnie sat on the end of his bed gazing out at the snow flakes falling past his window. He was grinning wildly as he watched them spiral downwards in the darkness, turning and falling like tiny delicate feathers. Using Simon's roof next door as a guide, he could see how deep the snow was already getting, and it had settled to least a few inches thick. It was getting exciting. He looked behind him at his Bart Simpson clock beside his bed. It was only nine o'clock. Three hours until Father Christmas would come down the chimney with his sack of presents. He was definitely going to stay up and wait for him this year.

From downstairs he could hear the chink and clatter of crockery, his parents clearing away the plates from their big Christmas dinner. Turkey and plum pudding and cream and after dinner mints. His stomach still ached with the load, and he patted it appreciatively, bulging nicely beneath his pyjamas. His official bedtime was half past eight, but his parents had allowed him to stay up until half past nine because it was Christmas, and he took the advantage of what available time there was left and slipped silently downstairs to double check the living room. His stocking still hung from the mantelpiece over the fire, but he knew that Santa would never get the mountain bike and Playstation he'd asked for in there. It was just to humour his parents more than anything else. Johnnie knew this, and Santa knew this too, and he would probably just leave the gifts next to the tree.

Johnnie went there now. There was sufficient space

for them both. Perhaps even space enough for the Pokemon he was after too. He'd put it on his list to the North Pole, along with the bike and the Playstation. It was a long shot, he knew, what with Pokemon being so highly sought after this Christmas, but he figured it was worth asking for nevertheless. From the dining room across the narrow hallway he could hear someone rummaging and the clinking of glass, and he hurried quickly out of the living room in case he was caught by the tree again. From the doorway, he could see that it was his mother, going through the drinks cabinet. He stood and watched her for a moment, as she filled a glass from one of the bottles. He didn't know what was in the bottles, and he didn't much care for any of them, but he watched as she took a quick sip and then refilled it furtively. He'd smelt the top of one of those bottles once. The stink was nasty, and why anyone would want to drink any of it was beyond him. His mother turned suddenly with it in her hand and saw him watching her. Their eyes locked briefly.

"Whiskey for Santa," she cried, and hurried away from the drinks cabinet and past him into the living room with it. Johnnie went after her and watched as she set the glass down on the mantelpiece, just above where his stocking hung. "Perhaps I should get some cookies for him too," she added. "What do you think?"

Johnnie nodded indifferently, his thoughts whirling elsewhere. This was outrageous. Santa would undoubtedly be unimpressed by that whiskey, perhaps he'd even be offended. He would probably feel just as sick as he had done the minute he smelt it, and would then not leave any presents. Johnnie went to see if he could get rid of the glass as soon as his mother left, but he just couldn't reach it, high up on the mantelpiece.

She came back a few moments later, holding a plate in her hand. On it was a circle of cookies, his favourite chocolate chip would you believe, and he pursed his lips at the sheer audacity of it. He just hoped that Santa would skip the drink and just have the cookies. That way he was sure to get his mountain bike and Playstation. If only his mother would put out some chocolate milk as well. He might even stand a chance of getting that Pokemon too.

She ruffled his hair as she set the plate down next to that glass of awful whiskey.

"It's getting close to your bedtime, honey," she said. "Santa won't come if he knows you're awake."

"I know," Johnnie replied, stalling for time, "I'll just go and see dad," and then he hurried out of the living room in search of him.

He found his father in the kitchen, sitting down with a glass of wine in his hand, flicking through the TV guide. Johnnie went and stood next to him, and glanced at the pictures as the glossy pages were turned. Here was Arnold Schwarzenegger, always a Christmas fave, and there were the Spice Girls, standing huddled beneath a glittering Christmas Tree. The stench from the wine glass drifted up and found his nostrils, and he took a step back away from it, missing the section about Nickelodeon's festive viewing. His dad glanced at him with a smile.

"Getting excited?" he asked. "It's the big day tomorrow. Christmas Day."

"Oh, yes," Johnnie replied, and secretly thought, And I'm going to stay up all night and wait for Santa to bring me my presents. You won't know I'll be awake, and neither will Santa, but I will be, oh yes I will be.

"Do you think he'll bring you everything you want?"

Not if mum doesn't get rid of that whiskey.

"Dad?" Johnnie asked out loud. "Do you think Santa would like some nice chocolate milk when he gets here?"

His father seemed to ponder the suggestion for a moment.

"I don't see why not," he said, and got up and went to the refrigerator. Mixing the milk with some chocolate powder in a glass from the cupboard, he took it through into the living room. Johnnie followed eagerly behind, and watched as his father set it down next to the plate of cookies.

"Looks like Santa's already got a drink," his father said, staring at the whiskey.

"I think he'd prefer chocolate milk," Johnnie urged.

His father turned to look at him, the smile still on his face.

"So do I," he said, and after swapping the glasses, downed the whiskey himself.

Johnnie winced as he watched him do it. He was sure Santa wouldn't have liked the stuff, but it was still one hell of a sacrifice for his dad to make rather than throw it away. But he seemed not to mind too much. He watched as his father took the empty glass and staggered out of the room. His smile had crept into a grin. At least his dad was happy to know that Santa would now be getting his milk.

His mother called from upstairs, telling him again that it was time to go to bed. Reluctantly he left the living room and traipsed upstairs. Back in his room, he closed the door behind him and went to the window to look outside once more. The snow was really beginning to come down now. It was probably about three or four inches thick on Simon's roof, and his high spirits came back at the sight of it. Down in the garden, the snow was a deep uninterrupted blanket of white, clean and deep and untouched by human footsteps or pawprints. Everything was white. Everything was there to be played in. It was going to be a wonderful Christmas.

His bedroom door opened a crack and his mother poked her head round.

"Come on, Jonathon, it's time for bed. I've told you twice now. Santa won't bring you any presents if he knows you're awake."

But he won't know I'm awake. I'll hide and wait for him, and then when I hear him, I'll creep down and surprise him. By then it'll be too late. He'll have to give me my presents.

"Bed," she commanded, as if she could hear these rebellious thoughts, and watched as he stomped away from the window and back towards his bed.

She came in again a few minutes later when he was under the blankets, and tucked them in around him. Kissing his forehead, she kindly ruffled his hair as she told him that she hoped he'd get all he wanted for Christmas. He smiled as she hugged him, and then watched as she left his room. Johnnie had left the curtains open, and now he turned his attentions back to watching the gentle flakes of snow flutter down on the other side of the glass. He couldn't wait to get his new presents, his mountain bike and his Playstation, and then he could go out to play in the deep snow with Simon from next door. He had a really big sledge and his dad used to take them both up to the big hill in the park. That was what Christmas was all about.

His bedroom door opened again, and his dad came into the room. Johnnie watched as he too went to the window to stare outside, to watch the world change before his eyes.

"Can't wait until the morning, eh, champ?" his dad said, turning to look at him.

You're right there. I can't wait. That's why I'm not going to wait. I'm going to see Santa this year, and he's going to give me my presents personally.

"Perhaps Mr Dresden from next door will take you sledging again," his dad added. "Would you like that?"

Johnnie nodded enthusiastically. His father came over, still with that grin on his face, and kissed him goodnight. The smell of the wine was still on him, sourly mixed with that terrible whiskey smell. It wasn't a good combination, but his dad was cheerful and he didn't want to upset him by telling him how much he stank. Johnnie waited until his dad had closed the door behind him, and then got up to sit on the end of the bed to watch the snow some more.

Bart Simpson told him it was ten minutes to midnight when he heard the first tinkle of bells. He hadn't realised, but he must have nodded off, because when the sound woke him, he was curled up on his bed. Thank God the reindeer had woken him, he thought, otherwise he would have missed Santa. Johnnie sprang to the window and looked out. There were no reindeer in sight, and there weren't any hoof prints on Simon's roof either. There were, however, marks in the snow in next door's garden, human footprints. Santa must have gone there first, Johnnie realised quickly. Perhaps Simon's house was nearer the North Pole than his. Oh well, he would just have to wait a few more minutes. Maybe he could get a look at him delivering presents inside Simon's house.

Johnnie gazed down at next door's living room window. The curtains were drawn, and the lights were out, and there was no Santa to be seen there. Then came the sound of tinkling bells again. Boy, those reindeer must be mighty close. A light was burning upstairs, and through the curtains Johnnie could see the silhouette of someone moving about. It looked like a man, with a fairly large build, so it must be Santa, bringing presents up to their bedrooms. Another light came on, and Johnnie wondered why Santa was not being as secretive as he was reported as being. The curtains at this other window were not completely drawn, and through the gap Johnnie could see the man moving about. It was the same man, fairly large, and was he, yes, he was wearing a suit of red. The excitement was almost too much to bear. Here was Santa.

Johnnie crept to his bedroom door so that he wouldn't wake his parents, eased it open, and then went downstairs as quietly as he could. Hiding in the living room, he huddled close to the tree, waiting for Santa to come down the chimney. The milk and cookies were still on the mantelpiece, he could see them from where he was, and hopefully that would put Father Christmas in a good enough mood for that Pokemon.

Then suddenly he heard the approach of the reindeer, but the tinkling of bells came not from the rooftop, but from the back of the house. Ears pricked now, Johnnie craned his neck forward to listen for the entrance of the mysterious Santa Claus. It was not a Ho Ho Ho that came, however, but a sort of gruff cursing, followed by more sounds of tinkling bells. It was then that Johnnie realised that the bells reminded him more of breaking glass than anything else. Slowly he crawled out from his hiding place and poked his head around the living room door. In the corner of the kitchen he could see a man in a suit, the same man in the same suit that he had seen inside Simon's house. It was red, this suit, a glistening red, but there was no white beard, no big shiny boots and no sack slung over his shoulder. What a swizz, Johnnie thought. He can't even be bothered to dress up like his Christmas cards. What he did have, Johnnie saw, and it was strange to even see him with it, was a long dark hook where his right hand should have been, dripping freely with blood. His suit glistened with the same blood, that was why it was red, and he was still cursing as he stepped over the glass from the broken kitchen window and into the house.

Johnnie had half a mind to go and tell him that this wasn't the way to deliver presents, and that he'd have his Playstation and mountain bike now please, before he broke anything else. But there was something in the hollow black eyes in Santa's head that told him to do otherwise, and so he stayed where he was, and watched the man in the red suit stalk through the house towards the stairs.

Johnnie could see his face more clearly now as he came into the hallway, but it was still distorted by shadows and blood. What little flesh he could see, was hideously bulbous and marked by bruises and nicks. His eyes were indeed hollow, and seemed little more than holes sunken into his head, and his mouth was nothing but an uneven slit, hacked open into a rough evil grin. Johnnie shivered now at the sight of him, and realised that this was not Santa. This was a creature, come in from the icy darkness outside. Was this even the same creature he had seen in Simon's house? Then an image came into his head, of his best friend Simon, slung on the end of this creature's hook like a lump of meat at the butchers. Was that why the lights had been on in their bedrooms? Because this thing hadn't cared whether they'd been awake when he'd killed them or not.

The man in the red suit was climbing the stairs now, not quietly like he had done, but noisily, his great boots clumping from one step to the next as he hauled his weight upstairs. My parents, thought Johnnie, and left the safety of the living room, hurrying into the hallway to stand at the bottom of the stairs. His motion must have been more significant than he'd intended, because the creature stopped and turned to look back. Johnnie's eyes locked with those of the beast, and in that connection, he could see the evil of this thing. There was death here, and malevolence, and it frightened him more than anything else ever had in his entire life. He took a step back, and as he did so, saw with absolute fear that the creature did likewise. It was turning, this thing, turning to face him. And now it was coming back down the stairs towards him, his great boots clumping like thunderclaps on every step. Darting back into the living room, Johnnie searched for someplace to hide, tears streaming now as his chest became stricken. He could find nowhere but behind the sofa, and even from there he could see the man in the red suit appear in the darkened doorway. His long black hook hung from his arm, still dripping blood onto the carpet, as his hollow eyes searched the gloom for him, his grimace ghastly as if enjoying this game. Then his eyes came to rest as they settled on him. He had found him, even in this darkness. The creature's human hand found the light switch, and the room was illuminated brightly. Johnnie let out a yelp as the thing came for him, but he managed to wriggle out from behind the sofa in time. The creature swung at him as Johnnie ducked past, and plunged his hook deep into the side of the sofa. Johnnie heard the material rip at the man tore his hook out, and headed for the kitchen and the back door. There was glass all across the tiled floor as he reached it, and it cut into his bare feet as he ran over it. His hands found the cold metal handle of the back door, and he tugged on it with all his strength as he turned it. But the door would not open. It was locked, and it just rattled in its jamb.

With his heart pumping wildly, Johnnie turned, only to find the creature stomping into the kitchen with his hook raised. From behind him, he could hear the sound of tinkling. More glass breaking. Were there more of these creatures now, coming in from the cold icy darkness? Johnnie stood trembling, terrified and helpless as he watched the man come towards him. His suit was the deepest red, glistening with fresh blood, and his ragged mouth dropped open to reveal a wider grin of broken and decaying teeth. He raised his hook higher as though he was about to bring it down upon him, and Johnnie shut his eyes as he put his hands over his head, but the blow never came.

Johnnie trembled as he opened his eyes. The kitchen was empty. Broken glass still littered the tiled floor, but of the creature there was no sign. Slowly, he took a step forward towards the hallway, and then from the living room, he suddenly heard a thump. Death was here, Johnnie kept thinking, and even though his senses protested, he followed the sound regardless.

In the middle of the living room were two forms. The one of the floor Johnnie recognised as the creature, only now he lay dead, his bloody hook motionless on the carpet. Above him stood another man, also in red, and he turned startled as Johnnie appeared in the doorway. In his hand was a long knife which he had used to open up the creature beneath him. His suit was also red, from head to foot, and also of blood. Beneath his bright eyes was a long fluffy beard of white, stained with the flecks of combat, and on his head he wore a cap of scarlet to match his suit. Behind him was a sack, leaning against the mantelpiece, and from the chimney came the same tinkling sound he had heard in the kitchen. This tinkling, however, was not the sound of breaking glass, he realised, but the real sound of sleigh-bells. Slay-bells, Johnnie thought with a grin of his own. This was Santa after all.

The man came towards him now, slipping his long knife back into its scabbard attached to his wide black belt. Going down on one knee in front of him, Santa said in a booming voice:

"What are you doing awake, little boy?"

"I stayed up to see you," Johnnie replied.

"Didn't your parents tell you of the dangers involved in staying awake on Christmas Eve?"

"They said you wouldn't give me any presents if you found me awake."

"Ho, ho, ho. I'm afraid it's a little more serious than that. These creatures only feed one night of the year, and they feed on human flesh on Christmas Eve. They know which households are awake and which households are not, and they only kill those that wait up for me. It is their punishment for those who would reward me for slaying their kind."

"You mean they knew I was awake?"

Santa nodded gravely.

"I'm afraid so."

"What about Simon next door? We both agreed that we would stay up to see you."

"He's okay," Father Christmas assured him. "It was a close one, but I got there in time."

Johnnie stared down at his feet as he tried to take this all in. Could it really be true that Santa Claus hunted demons all over the world as well as delivering presents? All on the same night? His eyes then went to the creature still lying dead on the living room carpet.

"What happens to him now," Johnnie asked, pointing at his twisted form.

"A little bit of Christmas magic sees to all that," Santa replied, and with a click of his large fingers, the creature's body rose into the air and was then spirited away up the chimney towards the waiting reindeer. A second click, and the blood stains went from the carpet. A third click, and Johnnie heard all the glass from the kitchen window repair itself back into the window frame. Johnnie stared agog at Father Christmas still kneeling in front of him. He had a large smile on his face now, his cheeks rosy and flushed, although Johnnie wasn't sure whether that had been from benevolence or slaying. Johnnie watched as he then pushed himself to his feet and stepped back towards the fireplace.

"I have to be going now," he said, "I have a lot more homes to visit tonight."

"Don't forget your milk and cookies," Johnnie told him, pointing.

"My favourite," Santa exclaimed, and took a

minute to wolf down the cookies and swallow the chocolate milk.

"Thank you for that," Santa said, with a wide grin. "I need to keep my strength up tonight. Well, have a Merry Christmas, and remember, never stay up on Christmas Eve again. Your life may depend on it. Goodbye."

Johnnie took a step after him.

"Santa -?"

He faltered, his right foot already in the hearth.

"Yes, my boy?"

"Have you forgotten something?"

Santa stared at him for a moment, perplexed. Then he remembered.

"Oh, how could I forget," he exclaimed, and then from his sack he produced a mountain bike, and then a Playstation, and set them down beside the Christmas tree.

Johnnie gazed down at them with joy, but before he could touch them, Santa cautioned:

"You can't play with them now. You'll have to wait until morning."

Father Christmas looked down at the disappointment on his face. Then, with a kindly smile, he reached into his sack once more.

"Here," he said, "something you can have now."

Johnnie took this last present from him and then watched as he disappeared in a shower of glittering dust back up the chimney towards his waiting reindeer. The sound of sleigh-bells tinkled from the roof, followed by the soft pad of hoofs disappearing into the night. Johnnie breathed a heavy sigh at the memory of the events of Christmas Eve, of the waiting until midnight, the creature in the suit of blood, and the meeting with Father Christmas himself. Turning to go back to bed, he remembered the last gift Santa had given him, and he glanced down now and saw Pikachu sitting in his hands. So Santa had got my Christmas list, Johnnie thought to himself, and held it to his chest as he ran all the way back to his bed.

# Nine Forty Two

Mr Springs was a salesman, a travelling salesman, and his business was encyclopaedias.

He was a short man, a stout man, and he lived out of a suitcase when he was away from home. The London night was a foul night, black and filthy with a grimy rain, and he'd dashed between the Underground Station and the hotel in Kensington to be out of it as soon as possible. The lobby had been packed, mostly with a stag party converging noisily on the hotel restaurant, others either filing in or filing out of the overcrowded bar. Mr Springs had to wait until most of them had been attended to first before he could even approach the reception desk, but it at least afforded him time to gaze around at the décor of the small but elegant chamber, a rewarding and stress-free hobby of his.

An old tall grandfather clock dominated one corner, eerily but impressively, its wood panelling dark and elaborately carved, a long silver pendulum tick-tocking rigidly in the frame behind the narrow glass door set in its front. Pendulum, he thought almost subconsciously to himself; a body suspended and swinging; the swinging piece in a clock which regulates its motion. Next along the wall hung a portrait of an old gent with a greying beard, dating back a century or more, a nameplate beneath it denoting it to be someone of importance somewhere within the history of the hotel. Further along still, and displayed inside a tall wooden cabinet, hung a series of ancient muskets and hunting rifles, little gold plaques under each of them, presumably with dates from when they were last fired.

It was all very fine and all very English, almost like a snapshot of an old gentleman's lodging. Gentleman, he mused quietly; a man of good social position; any man above the rank of yeoman; a man of good breeding or of high honour. Indeed, he thought, with a slight nod to himself. Indeed.

One of the reception staff caught his eye as he was gazing about, and Mr Springs stepped up briskly with a smile in order to sign in. It was still noisy at the desk even though most of the merrymakers from the stag party had shuffled through and into the restaurant, vacating the small chamber almost entirely. He took a room up on the fourth floor, and retired thankfully away to it, away from the hubbub of the merrymakers, away from the grim and grimy streets of London outside and away from the tick-tocking of the old tall grandfather clock. Hubbub, he thought carefully as he stepped into the lift; a great noise of many confused voices; a tumult; an uproar.

Room thirty three was small but quiet, and after the rain and bustle of the busy London streets, Mr Springs set his two heavy leather-bound suitcases down on the floor with a phew! One of the suitcases contained his encyclopaedias, the other his travelling arrangements - two changes of clothes, including undergarments neatly folded away in one half, shaving foam, razor, soap and toothbrush in the other. Everything had its place and Mr Springs was never at a loss. It had been a long day of travelling across North London, knocking on doors and selling sets of his wonderful encyclopaedias, but Mr Springs felt that his job was more than just a job. It was a calling, a duty. People would always need to know interesting and amazing facts about the world. And why on Earth wouldn't they?

After a shower in the overly small cubicle, Mr Springs had a shave and brushed his teeth, and then perched on the edge of the bed to trim his toenails. When they were all neat and even, he reached over to pick up the remote control off the bedside cabinet to switch on the television in the corner of the room. He flipped to the news and proceeded to nod intermittently at important points the newsreader was making about diplomats and presidents around the globe. Parliamentary dialectic, he mused thoughtfully. Very good.

Opening the other of his suitcases, Mr Springs carefully drew out one of the cherished volumes of his encyclopaedic range, and reverently began turning its pages. So many facts and references. So much work involved in categorising. The world must be a wonderful place to be so full of such interesting things. Of course, he'd only ever been outside the country himself just the once. A day trip to Calais. But the world still seemed jolly marvellous. And besides, people didn't need to see it for themselves, if they possessed such reference manuals as these.

Mr Springs reclined back on the bed and continued to leaf through the encyclopaedia. The room was lit only by the single wall-mounted lamp above his bed, not big enough to light the entire room, but more than sufficient to read by. On the other side of the single-glazed window, he could hear the sound of traffic, and from behind the wall at his head, probably room thirty one, a couple were talking rather more loudly than they should. The television still droned in the corner of the room, but it was quiet, and he didn't want to turn it off and have the traffic and arguing couple become more distinct than they already were.

Sabaism proved very informative, as did Sable and Sacrament, although he didn't care much for Sadism. Very distasteful. So many astonishing facts to be found about the world, he thought to himself, without the need for all that. There was a good long section on the archer Sagittarius, and he even read and re-read the two columns covering Saints and Sainthood. How much time elapsed between Sanskrit and Sesquipedalian, he had no idea, but by the time he reached Sombrero, everything around him was deathly quiet.

When he became conscious of how dead the silence actually was, Mr Springs let the encyclopaedia drop a little from his line of sight. His eyes went to the half-light of the room, and then strayed across to the patterned curtains drawn across the narrow window.

The traffic was gone, that was his first thought.

Not quiet or intermittent, but gone.

Strange, he thought, that there should be no cars out there at all. It must be later than he'd realised, but then there should still be some traffic about. This wasn't the middle of nowhere.

Even the couple next door weren't debating their marital issues as they had been, but then that seemed more of a godsend than a concern, and he smiled guiltily to himself at the notion.

But then there was the television too.

Although it was still on, the programmes themselves had apparently finished, leaving behind only a fuzzy and silent snow-show in their place.

Mr Springs took up the remote control from the bedside cabinet, pointed it at the set and pressed the off button. The snow disappeared instantly into a pulse of pale white that melted rapidly as he watched, leaving an echo of its nonsense behind in his sight.

It must just be bedtime, he reasoned, but he wasn't tired himself, and so he lifted the encyclopaedia back up in front of him and continued to read the passage concerning the origins of the large straw hat.

He had got only as far as the top of the next page with a piece concerning Sonatas, when a motion in the corner of the room caught his attention. It only seemed like a sort of grey shadow, floating and insignificant, but his peripheral vision had already given it the substance of a person entering the room. His hands lowered the book, his eyes staring uncomfortably at the wall that led round to where the main door stood, just out of sight. The urge rose in him to call out to see if anyone was there, but his heart was suddenly beating rapidly, and he realised that this was a hotel room. No one was supposed to be in here but him, not even a maid, and he would have heard if someone had opened the door.

Mr Springs shifted nervously on the bed so that he could continue reading while still keeping an eye on the corner of the room. The silence was still dead, deafening and unnatural, and although the room was warm, a shiver of unease shuddered across his body, ending up in his fingers as a tremble that wouldn't quit.

He forced his eyes down, pleading with them to follow the words that were printed there. Sonata, it began, a musical composition of several movements...

His eyes rose against his will.

There it was again.

Something was there.

Something grey.

Shifting across the room.

With shaking hands and hammering blood, Mr Springs lay the encyclopaedia down on the bed beside him, and pushed himself uneasily to his feet. Again, he wanted to call out to see if anyone was there, but a fear surfaced rapidly once more - suppose that there was someone, or even something, there? His voice came out timid, and then froze in his throat altogether, the words straining as though they were suddenly stuck on barbs. He stepped forward into the middle of the room, to a place where he could get a good look at both the door to the bathroom and the one that led out into the corridor. There was nothing there but those same two doors. He took a tentative step towards the bathroom, tugging quickly on the light cord and flooding the overly-small room with brightness. It stood empty, no grey shadows waiting inside to leap out at him. He looked around anyway, leaving the light on, before stepping back away from it.

The weight of the silence suddenly seemed even more oppressive than it had been, heavy and almost pushing down upon him, and he hurried quickly to the bedside cabinet in order to snatch up his wristwatch. The slender black hands showed nine forty two. He frowned to himself and shook his head slightly.

That wasn't right.

He pressed the gold wristwatch to his ear and listened.

Nothing.

How could that be? His watch had never stopped in all the years he'd had it.

He pursed his lips as he wound it, but then as he looked back at it, he saw that the second hand was still not moving. It was simply dead in his hands.

Mr Springs pocketed the watch regardless and then

looked behind him, although why he did that he didn't even know. Stepping warily back across the room, he looked about him as he went uneasily to the narrow window, another shiver crawling up his spine as he eased back the curtains just enough for him to peek through.

What had earlier been a busy Kensington street was now a deserted thoroughfare, and there was not a single car or pedestrian in sight. The streetlamps still burned with their usual dull yellow phosphor to illuminate the spears of rain that continued to pierce the cold dark night, but there was just no sign of anyone about.

London had become a ghost town.

Even across the street in the buildings opposite, a number of lights burned to themselves, but of anyone going about their lives inside their rooms there was simply no sight.

Deserted; he thought, abandoned, left, to quit a service without permission.

Mr Springs let the curtains drop before turning back to stare once more at the room, his ears pricked and listening intently.

No cars.

No voices.

No banging of doors.

This was a hotel in the middle of London, for God's sake. Where was everyone?

He went to the chair and picked up his shirt, dressing quickly before slipping on his expensive leather shoes. Even as he got to the door he wondered just what wandering through the hotel might achieve. Everyone was probably just in bed; all the drivers asleep, all the other guests asleep, the staff probably gone home for the night, except for the night staff who were probably... Well, perhaps they were just asleep as well. And as for his watch that had never stopped since he'd had it. Well, that was surely just a coincidence too.

The corridor outside was just as silent in both directions as the street when he finally stepped out into it. Even though he pulled his own door closed as quietly as he could so as not to wake anyone, its click still resounded loudly along the walls. His shoes somehow squeaked on the carpet as he started for the lift, something else that he had never noticed before, as he trod quietly past the first door on his right, number thirty one, the room of the disgruntled couple. He couldn't help himself, but he paused outside their door just long enough to incline his head a little towards it, but it was completely quiet inside, just as he had expected it would be. He leant nearer still, and even pressed his ear against the wood of the door, listening intently. Still there was nothing.

No talking.

No television.

No snoring.

It was all simply dead.

Mr Springs stepped away from the door and continued further along the corridor.

There were two more doors before the lift, number twenty seven and number twenty eight, and he stopped briefly in front of each. He had no idea if either room was occupied, but they were just as silent as the couple's in number thirty one. The lift chimed as it reached the fourth floor, and he took it down to the ground, where he headed straight for the small but elaborately decorated reception. He found it deserted, and after leaning over the counter and peering through the door which led round to the back, he relented and rang the small brass bell.

It let out a shrill ring that seemed to reverberate throughout the entire building, tinny and cold. That would get them running, Mr Springs thought to himself, as he stood waiting for them to appear, rolling backwards and forwards rather nervously on his heels. No one did, however. Not even after a minute or so. He pressed it again. The second ring seemed even louder than the first, but still no one appeared from the back room. Mr Springs turned to look round the lobby for some clue as to why he seemed to be the only one left alive in the building. Perhaps there had been a fire drill and someone had neglected to inform him of it. Perhaps there was even a fire.

As he looked about him, his fear beginning to creep up on him once more, he saw once again the old tall grandfather clock that stood in the corner. It wasn't until he idly wandered towards it that he realised how silent the lobby actually was, and it took a further moment to realise the exact reason why. The long silver pendulum that had tick-tocked so regularly behind the glass-panelled door now hung mute and motionless. His eyes rose hesitantly towards the clock face, an eerie feeling creeping over him like a cold slick fog. Its elegant hands were motionless and pointed to nine forty two.

Mr Springs staggered back away from it as though its deathly silence was infectious, and found himself stumbling back into the bar that adjoined the restaurant in his fear to get away from it. All the lights were burning here just as they had been in reception, and he took in the scene before him, observing quickly that the bar was clean and prepared, the glasses out, and the napkins laid evenly. Everything was here except the requisite barman and guests. It was wrong, he thought to himself, so very, very wrong.

Mr Springs took a breath and then crawled his way behind the bar to get himself a drink. If anyone actually turned up to catch him, he mused as his trembling hands shook a healthy measure out of one of the bottles and into a tumbler, then he'd be more than glad to be in trouble. As it turned out, no one did, and so he helped himself to another.

The whiskey was warming, and brought a welcome light-headedness with it. He took it with him back to the reception desk, which Mr Springs now ventured behind before making his way through into the back room. It was deserted, just as all the other rooms of the hotel had been, and he decided while he was there to have a quick look round. There was a fax machine and a computer here, a filing cabinet and a guest book, everything a hotel office should have, but then he started to have a quick nose through the papers on the desk as he took another draft from the tumbler. There were letters mostly, with reservations or slips attached to them, but then he found a staff book, a duty roster, and he flicked through it to find out just who was supposed to be on duty tonight. Sasha and Stewart were supposed to be here in reception, it read, as well as a guy called Taylor in the bar, and Romany the night porter. Here it all was in black and white. The only thing was, it begged the question, just where the hell were they?

As he went to leave, Mr Springs noticed a clock on the wall. He was not surprised to find that it too read nine forty two. But then a thought occurred, and with a wry smile, he glanced down at the computer, its standby light flashing dimly with a vague hope of life. He nudged the mouse to one side, the monitor flickered on, and he glanced down through the haze of whiskey already numbing his system, at the time being displayed in the corner of the screen.

It was nine forty two.

Oh for fuck's sake, this was impossible.

He was running now, darting out of the back room, out through reception, and heading back in the direction of the lift. He hovered impatiently, waiting in the dreadful deafening silence of the old hotel building, while the only discernible sound, his own heartbeat, thumped wildly away in his chest like a huge heavy drum. He scuttled into the lift when the doors finally opened, and he took it back up to the fourth floor, hugging his arms around himself now with a terrible creeping fear, before taking off in the direction of his own room. He stumbled to a halt as he passed number thirty one, the couple's room, and double-backed to press his ear against the wooden door once again to listen.

Still nothing.

Perhaps it was the unrepressed nature of the whiskey that made him do it, and if he had been asked about it at the time he would not have had an answer ready, but this time he knocked, loudly and insistently, banging on the door impatiently. There had better be someone in this time, he thought to himself. There was trouble brewing.

He stood rocking on his heels for a few moments, just as he had done in the lobby earlier, as he waited for someone to answer. But no one did. And barely another second had passed before he crossed the line of the door to door salesman, and entered uninvited.

The door was not even locked, and it swung open easily on its silent hinges. The room was lit, however, as bright as the hallway, and Mr Springs stepped over the threshold and carried on inside. The room was a mirror image of his own room, the bathroom on the right instead of the left, the bedroom on the left instead of the right, but as soon as he stood in the middle of the room and gazed around him, he could see that someone was at least staying here. There were bags standing in the corner of the room, open and partially unpacked.

He went towards the suitcases, his door to door code thrown right out the window now, as he began to poke about inside for anything unusual. Dresses, perfume, sweaters, this was the woman's case. He went to another. Trousers, razor, this the man's. On top of the dressing table in front of the window were a number of items, pocket change, deodorant, travel brochures, a watch. A watch! He snatched this up eagerly, his fingers clammy and shaking again, but this time with excitement and perhaps even a little panic. He looked at the face. It read nine forty three.

Nine forty three?

An edge of fear crept back over him as he looked at it again.

Nine forty three. There it was, the hands weren't wrong.

And then, from behind him, as the fear of what he was actually doing began to grow and grow, he heard the sound of someone laughing, muffled as though it was in another room, or maybe even outside in the corridor, and it boomed throughout the silence like a vast bronze bell. He turned, his weight suddenly unbalanced as his thoughts reeled with the realisation that somebody else was still alive in the building, only to find himself suddenly toppling awkwardly to the floor, and scattering the contents of both suitcases as he hit the ground hard. The door swung wide, and his eyes flickered upwards to find a couple standing at the threshold, their faces ashen with horror as they beheld the situation before them. Here was a thief, stealing their watches and their possessions while they'd been out on the town.

Mr Springs grappled forward to find his feet, to clamour for their forgiveness, to explain the unexplainable, but they were already screaming down the corridor, crying out for assistance. A hotel porter seemed to manifest beside them in the doorway almost immediately, rushing into the room to take charge, taking hold of Mr Springs' arm, twisting it and hauling him out of the room, his voice raised and with talk of police.

Mr Springs was stammering, excuses tumbling from his lips like those of a madman, but the porter ignored every word of lunacy he could utter as he was dragged along the corridor and past the faces of other shocked guests on their way towards the lift. The hotel suddenly seemed packed and bustling once again, the doors to both twenty seven and twenty eight opening quickly as their occupants stared out in both alarm and disbelief.

The lift delivered him back out into the lobby, the porter's grasp still painful upon the muscles of his arm. Sasha and Stewart were already stepping out from behind the counter, leaving two new guests to wait for their room keys, bewildered at the scene facing them. Guests even appeared from the busy restaurant and the bar, drinks half-full in their hands as they shook their heads in a disagreeable fashion at the state of the criminal caught red-handed.

Mr Springs stood helpless at the centre of a sudden and deafening din.

Guests debated him in the bar.

Voices whispered behind crooked turned hands.

The old tall grandfather clock tick-tocked its ceaseless chatter of time behind him.

And somewhere outside, the piercing siren of a police car cut through the rumble of late night traffic on the busy London streets, as it made its way towards the hotel. The din was unexplainable, bewildering, and he listened to it all with a distant notion of impending madness. Incarceration; he thought, imprisonment, to shut up or inclose.

The angel looked down from the white summit of the mountain as the warm sun sank beneath the horizon behind him. The city below him reached out like a glittering blanket as one by one the lights inside the houses began to burn. There was much happiness in the city, he could see, but there was also much sadness, and the hearts of the people who lived there glowed like tiny coloured fires inside their bodies and illuminated their world. Blue fires burned for love, yellow fires for rapture; red flames for rage, ochre flames despair. So many twinkling pyres, and each a different colour of the rainbow, the sight somehow both beautiful and disturbing at the same time. The watchers above him in the heavens would have it no other way, of course. To live without feeling would be not to live at all; without the sun there could be no night; without the anguished heart, no chance for love. A paradox to drive the human mind from sanity, for sure, but then that was what the human mind was made for.

As the evening sky continued towards night, and the first bright stars plotted the boundaries of their constellations, the angel descended from the heights of the mountain. His feet barely touched the smooth rock of the peak, or the soft blanket of pine needles as he broke the timberline, and as he made his way effortlessly across the river, he paused to watch the pale fires at work in the bodies of the fish beneath his feet.

As he neared the suburbs of the city, he came upon a car parked off a quiet road beneath the trees. There were no street lights here and the car's headlights were extinguished. It's engine still radiated heat, but it was towards the two fires inside the vehicle that he focussed his attention. Looking in through the rear window he could see a man and a woman, their hearts ablaze with scarlet flames that seared inside their bodies. As the angel stepped closer he could hear them arguing, and could feel the frustration in them both. The angel closed his eyes and smiled as he lifted his hand up toward the car, laying it palm down on the paintwork of the vehicle. The warmth from his own heart channelled through the tips of his fingers and flowed into the metal of the car, colours blossoming inside the vehicle like electric flowers, their glittering petals falling on the heads of the two people. The angry words subsided as their lips creased into smiles, and the angel opened his eyes to witness their subsequent embrace. The red flames inside their hearts dimmed into radiant hues of green, and flecks of blue and yellow swept through their arcs like fireflies. Turning his back on them, the calm restored to the trees, the angel headed on into the city along the quiet evening road.

The houses of the suburban streets had many wonderful sights to see as he passed by. Bright coloured fires burned in most of the people here, while others guttered with greys and browns. Some had to go their own way, he knew, and others were simply at the opposite end of the paradox. For an angel it was sometimes hard for him to keep his distance, but then it wasn't his place to question the rules. In times of uncertainty, he would often think of himself like the fish in the river; it was just his place to be, and that's all.

The houses had changed to shops, and inside one of their closed doorways he came upon a vagrant lying huddled. The angel looked down upon him, at his hands clasped to his chest beneath the soiled blanket drawn over him, and at his meagre possessions held in a cloth bag tied to his waist. He could see that the man had neither food nor water, and that he had no money in his pockets and was shivering from the cold wind that blew through the main street. The angel looked inside him and was surprised to find that the fire still burning in his heart was bright with vivid colours. Kneeling beside him, the angel smiled as he touched the vagrant's arm. Instantly his belly became full and the shivers went from his body, the wind changing direction to carry balmy summer fragrances from the south towards him.

A large white moon rose high overhead, and as the angel turned his head skyward to watch it's beauty, found another fire burning high on a ledge of a tall building in the heart of the city. The angel went quickly to him, and found a man standing beside an open window, his eyes clenched shut, his face pallid and vexed. The fire that burned inside his heart was not an eager one, and it's dark bruised flames guttered on the brink of extinction. The angel rose swiftly towards the ledge and as he reached the man's side, could hear the wind that threatened his heart howling inside him like a gale. It dimmed his fire, this wind of despair, and the angel spread his fingers against the man's trembling hand. Closing his eyes, the angel could see the images that tormented him, his fears and secrets, his dependants and the unseen future. These were branches of the life tree that could not be touched, the angel knew, but it was necessary that they all be faced without intervention. His fire would probably not be able to cope with the demands asked of it, but it was the gale raging inside him that had pushed him onto the ledge in the first place, only now it was threatening to snatch at his ankles and cast him over. The angel pressed his lips to the man's lips and inhaled a breath deeper than any lung could hold, and drew the gale out of the man's body and into his own. The dark fire ceased to gutter, and the angel watched as the flames caught a little, and then glimmered, as brighter flecks of hope sparked in its uncertain heat. The angel smiled as he watched the man climb back into his office, close the window behind him, and then retake his seat behind his desk.

Returning to the street, the angel noticed a young boy sat at the kerb, his feet crossed in front of him as he toyed idly with a stick. He was hitting the street with it, this boy, bringing the end of the stick down on the tarmac of the road. The angel could already see how dark the fire was that burned inside him, and as he moved closer, could see that it wasn't just the road the boy was hitting, but a beetle beneath. Standing over his shoulder, the angel could see that the beetle was dead, it's hard burnished shell broken into shards that remained glued to the yellow ooze of it's innards. The angel laid a hand on the boy's shoulder and felt the malice seething within him. There seemed to be no anger attached to it, however, just a single emotion to destroy. Closing his eyes, the angel drew the malice from the young boy, his concern lifting as the fire inside him glittered brightly once more. As he reopened his eyes, he smiled to himself as he watched the boy drop the stick and get to his feet, his malevolence forgotten, before striding away towards his home. Concern grew inside the angel again, however, as he watched the boy go, and wondered where such an isolated negative emotion could come from. There seemed nothing else the matter with him, no fears or anxieties that could warrant the purposeful death of the beetle, and he glanced down at it once more, it's armoured body still crackling as it's broken pieces continued to spread in the pool of yellow muck. The angel tried to dismiss it as he continued on his way, but as he turned another corner, he caught sight of another child, this time a young girl, skipping stones across the road at a parked car. She could perhaps have been about fifteen years of age, but her heart seemed to have bands of black arcing in it's otherwise colourful flames. Crossing the street swiftly towards her, the angel placed his hands, palms out, upon her shoulders and drew this spite out of her. Her eyes seemed to open to what she was doing, and in the instant that the car owner stepped from the house he was visiting and saw her, she took to her heels, her fire flickering with shafts of blue that encompassed her fear and guilt.

The angel stood in disbelief as he watched her dash across a number of lawns before disappearing from sight. His sight returned to the car owner as he stood with hands on hips inspecting the damage. His disappointment and anger at what the girl had done was expected, but the angel saw the healthiness inside him and left him to deal with it himself while he pondered the destructiveness the night had brought.

He took to walking once more, his attention on his thoughts. Sure, the human mind and heart was prone to harmful and thoughtless behaviour, they always had been since their creation, but such aggression was usually the outlet from building negative thoughts and feelings. In the two children he had just met, there had been no negative thoughts and feelings, just the aggressive outlet. It was troubling. A shout from up ahead distracted him, and he glanced up to see a man throwing insults across the street at a boy. The angel moved quickly to intercept the boy, and found the same isolated malice that the other two had possessed. This time, the child had pulled the man's hat from his head before running across the street with it, where he was now throwing it up in the air and cruelly taunting him with it. The angel touched the boy, dispelling the cruelty and unleashing a stream of repentant tears as he dropped the hat and began to run. The angel watched as the man strode towards him before stooping to retrieve his hat, cursing under his breath as he did so. The angel broke protocol as he brushed the man's hand, his anger dissipating instantly, but then from the corner of his eye, the angel caught sight of movement in one of the trees on the opposite side of the road.

Focussing on the heavy foliage, the angel caught a glimpse of a flash of white, like the zigzag pattern of a picket fence. The leaves parted again, but with little wind in the air, his curiosity increased, and the angel started towards the tree. The picket fence gleamed again, only this time the angel recognised the pattern as a jagged grin bared wide and white with evil laughter. He could hear that laughter now too, nasal and cackling, and he moved swiftly to intercept this creature before he escaped the partial cover of his hiding place and disappeared.

The angel reached the tree just as the demon toppled from its boughs, his ragged body bouncing off the grass before he was back up onto his feet. He was perhaps only three feet tall and the colour of burnt excrement, but his eyes shone brightly as he stared up at the angel, his grin faltering briefly as he realised who had discovered him, as though his night's mischief-making was already over.

The angel stooped to take hold of him, but the demon was quick, and rolled forward out of his reach with a scream in his throat, coming to a halt just a few yards from him. The angel stood and gazed at him, at his narrow slitty eyes and the wide gaping grin slashed in the middle of his face. He stank of rotten food and his body was a frenzy of tics. For a few minutes there seemed a kind of stalemate between them, each knowing the other's sway over the human heart, and the counter-sway the other could achieve. The angel wondered whether he would have the power in him to destroy the demon, but at the same moment wondered whether the demon was thinking the very same thought. There seemed little intelligence behind his shining narrow eyes, just an eerie mischievousness that knew no limits. A crash of breaking glass snatched him briefly from his dilemma, and he glanced up to see a broken window of a house, a boy standing in front of it clutching a second stone in his fist. Twenty yards behind him and chattering with a misshapen grin was another demon, tugging on his elfin claws with glee. The angel cast a look back at the demon in front of him. His hideous grin was mocking and defiant, and in his filthy hand he now held a snarling black flame. There was nothing the angel could do but watch as the demon scrambled to his feet and engulfed himself in that same protective black fire, the searing ebony flames licking eagerly across his body of filth. He let out a sickening laugh and then turned and scrambled away, the flames leaping from his burning head and into the sky like a runaway pyre, his cackles trailing behind him like a wake.

The angel watched him disappear into the night and then glanced back in the direction of the second demon. He too had gone, and so had they all, no doubt. Slowly the angel turned his head and gazed back up towards the mountain from which he had descended. Tomorrow night, he promised himself, he would not come alone. Tomorrow night, he would come with friends, and come with brighter fuel.

Once again she stepped along the dimly lit passageway, her footfalls echoing coldly off the grim stone walls. Her long black gown, tied at the neck, billowed behind her like an old rotten sail as she walked towards the flickering candlelight at the far end of the passage, as once more she had to honour her side of the pact. Her pace faltered and wavered, as it always did, yet she had no choice but to continue. After all, it was her own desires and dreams that had delivered her into this terrible place.

Stepping into the candle-lit chamber, her eyes traced the implements and ironwork of the room, a vast collection of hideous tools and weapons, sharpened scythes glinting their laceration potential in the grim yellow light, knives offering their tantalising delicacies as flames danced in the mirrors of their blades, mallets and clubs waiting patiently to crack open and splinter bones, and racks of wrought iron from which hung swarms of straps and buckles like cricking preying insects.

A cruel shiver crept across her cold spine as she cast her eyes at them again. Though she had seen them all so many times before, and knew from nightmarish memories what lay in their purpose, they still dug into her heart and her head to tempt the life and sanity out of them both. Standing huddled in the centre of the chamber, she called its name to lessen the agonising torment of the wait. There was silence. She took a breath and once again called its name. Still silence. Where was it? Was it here? Of course it was here. It was always here. Where else would it be?

A footstep behind the door in the far wall announced the creature's presence like a toll. She drew a ragged breath as her chest began to pound, hard and painfully, as she was made to wait like a slave. The large iron-braced door rattled in its jamb before it was slowly drawn open from the other side. The room beyond was utter blackness, a void of quiet that eventually delivered the creature that would soon do her harm. The candlelight was eager to explore its features, and they shocked her anew as they became visible, just as they always did. It was tall and dark skinned, its cranium devoid of hair that glinted in the feeble light to cast horrid misshapen shadows on the walls around it. The thin cruel smile on its lips broke into a grin at her presence, the furrows of razored teeth becoming visible between the slit in its face, but she tried hard not to look at them for she knew only too well what they too were capable of.

As it stepped unhurriedly across the floor towards her, it wrapped its dark sheet around its twisted frame like a death shroud. This creature should have died and been buried long before now but still it breathed and still it moved towards her like a ghostly nightmare.

"Hello," it said to her, its voice little more than a seething whisper. "So nice to see you again."

Its jagged mouth pressed against the falls of hair at her ear, but she did not move, nor attempt to sway from its proximity. What would be the point? This closeness was nothing compared with what was to come. Its clawed finger rose to her cheek and traced an imaginary scar across it, as its mouth pressed closer to the flesh of her ear, its teeth almost biting at the edge of the soft delicate morsel.

"Such flesh," it said softly. "So tempting. So tender. So full of hot blood."

She tried not to shudder against the touch of its words but she just couldn't help herself, and it grinned because of it. It traced more imaginary lines of promised lacerations across her jaw and down her neck with its cruel dark fingertips. They reached the ties of her long black gown and tugged at them, the ties releasing their grip and sending the gown silently to the floor, revealing her naked body that bestowed its radiance beneath the yellow caress of the candles' flames. The creature grinned again, like a street dog savouring the meat of a stolen bone, as she stepped slowly away from her only clothing towards one of the racks secured against the walls. She knew her place, and positioned her ankles and wrists into the shackles, awaiting the creature to buckle them fast, to strap her in so that she could not move. It stood for a while, deliberating as to the tools that hung from the walls of its domain, and oh, what a choice it had. At length it selected a razored blade with a profusion of barbs at its hilt, and then slowly it edged towards the woman restrained.

She clenched shut her teeth and tightened her limbs as she waited for the insurmountable pain that would soon come. She watched as it stepped in front of her, its teeth grinning, and like a madman happy in his lunacy, turned the implement lovingly in its grasp like a favourite scalpel. Tears streamed from her eyes, as did the screams from her throat, as the silvered blade ran red as it sliced the first of its crisp incisions into her white tender flesh, her rich blood running like hot honey onto the cold stone floor beneath.

It was raining. The coffee was cold. His butt ached from sitting on it all morning. And his feet were so cold that they stung him as he whiled away the hours sitting in his tiny metal booth at the front gate, seeing cars in, and seeing cars out. What a complete waste of bloody time. It was a shit job, and it paid shit wages. He could be out in the real world, having a life, being happy - what he would give to be happy - but no, he was stuck in this tiny metal booth, seeing cars in, and seeing cars out.

Brin had had this job for nearly two months and was sick of it already. He'd wanted to be an actor, or a rock'n'roll singer, or something of equal glamour or fame, but he had no talent for either and a will for success that just stunk. He'd had the ideas, he'd had the great plans, but when it all came down to it, he just couldn't be bothered to push himself. And so here he was, sitting on his aching butt in a tiny metal booth, seeing cars in, and seeing cars out.

The company he was employed with was some big American blue chip corporation; loads of money, and loads of loud brash Americans in coffin-black cars that made no noise when they pulled up at his tiny window. They'd sit behind their electric windows and flash an ID at him, before purring away and off into some hidden car park amongst the trees. That was the latest in corporate headquarters, he'd noticed. None of this inner-city smoke and pollution deal swamped by traffic, now it was sweeping offices built in the middle of a forest with nothing to fear but the occasional attack from a rabid squirrel. And here was his tiny booth at the gateway, jammed unceremoniously between the tarmac of the main road and the greenery of the corporate paradise, and well away on either side from anything that mattered.

He glanced up as a large coffin came to a halt in

front of him, the window sliding down like silk lingerie on one of his fantasy women. The male face that appeared was crisp and new, freshly made and blemish-free, his hair slicked meticulously, as too was his moustache, and as he spoke the breeze of classical music calmed to a whisper inside as he turned the knob on the Blaupunkt. Brin leant forward expectantly and put his elbows on the sill of his window.

"Good morning," came the oh-so-chirpy accent of the pompous executive. "I'm here to see Mister Downing. He's the financial director."

"I know who he is," Brin whispered under his breath, "I do fucking work here."

He peered past the man, deep inside the expanse of his car, and took note of the sumptuous leather seats. Oh how his buttocks yearned for their comfort. The interior seemed just as untouched and as new as the exterior and gleamed just as brightly. Brin focused back on its driver, asking him for his name and company in the same parrot-voice as always. The man supplied them with a cheery optimism that bordered on the theatrical, sickening and false, and Brin decided there and then that once you have the huge car and the expense account to match, the voice comes is the next to be supplied. Brin extended a pass towards him, and then waved him on towards the somewhere car park.

Slumping agitatedly back in his chair, his butt screaming at him once again for some kind of respite, he cursed his life once again for letting him down so badly. He got to his feet and rubbed his buttocks with the palms of his hands. The booth was tiny and his hair brushed the ceiling. He swore at it and tried to stretch as best he could in the confined space. His hands hit the sides of the booth before his arms were even straight, and he swore again. A small pile of crumpled envelopes sat on the counter in front of him, his own personal mail of the morning, mostly bills and threats of violence from his landlord; actually that wasn't quite true, he had received a love letter from an old girlfriend whose name he couldn't quite place, but then he had noticed that the address on the envelope was not his either and it had been delivered to him by mistake, but the bills and threats had put him in such a shit mood that he hadn't been bothered to forward the young lover's letter. There was a final demand for the electricity, a note in red writing informing him that his phone had just been disconnected, and one from the television hire people who were adamant that they weren't joking about repossessing their property. The final one was a scrap of paper that his landlord had slipped under his door, telling him that if he didn't see any of the rent money that was owing he'd be contacting not only his solicitors, but also a couple of guys who frequented gyms and were short of a few quid. Brin had no money to waste on the likes of things such as rent or electricity when he could barely scrap up the cash to afford luxuries like food. He dropped the letters back onto the counter and sunk into his chair, trying his best once again to ignore the complaints raised from his aching butt.

Friday morning came, and Brin was already looking forward to the end of the afternoon when he could get his hands on his pay-cheque and spend the evening getting drunk at his local. His dreams were inadvertently fractured when his eye became caught by the glint of an approaching car. Rubbing his fingers across his sleep-heavy eyes, he hauled himself to his feet as it pulled up at his booth. The rainclouds of the day had dissipated sufficiently to allow the sun's rays to revel in the paintwork of the large sparkling Mercedes. Its windows were black and deeply reflective, and as he leant forward on his sill, the driver's side purred slowly down. Brin exhaled heavily as he beheld the face of the beautiful woman driver. She was somewhere in her thirties and her skin was crisp and tight, the presence of a few wrinkles edging across it ever so slightly bringing elegance into the frame; it contrasted the youthfulness she was searching for and it made her face perfection. Her rich auburn hair, flashing scarlet in the sunlight, was bobbed just above her shoulder and swayed perfectly as she turned her head. Her suit jacket was delicate yet inspiring, as too was the gold that hung from her neck and ears, the combination of affluence and femininity complimenting themselves utterly. Only her eyes were hidden, chaste behind a hateful veil of black sunglasses. Oh how he would have wished for her to remove them so that he could see the vision absolute. But such prizes he knew were few and far between. Bless the heavens that he had laid eyes upon so much already.

They stared at each other for a while in silence, it could have been seconds, it could have been days, as far as Brin was concerned, so completely was he lost in her presence.

"Nice car," he stammered eventually, realising that he should perhaps be saying something. The woman, however, said nothing. Just the same cold stare from behind her unemotional black sunglasses, as though she were studying him also. He smiled at her as he handed her a pass, and tried to smile in a kind of 'I'm not really a loser working in this tiny metal booth, I'm really an actor and a rock'n'roll singer, so it would be perfectly alright for us to sleep together,' but he knew it had failed pathetically as soon as he watched the gleaming Mercedes pull silently away from his booth before disappearing into the trees. And it wasn't until the car had vanished from sight that he realised that he hadn't even asked her her name or her company or who she even wished to see. He cursed himself again, and vowed a promise that he would take any chance he got to be someone in this world, knowing even as he said it that he would never have the courage to action such a desire.

It was later that evening, as Brin whiled away the nightime hours in his local, swigging draught lager and munching crisps, that he found himself perched on a barstool in front of a silent television. Every night it showed a sparse array of films or sports from the satellite station, but it had the novelty of no sound to bother the pub's other patrons, a feat, Brin thought, that didn't wholly take too much away from the programmes. He had sat through the last half hour of a thriller where somebody had been stalked across beaches and through towns by some lumbering oaf with a knife who it had never occurred to that if he were to run after his victims he may actually catch up with them. The last ten minutes had seen a shabby detective explain silently who had done what and why. This probably would have annoyed him considerably had he given a toss about the whole affair, but he hadn't, and after the titles had rolled across the screen, the picture snowed, before delivering some ancient and obscure foreign football match.

Brin wasn't one of these guys who yelled at the teams or threw peanuts at the screen when somebody fucked up, he could sit and watch it passively for anything up to a minute, and that was about it. But tonight he couldn't even manage that. He downed the last of his pint before returning to the bar to order another of the same. The pub had less than a dozen people in it, and so every time the door swung open, all heads would turn to see if they recognised whoever it was that had strayed in off the streets. The door swung open now, and it was the stranger that stepped daintily across the threshold that caught Brin's eye. He was bored to the point of delirium and so any distraction was welcome. He watched as the stranger stepped up to the bar, waiting patiently while the landlord finished his conversation at the other end, and perched herself on one of the tall stools. Brin placed his pint back onto the bar, its base slithering on the sheen of spilt alcohol and cigarette ash, and wiped his greasy fingers on the backs of his jeans. The stranger at the bar was the woman in the Mercedes, he suddenly recognised her now, and he wondered in an instant just what was she might be doing in a place like this? He wanted desperately to go over and say hello, but what could he open a conversation with to a woman like that: 'Hello there, remember me? I'm the new corporate whizz-kid who earns more money than anyone, and I was only on the gate in that tiny metal booth for a laugh.' No, that was shite, he had to come up with something better than that. Something impressive. Something even true perhaps. But something definitely not about work. He got to his feet and started towards her, hoping that something would be forced onto his tongue when he at last reached her.

"Hello there," he said hesitantly, leaning against the bar beside her. "Remember me?" Not the next line, he told himself, something impressive, remember?

The woman at the bar sipped at the glass as it was set down in front of her, replacing it neatly on the beer-mat before looking back at him, wondering if there should be any reason why she should remember him. Brin simply stared back helplessly. Her hair was as rich and as perfect as it had been earlier, her skin just as crisp and fresh as though she had just been born. But this time he took special interest in her lips. Oh, how red they were, and how sweet, and how tempting. He longed to grab hold of her here in this grotty bar and press his lips to them, to taste this fine woman and have her taste him back. But more than that, freed from the restraints of her black sunglasses, he could now see her eyes. So deep brown and strong were they that they had no equal. He had no idea how long he stared into them, and nor did he much care, so blessed did he feel simply by her returning his gaze. It seemed, however, that she was not about to answer him at all, because she simply stared at him and now raised an eyebrow. The simple but perfect gesture broke his calm, and he panicked into further dialogue.

"In the Mercedes," he stammered, "this morning. I saw you in it. Remember?"

She cocked her head a little, her hair swaying like a sea of gilded grass, the effect was devastating. So sultry. So demure. He worshipped her eyes as she studied him, even if she did deem him a loser.

"On the gate," she said eventually. "Yes, I remember you."

Brin inwardly breathed a sigh of relief. She remembered him.

"Can I buy you a drink?" he offered quickly, not realising even as she lifted her glass to him, that he was too late.

"Can I get you a seat?" he asked eagerly, just as he noticed that she was already seated. He took a breath and forced himself onward.

"I'm Brin," he stated.

"Pleased to meet you," the woman replied, almost genuinely, holding out her hand for his. He lifted his hand into hers, cursing himself as he felt the warmth of her flesh that he hadn't thought of that.

"And you?" he asked.

"Tate," she said, shaking his hand delicately but firmly. Everything about this woman was perfect. "Beverley Tate."

He smiled warmly at her, and she even passed one back.

"So," he said to her, attempting to start a conversation while casually stepping up onto an adjacent stool, "what brings someone of your status into a place like this?"

She looked back at him, and then took another sip from her glass.

"What brings someone of your status here?" she asked him in return.

He was going to say worries and debts, but thought better of it.

"Just somewhere to hang out, meet people, you know," he added lamely.

She lifted her glass gently as if to salute such an ideal.

"Are you staying in town?" he enquired, innocently, he hoped.

"No," she said. "I'm driving back tonight."

Brin looked down at his drink and watched the ropes of bubbles string the golden beer to the surface of his glass. So close, he thought. She saw his heart sink and smiled.

"It's about a four hour drive," she said to him. "I'd better be going soon."

"Yes," Brin replied, downhearted. "I suppose so."

The fine woman crossed her legs beneath her long skirt and eyed this strange young man. He was spirited, she liked that, and it was obvious that he would do anything for her. She put her hand on his and squeezed it gently.

"Have you ever been in a Mercedes?" she asked him in a whisper.

He shook his head, his heart suddenly hammering.

"Finish your drink, then," she said. "It's a long drive home."


With the evening meal finished, Brin retired with the beautiful Beverley Tate to the drawing room of her estate house, to sip brandy in front of her large roaring fireplace. It still didn't seem right to him that he should even be here with her, but he sank back nevertheless into one of the sumptuous dark leather armchairs as he watched Beverley pour them both a measure of rich liquor. It swilled around the bowl of the glass as she handed it to him, and he put his nose to it, the aroma of potent alcohol excessively heavy. He watched her sit away from him a little in one of the other armchairs, slipping off her heels, before curling her stockinged feet up under her. The look she gave him was as warming as the brandy, and she smiled as she put the glass to her lips and took a little. Brin smiled back, and put the glass to his lips also, taking a mouthful of the neat alcohol, coughing violently as it burned his throat. It was bloody strong stuff. Beverley stifled a smile, but he saw it and it made him feel even more stupid.

"Have you been here long?" he tried asking her, changing the subject when he was sure his voice had returned sufficiently.

"A little while," she said, but offered no more.

"Is it… just you that lives here?"

She seemed to ponder the simple question for a few moments as if she were not sure of its answer, but then as she turned her glass gently in her hands, she replied that yes, it was only her.

"It's a big house for just one person."

"Yes," she replied. "But there's always something going on."

She took her eyes from him and stared into the fire, and in their reflection, Brin could see its flashes sparkling in them, as though he could see right through. He thought maybe this was as good a time as any to make a pass at her, so taking his heart in his hands, he placed his glass on the table beside him and got to his feet. Beverley did not look at him as he walked towards her, not even when he stopped and knelt down beside her. Her eyes stayed on the rituals that the flames performed, even as he put his hand over hers and bent his head towards hers. As his cheek brushed against the silk of her hair and his lips were just inches from hers, she spoke softly to him.

"I've set up one of the guestrooms for you. I think you'll find it comfortable."

Brin stopped where he was. What was she saying, that he wouldn't be spending the night in her bed.

Wasn't that why she had brought him here? With his fires of passion well and truly doused, he fell away from her side and returned back in his chair. He took another mouthful from his glass to soothe himself, and nearly choked as it seared his tongue and throat.

The evening continued uncomfortably after that until about eleven thirty, when Beverley showed him up to his room. On the threshold, as they said goodnight to each other, his eyes floated to her lips, her oh-so-perfect lips, once again. They were still a perfect shade of red, unblemished by their meal or their brandy, and they pouted to him like a beacon, a pout of desire and freedom that he so longed to touch. But no, he thought. He'd already made a fool of himself at least once tonight. He wasn't about to do it again. But as she said goodnight to him, and turned the key to his room in its lock, pushing the door wide into the murk, she leant forward and pressed her lips to his, their warm delicacy massaging her tender femininity into his very being. It took him completely by surprise, and by the time he had realised what was happening, she had pulled away and was retreating back along the corridor.

He put his fingertips to his mouth as if there was some trace of her left behind, as though he could somehow relive the moment, but as he watched her disappear into a darker part of the house, he cursed himself once again for being so slow, and swore that he would grasp the chance more firmly should it ever offer itself to him again, as he went into the dark guestroom and tried to locate the hidden light switch.

By twelve thirty, he was in bed with the light out. The mattress was large and comfortable, the sheets cool and fragrant, and he nestled his head into the plump pillow and took in the wonderful shadows of the room. A glow of moonlight at its highest point lit the chamber with a pale luminescence with which his eyes could pick out the shapes of the antique wardrobe and the dresser at the window. There were a few shapes that he had not noticed with the light on and try as he might, he could not discern their strangeness no matter how hard he strained his vision against the dark. The more he looked the heavier his eyes became, until it was a struggle simply to keep them open. The pale glow of the room became fused with the blackness of sleep and soon he started to lose himself to the whispers of dreams and the cradle of the bed. His heart slowed and his lungs sighed to its own gentle rhythm, and as he let his eyes roll closed for the night, he heard a quiet click from the door.

Brin didn't know whether he was actually awake or not, or even looking at the opening door of his room, but he was sure he heard the soft footfalls of someone entering. He lay still and quiet as his ears fought for more information, trying to confirm in the still silence of the night whether or not he was not alone.

There, another sound, a footfall brushing across the plush carpet. And there, another. Either he tried to look up, or he was asleep, because his eyes were just too heavy to open. Was it Beverley, come to rouse and arouse him in the middle of the night? No, he quickly decided. She would not be creeping about her own house, especially when she'd had the chance to do whatever it was that she had invited him here for when she had kissed him earlier. No, this was someone else altogether.

And then his eyes rolled open a little, just enough

for his vision to escape, but hopefully not so much that it should show this intruder that he was actually awake. His gaze dashed the room, looking for an unfamiliar shape that had not been there a moment ago. The wardrobe, the chair, the dresser by the window, all there, but wait, what was that that stood beside the chair, the chair on which lay his clothes? A thin hunched figure stooped over the antique chair, looking as though it was inspecting his clothes, examining them, analysing their owner. For a moment he thought he might have imagined the figure, or mistook it for a coat-stand or a lamp or something, but then it moved.

Its head rose on its twisted neck and turned and looked at him. And though the figure was dark in the gloom of the room, and he could see no features on its face, he could still feel its eyes piercing him, and he knew that it knew that he was awake and looking at it. Not a muscle moved in his body, not a bone twitched beneath the covers. His eyes stared straight ahead through the narrow slit between his lids and he hoped against hope that this creature could not see him awake. But now its body turned as its head had turned, moving round in order to face him. And then it was approaching, step by step, towards him, its whole frame twisted and bent over, its arms huddled close to its body, its head now craning round as if to see from a different angle. Brin's heart stopped. His lungs too. His fingers subconsciously gripped the sheets tighter in their ghostly-white knuckles. The thing was almost upon him. His eyes were open, yet almost so closed, but he could not shut them upon this intruder, or even so much as blink, for fear that it would see such movement. But know it must that he was awake and staring at it, for it came to a halt beside his bed, and rolled forward its head on its thin bony neck, and turned its dark blank face towards his.

Oh how he wished that he could see what features this thing had to offer, and how glad he was that he could not. The creature seemed to stare at him forever with its invisible but piercing eyes, and he could feel its hot and filthy breath brushing his cheek, coming and going in staggered rasps.

Then it touched him.

Brin felt a cold finger, tipped with a sharp hard nail, glance across his face, testing his flesh, tracing a line over and down across his neck. He could hardly stifle the muscles in his body as they itched to flee from its sickening touch. And then, resolved to do no more, the creature's hand lifted, and it slowly retreated from the room, pausing only momentarily at the door to stare back briefly, before slipping out of the room and away. Brin's body was knotted with both tension and fear, and eventually his eyes would stay open at the place where it had disappeared no longer. And so, heavy with strain and sleep, they closed, and his mind wandered from the dark room and away into some strange place filled with strange dreams and desires, like the dark creature who had left him just moments before.

Brin woke at daybreak, a chink of mellow warm sunlight spilling onto the floor, dividing the room in two. His eyes creaked open and he rolled about beneath the motherly covers as he tried to draw out the ecstasy of the delicate moment between waking and sleeping. As consciousness befell him completely, he sat up and looked about the room he was in. How different it looked out of the cold darkness of night. Here in the warm luminescence of dawn there were no horrors or anxieties lurking behind bedposts or wardrobes, only the comfort of the long bright curtains and his familiar clothes on the chair. He glanced at his watch. It was nearly five-thirty. He slipped from beneath the covers of the endearing bed and crossed silently to his clothes to dress, a plan in his head to wander the hallways of Beverley's grand house before she herself woke.

Stepping out into the hall a few minutes later, he was first surprised by how much larger the house appeared now that the shadows of nightime had been banished. The curtains hung light at their poles as the sun fell upon them through their windows, and the corridors through which he now crept seemed fresh and alive to him as if they themselves had been refreshed by their night's sleep. He wandered down the wondrous arcing staircase, his hand gliding over the solid dark banister as he went, like some grand actor in an old cult movie. His head was as light as the new day as he floated down and into the hall below. Could this one day be his, he thought, as he searched corridors new?

Through rooms and down hallways he wandered, taking in all the sights of porcelain and oak, tapestry and canvas, deep into his eyes and his heart, until his journey down one hallway ended abruptly at a door. This passage was different to those of the rest of the house, it had no windows in its length, nor any paintings or decoration to break its monotony. Indeed, it seemed as though it was maybe forgotten or ignored, yet the door at its end stood sturdy and strong. Brin's curiosity got the better of him, as it often did in such cases, and he tried the handle. Its steel was heavy and cold, and he was a little surprised at how freely the mechanism opened, even as if it were opening itself for him, and the door swung gently open to reveal the summit of a descending set of stairs, its path a secret from the blanket of darkness down below.

His hand went to the switch on the inside wall, a cold white light flickered to life and presented the remainder of the stairs. The electric light was cold and unyielding, and was prepared to tell him nothing about the lower chamber, no clue as to what the stairs lead to; it simply said, here are the stairs, they lead down, do you really want to know any more?

Brin thought for a moment whether he should actually be here. After all, he was a guest in Beverley's house, and now he was trespassing like an intruder. But just one look, his curiosity told him, what would it hurt?

It was not dusty or home to the webs of spiders as he presumed most basements to be, or even cluttered by boxes too ugly or commonplace to tarnish habitable rooms, but it was painted a stark white, against which the black structural beams pointed awkwardly at tangents. The floor was constructed of the same heavy wood as the stairs and it echoed uncomfortably around him as he stepped cautiously across it. The more he walked around the stark bare room, the more he felt out of place and distressed. Something was not right in this room; it was so very different from the rest of the house, as though it did not belong, did not want to belong, yet here it was, hiding away in its own depths. Until there, under the partial darkness of the stairs was another door, a small black uninteresting door. He could have almost missed it entirely yet like the room itself it seemed to be there for no reason whatsoever, and yet here it was.

Brin took a step towards it, his curiosity badgering him closer, but this time his consciousness fought to be heard. No, it said, it's not right, something's not right, leave it alone and be out of here. A spark of energy dashed across his spine and he lunged for the stairs, his sudden fear turning to hysterical panic as he desperately fought to be above ground once more. He was halfway up the steps when his head rose towards the door. And there in the doorway stood Beverley Tate; very still and very silent, her figure silhouetted against the light of day behind, her features not precise, yet he could feel a disturbing glare from somewhere in her head, and he suddenly felt very afraid.

He stood where he was, half up the stairs, half down, his eyes fixed on the motionless figure at the top. And then slowly, and inexplicably, she turned away from him and pulled the door closed behind her.

Oh God, what had she done?

His mind became a tumult.

What had he done? She'd sealed him below ground in her basement.

He leapt the remainder of the staircase three at a time, stumbling towards the handle. He put his full weight to it to try and break the lock, but it nearly threw him back down the stairs. She had not locked it at all, she had merely pulled it to behind her.

He started up the corridor, but she was nowhere in sight. Through the house he ran, hoping to catch up with her, hoping to explain, to plead, to cry, who knows what he wanted to do? His heart was pounding hard inside his chest, and his mind could control neither that nor itself until at last he found her in the kitchen. She was at the breakfast bar, her red silk robe wrapped neatly around her and flowing about the legs of the stool on which she was sat, a cup of steaming coffee in one hand, a page of the newspaper being turned in the other. As Brin entered, she looked up from the stories of the day and smiled sweetly at him, which took him completely by surprise.

"Good morning," she said to him, cheerfully. "Have you been jogging already this morning? You look tired out."

Brin gaped at her. He didn't know what to say.

"There's a bathroom next to your room if you want a shower," she said to him, a cheery smile still at her lips.

Brin was stunned by her almost inconsequential words. She had seemed so different, so cold, so domineering when she stood over him at the top of the stairs, or at least he had presumed it had been her. Had he imagined her, just as he had hoped he had imagined the weird creature last night who had studied him in his bed.

"Have you been up long?" he hesitantly enquired.

"Only a few minutes," she replied. "I thought I'd have some coffee before I took a shower."

"So you haven't been wandering about?"

She gave him a quizzical look.

"Through the house, I mean. This morning."

"Good Lord, no," she said. "Why on earth would I be doing that?"

Brin gazed at her, his heart still busy.

"You did say you lived alone," he persisted, changing his line of enquiry.

"Yes," she answered, a hint of suspicion starting to creep into her tone, as well as her eye.

"No one else," he continued. "No butlers, or servants, or anything."

"No. Why?"

"Oh nothing," he stammered. "It's just I thought I saw something - someone - last night, and this morning, just now, and it wasn't you, I think."

The smile dropped from Beverley Tate's face altogether and what remained made Brin feel very uncomfortable. "I know I shouldn't have been wandering about your house," he burst into apology, "but I just couldn't help myself..."

Beverley looked at him as he spoke, her complexion suddenly very pale, narrowing her eyes as she listened to where he had been, and what he had seen. When he had finished, she uncrossed her legs and got up from the stool. As she moved, the scarlet silk of her robe fluttered from her and exposed much of her thighs, a fine reward for whatever punishment was to come.

"Go upstairs and shower," she seemed to command him. "Then we will have breakfast." And with that, she drained the last of her coffee, neatly folded her barely touched newspaper and escorted him away from the kitchen and upstairs.

The shower had felt good on his body, its hot fingers massaging away his former fears and doubts. Once he had dried himself and dressed, he went in search of Beverley. He found the master bedroom further along the hallway and discovered the door to be slightly ajar. He rapped lightly on the jamb and called her name, but there was no reply. He pushed the door open a little further and stuck his head through the gap, calling her name once again. Still there was no answer. He pushed the door open fully now and wandered slowly through.

Never before had he seen a more splendid room, not even downstairs in the main living area. Here was a shrine to pleasure and aesthetic beauty. Rich fabrics hung at the windows, their bright colours dancing brighter for the sunlight that shone through them, fine-grained woods made up the furniture, the bed stood large and soft and elegant, and placed precisely in various corners and at shelves and on pedestals sat bouquets of beautiful flowers and crystalline china. He stepped further into the room, his eyes hungry for whatever they could find, and as he reached the bed, a figure emerged from the adjoining bathroom, a white towel wrapped scantily around her wet body. It was Beverley.

Brin gaped at the profusion of flesh now revealed to him and fought with himself not to show it. But Beverley did not turn away from embarrassment. Rather she walked casually towards him, a smile dancing across her lips.

"Couldn't help your curiosity this time either?" she asked him casually.

"I'm sorry," he stumbled. "I called but there was no answer."

"A likely story," she toyed with him, and beckoned him to sit. He obliged, perching on the edge of the bed, and avoided her sight by staring at the deep-carpeted floor.

"Do you find me attractive?" she asked him suddenly, as she reached her dressing table by the window and started to brush her silken hair.

Brin stared at her, and murmured something about not understanding her.

"Do I excite you?"

"Yes," he found himself confessing this time. "Very much."

"Would you like to see me naked?"

She looked at him through the reflection in the mirror, but still she was collected.

"Yes, very much so."

"From here," she pointed to the top of the towel, "to here," rolling her hand to the bottom.

"I'd give anything."

"Would you?" she asked. "What would you give?"

Brin looked blankly at her. Whatever she asked of him, he would unquestioningly give. Anything to see her naked before him.

"Just ask, and I will give it to you."

"The sight of my naked body, my naked flesh, will be your reward if you will tell me exactly what you were doing in my basement this morning."

Brin stared at her. So that was her that had stood over him at the top of the stairs. But why had she acted like nothing had happened in the kitchen, and why the sudden interest now? But then again, he hadn't really done anything wrong so why lie to her when he could see her very femininity once he had told her.

"I was just looking around," he told her.

"Not good enough," she retorted.

"It seemed so strange in the corridor," he continued, "so different, it didn't fit. And then the basement, it seemed so cold, so stark, so unnerving."

Beverley raised an eyebrow.

"And?" she said.

"There was a door," he continued, "a small black door. It didn't look as if it belonged either."

"Did you go through it?"

"No," he exclaimed. "I promise I didn't."

"Did you open it?"

"No."

"Did you touch it?"

"No."

Beverley paused for a moment while she studied the young man sat before her on the edge of her bed. He was undoubtedly troubled by her interrogation, and so it seemed that she finally relented and believed him.

"I think you are telling me the truth," she said at last. "And as promised, I shall give you your reward."

She took hold of the towel knotted at her chest and tugged it slowly from her body. As it fell away, her bosom rolled out freely to its full splendour, each breast perfect, plump and round, each nipple dark, red and hard. Her stomach was taut and flat, and sloped gracefully down to a small trimmed tuft of black hair between her legs that framed her sex. Brin stared uncontrollably as his eyes struggled to take her all in. She was indeed the most beautiful woman he had ever seen, and here she was displayed in all her bare beauty for only him to see and worship. She continued to stand before him, unabashed and unashamed, enjoying his enjoyment, showing her full naked glory as she had promised, her small white towel held redundant in one hand at her side.

Brin felt the tightening in his underwear as his member grew firm with excitement. His fingers itched and needed to touch her soft pale skin in order to pacify them. It was then that he moved from the edge of the bed and got to his feet, moving slowly step by step towards this exquisite beauty. His breaths were becoming heavy now as his hands drew themselves up to touch her breasts. But as they came within inches of her delicate flesh, she calmly spoke a warning to him.

"I only said you could look," she murmured. "I never said you could touch. At least not yet."

"Anything," he whispered helplessly, wanting only to please her, his fingertips hovering desperately over her body. "I'll do anything."

"Anything?" she tested.

"Anything," he confirmed. "I swear."

Beverley looked deep into his eyes, searching for his promise, but his sight was still fixed on her breasts just words away from his touch. She wondered how much he would give in one go, and tugged at his lead a little more.

"Go down to the basement," she told him, "and open the door beneath the stairs. Go through and tell me what you find there."

Brin hesitated. What was down there? Surely this woman knew what was buried below her own house.

His thoughts whirled between the fears of what had confronted him earlier and the touch of her silken skin against his. Perhaps if he pleased her now, who knows what she might reward him with?

"Do you want to touch me?" she asked. Her words shattered his thoughts, and filled them with fresh.

"Oh yes. Yes. Yes."

"Then go to the basement. Go through the door. And tell me what you find there."

"Can I... touch you now?"

"No," she said, turning away from him and wrapping the towel around her, covering her sights from his eyes once again. "Go to the basement. Go through the door. Then you may caress me for as long as you wish. That is the deal."

Brin's hands fell helpless at his sides. He turned from her and fled the room, racing back along the corridors and hallways until he reached the windowless forgotten passage that ended in the door that led to the basement. The metal was cold to his touch, but he gripped the handle firmly and turned its weight. The mechanism clicked, the door swung open, and a faint breeze of cool air escaped and whistled past his cheek, chilling him terribly. His eyes strained into the space now revealed but it was deathly black and he could see nothing.

Was this what Beverley wanted to know was behind the door, or was there something far worse to be seen here? His fears tugged at his mind, his hands itching to slam the door on such fears, but the promise of Beverley's body and what she would let him do to her urged him on, and so he took a step forward into the darkness.

With his arms outstretched in front of him, palms outward to touch for the far wall, he stepped warily into the gloom, but after maybe half a dozen steps his hands had still not found the other side of what he had presumed to be a closet or something. Perhaps it was another room, he thought, but after another dozen or more steps he still had not reached the other side. He pushed his arms out to the side and found a cold stone wall at each hand. He was in another corridor, a corridor that led to another room? Perhaps to one of many rooms? He continued forward, his hands guiding his uneasy path through the inky black void.

Through the still darkness ahead of him came a

faint rumble, a clamour of metal against metal, solid objects banging together, and somewhere beneath that a drone of human voices. The more he walked, the more he heard, and the more he heard, the deeper he seemed to go beneath the house. The walls on either side of the corridor slowly began to converge until it was no more than shoulder width apart, and the metallic bangs and clatters were loud in his ears, as too were the laments and moans of the many men and women he had heard earlier. That was when he reached the door.

He had more or less walked straight into it after such an unobstructed trek, but his fingers found the handle, and then they had turned it. The door was light and swung freely on its hinges, offering him easy access to what lay beyond. There was a warm glow of candle light in the chamber to greet him, and he wandered into its welcoming embrace after such cold and utter blackness. Strewn across the floor of this room stood piles of clothes and possessions, as well as the innumerable boxes that had once contained them, heaped high against the walls as if rummaged through hastily and without care.

The candle light, he discovered, was not in fact to be found in this room, but from its adjoining one, as too was the din of the ceaseless hammering that grew louder still as he approached the doorway. As he stepped through, the source of the dreadful clamour of many tongues, plus a foul stench of mixed origins, all of them acrid and thick, became horrifically apparent, as he found himself at the end of a long parapet that looked out over a deep chasm, opposite which ran a line of crude cells, their racks of rusting bars running from floor to ceiling like a sick black grin. Beneath this line of cells ran another, and beneath that, another, and another, and another. Down and down, deeper and deeper into the earth stretched these endless lines of tiny cages, and inside each and every one could be found a prisoner, soiled rags of dirt and excrement wrapped around their awkward frames, their flesh, where visible, bloodied from the obscene wounds that had been inflicted upon them.

Here was one whose words were unintelligible, barely formed from a throat that had been severed and by a tongue that had been removed, his toes taken too as he struggled for balance against the rotting rusted railings. And there, another, a similar figure, naked apart from a cloak of blackened blood and scarves of flesh that hung from his bones. His cries were not ones of words but ones of red tears from sockets that had long since lost their eyes.

Fleeing from such grievous torment, he dashed along the narrow parapet and ducked through an archway and down a flight of cold stone steps to the lower floor. Here he was to find the source of the thunderous metallic pounding.

Several new cages were under construction, their tenants already chained inside them, their ears dulled by the work carried out by huge beasts with assorted heavy tools. With maybe two or three of these brutes to each cage, the size of the operation became clearer. But where had all these poor wretches come from and why were they all here, Brin wanted to know?

The tall beasts stood maybe eight feet in height, their small heads crumpled and sunk low into their broad shoulders. The faces on them were equally small, puckered and squashed to fit such a space, giving the appearance of a dim intelligence behind.

They wore few garments over their tensed muscular frames as they laboured in the sweat-sodden chamber, and all were intent with the tools in their hands and the prisons on which they were using them. A foot on the step behind him announced another of the creatures descending, and as their eyes met, Brin flew from the spot while it seemed to struggle with the concept of what to do next. Eventually it arrived at a decision and lumbered after him in pursuit.

Some of the labourers looked up from their work as the pair rushed past, one or two even worked out the situation and dropped their tools to give chase, but as Brin scrambled between two frames of ironwork he tripped and stumbled, and fell sprawling to the filthy stone floor. As he looked up, he found himself face to face with one of the imprisoned wretches, chained to a post and lying motionless on the floor in a foetal position, his arms wrapped around himself, his legs tucked in, as he tried to hide the lacerations of his body and limbs. But he stared at Brin from behind bright eyes caged inside blood-crazed sockets as a strangled whisper slipped from the safety of his lips.

"Kill me," he pleaded. "Please kill me."

Brin stared at the man, stunned by his request, just as a huge hand seized him by the back of his neck, as another took hold of his ankle, and another by his arm, and by this triangle of aggression he was hoisted from the ground and carried headlong from the chamber.


The clatter of the latch behind him sealed Brin inside the small dank cell, a rough iron cage that had been laid into one of the sides of the chasm. He wandered tentatively to the edge where the metal grille was open to the sights and looked out upon the terrifying. On the other side of the pit he could see the layers upon layers of identical cages, each filled with desperate shadows of men and women wrapped in blankets of rags and fear, blood and shite. The rows were as endless from left to right as they were upwards and down, deep into the dark recesses of the chasm. His eyes fell to the floor in grief and saw his shoes coated in the filth that littered it. He made to scrape the worst off on the bars of the grille but stopped as he realised the futility of the action. It was then that he became aware of someone behind him in the darkness, and his eyes strained against the gloom to discern what it was that lurked there.

"Who are you?" he demanded of the dark.

"What does it matter?" came a weakened reply. It was the voice of a woman. A voice that carried words that it deemed useless and redundant. "What does it matter who I am, or who you are? It matters no more."

Brin stepped closer towards a dark mass slumped in a corner by the door at the back of the cell. A figure was wrapped there in a black cloak, her head bowed away from his prying eyes.

"How did you get to be here?" he asked.

She kept her silence, keeping her face from his scrutiny.

"Where is here?" Brin persisted. "And how did I get here?"

Again she chose to ignore him, seemingly to realise the futility of any explanation, even if she had one to offer.

"For God's sake answer me," Brin yelled at her, taking hold of her cloak. It was a coarse cloth, and wet, and as he pulled his hand back, found that it came

247

away reddened with the blood of fresh wounds.

"There is no God down here," she finally told him.

"And as to how you got here, it makes no difference now. You are here, and here you will stay. Until..."

"Until what?"

"I was going to say, until you die, but dying, I have learned, is a desire that can never be fulfilled. But as to why we are here, there are so many ways."

"Tell me yours," he asked of her, his voice quieter than it had been.

The woman lifted her head a little, her chin becoming visible beneath the cowl of her cloak. He could see a gash across her flesh as she spoke, narrow and bleeding, but she seemed to pay no heed to it.

"It happened some time ago," she began. "Maybe months, maybe years, maybe even another lifetime ago. I was confronted by a decision, many decisions. I had always known poverty. My house was small and run down. I had no money, no food, nobody to turn to. Then I met someone - something - that promised me everything, everything I ever wanted, everything I could dream of. I could have it all, but for one forfeit; to bargain away what I could offer for its own pleasures. I agreed out of desperation, and it gave me houses, and money, a smell of riches and of men. They came so easily that I forgot my poorer life. Then of course I wanted more, and more, and more. And with each yearning that was fulfilled, I bargained a little more. That was when they collected what was owing to them."

The woman shifted a little, and wrapped her cloak more tightly around her.

"It brought me here," she continued. "I had to come. That was the bargain. That was the deal."

"But surely you will be missed," Brin said to her.

"Oh no," she said. "It took care of that. It brought with it a sprite to take my place. It was a strange creature, I remember, not quite right, not properly made. That's when it took my place, that's when it became me. I saw it change, I saw its long thin arms become proportioned and slender, its awkward frame become voluptuous and curved; my perfected breasts grew at its chest, my toned body became its own, and my beautiful face came from the rise and falls of its own, its sunken eyes becoming angelic, its nose tightening and straightening into a narrow tilt, its furrows of razored teeth cultivating into a set white and even. And then before me stood myself, perfect in every naked detail. Then I was taken away, to a place I had never noticed before."

"The door beneath the stairs in the basement," Brin murmured beneath his breath, as he recalled his own mistake.

The woman lifted her head into full view as she nodded, and Brin saw the full extent of her injuries. Deep scars ran across both cheeks and over her jaw, their lines tracing further down her neck and on into the confines beneath her cloak. Her eyes, once round and sweet, were dark and heavy with tears of pain, but through these there was no mistaking the identity of this victim through all her agony and torment. This was the real Beverley Tate.

"What have they done to you?" he whispered. The recognition brought a tear from his eye.

Her hand strayed to her face, her fingers running along the healing scars of her once soft skin.

"These are its pleasures," she told him. "I had mine, these are its. And it will be the same with you also."

"No," Brin exclaimed defiantly. "I have made no such bargains, no such deals. I have promised nothing. I have had no pleasures."

Beverley looked at him, as though she knew that he had, and it was then that Brin remembered his pleas and his promises with the sprite in the bedroom. He had promised it anything. He cursed his stupidity. He had bargained his flesh away for the sight and touch of her body. But he had not received it. Was this a cruel twist of its deal?

"There is no way out," Beverley said to him, as though she could read his mind. "No escape. Not even through death. They cheat us even of that. Sit and rest, they will come for you soon."


The dull clangs of metal upon metal continued to resound against the walls of the bottomless chasm, so too did the moans and laments of the hundreds, maybe thousands, of prisoners trapped inside their rotting cells. Brin had not slept much in the forever that he had seemingly been held, though Beverley had urged him that sleep, even troubled nightmarish sleep, was the only respite from this never-ending hell. A sudden rattling at the small rusting iron door attracted his attention, but not hers; she knew what was to happen next. In the opening doorway stood two of the large beasts who had built this cell. They were not armed, nor did they need to be, any behaviour out of the unexpected could be dealt with by sheer brutality; a reign of muscle, not weapon. Weapons could be taken and used against them. It seemed the beasts were not that stupid.

He was led away then from Beverley and their

shared cell. He was reluctant to leave her but was certain that he would see her again only too soon. Along faceless corridors and passageways he was taken, an archway fronted by pillars tall and knurled, and tainted by grey dead flowers. The final stage he was left to travel alone. His huge escorts waited for his inevitable return while he stepped warily along the dark passage that led on from the archway, and the heart of all this suffering, he was sure, lay only at its end.

A gentle light came from the room that he now entered, and brought with it a soft warmth that could not touch the chill his flesh now ran with, as his sight fell upon the endless collection of savagery that had undoubtedly been the cause of such misery and cruelty throughout this hell. His thoughts were whirling and disjointed as he wandered amongst the tool-covered walls, each a shrine to a different family of razors and knives, hammers and clamps. And yet each was as meticulously clean and sorted as any surgeon's implements, and the very air around him was almost one of sterility.

As he approached one of the tall metal racks and let his fingers fall upon its cool surface, he heard the shuffling of footsteps behind him. He turned, startled, and saw a strange twisted shape wrapped inside a crisp black sheet. It carried its dark domed head low as its white bright eyes looked up to study him. Its skin seemed as cool and as murky as the stone chamber they stood in, and its feeble smile grew into a ghastly grin of jagged teeth as it made its way closer.

"Hello," it said quietly, like a street-walker to a small child, the familiar greeting sickening on such an unfamiliar face. "And who are you?"

Brin stared helplessly at it, but managed to keep his silence, despite his fear. He turned his head to follow it as it stepped casually in a circle around him as it looked him up and down, as though inspecting food for a meal. It extended a clawed hand to his arm and played one of its jagged fingers lightly across his skin.

"You are new here," it said softly. "No scars. No imperfections."

"Who are you?" Brin demanded, suddenly.

"I asked you first," it retorted childishly, and grinned at him defiantly.

Brin tried not to be baited by this, and answered this foul creature.

"My name is Brin," he said.

"Brin?" repeated the creature. "What kind of name is that?"

"Well who are you then?" Brin retorted, getting impatient with all its foolishness.

"Ah," spoke the creature. "Now that would be telling."

The dark figure shuffled about beneath its sheet, and stared up into Brin's eyes, its cruel grin becoming almost hypnotic.

"Who do you think I am?" it said.

"The devil?" muttered Brin under his breath.

"Ha!" it laughed out loud. "Such stories you people trouble yourselves with. I am no devil. I am no angel. But I can be somewhere in between. I am a businessman, I make deals. So it all depends on you."

"What do you mean?"

"What is it that you desire? More than anything else in the world."

Brin thought for a moment.

"Your world, that is," the creature pointed out

quickly, in case it should lead to any misunderstanding.

Brin thought back to his time at the house with Beverley, the fake Beverley, and the basement, and her bedroom. He had fallen for this before.

"I desire..." he started. "I desire nothing," and he hoped that to be the answer to the riddle.

"Don't be absurd," it said bluntly. "Just tell me what would you most truly want?"

"Beverley Tate," he said at last.

The creature raised an eyebrow, at least if it had one to raise, but the motion was there nevertheless.

"The real Beverley Tate?" it quizzed.

"The one you've been torturing in your cells, not the sprite you left to tempt me in her house."

"Her house?" it suddenly raged. "Her house? That is not her house, it never was. I gave her that, like I gave her the money, and the cars, and the men, and everything else she ever wanted. Her house was a crumbling rat-hole. She had nothing when I found her. I gave her everything she desired. Up to a point that is. There must always be a point."

It grinned suddenly to itself, its anger seemingly gone.

"Go on," Brin told it.

"She was poor, you see. A waster, a nobody, a nothing. I took her in. She longed for riches and power and love, and I gave it to her. And I gave it all under one condition. Just one small condition. When she grew bored with it all, she would belong to me, and then I could satisfy my desires. Of course, she thought she never would grow tired of such dreams, such fantasies, and so she agreed. But in time, and like all channels of greed, she grew discontent with all that I had given her. She wanted more and more, and like any businessman I made new deals with her, until one day I took what was owing to me. We made a deal. Pure and simple."

"Then why am I here? I wanted Beverley, the fake Beverley, but I was never given what I asked for. How could I ever get tired with something I never had?"

"You're right, you were never given Beverley," it said slyly. "I had her all along down here. You made a bargain with one of my sprites; they can be quite - devilish." It laughed at its own joke, its twisted chest shuddering beneath its dark sheet, its head falling back hard as if it should roll off and away.

Brin made towards it but it stopped him with an icy stare.

"But you're here now," it said to him, "and that's all I care about."

It picked up one of the long silver blades from its place at the wall and turned it slowly in its long slender fingers.

"I shall enjoy the sensation of my knife running through your flesh. The metal so much loves the lubrication of hot rich blood, and I do like to keep them all happy."

"I'll make a deal with you," Brin stammered quickly, backing away from the approaching blade.

"My knives," it said, his voice now like that of a scolded infant. "They want blood. They want your blood."

"Whatever I desire..." he continued, his mind racing.

"They want to know you," it said, stepping after Brin's retreat. "They want to know your flesh, know your blood, your bones."

"You asked for whatever I desired," he said, his back

hitting the wall behind and killing his escape.

The creature stopped in front of him, its blade hovering at his neck.

"What is it that you desire?" it asked, its curiosity to know the minds of men its second favourite pastime.

"To have you dead," he yelled, and snatched at one of the knives on the wall, plunging it deep into the creature's chest. It reeled back from the blow, its black sheet billowing in its wake like a whirlwind, before it spun full circle to turn its grinning head back towards him.

"Nice try," it said. "But you just made them hungry for more."

Brin was panicking, his heart pounding heavily in chest.

"I'll make a deal with you," he murmured.

"But you already made one with my sprite. Now you want to make another with me? No deal."

"No," he said. "Same deal."

The creature stood where it was and looked at him expectantly.

"Give me Beverley Tate," Brin told it. "Let us be together back in my world. When I get tired of her, you can do whatever you like with me."

The creature thought this over for a while. It liked to make deals, almost as much as it liked to collect on them.

"I accept your deal," it said after some deliberation. "I will have you both taken from here and left at her house. Her own house, rotten and penniless. That should make things far more interesting."

Brin stood and stared at it, his chest thudding with terror. Soon he would be alone with Beverley, away from this place, where they might both have a chance

255

to survive. She would not know about his deal until they were together but he was sure she would accept. What choice did either of them have? But the only threat to his deal that he could see, was the cloud of human nature that hung above their heads; the fear that they might someday grow tired of each other, and submit themselves to a continued living hell at the mercy of the knives of this creature.

Brin found himself in a hallway at the bottom of a flight of stairs in a dim and rotting old house. The carpet beneath his feet was ragged and threadbare and showed sections of the warped floorboards through its patchwork of holes. The ceiling was low and brown with grime, the air thick with decay, and it hurt his throat and lungs as he breathed it in. As he stumbled about the small dingy rooms, he heard the sound of sobbing coming from upstairs.

Finding one of the doors ajar, he stepped through and found Beverley, alone and kneeling in front of her dressing table, its mirror cracked. The tears rolled down her scarred cheeks as she saw for herself what a mutilated wretch she had become. Her black cloak hung like rags off her wasted frame, leaving her bloodied shoulders visible for him to see. Vast lines of wounds and incisions interlaced her once perfect skin like so many spiders webs. Blue-black smudges charted the vice-like holds of the straps that had bound her tightly. And as she heard him approach, she made to cover herself, but before she had even hidden as inch of her tainted flesh she gave up and allowed him to look at her.

Brin knelt down beside her and looked at the

reflection of her eyes in the mirror. Her beauty was still here, but locked behind pockets of pain, and now that he knew the truth, he loved her the more for it. Reaching down, he lifted up her cloak and wrapped it around her shoulders, against the chill, and for her dignity.

"Is it over?" she asked him weakly, her tears glistening on her ragged cheeks.

"It can be," he replied.

Her eyes searched his for an explanation.

"I made a deal with it," he explained softly.

She turned to him suddenly in horror, grabbing him by his shoulders, but he restrained her only with a smile.

"I told it that I wanted you more than anything else."

"No," she cried, shaking her head desperately. "You wanted the sprite, the replica, the rich duplicate in the big house. That's what you wished for."

"At first," Brin insisted, "that's true. I fell in love with your face, but I did not realise that it had been stolen. But it is you that I want."

Beverley turned back to look at herself in the mirror.

"How can you ever love someone like me? My face is torn and wasted, my body hangs like old meat, and I have nothing to offer you. I have no money, and this house is derelict. Can't you see why I traded all this. I traded this life for possessions, I traded it for money, to find happiness. I never thought I could grow discontent with all that it gave me. But I did, and I am ashamed of my own greed."

"But I made a different deal," Brin persisted. "If we never grow tired of each other, if we never stop loving each other, then we will be safe."

"But how can we be certain that we will?"

By noon the following day, a pact between Brin Lomax and Beverley Tate was made. With hearts declared and vows sworn, they made certain that day, legally and before God, that they would love each other until death did they part, living out the remainder of their lives as husband and wife, in a separate deal that would see them safe from the butchery of the creature that lived beneath their very feet.

# Coachman's Drive

David Willmet stood on the lawn at the front of the house and gazed up at the old weathered paintwork. His hands were deep in the pockets of his long heavy overcoat; his collar was pulled up snugly around his neck; his head was numb. A section of guttering had broken away, he could see, and a steady trickle of water dripped down to a noisy puddle at the base of the brickwork beneath the old kitchen window. It had been over twenty years since he had called this place home, twenty years since he had run away, twenty years since he had seen his parents, his father. He was an accountant now, working for local government, a long way from rural Kent. Things had changed some. A lot of things.

He'd heard that his father was dead over a decade ago, and he had called his mother shortly afterwards. For what reason he still wasn't quite sure of. Compassion? Perhaps. But just as likely Willmet wanted to make sure that the old man wasn't coming back. He never went to the funeral, or even phoned his mother in those ten years following. Now she was in the ground too. Maybe he'd go see both graves while he was here. It seemed fitting somehow, expected even, but it didn't carry any emotion. Maybe it would, he thought, once he was in the church grounds and looking down at the mounds of dark earth next to his feet, overshadowed by a slab of cold granite.

It was November, and an icy wind gnawed the whole of Coachman's Drive, chewing red exposed skin with a bite like rats' teeth and cutting late autumn leaves into vortices across the unkempt lawns. Grey rose bushes sagged in muddy overgrown flowerbeds, trapping the dead leaves against their twisted claws of spines, adding discarded debris to the already untidy pathways. Willmet had parked his silver Mercedes a little way up the road, a gleaming object of modernity and prosperity amongst all this that had turned to unruliness and decay. This had been his home once upon a time. And he was glad that he had left when he had.

He pulled his hand from the warmth of his coat pocket and glanced at his watch. It was getting close to three o'clock. It would only take perhaps ten minutes to get to the churchyard. Ten minutes to look around and find the graves - presumably they'd be next to each other - and then he'd be back at the hotel before half past. He turned to leave, his eyes not wanting to look around too closely for fear of what they might find, and as he made his way back along Coachman's Drive towards his car, he pretty much kept them cast down at the wet road as he walked.

There were few good memories of this place, but this walk along this stretch of road by the house brought its own troupe of ghosts, ghosts that he did not want to have haunting him any more. He wanted to be done with this place, and now he'd been brought back here once again. His parents were both dead, but that didn't stop those ghosts still clawing inside his chest, raking the insides of his ribcage like bony white talons, raking up feelings that should have erased themselves by now.

It wasn't until he pulled his keys from his trouser pocket and clicked the alarm off that he noticed the woman hovering at the rear of the car. He started at both her proximity and her scrutiny, and they gazed at each other for a few moments in an awkward silence. She was probably edging towards forty, the same as he, but her expression shifted like that of an autograph hunter come face to face with that week's movie star - should she, shouldn't she - her tongue seemed tied. Her bright inquisitive eyes tried to catch his, and even as Willmet grasped the door handle and began to pull, he only slowly began to recognise the features that he had fallen in love with over thirty years ago.

"Katie?" he asked breathlessly.

A tentative smile crept now across the woman's lips in confirmation, and she stepped round from the back of the car, her arms tentatively open to offer a welcoming embrace.

"I wasn't sure if it was you or not," she said gently. "I saw your car pull up, and I just couldn't believe…"

"It's good to see you again. It's been -"

"A long time," she said. "You never came to the funerals."

"No, I -"

"You don't have to explain. I went to your father's a few years back; you know, being a neighbour and all."

"Was he dead?" Willmet asked, his face straight.

The woman stared at him, apparently bewildered by his question.

"They buried him, if that's what you mean."

Willmet shook his head.

"I'm sorry, that was in poor taste."

"He was your father."

"I know."

An uneasy silence seemed to descend upon them again as they stood next to the unlocked silver Mercedes. They'd been the best of friends since before their memories began, in the same small sleepy village, and yet they hadn't spoken for over three decades. What was there to talk about? Old times? Old memories?

"You'll come in for a cup of tea?" she asked him finally.

Willmet gazed at her for a moment until her words sank in.

"You still live here?" he was incredulous.

The woman nodded with a half smile.

"I stayed with mum when she got sick. Dementia."

"I'm sorry."

"No need," she said with a shrug. "She's fine apart from the occasional bad spell. Nothing I can't handle, though."

"You're sure I wouldn't be imposing?"

"Of course not. She probably won't even recognise you anyway, probably think you're someone come to fix the telly. Come on."

Willmet pressed the clicker in his hand again, and as the alarm chirped twice, he went with her back along Coachman's Drive towards the big white house. She turned after a few steps, however, and with a full smile now on those still-beautiful lips, she said:

"And by the way, it's now Kathy."

"I missed you, you know," Willmet admitted, as he stirred his tea.

They were sitting at the kitchen table. Kathy had brought out some home-made scones and had set them in a small pyramid on a blue china plate. Willmet took one and placed it neatly on a small side plate. He wasn't sure if she'd heard him or not.

"No one's called me Katie for years," she said, as if they'd been talking non stop for hours. "Not since school. Not since you left in fact."

"Did you hear me?" he had to ask.

She looked at him. Her eyes were wide and seemed to see him fully, more fully than anyone had seen him in a long time.

"Yes," she said finally. "I heard you."

Willmet raised his eyebrows. He wanted something a little more than that.

"You left so suddenly, you left us all."

"I'm sorry," he said, his eyes dropping to the tea swirling round in his blue china cup. "It was difficult at home. One morning I just woke up and... well, you know the rest."

"No, David, I don't. You may know what happened to you that day, and what happened to you every day afterwards for over thirty years, but I don't. I haven't spoken to you or seen you in that time. You could have been dead for all I knew."

"I'm sorry," he said again. "Really."

"Don't be sorry," she exclaimed, reaching across the table and taking hold of his hand, "just be glad to be back here with me again. We've got a lot of catching up to do."

He smiled at her, at her face and at her hair and at those beautiful brown eyes that seemed to capture every part of him, just like they'd done all those years ago when they were kids.

"Now," she said, picking up a scone and taking a bite out of it, "tell me something I don't already know about you."

A heavy weight suddenly seemed to lift itself up out of his chest then as he let a grin of happiness come. He hadn't looked forward to coming back here, and certainly not to the house, but he'd now found something that he hadn't expected to find; little Katie Mote still sitting in the bare brick kitchen, her mother's copper pans still hanging in their places. She was older and she was taller but she was still little Katie Mote from down the road. Oh how he had loved her, how he had missed her. How best to begin then, he thought, something important from his life, something big, just to see how her expression might change, to see if she still cared.

"I met my wife when I was twenty two," he told her, watching her face without blinking.

"You're married?" she observed over the top of her cup.

"Divorced now, just over a year."

"I'm sorry. What happened - if it's any of my business?"

"No, it's okay. We just realised that we didn't really know each other. We were in love, I think, but we just didn't seem to share that much; emotionally, that is. There didn't seem to be anything to hold us together."

"Emotional glue," Kathy murmured.

Willmet looked up at her.

"Love - it sticks us together. I heard someone say it once, perhaps in a movie. I made a mental note for future use."

He tried to smile. It hadn't been an easy separation, and it hadn't been particularly messy, but it still hurt.

"The human heart can take a lot of punishment," he mused quietly. "Sometimes more than we realise."

Kathy nodded her agreement as she took another bite of her scone.

There was a brief moment of quiet as the weight of

their losses and misadventures sank in, until Kathy suddenly seemed to break out of her silence and blurt a sentence across the table in a fit of gossip:

"You'll never believe who runs the Post Office in the village now."

"Who?" Willmet asked, glad of the change of subject.

"Steve Satrick."

"No," Willmet cried, his mind reeling back to the days of chasing through the cornfields with the freckled ginger boy from over the road, little Katie Mote struggling to keep up behind them. "Not Satch."

"One and the same."

"He never left either?"

"He did for a while, for a couple of years I think. But he came back. We all came back in the end."

"You left too?"

"Only for a month. Then I heard about mum."

"Oh."

Willmet wanted to comment more than that, but he kept his words to himself. He'd only come back himself to look over the old house before it went on the market. The estate agent had put a price of £110,000 on it, a generous figure considering the work that needed doing to it. No doubt someone from London would come down and pick it up, renovate it into a country retreat or something. Perfect for the kids. Perfect for the dad to keep himself busy.

"I should give him a call," Kathy said.

"Who?" Willmet asked dumbly.

"Steve. He'd love to see you again, I'm sure."

"Yeah," he mused distantly, and watched as she got up from the table and went through into the hallway to pick up the phone.

"Just like old times," he murmured to himself.

Satch was sitting in the corner of the Jolly Woodman when they arrived shortly after seven o'clock. He half got up from the small table he was sat at, his hand cocked in the air to attract their attention, and they went swiftly towards him through the early evening throng. Willmet shook his hand - something they had never done, the contact between them feeling strange - while Kathy went to the bar to order drinks. Satch had a huge grin on his face. Obviously he was pleased to see him, and it quickly became infectious.

"This is quite some sight," the one-time ginger kid was saying. He was virtually bald now, no sign of that unruly ginger mop, but he now had a goatee that more than made up for it. He had been a geeky-looking child, Willmet half-remembered, but the shining domed head and fuzzy chin suited him more than he would have thought possible.

"I hear you're running the Post Office," Willmet said, not altogether sure how to start this conversation.

"Yeah, me and Janie, been a few years now too. You remember Janie? Janice Connelly."

"Little Janice Connelly from Hunton Secondary?"

"That's the one."

"I remember, long brown hair."

"Short and blonde now, but yeah. Got two kids too. One of each."

"Nice."

They stared at each other for a few awkward moments, huge dumb grins on their faces, until Kathy appeared at the table with three drinks and set them down in front of them. Willmet took up his pint of local brew and drank a good few throatfuls. He wasn't a big drinker, but he suddenly felt like he needed some alcohol in his system. This trip wasn't going at all how he'd imagined it. His memories he didn't like, but there was something nagging inside him, telling him that those memories were going to be getting a whole lot more painful before the night was out.

"Is Hunton Secondary still standing?" Willmet asked, as he set his pint back down.

"Sure is. I run the football squad there now. Weekend thing."

"What was the name of that bloke who was running it when we were there? Real nasty guy."

"Hilliard."

"That's it. I remember him."

"Things are a lot different now though. We've got proper facilities and everything."

Willmet picked up his pint and took another long throatful. There were things that he wanted to say, things that he would no doubt have to say later on. Dare he say them now? It seemed a bit early on in the evening. He'd only just met Satch again for Christ's sake. He didn't want to bring everything down just yet.

"I'm sorry to hear about your mother, by the way," Satch said, sipping his pint. "She was well liked around the village."

Willmet murmured non-committally and took another draw on his beer.

"It was quite a service," Satch went on.

"You went?" Willmet asked, looking up.

"Felt like I had to, you know? Known her a long time. And as you weren't there…"

"I had… I was busy. Work and all."

"Hey, there was no accusation intended."

"That's okay."

"I was there at your father's funeral as well."

Willmet looked hard at him now. He was returning his gaze more fully than was right for such a conversation. It was almost accusational, the way he looked at him. There was more than just words in his voice. There was something else. Something darker.

"I hadn't seen my father for a long time," Willmet confessed. "I didn't know until much later."

Satch didn't say anything, just took up his pint and sipped again. A glance seemed to pass between Kathy and Satch as they sat there too, a glance that seemed to carry some considerable weight. It was gone a moment later, but it tugged at his mind as the three of them continued to talk.

"Satch told me he married Janice Connelly," Willmet said to Kathy, watching as her eyes came back to look at him.

"It's been a few long years now, eh, Steve?" Kathy said.

"Fourteen years, come May."

"Have you never been tempted to go down the aisle yourself, Kathy?" Willmet asked her.

Her eyes flashed back at him, her gaze suddenly cold.

Her answer was just as icy.

An isolated:

"No."

That same glance flickered between her and Satch again, and suddenly Willmet felt even more uncomfortable. Something was definitely wrong, something even he wasn't aware of. Perhaps this was the right time to unload some of those ghosts. He glanced at his watch. It was only ten past eight. It should come later. Always later.

"I was thinking about moving into the old house

again," Willmet announced eventually, not even sure where such a statement could have come from. "You know, try and make it liveable again."

He hadn't even considered that eventuality until now, and where these words came from he had no idea. But he sat and watched the other two as they seemed to take in the news as though he was suggesting impromptu brain surgery on the pair of them, surgery with a hammer and chisel. It was Satch who spoke first.

"It'll need a lot of work, you know," he said. "I know a guy in Maidstone. Proper builder. I'll give you his card."

"What makes you want to live in the house again?" Kathy asked, her face now one of concern.

"I don't know. Why, don't you want me living on your doorstep again?"

"It's not that, it'd be great to have you in the road again, it's just -"

"Just what?"

"I thought you'd run away from that house for a reason."

Willmet sat and stared at her as he thought about it all for a moment. How much had this little girl known all those years ago? As far as he was aware nothing had changed in any of their lives. Actually, something had changed. His parents were both dead and in the ground. They weren't coming back.

"You know, the big oak tree is still standing," Satch told him suddenly.

Willmet shot him a gaze that could have knocked him off his chair if it'd had physical weight. His childhood friend sat there sipping his pint as though he had never said it. He didn't need to be told which oak tree. There was only one oak tree to talk about. He had thought it had been a secret, a deathly secret between him and his father, so how did Satch come to know about it? He had to know. Why else would he have mentioned it?

"Someone tried to burn it down shortly after you left," Satch continued as though nothing had happened, "but it's still alive."

"People thought it was you," Kathy said, "but you'd gone."

"People? What people? What are you talking about?"

Kathy suddenly reached across the small wooden table and put her hand over his. The cold of her hand made him realise just how hot he had become himself. He could feel himself shaking inside now, his body trembling as his nerves wracked themselves to pieces.

"We all knew what he did to you."

"Who?"

"At the time we just suspected, but when you went, the truth broke."

"What are you talking about?" Willmet said again, licking lips that had become as dry as dirt.

"We know why you left," Satch told him. "I tried to leave myself, but I just couldn't cope. I couldn't face up to anything. Not until I came back. Not until I met Janie. She helped me to talk. To open up."

Willmet stared from one of them to the other. His mouth felt like it was open, but he could feel his jaw muscles aching from where he had clenched them together. His stomach was turning over on itself, crawling and writhing as though it was full of maggots. He felt like he was going to throw up, as though he was going to wretch his whole damn childhood up over that tiny wooden table in front of them.

And then he felt Kathy's hand once again.

Her soft skin was cool against his own. His eyes were caught by hers. Cradled. And then his lips slowly parted, delicate words tumbling from them like petals held captive since the first brutal act upon the planet.

"They used to call me the purple-coloured boy at school," Willmet said slowly and quietly, as he began his confession. His eyes closed, and his memories drew themselves slowly in his head, painful, hollow, black and white. "I had marks over my back and buttocks, cuts and bruises, aches and welts. In the changing rooms I had nowhere to hide. I was exposed to jokes and ridicules."

"Kids can be so cruel," he heard Kathy murmur somewhere in the distance.

"Hilliard too. He didn't say the words but he knew what the others were saying. I used to catch him smirking near the showers while we dressed."

"It came back to the rest of us," Satch said. "When you went."

Willmet looked up and saw the wetness of his eyes.

"When you left," Satch continued, "your father took to walking…"

Willmet stared at him, and then he began to shake his head, but he was already beginning to see the bigger picture. How could this be, he kept wanting to say, but he knew, he knew deep down inside that it was true. He'd seen his father's evil mask face to face so many times. He knew what he was capable of. Maybe not every specific deed, not every sickening horror. But one crime led to another. No crime had a limit.

"He used to take me out to that big old oak tree,"

Willmet continued, the sight of its rough gnarled branches sketching themselves in black charcoal lines across the grained canvas inside his head. "He used to hang me from the big branch, hang me like I was a sack of laundry, and spin me round as he laughed. Then he'd lay into me with any branch that was lying around."

"You weren't the only one," he heard Satch say. "He did that to me too. When you were gone."

When Willmet looked up again, he saw that Satch was crying now, tears trickling down his once-freckled cheeks.

"I could see that big old oak tree from the edge of the woods," Kathy murmured quietly.

Willmet gazed at her now. What was coming here?

"Your father used to take me there," she said, "into the edge of the woods and lift my dress. I used to cry, to plead with him to stop, even before he started to touch me. His fingers used to enter me, I could feel his huge rough knuckles coarse inside me, inside..." she sniffed hard and pushed the back of her hand across her face. "I hated him. I wanted to die. But he said if I ever told anyone, he would kill me. He would kill me and my mother. I sometimes thought that my mother had found out. That was why her mind went the way it did."

Willmet stared at her. What was this she was telling him? That the girl he had loved since before he could remember had been... touched... by his own father? His stomach turned over again and a cold wet blanket of sickness seemed to descend around him, shrouding him. He felt distressingly isolated from these two friends, and yet bonded to them by some ancient despicable act. His father was dead. There could be no recriminations for him now. None of it had been his doing, and yet he still felt somehow responsible.

"I took the matches from my mother's kitchen," Kathy continued. "I wanted to burn that tree, burn myself too, but I just didn't have the strength inside me. I wanted to leave like you did, but I didn't have the courage for that either. I was just too ashamed. I put it off and I put it off, and then mum got sick and there was nobody else to help her."

Willmet stared from one to the other again in utter disbelief. The heavy glance that the two of them had passed so furtively between them, now enveloped him with its sickly glue. It seeped into his chest and into his head and promised to swallow him whole, swallow the three of them whole like some vast ugly fish. But somewhere in his gut, he knew that the circle of three would undoubtedly be bigger. And that circle would take a while to uncover. Only then perhaps could he feel something close to cleanliness, and allow his heart time to heal.


It was a little over a week later when Willmet returned to Coachman's Drive. He sat in his silver Mercedes outside the rundown exterior of what had once been his home and gazed up at the old weathered paintwork. He had spoken to Kathy and Satch twice on the phone since their reunion in the pub, and things had seemed a little brighter for them all, now that the truth was out.

He held the offer from the estate agent in his hand, and pondered over the For Sale sign hammered into the lawn out front. He'd come here with the intention of seeing the place once more before getting shot of it for good. Now it seemed there was reason to stay. Not just for himself, but for the two friends that had their own demons to slay. His father was dead, no doubt rotting away in the filth that had filled his body while he was alive. His mother too was in the ground, and although she had not laid a finger on him or anyone else he had known, he suspected that she must have known what his father was capable of. And because she had never done a thing to stop him, he was happy at her absence too.

The decaying stone pathway led up to a door that he knew would need a lot of work doing behind it, and he climbed out of the warmth of his car before glancing up at the For Sale sign on the front lawn once again. The icy November wind slashed at the late autumn leaves once more, darting them down the narrow country road he had known so intimately as a young boy, and sending them painfully on their way.

The sound of retching from upstairs interrupted the television, and Jude lifted her attention from the cat dozing in her lap. It looked like it was going to be yet another restless night for her husband, and it was only seven thirty. He'd been to see Doctor Williams three times already this month and each time he'd been told that he was all right - a few laboured breathing problems, some nausea, but nothing to worry about. He'd been prescribed some pills but they hadn't touched whatever was wrong with him. Jude knew that Michael wouldn't wake up with severe chest cramps every night for no good reason, and she pushed the cat down onto the carpet and got to her feet before heading upstairs to see him.

The single bulb up on the landing cast its light down the steps as she climbed, and once upstairs, she popped her head around the bathroom door. Michael was bent over the toilet panting, and he glanced up at her as she entered. Threads of spittle hung from his chin but he seemed not to care, his expression was pitiful.

Jude asked him if there was anything she could do, but he simply pushed himself to his feet and took a mouthful of water from the sink, before telling her that he'd rather just go back to bed. It was sleep that seemed to be the problem. He only ever got his cramps when he was asleep.

Jude followed him into the bedroom and watched him lay back down in their bed. With one hand pressed against his brow, his other against his chest, and his poor face held in a grimace of pain, it was hard for her to simply do nothing. There was nothing she could do, however. The doctor had said he would get better in time, and that had seemed to be an end to it. Yet here Michael was, struggling to get through another night and keep from crying. Jude bent to turn off the bedside lamp but Michael stopped her.

"Leave it on," he murmured. "I'd prefer to have some light."

"I'm the one who's supposed to be afraid of the dark around here, honey, remember?" Jude replied with a smile, and then left him to try and get some sleep, closing the bedroom door behind her.

Returning to the living room, Jude sat down once more in front of the television. She could hear Michael turning over in bed, even over the adverts, and she began to worry about him again. Pains didn't come for no good reason, but if the doctor couldn't do anything then who else was there? The light out in the kitchen suddenly flickered, and cast a blanket of shadow briefly across the whole room. Her heart skipped a beat and a shiver ran throughout her body. She hated the darkness, that's why she had to have all the lights on in the house, whether she was using the rooms or not. It annoyed Michael endlessly, especially when the electricity bill came each quarter, but it wasn't her fault. Not really. Something brushed past her leg and Jude let out a yelp as she clutched at the arm of the sofa. The black tail of the cat flicked into the air beside her shin like a flag and she cursed it before bending to scoop it up into her arms. Settling it into her lap, she leant back on the sofa once more and tried to compose herself into watching the rest of Eastenders.


When Jude got home the following evening, Michael's car was already in the driveway. All the lights were out, and she hurried trembling to the front door, fumbling with her keys and taking even longer to unlock it that if she'd simply approached the whole unlocking the door in the dark routine rationally. But then phobias were never rational things. Her hand slid in little rapid circles across the wall searching for the light switch, and only when the hallway was flooded with light and her stupid fears were alleviated, could she calm down and close the door behind her. Her first thought was to go through into the living and the kitchen and turn the lights on there too. Her second thought was to turn on the light on the landing and then go see how her husband was feeling.

She could hear his moans on the stairs as she ascended. Opening the bedroom door, a shaft of light spilled across the bed and illuminated his sprawled form, his hands clamped to his stomach and chest. Jude entered slowly, and perched on the edge of the bed beside him. Michael's eyes opened just a crack. She could see he was in so much pain.

"Have you taken your pills?" Jude asked him.

All Michael could manage was a fragile nod.

"Perhaps I should call him."

"No," he managed to utter. "I saw him again this morning. I'm usually fine during the day. It's just in the late afternoon when it starts to get dark, these cramps just seem to come. My boss tells me to go home to bed, and it just seems to get worse."

"I know, honey," Jude said, placing a hand to his brow. He didn't have a fever. It was just so strange.

Michael asked if she could put the bedside lamp on for him and she reached over and did so. Its soft light gently filled the room, and the sudden appearance of the shadows caught Jude's attention. Behind the books on the cupboard, across the floor behind the wicker chair, the shadows seemed to dance and move for just a moment before settling into their uniform shapes of darkness. There it was again. Darkness. You just couldn't get away from it. Jude forced herself to look away from it and change the subject.

"Is there anything you want?" she asked.

Michael managed to shake his head, accompanied by a little whimper of pain.

"Sure? Nothing to eat or anything."

"No thanks, love, I'm fine. Just leave me to rest."

"Okay, hon. Just cry out if you do."

Getting up from the bed, Jude left him and went back downstairs into the kitchen to get something to eat. It was getting too much, his leaving work most days to come home to bed. There was no sign of him improving, and Doctor Williams' pills were a joke. If there was no change over the next few days... Well, she didn't know what she'd do, but something would have to be done.


Jude heard Michael cry out, even over the end credits of Coronation Street. She sat motionless for a moment, her ears searching the quiet of the house, until a second cry came and she fled the sofa. Dashing upstairs, she hurried through into the bedroom where she found Michael doubled-up in agony. The shadows cast by the bedside lamp distorted his figure as he writhed, contorting themselves into eerie shapes that made Jude reach for the main bedroom light switch. The shadows that crawled over her husband went instantly, and she hurried to put her loving hands around him.

"What can I do? What can I do?" she cried, trying to hold him down.

"Make it stop. Please," he begged, his own hands clamped hard against his stomach and chest.

Jude gazed down at him helplessly. She just didn't know what to do. Twice an ambulance had taken him to casualty, and on both occasions they had scanned him and found nothing out of the ordinary. Severe indigestion, they'd claimed, or perhaps heartburn. Their answers were ridiculous.

Jude managed to calm him a little, and urge him to lie still. His breathing was rapid, probably more because of panic than anything else, and he was sweating profusely. Returning from the bathroom with a bowl of water and a washcloth, Jude began to bathe his forehead gently. His brow began to unknot as she soothed his face, and as he quietened, she lifted his t-shirt a little to bathe his stomach and chest too.

There was a mark there on his skin like a stain, a purple-black bruise the size of her fist than ran in fine strokes up and over his chest. It had not been there before, she was certain of it, but then she'd never really been looking for it. Gently she put her fingertips to it. Michael flinched in pain as she did so, his hands rising quickly to clutch at the air. Instantly she regretted it, and bent over quickly to kiss him and say sorry. How long had the bruise been there, she wanted to know? Michael had no answers for her, except that the pain had lessened in the last few minutes since she'd been with him. At least that was something. Jude glanced quickly at her watch. It was past nine o'clock - too late to call the doctor's surgery. She thought of an ambulance, or even driving him to the hospital across town herself, but after a moment decided that they'd done nothing before, so why would they do anything this time. She suggested the options to Michael.

"I don't want to travel," he gasped. "Just let me rest a while. I'll see what the bruise looks like in the morning. Wherever it came from, it won't be getting any worse tonight."

Jude decided to stay with him for a while. If she made him feel better while she was in the room, then all well and good; she'd be his good luck charm - whatever it took to make him get well again. He'd have to have the main bedroom light off, of course, but at least there was the bedside lamp, and that, if she was honest, was probably more for her sake than his.

Wandering back across the room, she switched off the main light as she pushed the bedroom door closed to hush the sound of the television downstairs, and then pulled up a chair at Michael's bedside, before taking hold of his hand and caressing it. It was hot and trembled in her touch, but he seemed to like the fact that she was close.

The only light in the room came from the lamp perched on the small bedside cabinet. Its glow was mediocre at most, spilling only a soft gentle luminescence over them both. The shadows were resurrected, of course, and in full strength, and she was glad that they were holding hands, even if his eyes weren't open and looking for ghosts. The darkness was there once again, lurking behind the books in the bookcase, crawling out from behind the bear Michael had bought her last Valentine's, and saturating the carpet beneath the bed and her dressing table. So much darkness, festering and shifting, and all of it on the brink of war, ready to take hold of her ankles and take her prisoner.

Michael grew quieter while she was with him. His trembling ceased and his breathing became peaceful until she thought he had at last begun to doze. For that at least she was thankful, and she began to wonder whether perhaps she was his good luck charm after all. She smiled to herself at the thought. As the silence of the room quieted her thoughts, and the warm lamplight urged her to succumb to her husband's blissful state, so Jude's eyes began to grow heavier. She glanced down at Michael's face once more but with effort now, in an attempt to keep a watchful gaze over him. His face was peaceful, his frown now gone, and his chest was rising and falling gently in the depths of much needed sleep. Yes, it was time for sleep, time for them both. Her eyes were growing ever more heavy, and the effort of keeping them open was matched only by the effort that it would take to push herself up from her chair.

Jude's eyes were flickering now, and the soft light from the bedside lamp seemed to be casting all sorts of protean shadows across the shelves and floor, all shifting and reaching between the efforts of keeping awake. The Valentine's bear was just a mass of dark crawling fur, the white of the wallpaper ebbed in patterns of its own, the books promised suicide by casting themselves off the edge of their own shelves, and the voids of deepest shadow stirred as though they were oceans of bottomless graves.

Her sight was teetering altogether now, and Jude felt herself slipping into the chasm between waking and sleeping. She was sure she still had conscious thoughts, and that she could still look down at Michael if she wanted to, and yet they seemed slippery and difficult to control, as though they were under their own influence, begging to become dreams. She imagined, or perhaps witnessed, the shadows coming to life. She saw them pluck themselves from behind her bear, creep across the wall behind the books, march like liquid soldiers across the floor. From out of the oceans they came too, sailing ghostly black galleons with tattered sails of sackcloth. Ebbing they came, on foot and by boat, swirling from their resting places like ribbons of Indian ink. From above her came the shape of a nearly human form, dark and angular, and Jude watched as it made its way slowly across the ceiling, before spilling down the patterned wallpaper towards her.

She was asleep now, of course she was asleep. So then why could she hear the television still playing to itself downstairs in the living room? Or still feel Michael's hand in her own? Her thoughts were a little more ordered now, and those last two were fairly self-explanatory in themselves. But then how could she be looking at this roving shadow if it were not a thing of dreams. It was reaching even now as she looked at it, this black ghost hovering in the air, and she could even see it growing solid. It had fingers, this shadow creature, and they stretched and grew in the air above her, writhing and contorting like slow awkward snakes. They seemed almost to have purpose, these snakes of phantom substance, purpose that her dream-mind, for some reason, was conjuring. But listen. Wasn't that the music at the end of the news? She could hear it distinctly. What would be the relevance of dreaming about the music at the end of the news, or even dreaming about hearing the music at the end of the news in another room? Dreams were stupid. They never made any sense. But then again, just as she thought this, Jude had the funny feeling that perhaps this was not a dream after all. The whole thing was irrational, for sure, but then so was her phobia, but that didn't make it any less real or terrifying. Jude squeezed Michael's hand ever so slightly. She could feel the resilience and warmth of his skin. That sort of thing could never be dreamt. She scrunched up her toes in her slippers. The wool lining was warm and familiar. That, too, was real. Slowly Jude swallowed, and let her eyes settle once again on the black apparition still hovering over her husband.

The slender fingers the ghost had flexed had now reached down and were out of sight inside the cavity of the sleeping Michael's chest. It seemed to be performing some kind of surgery, this ghost, manipulating or pulling at the organs of Michael's body, his lungs and his heart. What was it doing, she wanted to know? Why was it pulling at these things inside her husband's body? Then the thought came to her. Perhaps it was not some kind of surgery. Perhaps it was an evil thing, this ghost, this poltergeist, and it was trying to kill him slowly from the inside by ripping at his organs, tearing at them and bruising them.

Jude wanted to will herself to action, or if she was asleep then to wake, to shake herself from her static slumbers and do anything but sit there and helplessly watch her husband suffer at the mercy of this shadow creature. But her limbs were leaden, stricken with her fear of this thickening darkness, and they simply would not obey her. She wanted to cry out. She wanted to beat this thing back from her beloved Michael. But her voice would not come. Her fists were slack and useless.

Those ghostly fingers still roved beneath Michael's

t-shirt, working and contorting, and all Jude could think of was the evil this beast was performing. The source of the bruise was here now, and from internal bleeding, from such unnatural internal bleeding. The purple-black flesh was beginning to strain beneath the violations torn inside, the bruise darkening, glowering. Tears came to Jude's eyes as she watched. She so wanted to stop this. But it was the darkness, the very darkness, that had come from beneath her bed and from behind her books and Valentine's bear to tear at her husband's belly and heart that stopped her.

Her tears slipped their shackles and tracked down her cheeks, her chest loosing a sob of helplessness. Through her blurred vision, she thought she saw the shadow cease momentarily, its hand stopped, held poised. Involuntarily, she sniffed back her tears. A second movement. The shadow knew she was awake now. It was looking at her. It had no eyes in its head, nor even much of a head in the low-lit gloom, but she could sense its gaze upon her and it chilled her. How long it remained looking at her she had no way of knowing, but it seemed to go on, and on, until its hand suddenly lifted from Michael's chest, and then it retreated back across the wall altogether. Jude began to shake uncontrollably with fear as she watched it go, its dark supple form disappearing back into the oceans of darkness in the corner of the room.

Jude sat trembling for a few minutes, her sight fixed on the place the shadow creature had dissolved into, as more sobs came. There were things there, she knew. Things that don't exist. A shudder passed down her spine, and suddenly she couldn't help her sight raking the darkest areas of bedroom; the bookshelves, the wardrobe, her dressing table. So much darkness, and all of it total. A second shudder jolted her body, and this one she used to force herself into motion. She lurched forward with a cry in her throat, and grabbed hold of Michael. He was gasping again - how could she have missed that? - but she ignored his protestations and managed to haul him into a sitting position.

"We have to go," she yelled at him, tugging on his arms with strength she was certain she did not have. "Now!"

He clutched his stomach in pain, but she pushed herself to her feet regardless, pulling him up after her, before bearing his weight as she staggered with him towards the bedroom door. Only at the threshold did Jude cast a last glance back into the shadows of the room. The darkness was obedient, just as it should be, and lay motionless in the furthest reaches of the room. Michael was still protesting, even as she held him up on the landing. He didn't want to be moved, he kept insisting, the pains had returned and he just wanted to somehow get some sleep. Jude recalled the sight of the beast hovering over his chest, recalled too the vague memories of the shadows beneath her bed as a child. Something had been there. She had seen it. And there was no way that she was letting him get back into that room again tonight.

Together they started down the stairs, slowly, and one at a time. Michael's feet were unsteady, but Jude was insistent, and she just wanted to get them both out of the house, now. Even as she reached the kitchen, her befuddled fingers searching the worktops for her missing keys, she was overcome with the belief that the shadows of the house had taken them to stop her from leaving. She looked suddenly at Michael, his hands clasped to her side for support. What was she doing? She tried to look at herself through his eyes. How ludicrously was she acting? This was no way for a grown-up to behave.

"You're going crazy," she heard herself saying, even as she found her car keys and pushed them into her pocket. "Shadows don't move. And nor do they hurt people."

Michael groaned again as he clutched his stomach. Jude looked at him to see that he had lifted up his t-shirt to inspect the bruise there. It had grown more livid since last they had both looked, horrific purples, yellows and reds raking throughout his flesh. She glanced quickly over her shoulder at the door she had just come through, as though somehow the shadow creatures would be waiting there for her in the brightly lit living room, ready to claim back her husband. Only the cat was present, however, standing at the threshold looking up at her, the end of his tail flicking back and forth expectantly.

"I've got to get over this phobia," Jude murmured to herself, as she helped Michael back through into the living room. "It's just darkness."

The television was still playing to itself, and she sat down in front of it with Michael half-lying across her lap. He had been in pain in the kitchen, his breathing erratic after being moved through the house, but now that they were both sat down and quiet again, he seemed peaceful once more. Perhaps they could both get some sleep with the living room lights and the television on. Nothing was going to get them with protection like that.

Jude idly brushed the hair on Michael's scalp as she laid her head back on the sofa. The talk from the television was banal, politics or some such, and she let it drone in the background as she closed her eyes and tried to relax. She listened to the thump of the blood in her veins, and imagined it in her head, pounding away like the fuel of some incessant engine. Her breathing had steadied once again, she noticed, and she began to count its regularity with the rhythm of her blood. Something brushed against her arm, and she jumped, hard. Michael started in her arms as she snatched at him. Her eyes focussed on the cat half on her lap, his huge green eyes looking up at her optimistically.

"Damn stupid cat," Jude snapped, restraining herself from smacking it. "Don't do that again."

The cat seemed unrepentant and continued to gaze up at her, his whiskers twitching as he passed a tiny pink tongue up and over them. Jude watched as he then climbed up onto her legs and then settled himself, before she took a deep breath, closed her eyes and lay back again, cradling Michael who was thankfully still dozing.

The light from the room was still welcome, and the chat from the television still droned quietly to itself. A car passed by in the street outside, the wash of its headlights flickering across the folds of the curtains, and somewhere in the neighbourhood a dog was barking. All was well with the world once more, and she allowed herself the pleasure of another deep inhaling breath. Jude listened to the sound of her blood once again as it thumped around inside her head, filling it up with its dark viscous soup. As a distracting game, she tried to pinpoint the nearest vein that she could hear it thudding in, but her head was dull, and the game rapidly fell redundant. The search would have been an impossible one anyway, of course, but it took her mind off the nightmare she'd had in the bedroom, which in itself she something. Michael's own body was blissfully warm against her own, his skin soft and wonderful. The subtle rise and fall of his chest was hypnotic, and she eased her own rhythms into a kind of synchronicity with him. Her memories of what she had thought she'd seen in the bedroom tried to crawl in at the edges of her consciousness, but they suddenly seemed distant and powerless to her, and she gave them little regard as sleep came creeping to claim her.

Jude wasn't even certain that she had woken. Michael was not in her arms. The lights were off. So was the television. She blinked a few times into the darkness until she was sure that she was awake, her thoughts racing to try and remember how she had got where she was. She was still sitting on the sofa in the living room, that much she was aware of, but what she could not recall was helping Michael back to bed or even turning off the lights, (she was sure she wouldn't have turned off the lights). Even the cat was gone, although there was no news there. Nervously she got to her feet, the sheer depths of the darkness confounding her, and she wondered whether there might perhaps have been a power cut.

Wandering into the middle of the living room, Jude began to shake as she stared into the oppressive darkness, trying to make sense of its inky-black nothingness. She could discern nothing, not even the outline of the sofa she had just vacated. From somewhere upstairs the sound of Michael came through the darkness, a dull groaning of pain. The dark of the house was already getting too much for her, she could feel the fear creeping up inside her as she imagined just what it might contain unseen. Then she lost her self-control altogether and bolted towards the light switch by the stairs. She flicked it on but it wouldn't work. Damn bulb, she cursed, and dashed back towards the light switch in the kitchen. That wouldn't work either. Perhaps there had been a power cut, she reasoned. Or perhaps - and this she checked herself for as soon as she thought it - the shadow beasts had stolen the light. Her heart was pounding hard in her chest, she could feel it thumping in her head, and in her throat, and her body was shaking all over. It was getting bad again.

From upstairs Michael's agony suddenly turned into a shriek. Jude spun to face the stairs but couldn't move. There was too much darkness there, too much gathering darkness, and it seemed somehow to be growing thicker as the flight rose. Michael's shrieks grew but still Jude could not move, until a shape, as dark as the darkness itself, suddenly moved across the room in front of her. Her heart stopped. This was it. There was something there. And in that instant her entire body jolted. It was a moment of decision too. The darkness held creatures, or was made of creatures, of that she was now as certain as she was afraid, but Michael was still somewhere upstairs amongst them, alone and defenceless in their grasp. That moment of revelation did at least prove fruitful in some respect, however, for it caused Jude to move. She left the spot by the kitchen door and ran.

The shape in the darkness seemed to reach for her as that decision was made, but she either imagined its lunge or else managed to dodge out of its way. A second later and her feet were pounding up the stairs, Jude throwing herself forward to where the blackness grew more densely. She could see nothing on the landing as she reached it, and putting her hands out for the far wall so that she could trace its path, stumbled after the sound of Michael's agony, back to their own bedroom door.

A knot of restricting forms lay tangled on the other side of the threshold, converging and writhing above Michael's spread-eagled body. As she took a step towards him, the darkness seemed to reach for her, to either take hold of her or force her back the way she had come. But as she moved to evade them, she felt their substance press against the surface of her skin on her face and throat, clammy and constricting. She clawed a breath between their ghostly black fingers as she urged herself forward, just a few more steps until she was within reach of her husband, who even now was being violated inside his stomach and chest. The darkness grew, however, as yet more forms closed in to fill the space in front of her, their touch thickening like some murky grizzly soup.

It was difficult to even walk against them, but she caught a glimpse of Michael through the shreds of their matter, his limbs flailing against their assault on him, but the sheer sight of him gave her strength enough to reach his side. The shadow beasts were still at work inside Michael's body, and despite the claustrophobic murk of the room, Jude could see that his bruise had spread further, reaching now across his ribs and as high as his throat. The purple-yellow wounding of his skin seemed almost incandescent against the enveloping darkness surrounding it, and crying out now in pain from the intrusion, Michael's fingers reached out for her as she stretched past the blanket of twisting forms towards him, her grip tightening as soon as she took hold of him, before hauling him across the bed towards her. The creatures of the shadows loosed shrieks of their own at his departure, their cries shrill and piercing through the darkness, and Jude looked up to see them clawing their way through the very air towards her. They would not be denied their sport. Jude did not wait for their touch, however, but turned and ran, throwing herself towards the door with Michael held up in her arms, struggling past the pull of the shadow creatures.

With Michael now cradled in her arms, Jude forced them both onto the landing where there was now a tangled web of solidifying forms. She felt their wet and knitting shapes on her skin as she passed through them, strands of matter trailing her limbs like cobwebs behind her. They reached for her in turn, their unmade fingers slapping against her arms but failing to make any claim upon her. On the stairs she heard their chilling howls behind her as they gave pursuit, and Jude screamed with panic as she saw them fill the doorway to the kitchen ahead of her. Doubling back, she headed into the hallway towards the front door. More shadows were already growing out of the darkness there, she could see their twisting forms converging and congealing. She managed to get only one hand on the door handle, before she felt the first dominating touch of their muck upon her. It hauled them both back into the hallway, insistent that they stay in the house. Or at least to leave Michael with them. Neither were options, and with a cry of frustration, she threw herself forward and over the threshold, dragging Michael's heavy body after her.

Stumbling down the path towards the car, she fumbled in her pockets with her free hand for the keys, grateful that she had not left them on the kitchen worktop after all. The howls and cries were just behind her now, and as she wrestled the keys from her pocket, she felt their touch around her ankles like a tide, coursing up her legs and around her knees as she struggled to find the lock. They had hold of her waist now, and tugged her back with the strength of dogs as she tugged on the handle. Jude forced her helpless husband inside, scrambling after him, before clutching the steering wheel for support. The car began rocking furiously as she slammed shut the door, and Jude forced the key hard into the ignition, turning over the engine as the metal of the roof creaked and groaned beneath the onslaught of the night creatures.

Jude glanced up only briefly as she put the vehicle into gear. The world outside was no longer visible. The dark forms had all but covered up every window, and now they began to hammer against the glass, huge deep thuds that threatened to shatter each pane with every blow. Jude yelled out at them as she pushed her foot hard on the accelerator, the car veering blindly back down the driveway and into the road. The black forms resisted to let go at first, their ebony fingers clasping hold of anything they could, but as she put the car into first and sped away, they soon they began to slip from her sight, sliding from the glass and paintwork like scraps of filthy oil. Only once they had put a couple of streets between them and the house did Jude slow her pace and look down at Michael's condition.

He was sat huddled with his back partially to her, his arms clamped hard to his stomach. He was sobbing gently, and to look upon him in this state was a pitiful sight. With one hand she managed to coax him to face her a little, and as she lifted his t-shift, his injuries confirmed her worst fears. The bruises on his chest and stomach had indeed spread, and now covered most of his upper body, a distressing patchwork of livid colours, pitted with needle scars of blood. Just what the hell was going on? More tears came, but she sniffed them back hard. Crying was not going to help them, and she knew it. His injuries looked serious, and despite the distance she wanted to put between them and the shadows behind them, she knew that Michael needed attention, medical attention. Pressing her foot more firmly on the accelerator, Jude drove across town towards the hospital, hoping that someone on duty could see Michael quickly, and before the shadow creatures caught up with them.

The hospital finally found something that night, a problem inside Michael's body that their previous scans had not found. The severe bruising of his chest concerned them gravely, and caused them to ask Jude a great many questions, to which she had few sane answers. What was interesting, and perhaps it was more shocking than interesting, was the revelation concerning the nature of the problem in Michael's body. Whatever it was, or rather whatever it had been, was now gone. Only the remnants remained, but they held sufficient clues for the doctors to be confident that Michael would not have survived for much longer without whatever surgeries or manipulations had been performed on him. Of the identities of the surgeons, Jude was unable to help, not even when the local authorities became involved. Weeks passed and Michael and Jude were eventually permitted to return home, all outstanding enquiries left unanswerable. Michael stepped through the front door thankfully, Jude with reservations. Something had wanted to keep them in that house, but perhaps for their own benefit. Whatever the truth may have been fell by the wayside. Her husband was well again.

She had always been scared of the dark, especially as a child, and that fear had never left her. Her mother had told her stories about it, her boyfriends had teased her over it, and even Michael had despaired at times. But as she stood in the hallway and watched her husband climb the stairs towards their bedroom, she allowed herself a glance at the shadows of the house, given substance by the sunlight streaming in through the open front door. Could there really be things living unseen in the shadows? Were they looking back at her even now, knowing her uncertainty? Her thoughts drifted back to the problem that had been undetected for so long inside Michael's body. What might have happened if the shadow creatures had not intervened? Could Michael have died? Could he have had a defect so untraceable that their own doctor had not been able to find it? She shook her head in disbelief. Slowly she pressed the front door closed and turned to follow her husband upstairs. She paused, however, as she reached the first step, and whispered a faint thank you to the darkness. Perhaps a fear of the dark would not be such a bad thing after all, she thought. Not for what might be there, but for what might not be there.

## The Devil Owns A Xerox

There was a note waiting for him on the small reception desk when he unlocked the print room door and set his things down. Richard Stant recognised the handwriting immediately, his manager's even penmanship spelling his name in crisp letters across the white envelope. He'd respected Weldon once, years ago, and perhaps to some degree Weldon had respected him too. But that was gone now, all that remained between them, other than the thin shred of professional courtesy, was a resentment that got plain nasty at times. Even to see Weldon write his name so crisply seemed to patronise him, and he sneered as he peeled back the flap of the envelope and took out the note.

Mitchell brought a report down last night but you'd already gone home. It needs to be printed as a priority by 11.00AM. Make sure it's done and phone his secretary when it's ready. Weldon.

Richard half screwed the note into a ball but then straightened it back out in case Weldon saw it in the bin. Wouldn't that make a pleasant scene?

What's my note doing in the bin? You take your job that seriously, huh?

He'd found himself wishing more and more for something to happen, something that would either project himself up the job ladder and on to something better, or else take Weldon out of there altogether. But nothing happened, no secret god ever listened, and every year slipped effortlessly by him like a greased pig through a farmer's legs.

Richard picked up his things and took them across

the room to his work bench, before powering up the hulking grey Xerox machine behind him. It dominated much of the print room, it was long and heavy, and the cooling fans hummed smoothly as it booted itself, their white noise sounding almost like whispering voices, repeating the same words quickly over and over again until they became one big long word.

Richard stood in front of it as he reread the note, his eyes glancing up to see the stack of pages sitting on top of the Docutech. Mitchell would be lucky to get that lot done by 11.00AM. The copier was fast but not that fast. Why couldn't Weldon have started it last night? That would've helped some.

Slapping the note down irritably on the bench, Richard began unpacking his things, pulling his lunch out of his bag and setting it down in the corner of his bench for later. Beside it he put his latest copy of X-men, and beside that his old Coke bottle that he filled with cold water from the new drinks cooler.

The Docutech continued to hum lazily behind him, the voices indifferent about his frustration over the note and Mitchell's report; tedium, they said, so what? He'd already got his day's workload set out in his head, work that he'd already promised to people, and now he was going to have to look like an asshole when it wasn't ready. That useless fuck Weldon. He grabbed a pen from his desk tidy and then snatched up the note. With the tip of the pen hovering over the paper in his clenched fist, he hesitated for a moment, and then snatched a blank sheet of paper from stock and then wrote fuck in huge letters across that instead, the pen almost ripping the paper it half so hard did he drag it. Then he screwed that into a ball and hurled it angrily into the print room's tall blue recycling bin. It wasn't the greatest of retaliations but it made him feel a little better at least.

This hadn't been his first choice of careers, dragging out days of tedium in hot stuffy print rooms (and some of them had been hot and stuffy, oh yes), the dry burning stench of ozone thickening the air, the parched heat from thermal binders, the ventilation systems that just didn't work. He'd had his life of drawing comic books mapped out in his head while he was at school. A year at art college had been enough to put an end to that though. Ignorant tutors had bullied him each time he'd tried his work out on them. Fine art, they kept telling him, not shit art; that's the way. It wasn't until much later and he'd gotten himself trapped inside the print game that he'd realised that if they'd known half of what they'd tried teaching, they wouldn't be teaching in a second rate college in the first place. But still, hind sight was a cruel bitch and it got you every fucking time.

The Xerox machine was still warming up, the dull grey monitor passing through one boot up screen after another, and Richard took up the stack of pages that was Mitchell's report and stared disdainfully at it as he thumbed through its weight. The report was thick and heavy, the pages curled down at one edge, and as he shuffled them back into a stack, one of the edges sliced down through the knuckle of his right index finger, cutting it thinly and sharply. He sucked in air as the pain came. It was only a small paper cut, but it was deep enough to bring a glut of glistening blood quickly to the surface. Richard sucked at it, his own blood sweet on his tongue, and then shook his fingers to cool off the wound. But the cut was deeper than he'd thought and he only succeeded in landing a track of blood across the screen of the copier. He cursed as he wiped it off as best he could with the palm of his left hand, smearing it into a smudge of scarlet that now tracked down the monitor. He'd take that off later with some glass cleaner, he thought distantly, and took to sucking the knuckle joint again.

11.00AM they wanted it. No way. No way. Two o'clock at the earliest, and then if there weren't any machine breakdowns. Weldon would've known that but he would've been too spineless to say no to the Chief Exec.

Richard began feeding the pages into the document handler, the curl on the paper causing him concern about paper jams. It would be just his luck to rip a page in half. Wouldn't that delay things nicely? Weldon would love that too, no doubt. Only last week he'd found an extra backlog of work that needed doing. Shitty work too. All curled corners and torn edges. One copy of each for filing. Boy, that had torn a treat. A week and a half of Cellotape and copying it off the glass a page at a time.

Surprisingly, however, the pages fed through without a glitch, and Richard shuffled them back into a neat stack as he waited for the proof copy to come out of the printer. Three years he'd been in this print room under George Weldon, three years of doing the shittiest of jobs, as well as his manager's work. It had started off with Weldon unloading his end of month figures on him. It'll only take a couple of hours if you knuckle down. Couple of days more like. Weldon had dropped hints of nice bonuses and healthy promotions, but bonuses weren't given for any reason and there was only Weldon and himself in the print unit. Just where exactly was he expected to be promoted to?

And what came next? Doing the paperwork for all the satellite copiers around the building. That was definitely the manager's job. He tried to say he wouldn't have the time, he tried to tell him that he couldn't do it. Hell, he even tried doing it so badly that all the figures went haywire and wouldn't add up. But none of that seemed to matter. Just as long as someone else was doing it, and as long as he got to go to at least one meeting a day. Meetings, that's about all he did. In this building or the other building, it didn't matter. And nor did any of these meetings seem to make any difference to anything either. Nothing changed. The whole place stayed the same. It seemed like a daily dutiful ritual to some devil of indifference, with laptops for offerings and management reports for scriptures.

The Xerox machine finished its cycle and pushed a copy of Mitchell's report out of the stacker. Richard took it out and thumbed through it, checking for any dirty marks or deletions, and to make sure that all of the pages were there. You wouldn't want the scanner taking two sheets round instead of one. That would be a doozy.

Don't you check your work? Remember responsibility? Remember Best Value?

A chill crept across his shoulders and settled on his spine like broken ice as he flicked through pages still warm from the copier. He couldn't believe what he was seeing. On every page, over the text of the report, the word fuck appeared superimposed. And it wasn't small or just in any handwriting either. It was the same as what he had written just minutes before and hurled into the bin. But how had it gotten on all the copies? How?

Richard hurried to the tall blue recycling bin as a

grey dizziness fell across his eyes, threatening to take his consciousness and hurl him just as dismissively into insanity. He reached down into the bin, the motion forcing black shapes behind his eyes and causing him to sway uncertainly. He pulled out the ball regardless, struggling to unroll it, his sight slowly beginning to clear, but even through it, it was obvious that it was exactly the same as the word that had appeared on every page of Mitchell's report. He staggered back to the Docutech and stared at its huge grey screen.

"What do you think you're doing?" he said to it, clasping an unsteady hand to the cold sweat already turning clammy on his forehead.

The copier hummed smoothly to itself, the voices of its cooling fans unwavering, hypnotic. Why not? they said. This is what you really think.

Perhaps someone, some fucking comedian (Weldon perhaps? no, it wasn't his sense of humour, he didn't have one anyway) had put a whole bunch of copies with the word fuck on it in the paper tray they knew he'd be using. That would be a gas wouldn't it? Printing the Chief Exec's report on obscenity-coated paper. Especially if that someone suspected that he didn't check his own work either, which he did.

He pulled open tray three, and frantically tugged out sheet after sheet, checking both sides, but it was clean, all of it. Then he went back to the screen, but that was set up just as it should be. He shook his head slowly, feeling madness encroaching, like someone trying to convince themselves they're not going insane even as they're biting off their own tongue. But he wasn't going crazy, those words were there in black and white right in front of him. He deleted the first scan and put the report back in the scanner, double checking all the settings before pressing the big green start button on the front of the machine.

Round and round the pages went as the great Xerox beast eagerly devoured it. Eleven o'clock they wanted this by. This was the last shit he needed. Mechanical breakdowns aside, and this machine could go wrong spectacularly at times, he was still not going to get it done. But someone fucking with him as a joke, today of all days, well that was just plain asking for trouble, and he could feel his anger begin to throb in the temples of his head. Even the volume of the cooling fans seemed to increase as it almost seemed to become agitated in unison with him.

The second proof came out of the stacker a few minutes later and Richard picked it up with nervous hands. As he flicked through its warm pages, the word fuck appeared on every page, remaining in exactly the same place on every sheet, like a child's first animated flip book, only with less movement.

This was a joke, a sick joke, being played on him by some asshole somewhere. It wasn't the sort of thing Weldon would do, but then who else could? No one else knew how to use the kit in the print room, and besides, he'd unlocked it himself this morning. It had to be Weldon, that fuckwit Weldon, stopping him from getting on with Mitchell's report so that he'd get in trouble. But this was a new low. Mitchell's report could be running by now, and here he was trying to get to the bottom of this childish fucking prank.

Fine, he thought to himself, as he threw both proof copies into the recycling bin. If you can waste time then so can I.

Richard went back to his workbench and took out another sheet of paper, this time scrawling an ugly caricature image of Weldon on it - his thin sticky body, his balding head, his scrunched-up little face, a tiny penis sticking out of his fly - before feeding that into the scanner. He set the machine to copy it 100 times and then waited for it to print a stack of pictures of him with the word fuck emblazoned right across it. Wouldn't that be sweet revenge. His own plan backfiring, calling himself a fuck. How would that be? The printer's cycle wound down and out came the stacker. Richard had a huge grin on his face as he picked up the stack of 100 sheets. But that grin faltered quickly as he saw that each sheet only bore a copy of his sketch of Weldon. Of the word fuck there was now no sign.

That was crazy, just plain insanely crazy.

Not one sheet had the word fuck on it.

Not one.

But that just wasn't possible. There was no way that Weldon could have copied enough sheet so that they exactly ran out after two full sets of Mitchell's report. He wouldn't have spent that much time over a prank for his benefit. He wasn't that clever either, or organised. No, something weird was going on. And it was starting to make him nervous.

Richard went to dump the copies of the caricature in the tall blue recycling bin, but then held onto them for a moment. Maybe it wasn't wise leaving them so intact. They didn't have a shredder in the print room, but there was one upstairs in the main office, only he wasn't about to go walking through the building with abusive pictures of his manager in his hand. He decided he'd have to do the next best thing. Slice them up in the print room's guillotine and put them to the bottom of the bin like regular trimmings.

Standing in front of the heavy steel bulk of the guillotine, its lethally sharp blade looking like something used in a thousand aristocratic beheadings, Richard glanced nervously up at the clock on the wall and saw that it was getting close to eight thirty. He was more shocked about how quickly the morning had gone rather than the fact that he hadn't even started the Chief Exec's report, and realised that Weldon could come in at any minute and catch him red-handed holding these less than flattering pictures of him. Still, his not starting the report was Weldon's fault anyway, he could explain his fuck-emblazoned stationary to him when 11.00AM came and went. And as for the pictures? Shit, they needed going in the bin and quickly.

The blade came down silently and sliced the stack of paper neatly and with lethal precision. He'd hadn't been paying much attention to where the blade was going behind the dark plastic guard as long as the paper was shredded, but as he lifted the guard and looked down at it now, he saw that it had squarely cut through the narrow duck neck that he'd given Weldon, decapitating him, and that brought a very wide grin.

Cut your head right off. Cut it off and into the basket.

He remembered that Carry On film about the French Revolution, and the scene where Charles Hawtry gets a note delivered to him as he's putting his head under the guillotine, telling the messenger to drop it into the basket so he can read it later. Weldon's note, he thought, can go right in the bin along with the 100 copies of his head and all the paper marked fuck.

Then Richard turned the stack sideways and put the

guillotine blade straight down through the middle of his body, and took glee in seeing the tiny crooked torso splay sideways like a deck of cards, his tiny penis being split even tinier as the sharp steel blade bit it in two. The stack took three more cuts before the fistful of pornographic confetti found its way into the bin. And Richard glanced only once more back at the clock, it was now eight forty, before taking Mitchell's report up again and trying it for a third time. This time, however, the proof came out fine and he at last started the job for real.

By ten o'clock, half the report had been completed but Weldon had still not shown his face. It surprised Richard just how quickly the Docutech was running, and how sweetly too, but it was not like Weldon to be late. He was sure there must be meetings going on somewhere in the building that would be one fuckwit short (would they even notice?) but to not even have a phone call was just completely out of character.

The image of his cartoon head being sliced cleanly from his duck neck burned in his imagination suddenly like echoes of a candle left to burn in a darkened room. But it wasn't so comedic now. It had become an image that disturbed him. He tried to dismiss it and put it at the back of his mind. It had been something he'd drawn for a few laughs and then cut to shreds to hide it, nothing more. So why his manager's lateness was conjuring such unease he had no idea.

Ten thirty arrived and the Xerox machine had somehow managed to increase its capacity even further. There was now less than a quarter of the job to run, and the printer was running just as smoothly. Hell, it sounded effortless. Where before he could usually hear the burdened whirring of wheels and cogs or the heavy shunting of transports and conveyors, there was simply that effortless gliding sound of parts running efficiently, as smooth as oil.

The unease began to sink into him again, and Richard pulled out a copy of Mitchell's report to check again. He couldn't remember how many times he'd checked it since it had been running, but that practical joke had made him nervous about the whole job. He was expecting a repeat somewhere along the line, a stray sheet of paper with the fuck on it to crop up right in the middle of a bar chart or a lengthy paragraph. But everything seemed fine, no everything seemed better, as though somehow the text was clearer, sharper, and the images better than the originals that had come down from the top floor office.

It caught him offguard when the machine wound down to a halt. He got up from his chair, his mind lurching back to the present, cursing the breakdown he didn't need. But as he saw the neat pile of reports sitting on the stacker, and checked the counter on the screen to see that the job had actually finished, he glanced at his watch and saw that it was ten forty eight. Twelve minutes to spare. But that wasn't possible. The machine could only run at a certain pace. It couldn't speed up, not by itself, and it certainly couldn't continue to speed up of its own free will.

He stood there in a daze for a few moments, just staring at the pile of reports on the stacker of the quietly humming Xerox machine, telling himself that it just wasn't possible. But then the realisation came that he'd not only achieved the impossible and finished the Chief Exec's report ahead of time, but also that doing such a thing would undoubtedly piss Weldon off no end.

Gleefully, Richard began boxing the reports and shuffling them onto the print room flatbed before hurrying them through the building towards the service lift. Those precious twelve minutes had already diminished to ten as he'd stood staring at the printer and the finished reports, and had diminished yet further to eight whilst boxing them. He did however reach the top floor office with three minutes to spare, and he barely saw Mitchell's secretary so much was he gazing with disbelief at his watch.

Back in the print room, he discovered that Weldon still had not appeared, had still not even called. His eyes settled uneasily on the tall blue recycling bin, and although he could not see any of the shredded copies of the cruel caricature he'd drawn, a complete image suddenly bolted into his head, searing behind his eyes like phosphorus, before that scrunched up face came away from the duck neck in a shower of scarlet-tinged paper dust as the scythe-like guillotine blade sliced it in two. His own imagination disgusted him, turning his stomach to revolt, and he tried desperately to rid himself of his own imagination. And then his eyes fell upon the Xerox machine humming quietly to itself on the other side of the room, its voices hidden inside the whirling sound of its cooling fans insisting that he listen to it, insisting that he pay special heed.

Richard ran a coarse tongue over lips as dry as ancient parchment. A clammy sweat had already slickened his palms, alternating between temperatures both hot and cold. His fingers twitched uneasily, slimy across his damp skin, and an uneasy dread prickled across the back of his neck like a plague of insects.

Very slowly he went towards it.

The Xerox machine was a huge hulking grey beast,

its cooling fans humming like the breath of a great dormant dragon, and yet somewhere in that smooth noise there was almost definitely some ghostly or demonic communication. It was crazy, no, don't use that word, for Christ's sake don't use that word... It was strange, not much better, to think of it as something living, something sentient. And yet that humming, that relentless humming, if you stood in such a way and listened, you could almost hear... Stop it. For fuck's sake, stop it. That's crazy talk. It's a machine, a big box of gears and cogs and circuit boards and that's all, so fucking snap out of it. Weldon is just late, or off sick, that's all. You haven't killed him. You haven't.

He glanced down to see that his hand was hovering over the big green start button on the front of the machine. He hadn't realised he was even doing that. Had he? He wanted to pull it back, but then he thought what's the problem? I've done this a thousand times. It's only a copier.

He pressed the start button. The machine started.

He could hear the printer feed a sheet out of tray three, could hear it move from one area of the machine to another, from area one where it picked it up to area four where it laid down the toner, to area five where it fused it, up across the top transport of area eight and then ejected out the top tray, the copy born.

Richard moved on numb legs to the top tray and pulled the single sheet of paper up in front of him. His stomach lurched, heaving itself in two until he thought he was going to vomit, but it was still an hour or so before lunch and with nothing in his stomach the spasms dragged up nothing.

Upon the page was a single image, a photograph of George Weldon's head, decapitated and lying in what looked like a muddy ditch. His eyes were white and staring, his teeth biting together between slightly parted lips from which trickled a thin line of blood. Mud spattered his cheeks and chin and what was left of his neck, but what really gripped Richard's stomach and knotted it in two was the word fuck that had been slashed into Weldon's forehead with what looked like a scalpel blade, the thin slits forming knotted blood tracks right across his forehead from temple to temple. The letters were roughly carved, jagged even, as though... dear God no... as though the blade had almost ripped the flesh to the bone so hard had it been dragged across it. Something else about the word, he thought, even as his mind seemed to be coming apart, disconnecting, something familiar... the same... somehow the same... as the word... no, it wasn't possible...

He jerked violently as the Docutech started up again, this time of its own accord. Richard could do nothing but stand and stare at the sheet of paper now shaking in his trembling hands. The printer followed exactly the same cycle as before, and distantly Richard tracked the second single sheet of paper through its path, area one to area four, to five, through eight, and then out the top tray.

The new copy appeared just below his hands, out of focus and just beyond his sanity. His lips tried to dampen the grey parchment of his lips but either his mouth had no moisture or the parchment was too far gone. Something was already telling him about police cross-referencing the handwriting in the recycling bin with what had been carved across George Weldon's skull. But it wasn't too late to look at this new copy, he could still look away and keep his mind. But the humming voices inside the Xerox machine's cooling fans told him otherwise, coaxed him to cast his eyes down; look, they said, just look, what harm could that do? It's only your mind. You wanted this, remember? But what was left of his unsteady mind told him not to look, demanded that he not look, but his focus crept down regardless, away from the sheet in his hands, and down to the sheet still sitting in the top tray.

His brain struggled to make sense of the printed photograph, and then his right hand was reaching for it, pulling it towards him so that he could make it out more clearly. His stomach turned completely this time and wretched violently. Even though his stomach had nothing to heave up, it kept on trying, lurching so hard that he was soon struggling to breath. Long thin threads of acid-like spittle hung from his lips and chin, clinging to his shirt in wet loops. He stood for a few moments panting heavily once it subsided, wiping his mouth with the back of his hand before returning his sight to the second sheet.

The remainder of George Weldon's corpse lay in the ditch, severed from neck to groin, the torso opened up like racks of beef and pork in a butcher's shop window, his cock protruding from the fly of his slashed trousers and torn neatly in two. Glistening and red raw, flashes of white broke the monotony, of bone sheared clean in half by some unknown lethal force. He turned away now, dropping the sheets to the floor at his feet. His head was growing dark, his thoughts (those that hadn't deserted him completely) becoming difficult to decipher through the soup that had become a mire around them, as insanity slowly began to claim him.

He would never truly register the explanation the police would eventually arrive at, that George Weldon had been run off the road by the over-tired driver of an articulated lorry, his car hopelessly torn apart by the impact which had seen him hideously and fatally injured.

Nor would he ever comprehend his subsequent promotion to Weldon's position of manager, so impressed was the Chief Exec by the superb reproduction of his crucial report, which had been behind schedule since its inception only to be delivered on time when it finally mattered, and so desperate was the need to fill the position, the urgency and scale of work taking a sudden and unexpected upturn.

But the final terror that had perhaps pushed him over the edge was the fear that the police would cross-reference the word found (and never explained) across Weldon's decapitated head, with the word found copied and dumped in his own bin, which they would have found very quickly that they matched exactly. But the print room's tall blue recycling bin was emptied earlier than usual that night and no evidence was ever found of it. A shame really, because that's probably what drove Richard Stant to suicide, and that's what dragged him right down to Hell all the sooner.

Even as she parked the car, Melissa could not help the pangs of delight that skittered around inside her stomach. Tonight was the night, she was sure of it, more sure than she had ever been about anything before. From the first moment she had spoken to him, in that nightclub she had only occasionally frequented, she had felt something, something good, something right, but she had not wanted to let something as simple as lust destroy what relationship they might have waiting ahead of them. She'd denied his fullest advances so far, laying her hand against his to restrain his reach every time he had strayed, her breasts something to be savoured, her sex something to be cherished later on.

Melissa had never been one to sleep around, except for one regrettable night years ago when she had been a student; and that night had haunted her morals ever since, allowing herself to be undressed, groped and penetrated at a party, hidden away in an upstairs room of a stranger's house. She hadn't particularly regretted it at the time - she'd been drunk, she'd told herself, and that's what students did - but in the long run, it had tarnished her subsequent moralistic viewpoint on relationships to the point where if anyone asked if she'd ever had a one-nighter, she'd become embarrassed and would have to resort to either changing the subject, or simply outwardly accepting that casual sex was okay.

There was a clear sky overhead as she hurried across the small resident's car park towards the flats, the stars glittering, the moon pale and full and washing its surreal light across the path ahead of her. Mark lived in the ground floor apartment of a converted house, and she rapped on his window eagerly, waiting until the curtains were pulled back to reveal his handsome face before she smiled sweetly at him. Inside she was churning, desperate to have her arms around his broad frame and to have his hands spread across her body. She hoped he would not need too much coaxing tonight; she had rather a nice figure, she thought, and it would look so good draped across his, but then she didn't want to seem overly anxious in laying it out for him either. He had to instigate it all. It would make him feel better about himself anyway. Her body would be his reward for his patience these past three weeks.

The main entrance door opened and there he stood, bare-chested and wearing only tight-fitting jeans below. She stepped up into his arms and there they hugged for a few moments, nestling in the heat coming from him, until they finally pulled apart and stepped through the communal hallway and on into his flat.

"How's work?" Mark asked her, making small talk as he swept his dark wet hair back with one hand. She had been so enamoured of his beautiful face that she hadn't even realised that he'd just stepped out of the shower. Passing through the living room on their way to the kitchen, she could see his wet towel still draped across the sofa.

"You know, the usual," Melissa replied distantly, combing her brown silken hair away from her face with one hand. She was going for the Liz Hurley look tonight, bedazzle him with something sultry and willing. Her blouse was unbuttoned to her cleavage.

"Coffee?" he asked, glancing back at her with a warming smile.

She watched as he plugged in the kettle, and nodded affably as she set her keys down on the counter before leaning back against it. She watched him as he pulled two mugs down from one of the wall cupboards, the neat muscles of his back rippling in hypnotic formation as his shoulders moved, the muscles of his arms tightening. He was a sight of perfection, she thought, dark, graceful, divine. He glanced across his shoulder suddenly, enquiring about sugar, and caught her scrutiny of him, and his smile widened across his lips. She wanted him to kiss her then, to take hold of her and initiate the love that she hoped they would soon be making this night.

His smile grew into a grin, as though that thought had somehow managed to breach the gap between them, from her mind to his, and he suddenly turned and stepped towards her across the tiled kitchen floor. Melissa's lips parted in expectation of what was to come as he took hold of her in his strong bare arms, his lips like fire-brands as he pressed them against hers. She heard a sigh of bliss escape her as she tasted his hot thick tongue, pushing out between her lips, against her tongue, glancing across her teeth.

The kiss was exquisite, disorientating, and yet it was so distressingly brief. He pulled away from her all too soon, and her eyes flickered open with something close to alarm. He wore that same smile, his eyes bright and glittering, and she had to force one of her own just to keep from crying at his departure.

She was close to him now, just inches from his face, so close that she could see a mark of red next to his mouth. She raised her fingertips towards it but he shied away from her touch.

"What's that?" she asked gently.

"What's what?"

"You cut yourself shaving?"

He put his own hand to the nick of blood delicately.

"Yeah. Damn razors. Sorry. I'll go clean up."

She watched almost helplessly as he slipped out of the kitchen, his departure saddening as though it was somehow final. She gazed impatiently around the kitchen while he was gone, her eyes falling indifferently over his pans and mugs, the kettle in the corner. She caught her reflection in the kitchen window facing out into the night, straightened her bra beneath her blouse, evened her breasts, deepened her cleavage. Her hair hung over her shoulders like an expensive veil, cascading and sumptuous. She wanted his face to be in it, to be between her breasts.

"Sorry about that."

She looked up startled. Mark was coming through the kitchen door, his face now clean of blood. He had a grin of thanks on his face, barely concealing another one of embarrassment that lurked behind it, and he quickly returned to the mugs still sitting on the counter opposite her.

Her attention went briefly back to her reflection in the black window. Breasts, cleavage, hair; all that she wanted him to have. She returned to Mark. He was spooning coffee into each mug. Then he was reaching down to the fridge for a carton of milk. She studied him intently as he did so, like a zoologist studying a rare creature, lithe and fleeting, as though he were perhaps on the brink of extinction, this moment elusive, sacred. The kettle boiled behind him as she watched, a plume of steam encasing the area around him like a primordial fog rising up from a wild plain. He seemed like something free, something unique, and it was only after he'd stirred the mugs and dropped the spoon down into the sink with a clatter that it broke the magical moment. He looked up at her, as he carried their coffees through into the living room, with a slightly bemused expression, and it was only her eager smile as she followed after him that kept him from asking about her scrutiny.

Melissa took a seat next to the damp towel, and watched as he scooped it up with that same embarrassed smile on his lips, before taking it back through into the bathroom. Reaching for her coffee, she noticed a small notebook sitting on the edge of the coffee table partially obscured by a handful of well-thumbed magazines. She picked it up as she waited for him to return, leafing through it with mild curiosity, wondering if it might be his little black book. But there were no girl's names or strings of telephone numbers inside, just a few pages of scribbled notes accompanied by a handful of scratchy illustrations. She couldn't make much sense of the images, though, roughly scrawled in biro as they were, and she was about to set it back down before Mark came back and caught her with it, when her eye picked up a little tally of numbers on the inside front cover. This too was roughly etched in, and symbolised a series of four vertical strokes with the fifth angled through them. The number of strokes equalled twelve in all, and frowning at this tally without similar explanatory notes or captions such as what had appeared on the other pages, she wondered just what he had been adding up. The thought disappeared quickly out of her head as she heard his footsteps returning, and she quickly set it back down on the table as he reappeared through the door.

The smile was still on his face - it seemed he was genuinely glad to see her - and she now saw that in the few moments that he'd been away, he had combed his hair and put on a shirt too, which last detail now obscured much of his torso from her gaze. When he finally took a seat next to her, she realised that he had also put on some aftershave. He smelt divine now, strong and protective, and even before he had turned to look deep into her eyes, she realised how very wet she had already become.

A feeling of self-disgust rolled over her briefly, wondering how she could possibly have allowed herself to become so excited before anything had even been started between them. But then she realised that they were together now, that was the only important thing, and so she cherished the simple sight of him, realising even as she thought this how much she actually wanted him. He moved away from her a few inches to reach for his coffee, but Melissa laid a hand on his arm almost immediately and stopped him before he could do so. He looked back at her, a frown glancing his brow.

"What's wrong," he started, but Melissa did not want to reply with words, but instead took hold of his hand and began to stroke it tenderly. She had a smile of her own now, and leant forward to place a kiss upon his lips, a hazy fervour spreading throughout her body that felt almost like the luxuriant warmth of alcohol. The movement seemed to catch him off guard momentarily, Melissa having instigated the act, but he responded quickly enough, and turned now to take hold of her arms.

Melissa gasped with delirium as his hands moved passionately around to the soft flesh of her back, pulling her body against his as he pressed his lips hard against hers. His tongue came once again, tasting her wet lips as one hand moved round to take hold of her breast. She did not deny him this time, she had promised herself that much on her journey to his flat this night, and let him feel the softness of her flesh, the hardening of her nipple. She wanted him to touch her, to feel her body beneath his, and as she took hold of his hand, she urged him to knead her resilient flesh more firmly, to grasp it and squeeze it tightly, to pleasure her as fully as she wanted to be.

Mark complied with breathtaking speed now that he was no longer restrained by her chastity. His other hand left her back altogether and swept down between her legs, eager to be buried beneath the folds of her long skirt. A moan escaped her as he found her sex almost immediately, his fingertips firm as they sought out her own soft folds, teasing her private place, fingering her where she was most wet.

An image came into her head suddenly, a picture of how slutty she must look with her skirt pulled up between her legs, the front of it damp and dripping, darkened with her own fluids made slick from passion and want. But she suddenly didn't care. She wanted to look like that for him, she wanted to be touched like that by him, she wanted him to feel her, to be inside her; and then she took hold of his hands as roughly as she could, her head lurching forward, her eyes open, and she saw his gaze return hers, frustrated, sharp, anxious.

But she did not say no to him as he no doubt thought she would. No, she wanted him more fully than she had ever wanted anyone else before. This was no time for fancy or for sweetness. She wanted him inside her. She wanted heat.

"Take me to bed," was all that she said.

His hands found every crease that her body had, his tongue locating every part that could offer delight. His cock was large and it filled her utterly, and for a span of time that she would have sworn would have taken them well into the following day, he pleasured her steadily towards a heady climax.

Slumped back and sweating profusely, she lay on her back gazing up at the ceiling as her heart thumped and her pores oozed. Mark lay panting at her side, one hand on the flat of her stomach, his face nestled snugly against the curve of her breast. Oh but this was wonderful, she dreamed, and for a few moments she even wondered whether her morals had been right, or whether she should just let herself get fucked once in a while when the mood took her.

But these were just idle fancies, and they were soon gone from her head, chased away into the darkest recesses of her mind by the certainty that this was only good because they had known each other for a time; they had dated, they had spent time together, they had learned to look at each other and realise the magic of that passion. All that had been cultivated into an hour of blissful sex, two bodies churning together, writhing, contorting, both bringing and finding love. A foundation for their future had been made here this night, which, if they hadn't of waited, might never have been found.

They had parted the following morning a little after seven, Melissa making a reluctant departure to start her journey home in order to shower and change before continuing on to work. She had almost begged Mark to see her again that evening, not wanting to spend another night alone without his arms around her, his cock inside her. He agreed with a kiss, telling her that they would do so very much more that night, and as good as his word, as soon as Melissa crossed the threshold to his flat and sealed the world behind them, they tugged at each other's clothes like rabid animals and headed straight to the bedroom to begin a meal of flesh and love.

Melissa urged him on more than she would have ever though possible, clawing at him, demanding his cock, his fingers, raking her nails across his back until he cried out, dragging marks across his flesh. He took her with a heightened fervour too, grasping her breasts with both hands, squeezing them until she could no longer distinguish the boundaries between desire and distress. She lay on her back with his weight forced hard between her legs, almost crying out with alarm as his teeth sank deep into the meat of her shoulder, biting down and into her until she thought her blood would come. Only when he moved down her body towards her triangle of dark hair did she consciously put her hand there, lifting her fingertips up before her eyes to check for blood as Mark pressed his tongue deep into her sex. But her fingers came back soaked with nothing more than sweat, a slick mixture cultivated by their frenzied heat, but the memory of his teeth diminished quickly as his lips and tongue worked their former miracles once more on the churning heat of her pussy.

She knew exactly how wet she was, her fluids running down the insides of her legs, soaking the sheets and the mattress, so she was surprised at how readily Mark was to go down on her after an hour's passionate lovemaking. His tongue was firm and keen, however, and found her clitoris immediately, teasing and turning it with a vigour that shuddered through her spine, so that she was clutching at the top of his mop of dark hair within seconds, gasping at his touch. He seemed not to even notice how roughly she tugged at him, or even to care, but seemed genuinely urged on to penetrate her more deeply, his tongue lengthening to taste the soft wet walls of her vagina, arousing her so intensely that she began to roll her legs around him, crushing him hard. Melissa's hands went to her own hair now, grasping it and pulling at it as her hips bucked below him, her body now way beyond her control, slave to her lover's roving tongue.

But then her gasps slipped into a yelp of alarm as his teeth suddenly bit down on her clit, forcing her eyes wide with a sharp agony, and making her gaze down the length of her sweat-slick stomach to find Mark's eyes just as intense and staring back up at her. Even though much of his face was still engorged between her legs, she could still make out the grin of enjoyment plastered across his face. But his teeth had broken the moment of pleasure, shattered it irreparably, and she simply took hold of his face with both her hands and almost hauled him up right out of her lap.

She started to complain, but his lips were so intoxicating that her words soon fell short. His hands continued to roam across her wet skin, and so she laid back down and let him carry on as if nothing had happened. He seemed just as happy to pleasure her with his dick as he was with his tongue, however, and after a series of well placed kisses across her breasts and neck, he soon found his former rhythm once again. It still took a few moments for Melissa to be able to close her eyes against his face once more, so unnerved was she about his impromptu biting. But his lips had regained their former passion across her body once more, heightening her own pleasure, and it was simply too much to resist, no matter how annoyed she had been just moments before.

The rhythm of his hips escalated steadily, until he was suddenly bucking hard against her own, forcing his seed deep inside her, its heat almost burning. She lay gasping and holding him for a while after that, her head filled with so many thoughts, some good, some bad, some dirty, some even reproachful. Mark collapsed across her body as he had the previous night, one hand clasping her breast while the other drifted down to knead the top of her thigh. It felt good to have him on top of her though, she thought, so good to have him touch her the way he did. And yet he had no right to bite her the way that he had. That had hurt, and it had been too much. She could no longer feel the pain, however - her sex was too worn and numb after the aggressions his cock - but she'd wanted to smack him for it at the time. But now as she peered down at him, half-asleep already, she simply ran her fingers through his damp unruly hair, and told herself that perhaps it had been an accident. He hadn't forced anything subsequently, or tried to get her to do something that she hadn't wanted, so why did she want to put this stress on a relationship that had already proved more successful and more wonderful than any other she had ever known? Keep quiet about it for now, she told herself. She wanted him in her life, she knew, and she wasn't about to reprimand him for anything that he was doing, or even anything that he intended to do. He was wonderful, and that was the end of it.

The following evening they went out to dinner, a small restaurant in town that served a wonderful pasta. They ate well, a little too well, and were clutching their stomachs in pained but blissful extravagance on the short walk back to Mark's flat.

After a couple of glasses of red wine, the ache in their stomachs subsided and the heaviness of the wine drew a velvet veil across their minds, dulling their senses, but electrifying their groins. The sofa was small, but with the alcohol numbing their aches and forcing blood into their loins, they came quickly together in a long and passionate kiss.

Melissa already had her hands inside Mark's shirt, her fingers finding the deep grooves of his muscular frame, clawing at his flesh. His hands, meanwhile, had slipped beneath her skirt and were already inside her knickers, inching towards her sex held chastened by the angle of her body. Reclining back to allow him access, his fingers found their goal, and she loosed a delirious moan as they entered her. Oh how she had wanted them there during a day of answering telephone calls from frustrated customers, of meetings dragged on, of clients bullying and bargaining. She had hardly kept track of any of their wants or complaints, so much did the shape of his naked form fill her mind's eye. On the stroke of five thirty, she had been up from her desk and virtually running towards the lift, eager to be out and on her way home to ready herself for their special evening together.

He had pushed his fingers all the way inside her

now, filling her passage entirely as his tongue reached ever closer to the back of her throat. He was filling her so completely, so utterly, and still she wanted more of him inside her. Then his tongue suddenly slipped from her mouth, his lips hot and wet and tracking down across her cheeks and neck, searching out her shoulder as he eased back her silk blouse with his other hand. His teeth came again, biting at her soft flesh, and all she could do was whimper as her skin became pleasured first into pain and then back into pleasure, her pussy crying out for more length and girth than his fingers could offer in order to punish it.

Her head began to swim with a myriad of blurring thoughts, each one of them blissfully incoherent, but even as she felt his teeth sink even further into her shoulder, she could not help but let him taste her. Oh but this was good, that was what the cacophony of thoughts seemed to say in one mounting roar; this is good, don't let anything stop this.

Then Melissa's eyes flickered open as a wince of stinging pain came, her sight finding the top of Mark's head, buried at her shoulder. Vaguely, as though through some distant haze, she could see the place where his mouth had found its mark, and around it she could make out a dark crimson smear of blood. It almost seemed through this uncertain haze that he was drinking from her, drawing her blood out of the wound that he'd made, and swallowing it down just as he had swallowed down the wine earlier.

This sickening act seemed genuinely to be arousing him, the urge of his lips becoming more insistent than the motion of his fingers still buried inside her vagina. She struggled suddenly, the sharp pain in her shoulder disturbing her, but then she suddenly realised that he had her in a vice-like grip, her body stricken and wedged into the side of the small sofa. She gasped his name, clutching at his hair, and in a moment of panic thought that he would not let her go, that he would drink from her until she passed out.

But then after a final draw on her shoulder, his eyes suddenly lifted and found hers, his teeth lifted, and then a wave of something close to remorse suddenly seemed to wash over him. He started to stammer apologies, almost begging for her to forgive him, but for some reason she simply hushed him and told him that it was alright, they'd just got carried away.

He settled down somewhat as they both retook their seats, but it wasn't until they both turned their attentions back to the bite-wound still pulsing blood, that they both headed swiftly through into the bathroom to try and staunch the flow.

Melissa's blouse was ruined - a large red stain covered much of the top half - but as Mark applied a dressing to it, and apologised yet again, so they both gazed into each other's eyes and began to laugh out loud. The whole premise suddenly seemed ridiculous, an act of vampirism in a suburban neighbourhood, an act of blood-drinking in the middle of a feel-up.

"I'm sorry," he began to say again, putting his arm round her and pressing his face into her long brown hair.

"It's okay, Mark," she told him, hugging him hard against her. "I shouldn't have let you get so involved."

"It's just that…"

She looked at him.

"It's just what?"

He gazed up into her eyes now, his expression intense, yearning.

"It's just that you turn me on so much. I look at you, at your skin, and I just want to touch it, get under it, be inside it so totally."

"Oh Mark," she tried to hold back a sob of delight. "I want that too."

He looked hard at her, his eyes searching hers.

"You do?"

"Of course I do," she cried. "I love being with you. I love when we go to bed together. Can't you tell how crazy I am about you? There's nothing I'd say no to you for."

"Really?" he said.

His eyes gleamed as that smile of his returned once again, and it seemed so good to have it there, creasing the edges of his lips that had only just before been buried against her, laying kisses of desire against her skin.

"Really," Melissa continued. "I want us to be together. I want us both to be happy. I want you to do whatever you want to me, whatever you like, if you think it'll give me pleasure."

Mark's smile broke into a wonderful grin at this, and with their arms still wrapped around each other, they stumbled awkwardly out of the bathroom, only this time heading for the bedroom instead of the living room.

They didn't have sex that night, but slipped under the covers and drifted into sleep fully clothed, their arms still in the same embrace that they'd had on leaving the bathroom. It was a soundless slumber, no disturbances or ill dreams to stir the two lovers, nothing until dawn brought its pale light to the room and roused them gently into the promise of another new day.

Mark filled Melissa's thoughts for much of the morning - the touch of his fingers inside her, the heat of his lips against hers, the pressure of his body that had fixed her so tightly into the side of the sofa - but it was the pain that his teeth had inflicted upon her that dominated them all. At lunchtime, she sat alone and pondered his appetites.

Drinking her coffee as she nibbled absently on a tuna sandwich, she turned over the sight of him drinking hard upon the wound he had made. She had not thought that he had consumed that much, and yet all day she had felt light-headed. It was probably her imagination, she kept telling herself, he would have to drink a lot before she would lose consciousness altogether. But still, the memory of him almost gorging himself on her own blood made her feel uneasy.

She had shaken off her anxiety in the bathroom afterwards as he'd tended to her, the soreness of the wound dissipating. It still stung a little now when she put her fingertips to it through the fabric of her dress, but it would heal in a few days. The wound had not been that deep, after all. At one o'clock, she went to return to her desk, dismissing her over-reacting as mere foolishness. Mark was a wonderful man, a once in a lifetime catch, and she was not about to risk losing him just because she turned him on so much that he couldn't control himself.

For the fourth night in a row, Melissa drove to his flat after work. He was home as usual, and he greeted her on the threshold with a grin and a warm lingering hug. She sat in the living room as he made her a coffee, and once again she noticed his little notebook sitting on the edge of the coffee table, half concealed by the spread of magazines littering its surface. Once she could hear the clink of a spoon in the mugs, and knowing that he was occupied and not about to come back through the door and catch her reading it, she eased it out from beneath the magazines and had a quick leaf through.

There were a few more pages filled in, she could see, Mark's handwriting too spider-like to discern much of what he was making notes about, but here and there she could make out the odd word. 'Neck' was one, and later a reference to 'sickly blood', and towards the end of one paragraph a whole section about a 'warm glow burning inside'. She could only think that he was writing notes about her and about their relationship, but there was suddenly no time to read any more because she heard him coming back in from the kitchen. She just had time to set the notebook back down - her eye catching the inside cover where she was sure that his tally had now stepped up one notch to thirteen, although she couldn't be sure - before he reappeared in the doorway clutching two steaming mugs of coffee.

Glad of the warming drink inside her, she barely kept track of their conversation as she turned over the relevance of the numbers at the front of his notebook. Sure it was sweet that he was keeping a diary about their lovemaking, probably even making little asides about her and making notes for future reference - birthdays, that kind of thing - but it was the tally of numbers at the front that made no sense to her. They weren't the number of days that they'd known each other, or the number of times that they had actually dated, or even the number of times that they'd slept together. She thought momentarily, and with a turn of her stomach that made her feel sick, that perhaps it was the number of women that he'd been with. But that suddenly seemed ridiculous somehow. She had been with him for four consecutive nights. There wouldn't have been any time for him to squeeze in another. Surely. Unless he had found someone in a rapid space of time that didn't work during the day and didn't mind leaving the flat quickly before his girlfriend made an appearance. No, it was definitely not another lover. She ruled that out as best she could. It was something else entirely. She just didn't know what yet. They continued to chat for a while longer about work and about home, Melissa's doubts ebbing away by the second, until Mark suggested food and got back up to go into the kitchen to make something for them both to eat. She resisted the urge to linger behind in the living room just so that she could have another quick nose through his mysterious notebook, deciding that she should trust him, and that she wouldn't want her distrust of him returned, and have him have a secret nose through her diary instead, even if she did keep one, which she didn't. She got up and followed him through into the kitchen instead, giving him a hand with the meal, a brief supper of ham and potatoes, and another bottle of red.

It was not long after dinner, probably not much more than ten minutes, before they were back in one another's arms again and locked in a passionate kiss, their hands roving beneath each other's clothes, unbuttoning and unbuckling. Mark's head was at her lap before she had even hoisted her dress, his tongue tracing lines across the insides of her thighs, rising up towards her sex, where it found her already wet.

She gasped aloud as he raised her dress up and over her head, her hands clutching her own breasts firmly and squeezing them with ecstasy. Mark seemed not only eager to have the tip of his tongue flicker effortlessly across her clitoris, but also to push his mouth over the whole of her sex and drink deeply from her hole.

The sensation was more erotic than anything else he had done so far, his tongue stimulating her clit as his lips clamped around her and fed. A wave of stimulating heat coursed throughout her loins as she rocked back and forth against his mouth, inclining her hips to allow him even greater access to what he wanted.

With her head swirling as though drowned in some kind of glutinous soup, she barely noticed the change in his attentions, not even as his teeth found her clit once more and bit into it. Her buttocks clenched with the pain, her stomach churning with a sudden spasm, but so delirious was she with the headiness of his lips and tongue, that she could not stop the motions of her own body. A memory of something said before flitted briefly into her head, something about not denying him anything, and it gave a helpless credence to her apathy. She let him bite into it again, feeling the pain deep inside her, but letting it come, letting the pleasure still stimulating the rest of her overtake it, envelop it.

She grabbed hold of his hair as he bit into it a third time, this time much harder, twisting it between his teeth as though it was gristle from a bad steak. Melissa cried out in pain, her eyes stark, and as she gazed down at the man between her legs, saw that his face was once again stained with her blood.

Melissa had failed to notice through the pleasures and pains that he had instilled upon her, that he had been biting through the delicate layers of the flesh of her vagina, tearing them open in order to get to her more tender meat inside. Judging by the amount of blood smeared across his face, and it was so very awash with it, she must have lost a lot of it already. Even as she grasped his hair in two great fistfuls, attempting to yank back his skull, he strained to be back at her, strained to push his face back against her blood, to drink it and wash his skin in all that he could get.

The sight of him sickened her beyond measure. This was surely so far beyond forgiveness that she would not be able to even think about. She screamed at him to get the fuck away from her, yanking at his hair with all her strength now. But his grin came again, hideous through a mask of scarlet. And it came so very quickly, with his teeth stained red, his cheeks creasing and forcing rivulets of crawling blood out of them, that his fist, when it came, connected with her face so swiftly, that she saw nothing until her consciousness returned to her nearly an hour later.


When her eyes did finally open, it was to his bedroom ceiling. Her nose was throbbing incessantly, her eyes heavy and dulled, but even through all of that, an agonising sting of pain seared throughout her groin, up through her stomach, and shuddered the rest of her body. She remembered in an instant all that had happened, even through the haze of black shapes that still pulsed inside her head. Tears suddenly began to well, for herself and for her pain, for her anger and for

Mark, but mostly for how he had ripped her and punched her.

She lifted her head to see if he was near, but an agonising churn came as she realised that she could barely move. A cutting sensation burned at her wrists. She glanced sideways to see that he had tied her wrists to each bedpost, had tied her ankles at the bottom of the bed too. She struggled momentarily, but shafts of pain speared her body, and left echoes of fire burning throughout her groin and limbs.

A motion in the darkness at the edge of the room suddenly caught her attention, and she turned her head to try and make sense of the shadows. It was Mark, who else could it be, and it seemed that he was suddenly afraid to come any closer. Tears came freely now as she strained to make out his shape, standing there with his arms crossed, one hands playing nervously at his lips. She could not tell if he was sobbing himself, however, or just breathing heavily, but her tears began to obscure her vision even more, and she simply turned her head away from him and clenched her eyes shut against the whole room.

Between her own helpless sobs she could hear his footsteps pad slowly across the room until he was at her bedside. She resisted the urge to turn and look at him, but instead just listened to the hollow sound of his breaths, wondering what else he might do to her, how else he might hurt her in the name of passion. His breathing wasn't ragged as she had thought it might be, however, suggesting that he hadn't been sobbing, but it was irregular. It continued for a few minutes, drawing and fading, haggard breaths that came erratically as he gazed down upon her. But it wasn't until she eventually turned her head to find him, to find his eyes taking in the sight of her helpless naked body, of her bloodied hips, that he eventually spoke to her.

"I'm sorry," he said to her, his voice little more than a hoarse whisper.

The memory of her own words to him the last time he had apologised came rapidly into her head, urging her to repeat them this time also, but there would be no way they would ever come from her lips again. No way. Her eyes began to sting now with hatred for him, her nose still throbbing from where his punch had landed, and it felt like it had ballooned to twice its normal size, making it difficult for her eyes to even see past it.

Even as he apologised again, she could find no words to spit at him. Her body was wracked with pangs of agony, pulsing and churning deep inside her groin and her abdomen, her head a groggy soup where her thoughts struggled to keep coherence. Even as he leaned over her and pressed the gagging strip of black tape across her mouth, her throat could offer no final curse for him, bastard that he was.

And so Melissa's eyes clenched with a stifling agony as the man at her lap resumed his sickening meal of her, his fingertips peeling back folds that had been opened, his teeth opening new folds that he now made, tearing off slivers of red meat and swallowing them whole. Her body shuddered and writhed with an unequalled suffering as he assaulted her utterly, drinking her blood, devouring her flesh, undoing her body. The agonies seemed to last for hours until her consciousness finally slipped, allowing her passage into an inky black nothingness where she could feel no more harm.

Mark, however, continued his meal until he was done, leaving her where he had tied her while he went through into the bathroom to shower and wash her blood from his face and neck, removing all trace of her, cleaning his teeth twice, removing the sickly odour and taste from him altogether. He went back into the bedroom, opening the wardrobe where the hardening corpse of his thirteenth victim still hung from its wire noose, reaching past it to take out some of his clothes for the rest of the evening. Once he had dressed and combed his hair back neatly in the mirror, he went through into the living room, perched on the edge of the sofa as he took up his notebook hidden under the pile of magazines, and etched another line in his tally. Melissa could stay where she was, he thought to himself as he closed the book. He'd have a few weeks of gentlemanly behaviour before he'd have to worry about hanging up her body, a few weeks to dine at his new bedside table, her delicate menu open twenty four seven.

Pushing himself to his feet, he slipped on his black leather jacket and took up his keys from the counter, checking his look in the mirror one last time before making his way out into the night. It was only a few miles to the nightclub, a ten minute drive at the most. Best to plan ahead, he thought. Don't want to be left hungry in a fortnight's time.

I could tell you a lot of things about me. I could tell you I used to have bleach-blonde hair halfway to my ass. I could tell you I've had four motorcycles and crashed three of them. I could tell you that I kept my cherry until I was eighteen years old. I could even tell you that I've been to hell and back in a cable car made of green cheese. But none of that's important right now, because what I want to tell you about is that I used to play bass in a rock and roll band about twenty years ago in a town called High Wycombe.

We weren't much of a band, I think that's fair to say. But I don't think anyone is, not in the beginning. We had a short time of fame, of people coming up to us and asking us about our music, of thinking that maybe we had a shot at making it big time, of seeing a glimpse of something other than working nine to five on minimum wage. But it came to an end, just like most dreams do. It was fleeting, our fame, and it kept to a local level; but at least we had it for a while. Memories are important. That's something you don't realise until you're older.

Our band had a number of names over the couple of years we were together, but none of them are either important or worth listing here. We had a few arguments, and a couple of temporary splits, but none of them are important or worth mentioning here either. What was important and worth telling you about now was a guy we met along the way, a guy who had an unsurpassable passion for rock and roll, a guy who wasn't happy unless he was up on that stage with his guitar around his neck. My memories are important to me because I know I've done things, but those handful of years I've kept a secret until now because of the secret that they housed; I can not retell my story of life in a rock band without mentioning his name, and without mentioning his name there is no story.

You see, the reason I bring this all up now instead of leaving it a secret known only by myself and the other members of the band, is because I went back to the same pub where we first met him a few nights ago. I went back in a moment of nostalgia, perhaps to recapture something of my youth, but what I saw there up on that stage was something that I hadn't prepared myself for, at least not consciously.

His name was Moonshine, and I hadn't seen him in over twenty years, not since our last gig together. But there he was, some two decades later, playing his guitar like a pro. He hadn't changed, not his face, not his hair, nothing. The pub had changed, the stage lighting and the pa system, but Moonshine was exactly the same as his image that had become burned in my memories.

I'm sure he didn't see me, standing at the back of the hall in the dark unlit crowd, but I don't think he would have recognised me anyway. My long hair's gone, my belly no longer flat but sagging over my belt; I wear trousers and comfortable shoes now instead of leathers and boots, and those two decades are reflected deeply in the lines of my face. No, I don't think he would have recognised me at all. But I recognised him because he had not changed. I don't suppose I ever expected him to, not really, but then I didn't expect to ever see him again, not even here.

I first met Moonshine in this exact same pub, the

Nag's Head, back in the mid-eighties when we were a band. It was a dark and dingy pub back then, but the live music area is still upstairs at the back. It isn't much to look at, and it isn't particularly agreeable to bands - access to the stage is via a steep metal fire escape that's treacherous when it rains, and the backstage area is the size of a cardboard box - but it was still undeniably one of the best venues to play in the area.

We finished our first set in front of a slim audience, a crowd which probably numbered fifty if you were feeling generous, and the majority of those were either people we knew or other band members come to check out the local competition. As I took off my bass and leant it against my amp, I looked over to see this guy already in animated conversation with Andy, our singer. We were a rock band and we tried to take our image seriously. This guy, however, made us look like we hadn't even bothered. He looked the part and no mistake: he wore the obligatory leather jacket and jeans, he had long black hair right down to his ass, he wore silver rings across all his knuckles, and he carried himself like he was a signed guitar hero. I didn't think anything of it at the time, thinking he was just part of one of the other local bands come to take a shot at the new boys, and wandered into the crowd as the interval music started up and blared over the public address system. When I came back to the stage for the start of our second set, Andy grabbed hold of me and told me about the guy who I'd seen him talking to earlier. That's when he told me his name was Moonshine and he dug what we played. We only had one guitarist at the time, and it was pretty much agreed that the live sound suffered because of it (as if there was ever going to be a recorded sound!). During that gig on that fateful Saturday night, Moonshine basically signed himself in to fill our thin sound. We discussed it all later backstage, as we struggled to strip off sweat-soaked jeans and torn t-shirts, that he'd obviously have to audition. We were a pretty much unknown band then and it probably wouldn't have mattered much to have another average player join us, but we agreed that another player who might very well be worse than us would not help in the slightest. Even if it did fill out the guitar section.

The Nags' Head hired out their back room for rehearsals during the week, and it was there that we met regularly to try out new song ideas and tighten up our already short set. The following Thursday evening we asked Moonshine to come along to see just what he could do and where he could fit in, if anywhere. He was already there waiting for us with his Les Paul and his Marshall already set up. His talk was big, his eagerness and enthusiasm bigger, but when he plugged that baby in and started to wail over our first number, he blew everyone away. I can still remember that first grin spreading over my face as he took the first solo over Love Don't Give It Bad. I tell you, he wailed, and he threw that damn guitar all over the stage, pulling off licks quicker than I could see them. I felt sorry for Jon because he'd always covered both rhythm and lead. But after that first song, it was pretty much all agreed that Moonshine would be playing all lead guitar from there on in.

That Thursday night, the five of us played pretty much solidly for two hours and more, played tight too like we'd been best buddies for years. We all grinned and we all watched one another, and never once did any of our enthusiasm wane. I tell you it was infectious

337

how energetic that Moonshine was. We couldn't get enough of it, and it showed. Don't get me wrong; we'd played a lot of rehearsals and a lot of gigs before Moonshine came to see us that night, and there'd been as many ups as there had been downs. But just that one rehearsal almost made us see the whole band in an entirely new light. A single musician can do that. A single musician can walk in and take everyone else in a completely new direction. It doesn't have to be a new musical direction, it can be a mental one or one based on attitude. But that night, Moonshine somehow took us on all those trips in one go. And needless to say we hired him quick before anyone else got a whiff of him.

The following Thursday at rehearsal we brought in a tape recorder and taped the whole set for him, every song we played live. We gave it to him so that he could learn a few songs well enough for the following week instead of kind of just jamming over the top of them like he had done the previous week.

The Thursday night after that came and Moonshine had learned the lot: an hour and twenty minutes worth of chord progressions and changes: our entire set. We played it through without a glitch, Moonshine playing accurate solos which he then managed to repeat over and over again each time we played through the set.

On the night of our first gig as a five piece band, I for one was apprehensive about how well he would perform live. It was all very well reaming away in a backroom with four new mates, but it's another thing entirely to try and pull it off in front of people watching every string you pluck. But just like everything else about him, I needn't have worried about his skill or his stamina.

We played at the Elgiva, a support set in front of a packed crowd, and I watched with a mixture of awe and envy as he kept moving to the front of the stage, gyrating his hips with his guitar anchored to his groin, soloing with his head thrust back, and leaning against Jon whenever they played synchronised riffs. He'd told us that he'd played live before but he'd never gone into detail. I've played some well-known venues myself but I don't like to bore people. I've had it myself, been on the receiving end of some once-upon-a-time rock star's life story, and it gets stale pretty damn quickly, let me tell you. So I didn't pry into the where's and the when's of his history - and maybe if I had I wouldn't have believed him. But maybe if I had believed him then, I might have quit the band all the sooner, and perhaps joined another band in blissful ignorance.

So we played that first gig to a heaving audience, and it was probably one of the best shows I've ever had the privilege to be a part of. We partied backstage with the main band for a while afterwards, and then filtered back out into the crowd, some of whom we knew, most we didn't. Moonshine had brought a few of his own friends along, all of them dressed in rock and roll leathers and jeans, but none of us thought any more about the evening other than having some beers and chilling out. Even when we all went back to Andy's girlfriend's house for an after-gig party, we continued to drink beer and have a laugh, not thinking any more about the new friends that Moonshine had introduced into the fold. Indeed, it seemed the more the merrier. Some were older, others younger, but they all had the same enthusiasm and love for the kind of rock and roll that we'd been playing loud up on stage.

Over the coming months we learned more new

songs and played more live gigs and became a tighter and more professional band. We still only played local gigs - our name had not spread that far afield - but at least it was in front of growing audiences, and we began to enjoy a greater success than we probably would not have done if Moonshine had not been part of the band. He was no doubt the key member of the group, his skills as a musician gave him that title, and yet he seemed to desire no leadership status of any kind. He was there to play his guitar and that was all, and he'd made that clear right from that start. There was no political shit about him, and to this day I still give him credit for that. Music not only came first, but it was the only thing for him; there was no number two in his life so far as I knew.

Andy received a phone call not long after that gig at the Elgiva from a man at Arcane Promotions called Vince Carter, who said he'd seen us live and wanted to manage us. He could do great things for us, he promised; he could get us better gigs, he could pull in bigger crowds, but more importantly there was talk about a possible record deal. But when the news came about a support tour across the country, some thirty two dates spread across ten weeks, it was Moonshine who surprised us all by becoming vague and negative about the whole thing.

He gave us no reason as to why he was so dismissive, and it was perhaps that and the resultant doom that spread throughout the band that caused the first split. We all still knew that it was Moonshine's input that had snagged Vince Carter's attention in the first place, but to know that it was Moonshine that would ultimately deny the rest of us our shot at fame and fortune was too much to take; at least it was for Greg, our drummer.

He called Andy and told him how it was, and left it to him to pass round the cut-down version to the rest of us. He couldn't sit behind his drum kit with Moonshine in front of him, strutting his stuff like he gave a damn about anybody but himself, and continue to perform properly. He knew the chances of getting into another managed band with a shot at stardom was remote, but it was either that or sit and fume every time he played on stage or rehearsed with our newest member.

It was a dark time for us. Greg had been one of the original members, and there seemed to be a void without him. We also didn't know whether the band would or even could continue without him. We spoke about finding a replacement, but we just didn't know anything anymore. Was it even worth continuing if we could have no tour or record deal if it was offered? We tried to quiz Moonshine about his reasons for not wanting the success Vince Carter was both offering and, at times, promising, but he just wouldn't confess them to us - he had his reasons and that was it. He did, however, tell us that a friend of his was a drummer, and that he was interested in stepping into Greg's shoes. As I said, we didn't really know what to do anymore, and to be honest I don't think the rest of us particularly cared, so we had this guy Rags come along to audition on our usual Thursday night rehearsal, and were surprised at just how good he really was.

I wouldn't want to say that Rags was any better than Greg in case he ever reads this, but he really was; he pounded those skins like a demon, and added an extra dimension to our sound, a thunderous percussion that had been missing before, without us even knowing or even being aware of it.

Our first gig with Rags went down a storm. Vince Carter had booked us into the Axis Club, had rounded up a huge crowd too, and after the gig he came backstage to tell us how our new sound was even better. He pretty much promised a record deal right there and then, telling us that the record company executives would have to be crazy not to sign us. He told us that he would get things moving, and would try to put a showcase together. He had a couple of contacts at EMI and Geffen, and he'd do all he could to get them to come to our next show.

We went to our after-gig party elated. It was the closest we'd come to making it big, and only when Moonshine confessed to us that he still couldn't commit himself to anything that Vince Carter was working towards that we came down hard. What kicked us in the balls even harder, though, was Rags, who told us that he couldn't commit himself to a record contract of any kind either.

It was Jon who upped and left after that. We argued out in the street, the two of us, but I knew I could offer no justification for his staying. He wanted to get signed every bit as much as I did, and we both knew that that wasn't going to happen all the time Moonshine and Rags were in the band. It was a catch twenty two situation. We wouldn't get signed without them, and they didn't want the high life. The only benefit for staying was to be a local celebrity, and that was all.

So another of Moonshine's buddies joined the band, a rhythm guitarist called Axeman, whose heavy grinding rhythms managed to fill out our sound even more than it had been before. His tone was unbelievable, purer than anything Jon had been able to wring out of his old Fender tube amp, and once

342

again our sound stepped up another notch.

We played Vince Carter's showcase, but it was hard for either Andy or myself to conjure any kind of real enthusiasm. Moonshine, Rags and Axeman all played their usual flawless performances, but neither Andy nor I could fathom the reason why they bothered, other than for their genuine love of playing rock and roll. Why wouldn't they want to make it big, we kept asking ourselves? Why wouldn't they want to play in front of audiences all round the world? These and many more questions, we knew, just weren't going to be answered.

There were representatives from Music For Nations, Island, EMI and Sony, and without exception they all loved our music. Andy met them with Vince Carter after the show, but I didn't. I just couldn't bring myself to join them. I just couldn't stand there with my spirits being slowly raised like a sunken ship off the seabed knowing that it would be dashed again, knowing that we could never have anything that they were offering. And what were they offering? To this day I still don't know, and I don't want to know. I try and convince myself that it would have been a basic deal, nothing special, but there's always that nagging voice at the back of my head than hints that it could have been something huge, something major to rival the Bon Jovi's and the Metallica's of this world. We were that good. But who knows? Only those record company execs, Vince Carter (who left shortly afterwards), and Andy (who left even quicker).

"What's the fucking point?" Andy had said to me. "What's the fucking point of any of it?" And he left the band that night, on his own and in a taxi.

Moonshine found me at the bar. I was knocking

back shots of Jack Daniel's and he slung an arm around my shoulder and told me not to worry, we were still a kicking local band, and that was the most important thing of all.

It had been an energetic night, and the stench of his sweat was headier than it usually was. I'd probably subconsciously noticed before, but it wasn't until that moment that I realised how badly he actually smelled. The following day I met up with Moonshine to discuss just where the band was heading, and I noticed again the pungent smell that always seemed to hang around him, noticed it almost straight away. I wanted to quit the band, just as the others had done, but Moonshine said I should stay. We were one hell of a band, he told me, and to break that up would be criminal. The real scene was the local scene, he also told me, and to rock your home turf was the best thing in the world. I truly didn't know what I wanted, so I decided to stay, at least for the time being.

It seemed that more and more of Moonshine's friends were coming to our gigs. We played the Nag's Head regularly, and there they'd be, right at the front, dressed like rockers in their leather jackets and torn jeans, dancing and banging their heads all night long.

I began to lose touch with my friends, realising that most of them were friends of Andy's or Jon's or Greg's, and slowly began to get to know Moonshine's crowd. They didn't seem a bad bunch, and to give them credit they were all really into the music. But I noticed that same smell hanging around them that I'd smelled on Moonshine, a kind of dank musk that I just couldn't put my finger on. It wasn't sweat, although it was closer to body odour than anything else, and it would be a few months before I eventually realised what it was.

I had begun to grow close to one of the girls that came to the gigs. I don't want to use the word groupie because that conjures a bad impression of her. She was a nice girl, with shoulder length blonde hair and a pretty face, and she looked to be in her early twenties. Her name was Teresa, and we began to talk more and more in the intervals between our two sets, and again after the shows. We were getting close, or at least so I thought, but whenever I asked her out, she'd decline politely and say that she couldn't.

It was after my last gig at the Nag's Head - and it occurred to me then (strange that I hadn't noticed it before) that she only came to our gigs at that particular pub - that I made my move on her. We'd been chatting and giggling together, and it felt like the right moment, and I slipped my hand around her waist and pressed my lips against hers. She recoiled from my touch as though I was poison, struggling to get away in an almost hysterical fit, but it turned out that the damage had already been done. Right there in front of everyone, her top lip disintegrated. Only a little, but right there where I'd kissed her. She put her hand to it instinctively, but the decay had already begun. Her skin began to tumble away like dust, turning a foul grey colour as it dried and came away in flakes. Teresa ran screaming from the hall as everyone turned to look. I started after her but Moonshine appeared quickly at my side, his hand grasping my arm, stopping me from my pursuit of her. It was then that his odour came to my nostrils again and I recognised it as the stench of death.

I staggered back away from him but his hold kept me close. His eyes stared into mine as if to threaten me

345

to silence, as though their secret was now known, and I could not help but look from him to Rags to Axeman, and then to all of their friends as I realised the horrible truth.

They all stared at me in silence, and with Moonshine's hand still grasping my arm tightly, I feared that I would not make it out of there alive. But then his fingers slackened and I pulled free, and for a moment we just stared at one another, just Moonshine and me, and a kind of understanding passed between the two of us. Perhaps it was a kind of mutual respect, a kind of elation that we'd shared up on that stage, I have no idea and to this day still don't. But he let me go - they all let me go - out into the world with the knowledge of their dark secret.

I'd never returned to the Nag's Head again until a few nights ago, and to see them all still rocking that place as though no time had passed shocked me more than you could ever imagine. Moonshine was still there, gyrating his hips and pulling off licks quicker than my eyes could follow. Rags was still at the back pounding his drums. And Axeman was still grinding solid rhythm guitar with that same pure tone that maybe he'd sold his soul for. They had a new singer who I'd never seen before, and a new bass player too. I'd like to think that I laid down more solid bass lines than this new guy, especially on Love Don't Give It Bad, and hopefully Moonshine thought so too. But I never approached the stage to ask him, or even to show my face, not even at the interval between their two sets.

Instead I made my way out the back to the beer garden so I could take a breather and get my head into shape. I sat on one of the benches in the darkness for a while, just sitting alone and thinking about Moonshine and all that he'd done, not only for the band but for all of us as individuals. He'd brought me a lot of memories I wouldn't have otherwise got, and for that I had to at least be grateful.

I sat there for a while with the drone of voices emanating from the hall upstairs like a thunderous hive of bees, but when the band started up again, and I heard the familiar second set opener of Wildcat Woman, I smiled secretly to myself. There was no one else in the beer garden to see me, but I still covered my grin with my hand, and thought what great times they'd actually been, even if most of the band had been zombies.

My eyes drifted past my pint glass then, and settled upon a path that had been worn across the grass. To my recollection the beer garden had never been used that often, so enclosed was it by surrounding buildings and trees, and to see it lead all the way back to a gate in the fence kind of took me by surprise. I got to my feet and wandered over towards it, trying to peer over the top. There were mature trees on the other side, but I could not see over well enough to see what lay on the other side. My compulsion grew, though, enough to make me drag one of the heavy wooden benches across the lawn to the fence, climbing up onto its rickety surface, and looking over the top.

Even though I knew, or perhaps only suspected in my darkest nightmares, the truth about Moonshine and the others, for some reason I could still not believe my eyes. On the other side of the fence, on the other side of the gate and the well worn path, lay a graveyard. Set in the grounds of a small church and circumscribed on all sides by tall deciduous trees, their heavy foliage had camouflaged pretty much all of it. I thought I knew the area as well as anybody, and yet I'd never known this graveyard had even existed.

I looked again at the path that had been worn across the beer garden that led all the way to the fire escape which itself led up to the stage area. I gazed back again at the graveyard and traced its path between the headstones. My heart was hammering as I stared at the route that wound its way between their own graves as their rock and roll boomed from the building behind me.

And then without thinking, I clambered up and over the fence and jumped down into the graveyard. Wandering between the gravestones, I began examining the names engraved upon each one in turn by what frail moonlight filtered in through the trees around me. I had no doubt that the names Moonshine or Rags or Axeman would not appear upon any of them, and yet I continued to search and examine the inscriptions. Were his friends here too, I thought to myself? Or the groupies that had danced at the front of the stage. Had he been buried with his guitar, I thought crazily, his death shroud an outfit of leather jeans and jacket?

After perhaps half an hour I gave up my patrol and simply stood and gazed across the army of headstones. I had no idea where Moonshine had come from, but as I listened to his music echo around the small graveyard, I couldn't help but think that maybe his bones were indeed resting somewhere in this place, perhaps even resting somewhere near to where I stood, and that his passion for rock and roll had coaxed him up and out of his grave. Had the lure been too much, I thought to myself as I stood and listened to the familiar chord progression of Love On The Rocks, for him to listen to all these local bands without wanting to get involved once again? I did not know.

The feeling festered inside me that even now he was watching me from his grave, perhaps nodding with understanding because I now realised why he could not have accepted that elusive record deal and tour that the rest of us so desperately craved. I still don't think I fully accept or comprehend his condition, and to a certain extent I don't think it really matters, but I think it probably has something to do with the fact that he can only journey so far from his resting place. I think that's what he meant by the importance of playing on his home turf.

I smiled to myself again, yet I still couldn't shake the feeling that somebody was watching me, even though I knew that if he was up on stage and playing his guitar, then he couldn't possibly be here and watching me. I looked around, but there was no other living soul in the graveyard. But then as I went to leave, I noticed a figure perched on the edge of a mausoleum and looking down at me. It was dark where she sat, but I could just make out her shoulder length blonde hair, and guessed her pretty face, and suspected that she probably still looked to be in her early twenties.

"Teresa."

I mouthed her name and stood motionless as she slipped down from the stone tomb and came towards me, her arms at her sides, a smile upon her beautiful lips. I wanted to go to her, to slip my arms around her waist as I had done all those years before. But I stayed where I was, my arms at my side, petrified in case my touch began her destruction once again.

"I saw you in there," Teresa said to me, nodding towards the pub at my back. It was wonderful to hear her voice again, lilting and gentle. "When you came outside, I followed you. I thought you were leaving."

I shook my head.

"I needed some air," was all I could think to say.

Teresa smiled again.

"I'm glad you came back," she said. "It hasn't been the same since you left. Moonshine's missed you, I know that."

"And you?" I asked quickly.

Her smile became a coy grin.

"I've missed you too."

We spoke uncomfortably in this way for a while - it had been twenty years since we'd seen each other, and we'd parted on the back of a scream - but slowly the closeness that had begun to grow between us returned. I wanted to kiss her again, more now than ever, thinking of her alone and sleeping beneath cold dark earth. But I knew what would happen, and had to resolve myself to nothing more than words and sweet gestures.

It was during our conversation, however, that Teresa said something that did not fully strike me until later that night when I returned home to my empty flat and lay in bed not being able to sleep. She'd told me that Moonshine had never been able to find a decent replacement for me in the band, and as much as it could have been an innocuous compliment, it occurred to me that it might also be true.

The following day I ventured out to find the name of their graveyard, and discovered a plaque hidden amongst swathes of ivy which read St Constantine's, and wandered its grounds for much of the day, examining the gravestones by day as I had tried to do the previous night. It was quiet: no one else came to visit the graves, and no one rose from them either.

When I returned home, I sat down in front of a fresh sheet of paper, a pen in my hand, and held it over the blank page for more than an hour as I deliberated over the plan that had blundered its way to the forefront of my mind. Finally I wrote 'In the instance of my death, I request that I be buried in the grounds of St Constantine's Church, High Wycombe', and then folded it neatly and placed it safely in my wallet.

I sat for the remainder of the day in my flat alone, thinking about what I had done and how fate might do what I wasn't sure I could do myself. I think everyone has thought at some point or other just what might do the trick, but there's always that fear of pain that hinders us from stepping over the boundary, the terror of living with disfiguring burns or broken bones if death refuses to take us. As I sat there at the kitchen table I imagined a toaster in the bath, of running across the busy Bath Road, of taking a prescription of painkillers so that I might at least evade the pain of death. But instead I sat alone in my flat and decided to make no decision.

I was some twenty years older than Teresa, and I didn't even know for sure how Moonshine really felt about my playing. But there was another question that began to gnaw at my senses, one that was so obvious, and yet I hadn't even entertained it for a moment. Would I even be reanimated? How many of those buried at St Constantine's could not dig their way out of their own graves with the lure of live music, I wanted to know? How many of them were just rotting away as lifeless corpses are supposed to do?

In the end, however, it was not even my decision. Two days later I was found dead from a brain haemorrhage. Maybe it was stress, I don't know, and maybe it was somehow self-induced, but my note was found in my wallet where I'd put it, and I was duly buried in the grounds of St Constantine's Church.

My eyes opened that night to Moonshine's grinning face. I was barely even out of my freshly excavated grave before me was handing me my bass and telling me that he'd never seen a crazier old fool so desperate to play rock and roll in his life, or his death.

"Welcome back," he also added with a sly wink.

We didn't need a rehearsal. My fingers seemed to play all the old notes as though it hadn't been two decades that had passed since we'd last all played together. I found I could play better than I'd ever played before, too, as though my fingers could only remember the good notes, and had somehow managed the trick of ignoring all the bad. Our first reunion gig at the Nag's Head was a blast, our friends in front of the stage, the bodies of the dead amongst whose graves I had been buried, dancing like we were the best damned rock band in town. And right there amongst them, positioned in the space in front of me, was Teresa, laughing as her shoulder length blonde hair bobbed all around her, and turning like a ballerina as the music captured her. She smiled at me with beautiful red lips that I knew I would now be allowed to touch and kiss without fear of her degeneration, and I was happy for the first time in over twenty years, content that I had my music and a woman whom I could love forever.

She'd hurried to pick the dogs up just before dawn so that she could be the first one there. The short annex off the roundabout had been empty, and Amy had turned her van into the block of four spaces in front of the wide iron gate with almost a grin of victory on her face. The blue LED clock on the dashboard had read 7.05AM - was it any wonder that no one else was out with their dogs at Swinley Forest yet, especially on a weekday morning? Dog-walking was far from being a priority for most owners, it seemed, and that kind of thinking had both its good and bad points. The biggest plus point for Amy Randle, however, was that a lot of them were paying her six fifty an hour to walk their pets each day.

She'd converted the back of her white panel van herself, putting in six wire cages so that the dogs could travel safely. It was a good system too, with a narrow channel through the middle for her to crawl between where the locks were situated.

It was Wednesday and the middle of April, and the air was crisply cold and fragrant from the pine trees of the forest. Amy had four dogs with her, a collie, a labrador and two jack russells. They'd always got on well together, so it was usual for her to keep it that way and take them out at the same time, so it was relatively straight forward to unlatch the cages one at a time, attach their leads and then lock up the van.

The collie, who'd been named Cody after his owner's trip to Wyoming a couple of years ago, was the youngest and most exuberant, and they hadn't even halved the distance between the van and the gate before he was jumping up, jaws snapping with excitement. Amy coaxed him down with a firm hand to his chest, but she became distracted by a paper sign that had been pinned to the gate post just ahead of her. Lost, it said in thick felt tip pen at the top, Milo, one year old lurcher cross. Amy looked at the badly copied photograph of the missing hound, its tan and white face upturned and gazing out at the world with crazily-wide eyes. Owners should keep a closer watch over their dogs, Amy muttered beneath her breath as she negotiated her way around the gate with all four dogs straining at their leads, then they wouldn't get themselves lost, or worst still, wander onto a busy road and get themselves killed.

Once past the gate the pathway was wide and stretched up a long incline. She always wanted to let the dogs off their leads and let then run, but as they weren't her own dogs, she couldn't be sure whether they'd come when called every time. They were good with her, there was little doubt about that, but she'd hate having to return empty-handed to their owners, or worse still, with a dead or injured dog in the back of her van. It wasn't as fair to keep them on leads, but it was safer and a damn sight better than not taking them out at all.

The labrador was a chocolate male with the crazy name of Dave, Dave the dog, and he was the first to take a shit. They hadn't made a hundred yards before he tugged himself near the edge of the wide pathway and squatted. Amy could only guess what time his last walk must've been the previous night, but it couldn't have been late enough, so desperate was he. Her eye was caught by the glint of something silver as she stood there, and she craned her neck to see that it was an empty crisp packet. Frowning with disgust, she leant over and picked it up, stuffing it in her shoulder bag so that she could bin it later. She hated litter, especially up here in the woods. How difficult could it be, she always wanted to know, to take your litter home? It was probably kids. They can be bothered to bring the food up here, but they can't be bothered to take the wrappers back. Dave resumed his stance, shaking her off her soap box, and Amy checked what he'd passed just to make sure it looked okay. She had to peer over the top of one of the jack russell's heads as he strained to take a sniff, before she scooped it into one of her bags and slung it into her shoulder bag. It seemed fine - at least they seemed to be feeding him okay - and then they were off again.

There were so many benefits to walking dogs all day apart from the growing income - fresh air, exercise, not being stuck in an office - but the best one Amy had found was how it seemed to relieve tension. Just being outside with the dogs as they sniffed and found adventure in everything made her troubles seem to fade. Not completely, of course, (some troubles just hung in there for the duration), but most of the daily worries seemed less significant somehow after an hour's walk with excited dogs.

She loved dogs, that was the truth of it, and it had been for as long as she could remember. She'd always had a dog, too, even as a child, and now that she was working with them, it was a godsend.

A lemonade bottle and a biscuit wrapper had been thrown into the drainage ditch beside the pathway, and Amy stopped and simply stared at them in disgust. It wasn't as though she hated kids, it was just the ignorance or bloody-mindedness of them that got to her. How difficult was it to take your own shit home with you? Was it the parent's fault? Did they throw their shit down when they were out too? She stooped and picked them up, stuffing them into her shoulder bag along with the crisp packet and the bag of Dave's shit.

Always had dogs. Always would.

Kids had their positive moments, of course, she wasn't about to call for a national flogging or anything like that. It was just that they could be so thoughtless and ignorant at times. Her eyes rose into the depths of the woods as she thought this and settled on a stack of branches that had been set round the base of one of the pine trees like a wigwam. She didn't know why she even stared at it, or even why she'd looked at it for more than a few seconds in the first place. She'd seen them before countless times in the woods, presuming they were made by the same kids with the lemonade and the crisps, coming up into the forest to play. That she didn't mind, healthy adventure and creative imagination, it was just the littering that got her.

The dogs were pulling again, and it dragged her back to the moment. On she went with them, forward and up the incline.

Not every trouble faded with dog-walking. The mortgage in itself was fine, and the van repayments were okay, but she'd recently started getting into debt with the business itself. She'd run newspaper ads to get more business but they hadn't paid for themselves for a few weeks. Then the work picked up and she found that she had to put in some serious hours just to accommodate everyone. She knew it was a catch twenty two situation, it's just that on paper, all the numbers seemed great. It practice, there were a whole stack of other bills that kept adding up. Overheads, her bank manager had smugly informed her, as he'd charged her another twenty five pounds.

She hadn't been paying attention to what the dogs were doing, but now she looked down to see that the two jack russells had pulled a branch way too big for them out of the undergrowth and was systematically whacking it against her heels in their attempts to own it outright. They were brother and sister, the two russells, Pinky and Perky, and they were the easiest dogs to cope with out of all that she looked after. They belonged to an elderly lady who was getting too frail to take them out regularly. She clearly spent most of her time with them because they were so friendly. It was shame some of the other dogs she took out weren't quite so good-natured with her or the other dogs.

Passing through an area of land that had been stripped for timber, she made her way round and up towards the monument of Caesar's Camp. It was one of her favourite places to take the dogs, partly because it was an interesting walk, and partly because it was actually the remains of a real iron-age hill-fort. Her walks varied greatly, from the Thames at the end of the A329M, to the lakes at Dinton Pastures, and the routes through all the different woods in the area.

History itself, though, had never really appealed to Amy, not in any real sense of the word, but walking the perimeter of Caesar's Camp and seeing how the Romans or the ancient Britons or whoever had constructed such a place was awe-inspiring to her. The monument, although basically just a semi-cleared hill, had a handful of white information plaques stuck in the ground at various points, and on one of them she'd read something about how they'd dug trenches and built timber pole fences to keep out invaders. It was the sort of thing a university professor might've droned on about on a TV documentary, but to actually stand on the real-life perimeter and gaze out along the man-made banks or across the woodland sloping down and away made it all come alive. She was sure the dogs didn't give a shit about it, and that they'd probably much prefer chasing squirrels around the ancient land than taking in the heady aura of the place, but it took her breath away every time she stood up there, and for that reason alone she came here frequently.

On what would have been the north rampart, Amy stood for a few moments and gazed down at the sloping banks below her. The dogs were busy with the grass at her feet, she could hear them sniffing noisily, but she kept her eyes on the forest as if searches for those heathen invaders. She didn't see any marauders, however, but she did see another one of those wigwam constructions set deep into the trees, dead branches gathered roughly at its base and pitched to make a tent or a fortress. It could only be good for playing in for an hour or so, she thought distantly. There'd certainly be no shelter to had from them. It occurred to her then that she'd seen those wigwam structures dozens of times before and thought nothing of them. It seemed strange why she was paying so much attention to them now. Kids and their playthings, she conceded, they had their place up here too.

It had distracted her from her thoughts about the Romans and their hill-forts, and she tried to get back into it but the wigwams had disjointed her thoughts and they wouldn't reorder themselves. She glanced back down at the dogs. Cody was looking up at her, his tongue lolling as he panted with simple satisfaction, fogging the crisply cold air in front of him. Amy ruffled his ears affectionately as she cast a glance back out at the quiet woods, but the Roman aura had gone. She was just a dog walker out alone in the woods.

Amy was physically shaking as she hid in the small hollow. Her knuckles were clenched white as she grasped the three remaining leads in her trembling hands, her brow icy as the chill of the early morning dried the sweat that beaded there. Her cheeks were flushed and hot, she could hear her blood thumping in her ears, and her clothes had stuck to her back with a cold clammy sweat. Something was in the woods with her, and it had killed one of the dogs.

The wigwams weren't playthings, she'd seen the creatures that came out of them, hideous malformed beasts with unblinking white eyes. Motionless too, standing as still as the trees around them, staring back with those hideous eyes.

Branches snapped somewhere off to her right and her eyes jerked wildly in that direction. Her vision settled unsteadily on yet another rough wigwam of pine limbs stacked at the base of one of the trees. There was no movement though, no sign of anything out there, just the motionless vertical trunks of a hundred thousand pine trees.

Her skin crawled again as the memory of the creature returned. Cody, the black and white collie who had been the first to start barking out into the silent wood, hadn't come back. She'd pulled on his lead as he'd stood his ground, barking ferociously into the eerie dark depths, but as much as she'd tried to coax him and pull him, Cody just wouldn't budge.

Even now, sitting hunched in her small hollow, she couldn't quite remember what had distracted her, what had happened, but something had, that's all she was certain of, and it had been in that moment when Cody had yanked the lead out of her hand and bolted for the wigwam.

The wind picked up suddenly through the trees, bringing voices that screeched overhead like shrieking owls. The muscles of her arms had almost knotted themselves into old rope so hard were they tensed and shaking, but all Amy could do was huddle with the three remaining dogs as they growled and slavered around her.

The small black and white collie had hurdled through the undergrowth like a wild animal, and it was as it neared that hateful wigwam that she'd caught sight of the monster. It had almost evolved out of the conical stack of branches, so slight did it appear, its reedy twisted body emerging from where before had been nothing but dark grey bark and needleless twigs.

Its white soulless eyes had stared back at her with utter blankness until Cody was within yards of it. What had happened then she could still hardly decipher, but the dog had let out a dismembered yelp inside a shower of scarlet rain, and that had been the end of its attack. The creature remained in view for a moment, its claws stained crimson and steaming with hot blood in the cold of the morning air, and then went from her sight.

Maybe they couldn't always be seen, Amy had no idea, but she'd searched those trees for a handful of terrible seconds as the three dogs at her side had pulled and lurched, before the chill of fear grasped her utterly and she turned and ran for her life.

It was not easy to run with any kind of useful speed with three dogs bounding into her path with every step, and so she could make little more than a stumbling flight. She wanted to simply let go of their leads and make a run for it herself, but part of her said that she was responsible for them being out here in the first place - and just what was she going to tell Cody's owners? - and part of her said that if whatever had butchered the collie wanted a piece of her too, then it would have to get past three sets of snapping jaws first. No walk was ever really the same - how crazy did that statement sound now? - but it occurred to her suddenly, as she darted off the path and between the trees, that she'd only seen these wigwam structures at Swinley Forest. It was Forestry Commission land, she thought insanely to herself as she stumbled up an incline that led to the pathway back, and she should call them when she got home to tell them to patrol their woods more closely.

Branches snapped off to her left now, less than twenty yards away, but her eyes would only make little sense of her surroundings, so that she was almost running blind in a place she was familiar with. A scream was being held at the back of her throat, she could feel it clogging her breaths, but with her chest struggling to keep oxygen in it, it had no chance of escaping. She didn't want to look anyway, something was there, she'd seen it, and she knew that she didn't want its grey talons raking at her flesh, or its eyes falling upon her flesh.

The undergrowth crunched again, more loudly this time, and one of the dogs lurched sideways towards it, sending her sprawling to the ground. She put one hand down into the cold dank earth to steady herself, snatching a heart-stopping glance into the trees. She was running again before she had even registered what she had seen, throwing herself over the ridge and onto the path on the other side, her head swimming wildly as she thought she had seen two eyes gouging the space in front of her.

Amy gazed down at her feet and saw that only two dogs were with her, the two jack russells. She staggered to a circling halt as she tried to untangle the knot of leads in her hand, as her head tried to make sense of what was happening. Dave the chocolate labrador was no longer with her. Had he been the one that had pulled her to the ground? Had he managed to pull himself free and she'd not even noticed? Her heart lurched at the thought. She'd heard nothing from the woods to prove that he was dead, nothing to prove that he was alive either.

She stood for a few terrifying moments with her heart thudding in her chest and head like a heavy diesel engine as she tried to make out any sign that he was still close. One of the dogs at her heels barked gruffly into the woods, only a short warning bark, but enough to make her circle slowly once more, checking all the trees around her for the beasts with the wide albino eyes. It was then that she realised just how deathly silent the forest had become. Not a single creature moved or made a sound, no birds, no rabbits, nothing.

Somewhere off in the distance she could make out a string of pitiful whimpering yelps just above the call of the wind as it suddenly picked up once again through the pine trees, but she couldn't be sure whether it was Cody or Dave. She held her breath to try and make out the distance, but the yelps stopped all too soon and never picked up again.

Then something growled behind her, and she knew that it wasn't one of the dogs. Amy spun wildly, the leads slipping from her numb fingers as the scream that had been promised finally came. Once in the air it was loud and it wouldn't stop. Her lungs fed it until they began to burn, and it sliced the air in two even as she watched the last two dogs dash madly back the way they'd come, over the ridge they'd scrambled up, and out of sight, barking all the way. It dawned on her as her scream died, that she was suddenly all alone. It was still early light, she'd been the first vehicle in the handful of parking spaces, and it was reasonable to expect that no one else would have arrived yet. She'd only been walking perhaps twenty minutes or so until Cody had first started barking, and even after her short staggering run, it would still take her at least five or ten minutes to get back to where she'd parked her van. It was not the most desolate of woods, but it was out of the way enough to not be heard screaming.

Very slowly Amy began to edge herself back, her eyes straining to try and make out shapes amongst the ferns slowly nodding in the early morning breeze, but there was simply nothing there to be seen. But the monster had simply appeared out of nothing, hadn't it? Its hideous form had unpacked itself out of the branches that made up those frightening wigwam structures at the base of the trees. Her eyes moved round again, scanning the darkest depths of the forest, until they settled upon another tent of branches stacked up in its sickening conical formation. Her blood turned to ice, and her teeth rattled in her skull like dice in a bone-white shaker, as the image of its simple shape burned into her head. And then three feet to the left of it, she saw its occupant standing there, the thing of nightmares, as emaciated and as grey as the dead pine branches around it. Its eyes shone white and pupil-less and glared at her with a hollow weight that seemed almost to bury inside her. Its slitty maw opened like a grizzly trap, and inside she saw the threat of its needle teeth stark white against the chasm of blackness beyond.

Then she ran, as hard as she could across the uneven pathway worn between the trees, back towards her van. With no dogs to hinder her, Amy was able to cover ground more swiftly, and hoped that the creatures that were no doubt following would not be able to keep up. They had the dogs, she wanted to scream at them, keep them and leave her be.

The wide iron gate appeared suddenly through the trees as she rounded a corner, and she gasped with relief at the sight of it. She could feel tears of relief streaming from the corners of her eyes as she ran, dangerously blurring her vision as she tried to keep her ragged pace as best she could, until finally she reached the gate and stumbled through the narrow gap beside it and onto the short strip of tarmac that made up the parking spaces.

The blackness of fatigue was already crippling much of her vision, but as she lifted her head to the sky and sucked in breaths that bit icily at her throat, she saw the troubled and wary faces of two people clutching the lead of their brown and white spaniel. Her breath was coming out in haggard bursts, but she tried to stop them from going past her with what few words she could get out.

"Don't…" she managed to say, clasping both hands to her chest now. "Dogs dead. You mustn't go…"

She heard one of them hiss something to the other before they both tried to skirt around her. She grabbed hold of the sleeve of the man, an elderly man with receding grey hair, easy meat for the monsters of the forest, but the woman huffed her indignance as he swiftly wrenched it from her grasp. Amy had no strength left to hang on, but she tried once again to verbally stop them both from entering the forest.

"Killers in there..." she stammered. "They'll kill you, kill you both..."

But they were already past her now and both had their backs to her. Only the spaniel looked her way, its eyes fixed on the madwoman, before it too returned its attention to the early morning walk ahead of them.

Amy stood breathing hard in the small car park until the couple and their dog were out of sight, and only then did she turn and trudge back to her van. The dogs were dead, she was sure of that, and as she tugged the keys from her pocket and unlocked the door, realised how close she had been to joining them. It was only once she was back inside her van and looking round at the familiar interior that her doubts began to surface. Had the dogs been killed? Had she really seen something in the woods?

The dogs had slipped their leads and run off, that was still evident by the empty van, but where had they gone? If she returned to their owners now with that story, she'd have no excuse as to why she'd not gone after them, except for the creature that she thought she'd seen. But had she even seen it? She'd been spooked by Cody's barking, spooked into hysteria maybe. Perhaps he was still dashing through the woods looking for her, looking for a way back to where the van was parked. Perhaps they all were.

No, it was crazy to think there were weird creatures alive and living in the woods, despite how much her chest was still thudding with terror. It just didn't happen, not today. Her fingers went back to the door handle beside her, just as her eyes flickered up to the rear view mirror. She just had time to see two savage white eyes glaring at her from the back of the van, before its talons slashed the fabric of the seat from behind, and sprayed the inside of the windscreen scarlet before she could even loose a scream.

# The Black Woods

I had been lucky to save it on the wet road, that's all I could think at the time. The rain had washed so much mud and muck down off the steep banks that the hill had become more treacherous than it might otherwise have been.

But the blown tyre's not the only thing that's shaken me up tonight. There's something else, something that I'm not sure even happened now. The only thing that holds my certainty are the jitters that still have hold of my chest. My hands are still shaking after my third measure of Remy Martin, downed from one of the tumblers we'd received last anniversary from my wife's sister. My wife; I was supposed to pick her up over an hour ago - she's going to be mad. But I don't want to go back out there, not just yet, not through the Black Woods outside Cookham.

Its just gone four past midnight, a chilling coincidence that echoes the title of that Stephen King novel. The sight of the narrow hands on my watch that point to that time turns a dull flat slab over in my stomach that has the weight of a gravestone. I know Kathryn will be waiting, twitching the curtains at Jenny's house with every car that passes, but I can't face driving back out into the dark and the rain, not just yet, and not on that silent hill that has no streetlights.

My tumbler's empty, and I try to pour another measure as steadily as I can. Some of the sombre liquor spills down the side of the crystal and drips in perfect circles across the dark wood of the table. I can see an ebony reflection of myself in the wall of the tumbler, distorted against the cut glass and the deep rich colour of the brandy. I do not look well.

Did I see anything at all?

That's what I keep asking myself.

It's starting to become vague now, what actually happened, just a series of blurred static images clutched together with uncertainty and irrational childhood fear. I was out in the woods alone, out in the Black Woods, no less, and that's all that I really know for sure. Who knows what's out there, in an ancient woodland unbounded by any fence or city. This is rural country, out in the sticks.

Let me first explain what I was doing out there, it may well help me get the events in some sort of rational order at least. Kathryn, that's my wife, had one of her socials at Jenny Maxwell's, and I took her over there around nine o'clock. It's only a short drive between Burnham and Cookham, but there's no real direct route, and the country roads are generally quicker anyway. The outward trip was nothing special. The rain had picked up from a drizzle to a light squall, a cold wind whipping it up and making visibility a bit of a handful, but it was nothing too untoward. Hedsor Hill was a little slippery, but then with the steep muddy banks either side, it usually is when it's wet. All was fine when I dropped her off, but with a miserable selection of programmes on TV, I thought I'd stop off for a quick pint on the way back. One pint led to two, however, and by the time I came out, the rain had picked up considerably. It wasn't yet ten o'clock, and I still had an hour or more to go before Kathryn would be ready, so I hurried back to the car with the collar of my coat pulled up over my head.

Heading out over the river, I took the next turning

right towards Hedsor Hill, out of the lit B-roads of Cookham and onto the unlit narrow thoroughfares cutting through the farmers' fields and open woodland. I'd only gone a few hundred yards at most, when suddenly through the heavy rain, I made out the shape of a walker hunched miserably against the downpour with a wretched hound soaked on the end of a sagging lead. I remember thinking what a pitiful sight it was to see a man and his friend out taking a constitutional in such foul weather, but then that's the burden of dogs, I guess. They've got to be walked, rain or shine. It was only a passing sight, and they were both gone from my mind once I was past.

The phone's started to ring out in the hallway. It'll be Kathryn. If I answer she'll want to know where the hell I am and why I haven't picked her up yet. What could I tell her? I have no idea. She'll have to wait for now, I'm in no condition to drive.

I reached Hedsor Hill shortly afterwards and started up the incline. I could see the washes and rivulets of the rainwater cascading down the road from the light of my headlamps. I drove steadily in third gear, an easy forty mph, towards the summit. It would be slippery, mud and all, but by no means treacherous. The beer had made me slightly light-headed, I'll admit, perhaps even a little distant and lacking in concentration, but I still sat bolt upright when the tyre blew and threw the car across the road. Mud or no mud, the car slid sideways, lurching towards the ditch at the side of the road like a felled ox. I wasn't going that fast, I'm certain of that, no more than forty. But I was still lucky to save it.

Hush. The phone's stopped ringing. I'm probably making her worry unneedlessly, I know, but what can

I do? She'll phone again in a bit. Perhaps I'll be calmer then. Have a better story to tell. A sane one.

I crawled out into the horrible night cursing. The overhanging trees seemed almost to act like some kind of cruel wind tunnel, and it whipped the rain hard into my face and is fell through the canopy, stinging my skin like tiny needles of cold and wet, almost blinding me as I stomped round to the front of the car to find the tyre bunched up at the base of the wheel.

I gazed back the way I'd come, back down the dark unlit hill, the lights of Cookham spread out and glittering snugly on the other side of the curving black mass of the Thames. It was probably only about a mile and a half back to the village, but I wasn't about to start walking back to Jenny Maxwell's house just to phone the RAC. My hair was already soaked, and trickles of icy water slid down my collar and settled at the base of my neck like a cold washcloth. My coat was still damp from when I'd left the pub, but now it was pretty much sodden just from stepping round to the front of the car. I had very little choice, I knew, although I wish now that I'd left the car where it was and ran all the way back to the village. But for some reason I had already resolved myself to going back home soaked to the skin. I was going to fix the tyre myself and drive back. I guess you'd call it dumb stubbornness or something, I don't know, but I trudged round to the back of the car, unlocked the boot, and set about tugging the spare out from beneath the coarse grey carpet.

The canopy of beech trees that towered overhead showered me with huge drops of water with every blast of wind that came, adding to the fury that gusted down the hill and the freight of rain that it carried. My clothes were wet through and stuck to my skin like freezing adhesive before I had even jacked up the car. I began to shiver violently with the cold, the wrench slipping repeatedly in my numbed and weakened fingers, but once the nuts were loose, I knew I could no longer change my mind. I had to continue.

I could feel the steam of frustration and hard work rising off my forehead as I tugged at the wheel, lifting skyward like some fragile and benign ghost, losing its tentative substance almost immediately in the cold midnight air. No traffic passed me on that quiet winding hill, and I was too far from the village to distinguish any sounds coming from its streets, the shrouding grasp of the rain suffocating any noise that might have come from as far away as the river. The only sound around me was the metallic grind of the wrench slipping against the wheel nuts, the car gently ticking towards silence, and my own heartbeat thudding erratically in my ears.

My watch now reads twenty minutes past midnight. No novels about that particular time I'm sure. Kathryn will be getting really concerned by now. I should phone her really, but what excuse could I possibly think of? Sorry honey, I'm going to be a bit late because I'm chicken-shit scared of the dark. I'm acting like a kid, a big dumb kid, and I know it's irrational and I know that if I even had kids and one of them was behaving like this I'd grab hold of them and shake some good honest sense into them. Except now perhaps I wouldn't. Perhaps now if I had a kid and he gave me good reason why he was scared of the dark, like the reason I have now, then maybe I wouldn't shake him. Maybe I would settle him down and say, yes son, there are things to be scared of in the dark. It used to be irrational, but now it's not. Not after what

I've seen. But who am I to say any of that? I'm still here, aren't I? I haven't been killed by the dark, or what lurks behind its grim translucent veil. I'm still sitting here in my own home throwing brandy down my neck like it was water. I'm not even sure now whether I saw that shit or not. God, I've got to get a grip. Go pick Kathryn up. That's the sane thing to do, the rational thing to do. At the very least, then there'd be two of us in the house.

I'm getting lost again, nervous, perhaps it's even hysteria. I've never felt like this before so it's kind of hard to tell if it is hysteria. I'm sure I don't look like one of those hysterics in films that need to be slapped. It's all in the mind, sitting there, shaking. Shit, where was I? Oh yes, the wheel.

It wasn't until I'd managed to fit the spare and was doing the nuts back up by hand that I first paid any attention to the crackling sounds coming from amongst the trees at my back. I must have been vaguely aware of the sounds of the woods - the wind gusting through the boughs, the scrabbling of some midnight creature - and yet the branches that began to break so very close to me suddenly caused a shiver to run down my spine. Resisting that dumb kid's fear of spinning round to study what might be lurking there in the dark, I continued to tighten the wheel nuts without slowing, picking up the wrench beside me in a measured fashion, feeling a sense of comfort at its weight in my hand. The sound of branches breaking came again, and this time only yards behind me. My mind ran with images of some horrible mutated being, something shambling and groaning like a rotting zombie pulled straight out of one of George A Romero's undead movies. I fought the urge to yell out, to swing that wrench about my head like it was an axe, but allowed myself the simple but ridiculous comfort of a quick glance over my shoulder.

The woods were black, the darkness total, enveloping, almost as though it was sucking me into its deathly void, and I could see nothing but the trees. If there had been a moon that night, the rain clouds had simply swallowed it whole. I was in darkness. The world outside was not to be scrutinised this cold wet night. I was alone with a broken car, easy pickings for whatever might live out in the woods.

And then my imagination played me a desperate card of sanity.

The dog walker.

Perhaps it was him, made his way up this far, marking his route home through the woods away from the danger of the unlit roads where he might not have been so easy to see. That must be it, I remember thinking, and yet my unease would not go, despite the reassurance my subconscious sanity had offered me.

I had at least a few more minutes outside in the dark shrouding rain before I could return to the safety of my car and lock the doors to seal me in. The creaking and cracking of the woods halted and yet I continued to flap at my labours, my stupid fingers fumbling with everything they sought to touch, the wrench, the tyre, the coarse grey carpet. I returned it all to the boot without incident, however, with no zombies, and no ghosts, even though my heart was hammering like a smithy's anvil, pounding blood like hard steel.

I wanted to run, wanted to fall down onto the ground and cry out the admission that I was scared, terrified, but I didn't want this stranger, this midnight dog walker, creeping around the woods in the middle of the night, to see how petrified he had made me. I strode back to the car as collectively as I thought I could manage, puffing out my chest to ward off any thought of his scaring me further. I pulled open the car door and clambered inside, shutting it firmly before the chill of fear returned to my trembling bones and caused my hand to fly to the lock to hammer it down. I was thankful for central locking that night, and breathed a sigh of relief rather more loudly than I would have thought possible as they all clunked around me. And then, with a deep breath of resolution, I reached down to take a firm hold of the key in the ignition.

It sounds like the wind is gusting up again outside. I can hear it whistling through the trees out back, hear the rain begin to slap against the window pane too. The storm isn't subsiding yet. I can't go out in this. Not yet.

The engine turned immediately, and I put the car into gear. Then a motion to my right snagged my attention like a fish snagged on a hook, a movement out in the Black Woods. Without thinking, I turned my eyes towards it. Something was gazing back at me from the depths of the woods, something black and with a face twisted from matted fur and death. Teeth grew from its maw in a ghastly growl. It bore no resemblance to anything I had ever seen before, not animal, not alien, and certainly not human. It was horrid, and even through the glass I could hear it grunt and snort at the air. I shook with absolute terror as it stood there and watched me, our eyes connected in an icy gaze that clutched at my heart. And then suddenly, as the wind gusted up again and lifted the branches of the trees, the blackness of the woods shifted and swirled, and stole the face of the fleeting beast. My eyes clutched at the darkness in the wake of its disappearance, but it had simply vanished.

Its eyes still hang before me now, orange and sharp, focussed like that of a hunting animal, even as I gaze at the familiar objects of my house through an ever-thickening fervour of brandy. It chilled me more than the cold and the wet, chilled me in a far deeper place than any weather ever could. Did I even see it? That's the question that still remains. I'm sure I did, I'm certain that I did, but what could I possibly say? It's not rational. The darkness has no monsters.

The phone in the hallway has started ringing again. Kathryn must be getting furious by now, and the wind and rain are coming even stronger now. I can hear the tips of the branches tapping on the glass now. They sound like bony little fingers. Or even bony little claws.

Tap. Tap. Tap.

# Chaos Of Calm

The air in the dark hallway was dank and stale as Jack opened the door to his mother's house for the first time in over eight years. She had died suddenly at the age of fifty-five, leaving her home full of antiques and memories. He had not been in this house since he was sixteen, when he had left at the first opportunity to escape his father's drunken beatings. His father had subsequently left the house shortly after in search of new dens of squalor and alcohol, but Jack had not had such knowledge to return by. He'd been cheated of a lot of family life, that's what it felt like. Now all that was gone, only this time for good.

The new tenant stepped over the weathered threshold, his shadow casting long shapes into the room ahead, the halo of bright morning sunlight around him beginning to excite the film of dust that had laid dormant for so long into an agitated desire to soar upward and to dance in his wake as he trod slowly across the silent boards. He crossed carefully to the bay window in the front room that looked out over the driveway, his memory surpassing eyes unable to guide his feet through the gloom. Grasping the coarse fabric of the long heavy curtains, he tugged them back only to release the infinite motes of dust that had long awaited their freedom into a billowing cloud that seemed to glitter and ignite inside the bright rays of the early Spring sunlight that now flooded in through the glass behind.

Jack turned to study the room that he had played in as a child, only now with the strangeness of a taller perspective, as he put a cigarette to his lips and lit it.

The hearth where he had built villages and towns for his toy cars and trains stood decaying and dirty, the cushions of the armchairs and sofa that he had created castles from now worn and frayed, the thick brown carpet that had enticed dreams from him lay threadbare and discoloured, and the table and chairs that held within their dark knurled legs a forest as dense as any fairy tale kingdom held their own dark secrets behind each and every trunk. Had they always been so worn and decrepit, he wondered, as the blue smoke from his cigarette curled about him? Always so weathered and torn? Perhaps his isolated and lonely games had coloured them differently, who knows? But he was home now. That was all that mattered. Jack caught the movement of another figure lurking in the gloom of the hallway, and it jerked him swiftly back to reality with a quickened heartbeat. He issued for Susie to come forward, and her smile came reluctantly as she walked across the room to join him, the virgin sunlight catching the distaste in her features as she passed through its illuminating rays.

"Come on, honey," he said to her, drawing on his cigarette. "Just try and show a little interest. For me."

She widened her smile for him, then lost it all too quickly as she too stared about the small dusty room, her eyes finding old rickety furniture cluttering what awkward cramped spaces there were.

"It'll all have to go," she said to him.

"No," Jack returned, defiantly. "It all stays."

"But we'll have to get new stuff."

"It all stays."

Susie walked away from him and stomped back out into the hallway in search of anything that might possibly pass for a home. She poked her head around another door and found the murk of a similarly dismal kitchen, its floor grimy, its walls streaked with condensation, its sink slung haphazardly beneath the boarded windows still home to a number of soiled plates and cups. She slunk from this in disgust and found the stairs further on.

Its banister was large and grand, out of place to what she had already seen in the other rooms, its timbers turned and lathed by some fine craftsman, its bare steps smooth and dark from care and polish. As she slowly ascended, her eyes drawn to the landing at its summit, her tread brought forth from the third step a low jagged creak, perhaps a reminder of the rot and decay of the lower floor, while the subsequent steps, however, remained as silent and as solid as the first two.

The landing was as dark as the boarded ground floor and she had a choice of three doors at the top. Out of the two to her left - one was the bathroom, and the other a kind of junk room - she found nothing of any interest to entice her over either threshold. The door to her right, however, stood slightly ajar and as she pressed it further to reveal the room's secrets, it swung gently open on silent hinges before coming to rest against the wall behind. She remained at the doorway for a while as her eyes grew accustomed to what lay inside. From the weak glow that permeated the edges of the curtains she could just make out a large bed at one end, an assortment of cupboards and closets at the other, and in the centre of the wall opposite stood a fireplace with an ornament-topped mantelpiece above. Tentatively she stepped across the carpeted floor, her steps as deathly silent as the chamber itself, through the dark room towards the darker window. As she grasped a curtain in each hand she felt a light breath against the back of her neck, a delicate whisper of both promise and passion, and she inclined her head as if she expected her husband to have found his way just as silently behind her. But her eyes traced the shadows of the room and found herself to be strangely still alone in the room.

Returning her attentions to the coarse dark fabric in her hands, she stretched her arms wide and submitted the gloom of the chamber to the bright world outside, and sent the shadows from their kingdoms, and the darkness back to the shallows beneath the cabinets and the bed. Susie leant forward to unlatch the windows, setting them back as far as they would go, allowing the gentle breeze outside to fill the fibres of the curtains with its fresh sweetness, and to billow appreciatively against its touch. She leant forward on the sill and closed her eyes, letting the dream-like potency of the Spring air carry her readily from the room, the breath of warm promise once again at her neck to tease the despondent gloom and murkiness from her soft flesh. The creak of the third stair from back inside the house brought her unwittingly from her dreams and she reluctantly glanced over her shoulder this time to find her husband crossing the threshold in search for her.

"I see you've found the main bedroom," he said to her, with a smile.

"Yes," she replied simply, her thoughts still yearning for the distraction of the balmy fresh air.

"That was my parent's bed," Jack continued.

"Really?" Susie answered, the air making her more tetchy than she actually felt, "you do surprise me."

"Don't be like that," Jack said to her. "This is our home now, but I can't help thinking about what it used to be like, you know, before..."

Susie left the pleasures of the window and crossed the room to join her husband. She loved him dearly, even though she had objected to his decision that they should both live here in this place. She knew a little of his life here as a child, that much he had told her about anyway, the frequent beatings he had received and the unhappiness he'd felt, but she still thought that he was maybe keeping one or two secrets from her. All families had a few problems, she realised, but she just got the impression that Jack's had more than its fair share.

"I'm sorry," she said at last, threading an arm through his as she kissed him gently. "I promise that I'll try and make an effort."

Jack returned her kiss and then turned back towards the bed.

"This is where it happened, apparently," he told her.

"What?"

"Where she died," Jack explained. "In her sleep, the coroner told me, as tranquil and as sedate as a new-born and at total peace when she left. He was quite adamant about how peacefully she had died."

Jack smiled to himself now, happy in the knowledge that she had at least left this earth in a better state than she had endured it with his father.

"We'll change the bed of course," he added quickly.

"Of course."

"And then we can move in properly."

"You're sure that's what you want?"

"It is," Jack replied, and then turned to kiss her once again

It was later that afternoon that their explorations were disturbed by the clattering of a large near-white box van that had pulled up outside in the driveway. Jack was the first to spring to arms, dropping his memories back into the dust and charging through the house to open the front door for the two men who had by now climbed from the cab and were busy staring up at the  front of the house, their hands portentously idle at their hips. As the door swung wide and the figure of its occupant loomed from the dark corridor behind, the larger of the two men slouched forward to intercept him. He was a big man, overweight not from the plate but from the glass, and his dowdy baggy clothes hung about him through no choice of their own; had they been given the choice they would surely have chosen incineration.

"Hello again," Jack greeted them, as he leapt the three steps between the front door and the drive.

"Art'noon," the large man returned, with as little fervour as he could muster. "Sorry we're so late, but dickhead here c'nt read the bloody map," highlighting his partner behind him with a nod of his head.

The partner shuffled behind in disciplined shame, his defence unforthcoming.

"I'm Jack," said Jack, extending his hand to them both. "Jack Darwin."

"Barry," replied the larger of the two. "And this is dickhead."

"Corey," corrected the other quietly, his arm extending hesitantly.

Jack took it nevertheless.

"Where shall we start?" Jack asked the two professionals. "We've got a few things that need to be got rid of first..."

"We don't dump stuff," pointed out Barry rather quickly, "unless our expenses is covered."

Jack caught his meaning and assured him that all parties would be taken care of.

Susie watched her husband offer the two men over the threshold before following them inside himself. She was in the main bedroom once again. Although she felt a little uneasy that her mother-in-law had passed away here in this room, she also felt strangely content as she stood by the window, the warm breeze once again caressing her as it gently billowed the curtains beside her. She turned as she heard the creak of the third stair and moved from the window to the door to greet the three men to her bedroom.

"Art'noon," the larger of the three mumbled as he stepped past her.

Susie smiled her reply, faintly uncomfortable at this stranger's presence here.

"All this goin', is it?" the man asked, as he looked round at the antiques of the chamber.

"No," Susie told him sternly, as he tapped the base of an old wardrobe with the toe of his boot. "Just the bed."

He lumbered across the room toward the furniture in question, and proceeded to tap that with the toe of his boot.

"Looks all right to me," he stated, as much to himself as to the rest of those present, his guide to quality furnishings now replaced back upon the floor.

"What's wrong wi' it?"

"We -"

"We bought our own," finished Jack, as he stepped to his wife's side.

Barry eyed the weight of the bed with an eye that

seemed used to such things.

"Get your arse over 'ere, Corey, and do some bloody work."

Corey shuffled over to his employer's side to appraise the bed with an apprentice's boot.

"That end, stoopid," he said, shoving him toward that end.

"Sheets'n'all?" asked Barry to the couple.

They both nodded.

The two men hauled the bed away from the wall before heaving it over onto its side. Lifting it up and away by any means they could, they manhandled it precariously to the door and slowly edged it through, the jamb harried under frequent assault, before losing it to gravity at the stairs. For his part, Corey earned himself a string of abuse and threats, most of which were surely untrue, while Jack and Susie watched from the bedroom window as the two men staggered back across the driveway, a bed beneath their tensed crooked arms, before they dropped their burden unceremoniously at the back of their near-white box van. They also watched as the larger of the two shoved the smaller of the two in an order to open up, only to follow after him and appear seconds later with a second bed wrapped in plastic which they then manhandled back in much the same manner as the first.

With the two men gone and their new bed in place, Jack went in search of his wife. Her voice trailed from the kitchen, and as he entered, he found her up to her arms in thick white suds at the sink, a chaos of assorted crockery lined up to her left, a stack of glimmering soapy crockery to her right.

"Thought I'd make a start in here," she told him.

"We'll have to eat sometime."

Jack walked up behind her, slipped his arms around her waist, and kissed her gently on the back of her neck.

"See? It's not so bad," he said, his voice muffled as his lips moved round to nibble at her ear.

Susie's head reclined into her shoulders at his touch, as she recoiled against the tickling sensation he was inducing.

"I've got this to do," she said as she turned, dousing his fires of passion with a handful of soapy water.

Jack kissed her forehead in mock surrender, and then sloped from the kitchen with a sly grin as he went in search of wonders new.

The electrician was due that afternoon, as well as the removal men, to turn the power back on, yet he did not appear. Neither had he appeared after their evening meal which they took outside at dusk, a combination of bread and cold meats along with anything else they could find that did not require any cooking. By eight-thirty it was getting too dark to see outside, so deciding that there was no chance of a miraculous visit at this hour, Jack searched the recesses of the kitchen cupboards for a sign of any candles with the aid of his cigarette lighter.

His mother had always been a just-in-case sort of woman and she was never to be found without the most obscure of apparatus given any crisis, and so sure enough, in one of the cupboards beneath the sink, he found a large box crammed with thick white candles. Withdrawing a fistful of them, he closed the cupboard door and picked out one from the bunch, marrying the small flame of his lighter to the virginal wick producing a weak soft glow that grew as it crept eagerly towards the wax. As he turned from the sink, the flame's flickering light cast dense shadows across the walls and the ceiling, dancing and creeping as he moved through the house.

"What now?" asked Susie, as the beacon approached out of the gloom.

Jack screwed his face in thought, the light from the candle contorting the potency of the creases making him look weird and disfigured.

"We might as well go to bed," he suggested, "there's nothing else to do."

"Ever the romantic," she returned, as he and the light joined her at the bottom of the stairs.

They had placed the new bed in the same place as the old, its vividly coloured covers contrasting violently with the subtly decorated timbers and off-whites of the remainder of his mother's bedroom. Jack had brought with him the bottle wine that they'd consumed over dinner to use as a candle holder. He drew its lip to his and drained the last dregs of the warm sweet liquor before running a line of molten wax around its rim to press the butt of the candle into, before setting it down on the bedside cabinet. Finished with his labours, he turned to catch the flickering shadow of his wife discarding the last of her clothes to the floor, and then searched for her amongst the gloom to view the flesh. She did not see him looking at her at first, but she did so now and saw him standing by the edge of the bed gazing at the smooth planes of her body. At first she wondered just what he was looking at and checked herself for defect, but when he smiled affectionately up at her, the glow from the candle masking one side of his face and sending it into deep shadow, she returned it happily, and walked from her spot and round to the other side of the bed, offering him more sights of illumination.

She was not a large woman, and nor was she willowy. She was slightly shorter than he, as is often the case in such matters, and although her figure was not the most voluptuous he could have hoped for, it was nevertheless very pleasing for him to look at. Her soft curved breasts bobbed as she walked, the candle's flame catching their round beauty and displaying their perfection for this private audience. He had spent much time at these in the past, taking his time to grow more and more familiar with them as time went on, stroking them tenderly, holding their firmness with the palms of his hands and massaging them against her chest, lowering his mouth to them and drawing on them gently yet firmly like a child, to be fed with their eroticism rather than their sweet milk. The arch of her spine curved perfectly into her tight bottom, the gentle glow of the flame caressing her inviting cheeks with its yellow warmth as she stopped at the end of the bed. As she turned towards him and lifted back the covers, his eyes went to the dark mound between her legs, as her voyeur overdosed on the rampaging thoughts that whirled from his mind and snaked to his member as he studied her. As she climbed into bed and slid her silken legs beneath the covers, he caught sight of the sacred folds of flesh that dwelled amongst the haven of dark hair, and he longed to tread there once again. As she pulled the covers up over her body, both the journey of his roving sight and that of the candle's flame was at an end, and he slipped from his clothing in a light that seemed less erotic than the one that his wife had bathed in. Yet he slipped beneath the same covers as she and lay next to the enchanting creature of whom he knew so much, and as he pressed his lips to hers in a loving kiss, he ran his palm across the precious flesh of those resilient breasts and kneaded them tenderly.

He was not altogether sure that she was quite in the mood for his advances for she did not return his tongue with as much fervour as he gave it, but as they kissed, and his fingertips found her nipples and rolled them into their surrounding soft flesh, she slowly drew him closer, reaching a hand out to him and gently running her nails across his chest, and down across his stomach, before straying at the pleasure of his loins. Jack moved his hips towards her in order to guide himself closer to her touch. She responded to such obvious intent and let her fingers play down the length of his shaft before encircling him with her hand and pulling gently at him.

He muffled a sigh of ecstasy through their kisses as she slowly slid her hand up and down over him, her hand releasing shuddering spasms throughout his body as he swayed to her rhythm. She slid her fingers gracefully away from his shaft and down over his balls, squeezing them gently before running her nails over its sensitive skin. Jack moved his attentions from his wife's breasts, his fingers stroking her flat stomach in circles, edging down her body in slow lingering motions, increasing her expectancy but heightening such agonies of release, until he felt his touch amongst the growth of her coarse dark hair. His hand swept swiftly between her opening legs as he played his middle finger across the soft folds of her sex, probing deeper to find the warm pool of her vagina and slip effortlessly into its enticing promise.

Susie breathed heavily as he began to rub at her, gripping his cock harder and opening her mouth to the heavens as she herself opened up to such primordial pleasures. She rolled away from him onto her side in order to give him greater access, and slid one leg back over his to widen the breach. With one hand she continued to play with him behind her while the other she used to guide Jack's fingers to the heights of her passion. She tossed and bucked beneath his violation, her mouth wide as staggered gasps erupted from it with ever-increasing potency, and as her sex started to overcome her mind and her body, her eyes flickered open in her fits for the briefest of seconds.

Her gaze caught the shimmering glow of the candle against the wall, and there below it the swirling forms of two lovers locked in writhes of pleasure and sin. The vision enticed her eyes still further, but amongst the glimmering shadows from the warm glow stood another form, a dark and twisted form, a head set at an angle upon narrow shoulders, an arm reaching out, clawed fingers of a hand.

She wrenched away from her husband's touch in a violent movement and sat bolt upright, checking the shadow on the wall before turning sharply as if to catch its projecting figure behind. Her eyes strained against the gloom beyond the glow but it was obvious even in the half-light that they were alone.

"What's wrong?" stammered Jack, as he hauled himself up beside her. "Did I hurt you? I'm sorry."

Susie did not reply, or even acknowledge him, but simply stared out at the dark murk of the room.

"Someone was in here..." she murmured, a waver in her throat.

Jack frowned at her.

Susie smacked him in the chest with frustration.

"I tell you someone was in here!" she snapped.

"Who?" he asked.

"I don't know," she insisted, "but someone was definitely in here. I saw them."

Jack followed her gaze as he too scanned the room for unlikely intruders.

They were definitely alone.

Jack turned back to her, a look on his face that contradicted her argument. Susie slumped back into the mattress. Jack lay down beside her. He slid an arm around her waist and offered a kiss to her cheek, but it was obvious that that wasn't what she wanted. She was flustered, perhaps even a little scared.

"It was probably just a shadow or something," he told her.

Susie looked at him.

"That's all," he said.

Her eyes went past him to the emptiness of the room behind, the threads of her former panic giving way to the authority of common sense. How could anyone else be here in the room with them? It just couldn't happen. They were alone.

By mid-morning the electrician had still not arrived. Susie made further attempts to reveal the true colours of the work surfaces and the tiled floor from the resident dictators of grime and grease in the kitchen. She had brought a handful of detergent bottles and scourers to the house with her but had nearly exhausted her supplies on this room alone; the whole house, it seemed, had a love for its stain and was loathe to lose it. Heaven knows what her mother-in-law had done in here, she wondered, as she broke the seal on yet another bottle of cleaner, because she had appeared to distribute all kinds of stuff in the most peculiar of places. Dragging forward the refrigerator, the most common haven for mutated fuzz, she expected to be confronted by a jungle of mould, yet she discovered this to be far cleaner than the rest of the room. There was little in the way of dust, let alone anything else. Susie shoved the white cabinet back into its hole and turned once more to the shrine of degradation. She sighed in surrender, turned her back to the altar, and went in search of her husband.

The riot of coarse swaying grasses rose up like a vast green sea, its waves rolling under the influence of the morning wind as it buffeted the back garden. Wading through the ragged tide, Jack struggled warily against the tangled mess, attempting to discern the borders between the lawn and what were once flowerbeds. An unruly fence of conifers ran the perimeter of the garden, their billowing limbs as rebellious as the grasses that also reached out for attention. But standing alone in the centre of all this bedlam stood a solitary tree, the apple tree that he had planted from a small black pip from a once-ravaged core. Jack stared at the twisted branches and at its awkward frame, a pitiful example of nature, but oh how good it was to see it after so many years, still alive and thriving amongst all this disorder. He had gone to the same spot of tilled earth every day for weeks after it had been sown and he had seen nothing. His parents had told him on each disappointed visit that it would not grow, and even he believed it after a while, yet he persevered with his tree and he watered it and he tended it, even spoke to it on occasion, and after a month of pleads and promises a small shoot had dared to appear from the dark earth one morning.

His excitement grew in proportion to his love for the sapling as it grew larger and stronger. As he gazed now upon his creation, this plant that he had given life to by the will of his own hand, he smiled at what he had created, at what he had made. True, it was contorted and not the most beautiful tree in the whole world, and it had never born him a single fruit in appreciation of his efforts, but he had made it nevertheless and it was his, and now after all these years they were reunited once again. His memory jolted from the past as the sound of his name echoed around the garden, and he glanced round to see his wife hovering on the step at the back door.

"What are you doing?" she called across the sea of green to him.

Jack visualised his position from her perspective. Here he was, standing alone up to his waist in swathes of grass, staring at a small crooked tree.

"My tree," he explained, pointing behind him. "I planted it. Years ago."

"Got any apples on it?" she called again, hopefully.

"Nope," he replied, disdainfully, and turned back once more to the tree. He supposed it was a bit naff really. And half-turning back to his wife he added: "Never has, never will."

Suddenly there was a ring from the front door and he watched as she disappeared back into the house. He looked around the garden once again, at the disorder and the unruly claim of the overgrowing weeds, and decided that he would assault its defiance of order with whatever equipment lived in the garage and transform it into some kind of liveable state. Tomorrow, he thought quickly, and traipsed back through the swirling and untamed sea, back into the house that was now his.

Following the murmur of voices from inside, he tracked them to the stairs where his wife was in discussion with the darkness of the cupboard beneath. As he approached, she paused mid-sentence and turned to him.

"Guess what?" she said. "The electrician's here."

Jack gazed into the dark depths of the cupboard beneath the stairs. A head appeared, followed by a pair of blue overalls.

"Sorry I'm so late," he apologised, "but we've been backed up in these parts for weeks with call-outs and I just couldn't find the place this morning."

"Well at least you're here now," Jack conceded.

"I only need to reconnect a few things anyway and then you'll be back in business," he said, disappearing back into the gloom.

Jack stood beside Susie as they watched the darkness and listened to the clamour of his tools and instruments emanating from inside. After a couple of minutes the noises ceased and his head came into view once again.

"You now have power," he declared cheerily.

Sorting his instruments back into his company-supplied case, he declined the Darwin's offer of morning tea, part due to his workload, and part due to the numerous cups of tea that were already swirling through his system from his earlier jobs that day, so after the banter of thank you's and appreciation's they closed the door on him and went in search of something to initiate their electrical account with.

After another day of cleaning and foraging, the new occupants decided that another early night was in order, and so a little after nine o'clock they turned out the downstairs lights and retired to the master bedroom. The candle in the bottle had lost its vocation after only one night and had been replaced by a modern white table lamp, its glow bright and constant and its illumination of the chamber both warm and comforting, yet the bottle remained next to its counterpart, its presence stronger by sheer aesthetic simplicity. Jack watched his wife slip from her clothes once more, as he slipped from his, yet as attractive as she was, and as erotic as she had seemed the night before, she did not look quite so alluring or so inviting under this blanket of electric light. Climbing beneath the covers first, he watched her walk round the corner of the bed before pulling aside the covers and climbing in also. The light seemed indifferent to her femininity and did not search to find her secrets, nor try to tempt its fingertips around either breast or buttock. Neither did it revel in the wonder of her sex nor dance between her legs. It appeared content to illuminate her figure and to cast her shadow against the wall behind her, leaving him to conjure his own desires.

As Susie pulled the covers up over her body Jack reached out a hand to her chest, his fingers light upon her warm soft skin, and she turned her head to his and smiled at him. As they came together in embrace, their lips connecting in a lingering passion, their fingers set forth on a quest from their mind's persuasion and travelled the contours of each other's bodies. Jack was soon hard once again inside Susie's grasp and she caressed him tenderly as he traversed the heat between her legs with his broad fingers. He urged her closer to him, inviting her to cross the boundary between them and climb astride him. With her knees at his sides she slowly lowered herself over him, guiding the head of his cock with one hand to nestle amongst the damp folds of her most private of flesh. Slowly he lifted his hips, his penis entering her with agonising delirium, and as one they came down together. She started to writhe atop him, urging herself over him, his hands drawn to her firm breasts now, squeezing and rolling the full flesh like clay with ever-increasing fervour. Her head began to sway from side to side and loll forwards and back as her eyelids became heavy with the sensation that was coursing through the depths of her body. Together they surged, their love for each other transporting themselves to familiar provinces of ecstasy, their hands grasping flesh, knuckles white from spasms deep within, their muscles taut, as their blood coursed red with the heat of their convulsing loins. With eruption imminent and the desire to sustain such passions utmost in their bodies, Susie drew back her knees and lay her legs down beside his, and as they rolled over together, his hips pushed hard against her to maintain contact, she wrapped her legs up around his waist with such strength in her thighs as to urge him on to pound deeper inside her. His mouth was once more at hers, their tongues fighting in glorious combat over the territory in a swirling desperate rampage of passion and saliva. Their breaths grew heavy once again as their lungs succumbed to the potent beats of their hearts as they writhed together in the pools of sweat between them, struggling for traction as they slid against each others saturated flesh. Susie's eyes had been clamped throughout but they now flickered open to catch sight of her husband's beautiful sweat-soaked face. As she ran her hand through his wet tangled hair, her fingers tugging at the mane of her beast, she noticed a dark patch of irregular form on the far wall beyond her husband, too still to be a shadow cast by them, too fluid to be a shadow grown by furniture. She lay still and wide-eyed as she stared hard at the alien shadow, her husband still writhing and pounding atop her and caught up in his own delirium to realise her sudden passivity, and studied its structure. Although it appeared mainly human in proportion, its head sprouted two prongs and was slightly more angular. Its torso was muscular and yet it seemed unlikely that the human skeleton could support such extremes of sinew, its chest large while its waist hung sleek and restrained. Its limbs, though too sporting a distinctive array of muscle and sinew, looked somehow twisted and contorted and surely unable to function properly. And yet as disfigured and as weird as this figure appeared to be, it drifted and rippled across the surface of the wall in as fluid a motion as a tide across a pebbled beach.

Jack stopped suddenly and stared at her, now aware that her mind was elsewhere. She was lying perfectly still beneath him and gazing straight past his shoulder, her hand gripping his hair so tightly that it strained hard at the roots. His hand went to hers to relinquish the painful grip.

"What's wrong?" he wanted to know, his harried breathing staggering his speech, while the sweat from his brow ran in rivulets down his face, the droplets converging at his lip and running onto his tongue.

Susie did not reply.

She stared straight past him, her grip on his head still absolute.

"Susie..," he pleaded, his hand trying desperately to free his mind from the agonising pain she was inflicting upon him.

"On the wall..." she whispered, her hand tugging at his head to direct his attention.

"What?" he asked her.

"That shadow," she said, her voice still hushed and anguished.

Jack looked at the shadows cast on the wall. With the table lamp beside them, its glow cast several dark forms upon the white wall. There was the silhouette of himself and his wife, and those of the cupboards and wardrobes...

"What?" he asked her again, getting a little impatient.

Susie's hand lifted from his scalp and pointed towards a twisted dark mass in the corner of the room.

"There," she said, her voice almost inaudible in the deafening silence of the room.

As she spoke, however, the shadow seemed to ripple with new agitation. Now it had been spotted by them both and its camouflage been made redundant, it shifted from its place as though it were pondering what to do next. The two lovers stared in silence and without movement as the shadow flowed back across the surface of the wall like a gentle tide. Now its shape began to grow clearer, its irregular edges swelling to form distinct features. Its arms sprouted further sinew and pointed digits sprang from its palms. Its swollen torso ebbed against the plaster and then flowed on through its stomach to its hips that rolled beneath. Now it started to seep up the wall towards the ceiling, the dark shadow swirling like a brook as effortlessly it climbed higher. Drifting over the plane of the ceiling it rippled until it came to rest like a pool directly above them. Jack and Susie were without movement or heartbeat as they stared agog up at the purling mass above them. And then its form began to contort once again, only this time not to discern its borders, rather to discern its properties.

The blank characterless shadow started to create both its features and its anatomy, and as they stared harder, they began to make out differences in its darkness, only subtle at first, but growing more vivid as it reconfigured itself. Eyes grew in dark sockets beneath a black brow, grey teeth started to glisten between darker lips, and the prongs at its forehead grew sharper and stronger until there could be no doubt that they were in fact horns. The figure continued to create itself until its solid form hung unsuspended over the two of them, who stared helplessly up at the beast above them.

Covering its valleys of sinew stretched a hide of dark skin. Its forearms and legs were coated in the same coarse black hair as that that flowed like a long mane from its head, and between its legs hung not one but two members, each approximately a foot in length, with a line of tiny barbs running along the top of each. Protruding from its forehead stood two dark horns, their points long and sharp, and below these, nestled by blackened pits, lay two eyes, their tiny black pupils piercing the skulls of the two bodies beneath with a gaze of pure cold evil. And then, just as it spread wide its limbs in an encompassing embrace, it gave way to the forces of gravity and dropped downward like a rock.

Jack struggled helplessly under the insurmountable and sudden weight of the beast, while Susie struggled under them both. His back was still to the shadow demon yet the covers of the bed still separated their naked bodies. The two humans writhed in panic but the sheer strength of the beast held them fast, one of its hands pinning them down, the other tearing at the sheets, ripping the fibres to shreds with its claws in its efforts to be at them. Soon the sight of Jack's bare buttocks became visible through the scraps of cloth that remained, and as the beast shifted its weight above them, Jack turned his head only to see its grotesque features as it forced itself down upon him.

Jack cried out in pain as one of its barbed erections nudged at his anus before being thrust into the restrictive hole. The beast took hold of Jack's shoulders, throwing its own back, as it ground its hips down against the soft fleshy buttocks. In and out stormed the ravaging weapon, now hardened to twice its size inside him, the spines along its length tearing at the tender walls of meat. Jack's screams and cries of agony were deafening in his wife's ears as he was torn apart, as she herself encountered the assault from beneath, the bludgeoning weight of both beginning to crush her frame.

Jack had no sensation other than that of his desecrated rectum. The onslaught of the monstrous erection inside him had battered his muscle tissue greatly while the tiny barbs had ripped fissures amongst them, opening them up so that torrents of hot red blood poured from his anus with every thrust of the beast's pelvis, to run down his legs and down over his wife's, coating them all and saturating the sheets of the bed with a deep scarlet blanket.

The thrusts of the beast grew stronger and harder and more urgent. Its head pounded the air violently, sending its black mane coursing like a rabid tornado. And then, just as Jack felt his mind begin to crack and surrender, the pelvis behind him pounded with a colossal weight and a sharp deluge of acrid semen stung him hard, its evil fluid like acid as it burned into every internal wound and fissure, penetrating his innermost organs and intestines with a furious fire. The beast withdrew swiftly and then sat back in the pools of rich blood, its penis still vertical and glistening with the fused spatter of scarlet and white. It reached out a hand and took hold of Jack by a fistful of his matted hair, and dragging him up and away from the woman beneath, hurled him effortlessly from the bed. Jack's wretched frame landed untidily on the floor, his arms twisted under him and his legs buckled as more and more of his blood continued to pour from the gaping wound behind. It was then that the beast moved forward over Susie's petrified figure, and she found herself reaching up with her arms to pathetically push the demon from her. It was no defence against such a thing, and she watched helplessly as its head bent down towards her sex, its tongue long and pointed, its rasping texture exciting her sensations even though her will fought to revulse them. The hot tongue probed deeper, and deeper, and deeper, until its whole mouth was clamped hard around her vagina, the creature's razored teeth piercing her to the bone while its tongue continued to explore her most private cavity further as it thrashed inside against the folds of her sweet soft flesh.

After what seemed like an hour of monstrous violation, the demon withdrew, its pointed tongue running an abrasive line back along the inside, its sexual potency requiting such sickened delirium from the woman beneath that her hips involuntarily moved towards its contact. The beast moved up over her body, its hot tongue tracing interlacing lines across her taut pale skin, up over her stomach, around her navel, across her breasts, savouring her dark hard nipples, circling her neck, exploring an ear and sucking hard upon its sweet lobe, then round and across her light cheek and jawline, before finding her inviting mouth, his tongue for once in competition with hers as she fought him hard with her own primordial fits of desire. Its hips bore down upon her's with such ferocity that a tear of pain seeped from one of her eyes as the beast entered her more fully than she could have thought possible. With one barbed penis speared violently into her vagina and the other pierced hard into her anus, and with hard urgent bursts, it thrust its twin erect members deep inside her so fully and so absolutely that her mind knew not how to deal with such an influx of sinful pleasure and desperate injury. Harder and harder, faster and faster, they pounded together as one convulsing unnatural animal, Susie's body urging on the rampaging beast even though it was being torn apart under the hideous assault. Blood poured from both entries but her body could not halt itself. Constantly ripped to shredded flesh like that of her husbands earlier, but at such heights of primitive ecstasy and passion, every thought was redundant and every desire was surpassed. Her mind began to blacken as her body suffered terminal fissures deep inside, and as the demon burst harder with its final destructive thrust, her mind aborted altogether as the burning floods of vile semen exploded from the demon's twin members, coursing through every tear and laceration that they had inflicted.

Slowly the beast withdrew from the still shuddering figure beneath it, its brow dripping evil droplets of sweat from such lethal activity. Strangely, it ran a tender hand across her face and through her sweat-soaked hair.

"Sweet child," it whispered, its voice dark and rasping, as it kissed her softly at the gaping wounds between her legs, so that trickles of her life-blood flowed over and between its lips and glistened as it ran down his throat. "I found such perfect pleasure in this house over four weeks ago, but I have had to wait until tonight to taste such pleasures again. She was not as supple or as responsive as you, my love. Her flesh was much older. But you, you are something else. I will remember you for a long time, my sweet. I will think of you until the next one arrives. Our passion will comfort me."

It was then that the black beast climbed from the scarlet bed and stood to view the carnage of the room. Two figures lay crippled, their blood coursing from gashes inflicted by a brutal assault of intense primitive and bestial proportions. As it walked away from the ill-lit chamber, so its form changed once again as its flesh recreated itself and grew darker, and its limbs realigned themselves once more, until it no longer trod the boards of the room but swept across them like a black aqueous tide, seeping beneath the door before flowing down and across the stairs. And then as it washed down through a crack in the third step, the demon disappeared and was gone, and the shadows of the house settled, and the building was at peace once again.

The car was filled with excited chatter as the girls offered vivid accounts of past glories and failures with their nocturnal partners - with one exception. Catherine had sat in silence - her arms folded and her gaze directed at the world that rushed past outside - for the majority of the journey. It was the eve of her friend Julie's wedding and she was at the epicentre of the story telling. Catherine had known her since secondary school some twelve years previous and they had been friends ever since; not the best of friends, but friends nevertheless. Julie's closest companion and confident, who also happened to be sitting beside her and throwing most of her voice into the proceedings, was a short tubby woman of unrivalled ill repute. She had many a tale, at any given moment, to tell of adventures with incredulously endowed men, legends of stupendous feats of athleticism and stamina performed in beds and on floors, in car parks and in all manner of cars, in fields and in woods. The list seemed to be as endless as her imagination. Her reputation preceded her of course, and attracted many a wanton man to her side, all of whom guided by the guaranteed satisfaction of a no-strings one night stand. She received her fair share of abuse from the populous, as one would imagine, especially from the women, but why should she care? After all, she enjoyed it just as much as the men who came to her, and if they were too prudish or too ugly to attract the opposite sex in such a way then they could go fuck themselves in her opinion - literally. Julie enjoyed the relationship she had with her best friend Di. It gave her the opportunity to go to pubs and parties safe in the knowledge that any undesirable men just looking for sex would be picked off by her. It was a great play for both of them at first, Julie drawing the attentions of the men by her looks and Di's uncanny knack for sleeping with anyone, to comb through the low-lifes. In fact, that's how Julie had met her husband-to-be. He and his friend had gone to the same club, their eyes had met though they were both too shy to actually go over and talk to one another, but their respective friends had instigated a meeting by the luck that they were both as interested in one-nighters as each other. They had continued to court each other for the next year and a half until he had finally proposed to her, and it was then that she had eagerly accepted.

Mandy, who was sat next to her sister Chrissie at the wheel of the car, turned round to point out to the three behind that their destination lay at the end of the road, a fact blatantly ridiculous considering how often they frequented the place of a weekend, but it was sanctioned because of the excited fervour of Julie's final night as a single woman. As the car's headlights illuminated the night-club's sign against the black of the night, a cheer rose up from the throats of the would-be merrymakers. Di poked Catherine in the ribs, drawing her attention sharply from the window.

"Cheer up, misery guts," she said. "We're supposed to be celebrating with Julie."

Catherine did not like Di. She shared the opinion of many and thought that she was a cheap slut. If they had not both been Julie's friends she could have quite easily pushed her from the car as a truck rushed by. She did not reply to Di's comment but gave her a less than friendly stare, and then looked past her to Julie who gave her a tiny smile. Julie knew that Catherine was to have been married some six months ago but she had called it off the day before when she had discovered that her fiancé had slept around quite considerably behind her back. As part of her cancellation announcement she had driven to his house and inserted house bricks through as many windows as she had bricks, before dousing his car in paraffin and putting a match to it. Her antics had been witnessed by many bemused neighbours and had even caught the attention of the local paper, but after she had been arrested all charges against her had been dropped, after her fiancé saw the error of his ways when her two older brothers had dropped round for coffee. Needless to say she still had a passion to hate men, but she had promised Julie, as well as herself, that she would behave herself and control her anger as best she could, and try to participate in her wedding-to-be celebrations.

As Chrissie drove into the club's car park and located one of the few remaining spaces, Di spotted a handful of young men entering the building and proceeded to inform the rest of the car's occupants of her aspirations to know the flesh of their bodies under close scrutiny. This brought forth the intended reaction of the night, and cries and whoops filled the car from all but the window-watcher who seethed with heightened hatred of the slut beside her.

Once inside, the small group methodically scanned the profusion of patrons that the club had to offer; some were thrashing wildly on the light-toxic dance floor like bees round their chosen queen, some sat huddled at the few tables that hid in its darkened corners, while the remainder filled the halls and floors in various stages of undress and alcoholic incompetence, staring around at each other in the hope of an easy lay. Di was first to the bar, pushing past a number of hopefuls to lean over the counter, thrusting her cleavage forward, as well as a twenty pound note, in order to gain the attention of one of the male bar staff. Ordering two of everything to save time and to get the evening started as she meant it to go on, she offered the twin cocktails to Catherine, who accepted the first but declined the second, informing her that she had no intention of befriending any man through some drunken stupor. Di told her that she intended to and drained it herself.

Throughout the night, the small party of women became more drunk and more receptive to the advances of any of the surrounding males, with the exception of Catherine, who watched quietly as they swayed and giggled and acted coyly in and out of the arms of various men for the duration of the club's opening hours, where said men invited them to dance or to view their new cars that were parked just outside. Julie tried her hardest to resist such attention, Catherine could see that, but with such potent alcohol in her stomach and Di's encouragement in her ear, she soon found a tongue down her throat and a hand on her breast.

Catherine had attempted to prize the ill-matched couple apart but they had both grown fond of each other through the pursuit of flesh groping and saliva exchange that they just pushed her aside, so once again she sat back from the evening's entertainment and just let them get on with it. As she sat at the bar, her interest flitting between the jaunts of her friends and the vertical flights of the tiny bubbles in her glass, she noticed little of the other people in the club despite the intense noise of amplified sound coupled with the competition of two hundred raised voices. But her gaze inevitably wandered towards the dance floor, just for the briefest of seconds, and as she did so her eye was caught by a face that was captured and stilled in the glare of a bright strobe light.

It was there in just one of the breaches between the flashes of white. He was there, and then he was gone, but his face had stared at her with such focused intensity, and with such adored passion, that her heart had faltered with the following wash of light. Her sight returned immediately to her glass as her heart pounded, where she studied the rich burgundy of the liquor and the crystal purity of the shards of ice to try and steady the throngs in her chest. She struggled to control her fevered breathlessness, angry at herself for succumbing in such a way to the simple sight of a man, but when she could resist no longer and she looked once again to the dance floor where the strobe still governed, the face was no longer there amongst the mass of monochrome statues. The man had gone.

Her heart faltered again though she knew not why. What had she felt, she wanted to know? She had hated all men since her fiancé's secret romances had come to light, yet she had reacted to this unforeseen stranger with an emotion that she could not consciously comprehend. Hadn't she? She wasn't sure now. It certainly wasn't love at first sight, that much she was sure of. But neither was it revulsion, nor the desire to spill his blood. She was certain that she would never find out. In a place of this size, where a population of hundreds swarmed beneath a sky of flashing bulbs, how could she find the man whose face she had snatched so briefly?

As her face drifted over the horizon of shimmering faces, her gaze came to rest on a familiar figure; a figure stumbling through the crowd with a man on either arm. It was Di. And she had acquired two of the locals and was heading towards the exit with them both. One had his hand at her buttocks, rubbing its lycra-clad cheeks generously with excited drunken fervour, while the other had a hand at her sex, groping with equal vigour. Catherine found herself mouthing the word 'slut' at her before she withdrew her gaze and returned it to her drink.

As the night drew on, and the crowds of the club waned and dispersed as couples were formed and friendships were acquainted, Catherine rose from her seat and went to join her friends at the eve of their merriment. Chrissie was exchanging small scraps of paper with a tall dark-haired lad before they kissed and were separated. Mandy was lingering behind them waiting to be informed of all the details. And Julie was in the process of untangling herself from the tongue and grope beast. Catherine stood quietly as they said their goodbyes and then they stumbled as one towards the door.

Pushing through the crowd of bustling youths who had congregated at the exit, a figure suddenly emerged from the throng and caught Catherine's eye before he became swallowed up once more by the enveloping mass of bodies. She had forgotten the man held captured in the glare of the strobe, and she had not been prepared for this second sight. As her head turned and her eyes fell upon his features, her heart had faltered once again, her breath stricken in her throat and detaining all advances of speech, not as though anything had come to mind anyway. But he was gone again before the moment had ticked its completion, and she stopped and spun around to look for him, but he was simply nowhere in sight.

"You can drive," Catherine was suddenly instructed, as Chrissie attempted to locate the keys in her small bag. "You're the only one who's sober," and she giggled helplessly as she fell hysterical against the side of the car.

Julie toppled against the car beside her, clutching her head as dizziness overwhelmed her suddenly. Mandy tried her best to guide her to one of the doors, but she had problems finding one herself. Catherine took up the challenge of finding the elusive keys, and reached her hand into Chrissie's bag, and shortly withdrew them from the sparse collection of objects within. She unlocked one of the doors and they all piled in together, accompanied by bouts of drunken laughter and whoops of nonsense. She ignored the boisterous passengers as best she could and started the car. As she reversed out of the space and made to drive away, a face flashed in the side mirror of the car and her foot stomped on the brake. The mass of swaying limbs and bobbing heads lurched forward before further bouts of whoops and laughter were released. She spun round in her seat to locate the figure behind her but once again the man had gone.

Pulling out of the car park and back onto the main road, her mind became obsessed with the elusive stranger, even as her memory struggled to recall the briefest of glances of him. Who was he, she wanted to know? And why had he instigated such a reaction from her? His presence, however brief, had been enough to stir unheard of emotions deep inside her, emotions she wasn't even sure she had, or even knew existed. But he had nevertheless touched something deep within her, something she had never felt before.

It wasn't just sexual, that much she was certain of, yet the primeval fibres of her desires seemed almost to twitch in anticipation of something that she just couldn't name.

Detective Morgan was a troubled man to say the least. He had been there when the first killing had taken place, a vile perverted killing where no motive, no comprehension, and not even a hint of a suspect, had been left behind to cleanse the pools of blood of its dark depraved mystery. He remembered vividly how he had been one of the first to witness the aftermath, and he felt sick once again as the visions returned to his skull. He had crossed the threshold of the bedroom with a crisp notepad in one hand and a new fountain pen in the other, but as his sight fell upon the naked figure left butchered in the centre of the room, these two items had slipped swiftly from his fingers, and skipped in circles across the filthy scarlet soup at his feet.

He had gazed hard at the deathly scene, no hint of breath at his parted lips as his jaw had dropped open. Sprawled awkwardly on the ravaged and torn bed stretched the figure of possibly a woman. She lay face down, her arms outstretched in front of her and strapped to the metal bars of the headboard, her buttocks high in the air and held aloft by the rigor mortis that had seized her limbs. Her flesh, where untouched, was coated in the rich deep blood that had literally poured from the flesh that was torn. Her thighs were heavily lacerated, as too was her upper back, as if a maniac with a razor had mercilessly and ferociously slashed at her in a fit of frenzy. Her face was pressed into the pillow, and on slightly closer investigation, showed that it too bore its own array of gashes as the muscles in her cheeks had been torn away to reveal the bloodied whiteness of her teeth. Her greying hair had been ripped from her skull in places and lay in clumps about the pillow and on the floor below. And last, and most disturbing and prominent of all, was her backside, raised up to full view.

Her vagina and her arse, torn and shredded as if the very skin outside had been hacked away by a saw blade before the soft flesh inside had been pulled out after it. The outflow of her blood had saturated not only her buttocks and legs and the majority of the mattress, but had been thrown and smeared across the floor and walls as well. The bloody murder had been committed maybe a week before it had been discovered and the acrid stench had still filled the room. It was as potent in his nostrils then as it was now, as he found himself staring at the memory of it for the second time in just over a month.

"Detective Morgan?"

He looked up from the scene to find a young detective in the hospital corridor behind him, as keen and as enthusiastic as he had been once, when he had thought he could change the world and bring justice back into it. He had seen a lot since then, and he had changed. After that day four weeks ago, he had stopped taking the first calls of the day. He had faltered before rushing to the scenes of new cases, and he had lingered around the station and seen to the missing persons or the latest car thefts. Maybe he had attended a burglary now and again, he could barely remember, but not homicide, not after that day, and certainly not in that house. Not until now anyway. When he had no choice.

"The nurse says we can go in now."

"What?"

"We can talk to him. You know, find out just what might have torn him up like that."

"Leave it alone, Hoskin," Morgan said to him, under his breath. "Some things just need to be left alone."

"Are you saying you don't want to find out what fucker did this?"

"Maybe I am," Morgan murmured, closing his eyes, and allowing the horrors back in. "People hurt, and people bleed. This isn't a game, and sometimes the poor bastards escape death and live."

Morgan jabbed out his cigarette and then stepped out of the waiting room in a plume of blue smoke. He found a nurse in the corridor and stopped her to ask after the patient's condition.

"He's about as stable as you could expect, after what he's been through. We've filled him full of painkillers to lessen the torment but he's still got to be hurting like hell, even in sleep."

"What was he like inside? Just as torn up?"

"The surgeons who stitched him back together were glad to be finished and be out of there. None of them had seen anything like it before, and they all hope that they never will again, myself included."

Morgan thanked her for her opinion and then left her to speak to the patient himself. As he slowly pushed open the door and stepped into the private room, Hoskin now in tow behind him, his eyes fell awkwardly onto the figure lying in the bed, motionless except for the harried rise and fall of his chest beneath the covers. He had honestly expected to see him straining in agony and anguish like the bloodied wretch a month ago, yet here lay a face that spoke of

411

no such horrors. The human consciousness could hide a great deal when it wanted to.

As he stood over him, he noticed that his eyes flickered beneath their lids, and his forehead wrinkled occasionally as though there were still terrors that tore at him inside his head. Morgan plucked the clipboard from the foot of the bed and read its profusion of information, none of which made any sense to him. He replaced it and then stepped round to the patient's side, perching on the only seat provided, and leaving Hoskin to stand.

"Jack?" he said to the man, laying a hand upon his shoulder to stir him. "Jack Darwin?"

The man's eyes flickered open and pierced Morgan's gaze for the briefest of moments, before the drugs in his bloodstream took control and half-lidded them, leaving behind a barely responsive being to look through them.

"Jack Darwin? Can you hear me?"

A faint sound emanated from the back of his throat, coupled with the smallest of nods from his head.

"Yes. I can... hear you," the breath that carried his words barely able to break the seal of his dry lips.

"My name is Detective Morgan. I need to ask you a few questions."

The pitiful shape of the man swallowed uncomfortably as he stared up at him, his eyes glazing one moment and then focussing sharply the next.

"Who did this to you?" Morgan asked him.

"I have seen Hell," the man said slowly, his words measured. "I have seen Hell and the demons that live there."

"Who did this to you?" Morgan asked again.

"It could have taken me. It should have taken me. But why am I still here?"

"Jack, listen to me," said Morgan, trying to calm him. "What happened to you? Who did this?"

"The demon. The demon of the shadows. The demon from Hell..."

"Tell me who did this," Morgan insisted. "Just tell me who did this to you and your wife, and I'll go and get him."

"My... wife?"

Morgan stopped suddenly, only realising now just what he had said. It was obvious that Jack Darwin had not been told about the terrible death of his wife.

"Susie?" the man whispered, his eyes searching the face of Morgan for an answer.

Morgan could only offer a shallow nod, and then watch with regret as the man's eyes flickered closed and then clenched, as the breath that had barely conveyed his words went from his body altogether. His teeth ground hard against themselves, his head began to roll from side to side as though in the midst of a horrid fit, and all Morgan could do was watch as whatever terrors this man had seen revisited him yet again.

Morgan himself had seen the re-enactment of the most evil and brutal murder that he had ever seen, that defied any explanation, and yet this time it offered twice the carnage, as well as a survivor to confirm that this was not just another brutal assault, but an act of depraved carnality of truly hellish proportions.


It had been a few days since the girls' night out and the stranger in Catherine's thoughts had faded almost entirely. She had long forgotten the emotion she had felt that night, although she had kind of enjoyed it inside her and had fought to keep its potency alive, but now she could not even conjure the remotest of images that bore any true resemblance to his face. Even as she wandered through the endless shops in town, musing at the many fine fabrics of the finer clothes she knew she could not afford, the memories of him remained elusive to all her efforts to recall him. She couldn't believe that she had even been affected, perhaps afflicted, by the mere presence of a man, and she still felt angry at herself for reacting in such a way as she had.

She passed through the busy precinct, past shops displaying their bright assortment of glittering goods that carried with them guarantees of unrivalled pleasures and fulfilled contentment. Her ex-fiancé had given her such promises also, as he had done, no doubt, to numerous other women throughout his reign of ejaculations, but she had found the flaw in such a contract, albeit far too late, and was subsequently more than aware of similar lies. But it was as she stepped through the doorway of a busy electrical store that she suddenly ran cold, stopping at the threshold, so that the couple trailing behind walked into her and nudged her aside with a brusque comment. She stared hard into the shop, her eyes placing every customer as they grazed slowly on the fodder of televisions and refrigerators. Every muscle and every sinew became taut in her body, as the realisation dawned on her. He was here.

She took a few steps across the deep blue carpet and headed further into the shop, padding cautiously between two pensioners and their television display, who tutted their disapproval at her impudence, her eyes busy on the crowded aisles. And there, at the back of the store by a rack of video recorders swept an agile figure, his torso camouflaged against the swathes of floating shoppers. Catherine's pace quickened as she hurried past customers and appliances, frequently bumping into both, as her eyes strained to stay with the elusive figure. She lost him momentarily as he disappeared behind a stand of cookers, but caught him again in another aisle, only to lose him once more by the crowded cashier area. By now she was running as best she could against the tide, and jostling past those who blocked her path as they checked out the relevant finance details of the hire purchase agreements that were available, she cursed them all for their financial inability.

Catherine reached the tills and shoved her way through the queue, receiving a crescendo of stifled complaints for her actions, and stood where she expected him to be. But the area beheld a mystery of its own. It was the only area of the shop devoid of any people.

Her heart sank as she turned away from the shelves of kettles and pop-up toasters, and looked back to the scowling faces of the queue. Sloping across to the other side of the store to avoid their wrath she went to make her way out, but as she neared the exit the face of the stranger swept across the screen of one of the televisions by her side. It lingered but a moment, just long enough to catch her attention and hold a chill to her skin. Catherine spun around to look for its originator but she was alone in the aisle. And with panic beginning to set in she ran from the shop, out into the hallways of the precinct, and away.

Her quickened heartbeat remained with her even in the car, and she broke all the speed limits as she headed to Mandy's house, some quarter of an hour's trek from the town centre. With all the windows wound down, the rush of cool air helped to at least clear some of the knots inside her head, but those same images of the stranger's face were burned into her imagination once again, and she could do little to dispel them. Distractions was what she needed, and Mandy was closest, the drive taking her past the outskirts of town where the houses and main roads conceded their purpose and gave way to trees and fields and narrow winding lanes.

Catherine had loved Mandy's idyllic house ever since she had first moved in nearly a year ago, and the whole world seemed to share her view, the bright summer sunlight flashing through the canopies of leaves that stretched overhead. As she drove along the hedgerow-lined lanes, fields of green to either side, her mood lifted into a kind of balmy calm and by the time she reached her destination and had crunched into Mandy's driveway, she had almost forgotten her former panic and her need for distracting conversation. The afternoon passed pleasantly enough, Catherine resisting the urge to tell her about the mysterious stranger who had haunted her since Julie's night out, and Mandy fulfilling her urge to show off the new patio that she had just had laid. They lost all track of time throughout the afternoon and were surprised when Mandy's live-in boyfriend returned home at a little after six thirty, curious as to the distinct lack of aroma from the evening meal. Mandy had repented furiously as she batted her eyelids at him, and he had replied by saying that as Cathy was there, and it was a warm evening, that after he had showered and changed, he should light the barbecue and incinerate a fridgeful of meat for them. Mandy vehemently agreed, whispering out of earshot that as long as she didn't have to cook she'd be happy.

"Watch those new slabs outside," she said to him. "I don't want any charcoal or fat all over them."

"Yes, dear," he replied playfully, even as a lump of charcoal slipped from the bag he was carrying and scuttled across the crisp stones, leaving a fragmented black trail in its wake. He was instantly reprimanded for his crime as Mandy threw a cold sausage at him.

By eleven forty Catherine stood up and announced that it was time she left. Between them they had consumed the best part of three bottles of wine, and Mandy told her that she was indeed welcome to stay the night, partly to save her a trip home in the dark and partly to give them a hand with the washing up. Catherine declined the offer with a smile, and after walking her to the door, waved her off into the night. The former balm and tranquillity of the country roads had dissolved while she had been in the company of her friends. The once welcoming arms of the warm sunshine and comforting veldt had been folded away, the beauty of the trees and the hedgerows replaced with the deadly still and solitude of the cold dark wilderness. Every turn of the road ahead rolled into a stretch of stark barren lane, setting her heart into new rhythms of nervous palpitation. As she pulled up at a small junction, the pale ghost of an owl flashed across the flood of her headlights as it announced its territory. Her foot faltered at the clutch. The car lurched forward. And the life of the cold engine died.

She had physically jumped in her seat, subconsciously smacking down the lock on the door, before trying the key in the ignition again. Her sudden desperation forced tremors into her fingers, and at first the engine would have none of it. It coughed at her and mocked her efforts. It wheezed and groaned. But after a number of frantic attempts it conceded and spluttered begrudgingly to life. Catherine praised all the gods she could think of and headed off up the road at speed.

A few corners further on and the engine coughed at her again, and stalled, illuminating so many red lights on the instrument panel in front of her that she caught her own scarlet reflection on the windscreen in front of her. This time there would be no such concessions. Again and again she turned the key in its mechanism, promising deals under her breath of washes, waxes and full valets if only it would start. But it was dead to the world.

Eventually she slumped back in her seat, her body shivering from cold and panic, and looked fearfully around her. The only light she could see came from her own dim headlights and that of the bright crisp moon in the blackened sky overhead. The thought of walking for help whispered at the edge of her mind though she fought hard not to even consider it. She had driven for less than a few minutes from Mandy's house and would probably take her no more than ten to walk back, and probably only twice that to walk ahead into the first reaches of town. She knew she couldn't stay in the car for another six hours or more until dawn inched onto the horizon and she was angry at herself for even being afraid of the dark at her age. Yet afraid she was, petrified in fact, and she cursed her fear constantly, even as she reached for the lock of the door and clicked it open, as it peppered her imagination with images of stalkers and monsters and whatever else might be lurking in the night.

The unfeeling enormity of the openness seemed far vaster than it had been from inside the car, but she knew that she had to go back to Mandy's house, so once she had locked the car door, she turned her back on it and unwittingly stepped away. Her only guide to the road ahead was the bare illumination of the pale white moon above, and it cast its pale embrace across the tarmac and the hedgerows, adding to her trek the cool tones of its touch, devoid of any warming or comforting colour. Catherine turned the first bend of the lane and looked back from its apex to see that her car had disappeared from sight altogether. She knew she was alone now, with nothing familiar to comfort her, and it was only then that her worst fears began to come to life, as one by one the nocturnal creatures began to crackle and crawl in the undergrowth about her. Leaves rustled and grass twitched, branches snapped, roots creaked. She quickened her pace slightly, her feet suddenly more purposeful. her heart hammering faster as it thudded a harder rhythm against her chest. The sky looming above her seemed to amplify her fears as the creatures of the air sought out meals of moths and flies; the flutter of a bat as it flickered overhead in endless cycles of sonar exploration, the swooping navigation of a huge dark owl, strange contorted shaes silhouetted against the still silver heavens.

Catherine turned to look behind her once again, and her panic heightened as she thought she saw a figure moving in the tangle of the hedgerows. She looked harder as her heart frantically pounded at her ribs and in her throat, as though it should escape and seek some saner refuge. And though the road was dimly lit, she was certain that she saw a crooked shadow wash across the monochrome tarmac from one side of the road to the other, yet she could discern nothing that could have created such a shadow. It disappeared from the road then, escaping into the hedge and then from her sight completely.

Then her heart began to affect her lungs, her breaths coming heavy now, stricken in her throat. There was a crackle of a snapping branch, followed by the rush of a curtain of grasses as they were swept aside, and as she took to her heels in terror, a huge black mass stormed through a gap in the hedgerow to swallow the road behind her.

It shifted and changed as it raged, the shadow that washed across the tarmac, bubbling and thrashing like the tide of some vast foaming sea, transforming with every inch of solid ground it covered, its tempestuous waves turning to limbs and then to razored claws, the head of the tumult converging to a point where teeth erupted from the surf into lethal fangs, the body of the wash contorting upon itself until a sleek spine and slender torso assimilated solidity from the chaos of the hellish blackness.

Catherine hammered hard across the surface of the road, the wash of the pale white moon above her useless as tears streamed from her eyes to blind her vision. Her cries for help competed with the need for oxygen in her restricting throat, and her mind began to pump with tides as black as those at her heels as the blood in her brain grew thick, filling her head to saturation with its sickly potency. Step by step, yard by yard, the demon of the shadows gained upon her, its teeth just inches from her tender flesh. But through the black totality of the deathly-still night, the road ahead suddenly became filled by the violent glare of white light, the approaching car hurtling towards them at speed.

Catherine's arms flew to her face as she fell sideways into the hedge to avoid the impact, resolved to the inevitable needle-teeth that would be upon her. Yet as she hit the hard earth of the bank and felt the barbs of the hedge tear at her clothes and skin, she just caught a flash of the car as it rushed past. Did she even hear the thud and crack of bone against metal, as the vehicle careered into the beast? She wasn't sure. Her eyes fell to the scene behind her. The car had skidded to a halt, and there, caught in the glare of its headlights, she could see the beast's crippled frame, its dark fluid shadow ebbing rapidly back into the side of the hedge.

Her head became heavy and dull as she heard the door to the car open and its driver clamber out to race to her aid. As the welcome footsteps padded closer, so her vision became clouded. She felt the figure go down on one knee, taking her head in his hand, lifting her face towards his, and she saw him then for just a moment. It was the mysterious stranger from the night club, the mysterious stranger from the electrical store, the man who had rallied her emotions to peaks she could not control, the man who was her saviour. Her eyes tried desperately to fix on his, her lips parting to expel words, but her throat tightened and her mind blackened, and her consciousness let him slip from her clutches once again.


A reluctant breath passed uneasily between Morgan's lips as he stooped under the police restriction tape. Standing at the base of the three steps that led up to the front door, he drew deeply on his cigarette as he stared up at the unimposing facade that held behind its lacklustre bricks such dark and morbid secrets. The faceless windows showed him no hint of repentance from the dark rooms that they fronted, while the long curtains hung from their poles in still silence, both of them witnesses to evil crimes that could never tell their stories. Stepping through the heavy door and into the dim hallway, he found it almost impossible to believe the bloodlust atrocities that had occurred upstairs, for the rest of the house showed no evidence of the acts of brutality or depravity and were as wholesome and as familiar as any home could be. He paused at the foot of the stairs, his hand on the post at the end of the banister, and gazed through into the kitchen. The floor and work surfaces had remained partially cleaned where the new owner had left them until the following day, unaware of the fate that would deprive them of rediscovered cleanliness.

Morgan turned and stepped slowly up the staircase, his mind wandering elsewhere in a ragged terrain of uncertain thought. The third stair creaked beneath his weight, dragging his mind back to the present, and he looked down at the bare boards of the step before going down on his haunches to inspect the groaning timber. The wood that formed the step was ill-fitting and there lay a gap of maybe an inch between it and the top of the step below. Morgan peered hard into the shadows but saw only the darkness inside. Reaching into his inside overcoat pocket he withdrew a pen and played its length into the black void in the hope of perhaps finding a murder weapon or some such clue discarded after the crime, his comprehension of events as lost on him as his efforts at the stairs. But as he probed as far as his fingers would allow in the restricting gap, the pen slipped from his grasp and fell down into the darkness. He cursed his incompetence as well as his luck for it was his only pen. But his distress was short lived for even as these thoughts sparked his irritation, they were soon extinguished when no audible trace of his pen's descent came. It was only the third step and it should have clattered to the floor about two feet below. But there was just no sound at all.

He pressed his face closer to the slim gap and narrowed his eyes against the gloom, attempting to discern any shapes of the staircase's construction, but the blackness was absolute and he could see nothing. He fished into his pocket for means of a further test, and brought forth his cigarette lighter. Holding the cheap disposable between his thumb and fore-finger, he manoeuvred it into the dark space and let go, pinning his ear to the step as he did so.

He listened.

And listened.

And then, as he was about to get to his feet, a distant clatter emanated from somewhere deep below. Something in this house was indeed strange, and it ran a shiver of dread throughout his body and he would have no further part in it alone. His mind screamed at him of ghosts, beasts and hidden dungeons, but he desperately tried to tell his mind that there were no such things as ghosts, or beasts, and that hidden dungeons belonged only in horror films, and not in the working lives of policemen. He backed down the stairs, his eyes wide and unfocussed and flitting between the gap at the third step and the summit of the staircase that led on towards the bedroom. And then as his feet touched the floor of the hallway, he turned his back on the wooden flight for the first time, and ran headlong for the front door before bursting out of the house and into the bright sunshine of the day.

As he reached his car and fumbled in his pockets for the key, his gaze drifted back to the window of the bedroom. His sight settled on the pane of glass, the hang of the curtains twitching slightly in the draftless house, as shadows seemed to realign themselves after the disturbance of the day. He stared for what seemed like hours, as those very shadows watched him flee in terror from them. They seemed to mock him, to laugh at him, for they knew that he could do nothing to harm them.


The mists started to clear a little as she stepped ahead through the tangled forest, her feet occasionally catching amongst the vines and fallen branches that tried to hold her back. Yet she persevered, although she did not know why she was here or even where she was headed, the thinning fog drawing her at last into the clearing.

As she stepped past the last few trees and out into the open space, the dense vapour behind her dissolved entirely taking with it the forest as well. Catherine turned in a flustered panic to catch her bearings but caught only snatches - a playground that bore children fused with toys, their laughter and the games that caused it generating the multi-coloured plastics from their limbs, and teddy bear's heads from their shoulders, yet they minded it not as their excitement grew because of it. Then a dark quiet alleyway, she could see a young girl walking hurriedly along the ill-lit path, one arm clutching her bag to her side in fearful trepidation. As she reached the darkest point beneath the encompassing shadow of an overhanging tree, Catherine witnessed the assault as three men entered the alleyway in front of her from a gate in its length. Beyond that sprung open fields, so vast and so desolate and with no tree or house or city at any horizon, she stood alone amongst the tall swaying grasses as they bowed beneath the kiss of the gentle breeze. And as her head dizzied, the bright lights of an approaching car blinded her with their intensity, and her hands went to shield her face, leaving her once more alone in the darkness.

As her hands fell away, she looked up to see a house. It was a house that she had never seen before, and yet it offered her the comfort of a welcoming home. The windows looked down favourably upon her as their dark interiors ebbed gently upon themselves like warm tides. The door stood open and from it sweet odours of honeysuckle and amber drifted on a balmy current towards her, inviting her away from the tremors and fears outside.

Catherine knew no reason not to enter and soon took her first steps towards the house, its sweet smells ripening as she walked, bringing with them fresh new delights to enchant and entice her. With each subsequent step her nostrils became the pinnacle of her fantasy, as she savoured the richest of delicacies that floated on the palette of the air. Up the steps she went, and on through the front door, her eyes almost closed to accept the full generosity of the breeze. On through the hallway the fragrances carried her, past the open door to the living room, and the half-touched kitchen, until she reached the bottom of a flight of stairs, where her hand explored for the edge of the banister. The stairway was illuminated only by the warm soft glow at the top, and she stepped forward willingly into its embrace.

As her foot touched the first step, however, a chink opened up at the base of the third, allowing a thin shaft of darkness to spill out across the stair. As her foot touched the second, the chink opened up further into a gash, and a wave of darkness washed down over her feet and out into the hall behind her. As her foot touched the third, though, the step disappeared entirely, as well as the rest of the staircase, and the gash became a deep black chasm. She fell headlong then, down into the abyss, her hands clawing at the air for some hopeless respite.

Down and down she fell, faster and faster, the wind raised by her descent raging as she plummeted, wrapping her hair into violent snakes behind her. And as she hurtled down through the darkness, there seemed to be hands and fingers in that darkness that stung her flesh as she fell through them. They tried to hold on to her, it seemed, to claw her back to them, their tentacle-like grip tightening across her skin and restricting her movements. And then, just as suddenly as her descent had started, her body slowly almost immediately to a halt.

The invisible fingers readjusted their hold upon her and tightened. So solid was their grip upon her flesh that she could not even struggle against it and she stood, at least if there had been any ground to stand on, waiting uncertain and afraid in the blackest pitch, waiting until she was finally addressed.

"Catherine..." came a voice ahead of her, a voice

that brought with it hot breath that brushed across her face, a breath that carried with it the spice of incense.

Catherine rolled her eyes in her head and looked hard for the speaker, though she could not be certain whether her eyes were even open or not.

"Catherine..." it said again, and again came the scented breath upon her face.

Catherine thought that perhaps she should answer, yet no words came from her lips, or if they did she did not hear them.

"Why do you live, Catherine?" it asked her, its question lingering in the air before her like dancing dust. "You live because others die. Your world turns because its surface needs equal amounts of hot and cold from the sun."

The voice paused.

"Hot and cold. Right and wrong. Good and evil. Light and dark. One cannot exist without the other. But while one may hold more of an advantage than the other at any one time, it doesn't mean that the other cannot dance in its opponent's dominance."

Catherine remained silent. What could she say to such things?

"You have seen, haven't you, Catherine?" it continued, its tone darkening to that of the air around her and the hold on her flesh. "You've seen us. Glimpses. Snatches. Brief sightings you didn't even know you'd seen. But you knew. And we knew. It's not your fault, it's nobody's fault, but some things just have to be kept unseen..."

There was silence after that, and then the scents of the sweet fragrances blew upon the breeze once more. The fingers that bound her body loosened and slipped away, and she felt herself floating on a sea of nectar

427

and blossom. Her thoughts ebbed with the influence of the tides around her, and she felt herself being rocked into a far deeper slumber, the words of the darkness slowly dissolving in her memory, their meanings with them, as her mind became as black as the warm ocean around her.

She looked up and around at the room she had woken in. The loose covers of the bed she had been laid in were ragged from her distressed sleep and hung from her body in loose folds. To her left she could see the closed door to the room, and from beneath it there penetrated a narrow chink of light that bravely spilled its radiance across the dark floor. At the far wall opposite there was set a large window, its horizontal blinds tilted against the approaching dawn. And skirting the walls stood a number of wardrobes and cabinets as well as a chair on which lay some of her clothes.

Catherine slid silently from beneath the covers and crossed to the chair, pulling on her sweater and jacket, before cautiously approaching the door. As she gripped the handle and eased it open, the wash of light from the other side flooded into the room as if it were eager to absorb her and give away her attempt at escape. She followed its path a short way along the hall to where a door stood ajar, and as she put her head to the gap to see in, a voice came from the other side to beckon her in.

It was a welcoming voice, its tone gentle and peaceful, and yet it managed to carry with it an air of authority and intention. Although she felt a little afraid of her very presence in this strange house the voice comforted her and she was curious to enter. The source of the light, she discovered, came from a number of candles placed about the room, their heights somewhat diminished by perhaps the whole nights employ. The majority, she saw, were crowded upon a table beside the figure who sat in a sumptuous chair, a leather-bound book in one hand, a glass of wine in the other. By his feet stood three bottles; one full, one empty, and one neither full nor empty but obviously working towards the latter.

The pounding started again in Catherine's chest as the figure's features flickered in the light of the bright flames. It was the face of her mysterious saviour, and he spoke to her again as she entered, but his eyes did not lift once from the book in his hand as he did so.

"I think perhaps you should be seated," he said to her, his voice as gentle and serene as the flames that illuminated him. "Would you like a drink?"

Catherine said she was fine and took a seat opposite him, her voice silent as she awaited his.

"There are some things in this world and in others," he began, his eyes still at the pages of his book, "that should be understood. And then there are those that shouldn't. Some things need their secrets. Some things just need to be taken for granted and remain unexplained. Some things are explained and then they lose their..." he paused, as if trying to find the right word, "beauty," he said.

"What are you talking about?" Catherine wanted to know. "Who are you?"

"So many questions," the man replied. "So much trouble."

"What are you on about? What trouble?"

"There you go again," the man said. "More

questions. That's why they want you, Catherine. That's why they want you with them. Down in the darkness and away from those in the light."

Catherine sat through the silence that followed as her memory dragged back her dream of the darkness. It seemed as though this stranger of hers thought that shadows were alive, and that he might also have known about her dream, but all she could remember beyond that was her car left in the road near Mandy's house, and avoiding his car which had nearly mown her down. She began to wonder, as the silence lingered, that perhaps she should have answered him in some way, or perhaps have said something to him, but she could think of nothing at the moment and so kept her silence. She was thankful when at last he spoke again.

"My name is Roker," he told her, as he snapped shut the book and directed his gaze at her for the first time since their conversation began. "I'm glad to have finally met you after all this time."

"What time?" she wanted to know.

"Since the first time you saw them."

"Saw who?"

"The shadows, Catherine," he said, leaning forward. "You remember them, don't you?"

Catherine tried to think. What shadows? What was he talking about?

"At kindergarten," Roker jogged her memory. "You saw, in the tall oak by the main gate. It saw you. We saw you."

Catherine struggled with her mind, as though any of this made sense.

"And when you were fifteen, walking home from that party that your parents told you not to go to. The shadows, Catherine. The shadows on your way home. I saved you then, as I saved you last night. You must remember, surely."

A terrible fear crept over her, as Roker recounted again and again the different incidents of her childhood and adolescence. A tear came, and trickled down her soft cheek, as the horror took her over. She remembered.

Roker continued to talk as she listened, telling her about the laws and the agreements that bound everything together, and the way that she had unwittingly breached them. It had been decided that her failing memory was not enough. Time and again she had seen the shadows, and her memory had faltered shortly afterwards, but the dominance of the dark world had made a decision. No more. It must stop. "So what now?" she heard herself murmur, although she knew that to ask such a question must surely invite insanity.

"We have decided that it is your decision."

Catherine looked up at him.

"I can continue to protect you as I have done," Roker explained, "or you can say enough is enough and let them take you."

She stared at him speechless. What kind of choice was that? What was she supposed to make of all this? This was insane. She slumped back into the chair and closed her eyes, and as the darkness began to soothe her, the ghosts of the candles' flames danced behind her eyelids, the strange sensation of apple blossom and sweet honey arousing her senses as they had done in her dream. Her eyes shot open and she stared hard at Roker. He was already standing, his book still in one hand, his other extended towards hers, as though he already knew her decision, a decision that she had not even consciously made herself.

"We should go," he said to her softly. "They will be here soon."

Catherine took his hand and he helped her to her feet, and turning their backs to the candle-lit room, they hurried from the house. Outside in the quiet street stood a plain-looking car, its exterior devoid of décor, badge or interest. Fishing a single key from his pocket, Roker escorted Catherine to the passenger side before hurrying round to the other, the street falling quiet once again after the car disappeared into the night at a little under the designated speed limit.


Hoskin shoved the end of the crowbar into the hole and poked about in the darkness.

"It's just a gap in the wood," he muttered. "I don't see what's so special about it."

"Just rip out the step," Morgan retorted.

Hoskin turned back to the iron in his hand and gave it his full weight, twisting its length against the timbers. At first they would not budge, but a tiny creak gave way to a groan and then a splintered shaft came away from the stair. Hoskin continued at the third step until it was nothing but a small pile of fragmented shards on the step below. It was then that Morgan tentatively stepped forward for the first time and peered over his shoulder into the darkness.

He had come prepared this time and drawing a handful of small rocks from his inside coat pocket, held it aloft over the chasm in the staircase, before releasing it. He expected to hear nothing for the majority of its descent, and was about to confirm his fears to Hoskin, when the rock clattered instantly across the wooden framework beneath the stairs and rattled down its slope under the tug of gravity. Hoskin gave him a very odd look, but he indignantly persevered and picked another of the rocks before casting that into the darkness. Again it hit the structure of the staircase immediately and rattled down to the floor.

Morgan began to grow anxious and frustrated, for he knew its hidden depths. And he was more than certain that he wasn't going as mad as the savaged patient in the hospital. Raising his arm high above him, he cast the remainder of the rocks down angrily into the hole. This time the thunder of the assault echoed throughout the very walls of the silent house.

"Where's the torch?" Morgan demanded, obstinately. "We'll just have to see what's down there."

"Are you sure no one's going to mind us ripping out this staircase?" Hoskin murmured, under his breath.

Morgan ignored him, and reached past to snatch the torch out of Hoskin's hands. He flicked it on and shone its powerful beam into the hole. All he could see was the interior of a staircase - wooden planks, struts and pillars. He switched off the torch, and handed it back to Hoskin. Then he stepped quietly back down the remaining two stairs and into the hallway to collect the whirling thoughts that tumbled like lunatic acrobats in his clouded skull.

Hoskin sat on the stairs and watched him pace the length of the hall. He had his hands in his pockets and his eyes on the floor. He was a sorry sight indeed. He left Morgan to his worries and turned his attention back to the troublesome stair that he had ripped out. Flicking on the torch, he aimed its beam back down into the hole to play its light across the struts and timbers. But as the bright shaft spilled into the black chasm, its beam travelled on an endless journey into the void, its luminescence eventually swallowed by the enveloping blackness when it could find nothing to cling on to. Hoskin watched spellbound as he swept the light back and forth beneath the staircase, its path unable to find anything to fall upon, the blackness total and consuming.

He moved his head closer to the hole in the vain hope that he could possibly catch something that the flashlight couldn't, but somewhere in his vision the blackness started to ebb against itself, curling and turning. Like waves in some bottomless coastless ocean, the air of the dark pit began to flow and to swirl, its motion fluid and almost hypnotic in its unnatural ceaseless patterns. The inky tides seemed to consume the man at its shore and draw him closer to meet its tenebrous pleasures. The torch slipped easily from his light fingertips, spiralling silently into the sea, its swirling beacon the only warning to the innocent straying too close to the dashing rocks at its mouth as it flashed through the murk.

So consumed by the black mesmerising ocean was he that he barely noticed the contorted shadow that rose and issued forth from the darkness, out into the space between the second and fourth steps, its dark form solidifying and converging in the light of day, its mist becoming whole, its vapour becoming flesh, and as his eyes looked up to see what had risen before him, the beast took them swiftly from his skull with the twin barbs of its forehead, as it butted him sharply and mercilessly.

Morgan looked up from his perplexing quandary for just long enough to witness the demon of the

434

darkness clamp its embrace around the young man's body. Its black-haired forearms wrapped themselves tightly around his torso, before tumbling back into the chasm in the staircase with him. Even as Morgan raced back to the step, he just had time to catch sight of the two entwined forms falling into the black enveloping sea, before being consumed entirely by the swirling shadows of darkness.

Morgan stood over the void for what seemed like hours, his sight fixed upon the point where Hoskin had finally disappeared, as if he somehow expected to see him rise back up. Then his hand reached almost subconsciously into his inside coat pocket, his numbed fingers plucking out a small rock, before releasing it down into the unnatural darkness. The rock was airborne for only a few seconds before it too clattered onto the wooden structure of the staircase before rattling down the incline and onto the floor below.


The endless yellow streetlamps stood rhythmical distances between each other on the quiet endless motorway. The drone of the engine and the hum of the tyres on the tarmac seemed eerily syncopated with the hypnotic blur of the lights and Catherine soon found it hard to keep her mind detached from their persuasions, her eyes starting to flicker and grow as heavy as her thoughts, as she soon drifted asleep as her body rocked gently to the sways of the car. Her eyes only opened again to a bright light that her tired eyes fought to focus on, but the vacancy sign swung nevertheless from its bracket attached to the front of the guest house. After stretching out the cramps from her muscles, she rubbed the mists from her eyes and studied the complex of their night's lodgings. There were already three cars in the small gravel car park at the rear of the building, Roker choosing a spot nearest the solitary bulb that hung by the back door. As he extinguished the car's headlights and took the key from the ignition, Catherine turned to him for the first time since leaving the house that morning.

"Where are we?" she asked, a yawn creeping unexpectedly into her question.

"Further away than we were," he told her.

She eyed him suspiciously as he reached across and fumbled about in the glove compartment. As he found what he was looking for, he leant back and opened the door.

"We'd better go," he said to her, attempting a smile.

"We can get a few hours sleep here."

Catherine agreed without comment, a simple nod that surprised even her that she had not so much as questioned anything that Roker had said or done. She felt as though he were somehow above all these earthly things, even though he had said he would protect her. He seemed strangely more than just a man, though his face and his body would suggest that that was all he was. He was no thing of great beauty, despite how he had captured her attentions in the club and in the electrical store, but nor was he ugly. He was not wrapped in layers of sinew, but his gait professed strength. His eyes inspired her while his words soothed, his spirit seemed betrothed to her, yet instead of showing passion, he showed compassion. But in her heart of hearts, and though her mind threw up a barrage of every conceivable contrary argument against it, she felt that he was perhaps more a part of her than she was, and that this man, whose snatched glimpses were enough to snare her emotions and throw them into turmoil, would mean more to her than anyone else ever could.

The landlord was reluctant to show them up to their room at such an hour, and wrapped his gown hastily around his frame, his hair greased back into respectability with just a few sweeps of his hand. Handing them their key at the top of the stairs, he left them to it as he turned and shuffled back down to continue his interrupted sleep. They found their room at the corner of the building, Catherine allowing Roker to unlock the door and step over the threshold first, before following in his wake.

It was a small room, consisting of the usual furnishings; a small table beside the bed, a chair, a wardrobe, a television, but only one bed - a solitary double bed. Roker looked to Catherine but he didn't speak. They were only passing through and any kind of a bed was better than the seats in the car outside. He stepped into the room and fished out the contents of his coat, placing them on the bedside table before removing his coat altogether and discarding it over the back of the chair. At first glance it would seem that the objects in his pockets had been chosen at random, but his attentions in finding them in the car had maybe been too precise. Even their functions could have been mistaken as some random choice, yet maybe there too lurked some hidden agenda - a small leather-bound book, a cigarette lighter but no cigarettes, a pocket-sized torch, a small tin box, a black-handled penknife. They were arranged together with no thought, yet they appeared equidistant from each other as though frequency had taken their juxtaposition for granted. It seemed obvious to Catherine that he had done this many times before.

She crossed the room now and located the en-suite bathroom. It had the minimum essentials of course, but at least offered a useable shower. She looked at herself in the mirror above the sink and ran her fingers through her bedraggled hair. She felt light-headed after the long journey they had taken, and she presumed it to be the first of many, her bones aching from being awake at this hour of the night, her skin seeming pale beneath the single dull bulb that hung over her head. Glancing back into the other room, she saw Roker perched on the edge of the bed, his fingers busy at the pages of his small book, his eyes likewise at the words written upon them. She watched him for a moment, and then half-closed the door behind her before turning her attention to the shower.

The water was hot and welcome, and she gratefully let it douse her. She could feel the dull aches draining from her body as she stood there, massaging her skin as she watched the plumes of steam roll up and around the ceiling. Reluctantly stepping from its delights after an age of luxuriating, she wrapped one towel around her hair while she dried her skin with another. But it was as she bent down to dry her legs that she looked up and through the crack in the door. She found Roker staring back at her, her body naked and illuminated beneath the solitary light bulb, its radiance glimmering in the haze of steam and dancing in the layer of moisture on her skin.

As she caught his glance, he lingered but a moment, as did she, their eyes linked in silent whimsy, before he finally turned away. Her first instinct was not one of violation or of privacy, but of warmth and feeling. It was like the touch of a lover, precious and delicate and caressing, but there was even more to it than that, because it held the secrets and promises of the unknown between them. She was even perhaps sorry that he did not look a little longer. Or maybe he had. How long had he been watching her as she ran the towel over her wet body, she wondered? And would he take her in his arms or would she be greeted with indifference?

She said nothing as she slipped her sweater back over her head and returned to the bedroom. She wandered about the room as she towel-dried her hair, her eyes drifting occasionally to the man sat at the edge of the bed. But his eyes would not stray again from the pages of his book. Had his glimpse of her been unintentional after all? It perhaps seemed so.

"We should get some sleep?" he eventually said to her, as she put the towel back into the bathroom. "It'll be dawn in a few hours."

"Are you joining me?" she tested, as she drew back the covers of the bed.

Roker looked up at her, a look that seemed to hold both of them entirely, from the minds in their skulls to the souls behind, and from the rapture in their unison to the severity of their situation.

"No," he said simply, and his eyes returned to the book in his hands.

Catherine clambered under the covers and shuffled beneath them, fluffing the pillows before turning back to him once more.

"What is that you're reading?" she asked. "You were reading that back at the house, weren't you?"

"It's just poetry," he replied, again without lifting his eyes from the page.

"What kind of poetry?" she persisted, curious to find out more about this guy.

This time, Roker put the book down and placed it on his lap, before turning his head to look at her.

"Love poetry," he said.

Catherine studied his expression and tried to decipher the lines upon them. But they were too well used and their plainness told her nothing, and she herself offered no more. She wanted to say something to him but no words would come. She simply smiled to him and then rolled over and closed her eyes to sleep. She wondered, as she lay there, certain that he was watching her sleep, what kind of man would read love poems, but she didn't even know what kind of man it was that was perched beside her on the bed. No man she had ever known had read any poetry, or written her any, despite how much she longed for it. With her back to him, she heard him replace the small book on the table, and felt him shuffle down the bed to lay beside her. Something was indeed not right with him for it seemed that he took great pains in lying away from her so that he wouldn't so much as touch her accidentally during the night in the course of dreams. He also lay above the covers in order that their flesh might not brush against each other's by equal chance. Catherine felt that she could relax with him beside her, and closed her eyes as she exhaled the heavy breaths of consciousness so that the calmer breaths of sleep could replace them. Morning would come soon enough, she thought, and with it a brand new day.

Jack Darwin had been taken from casualty and moved to the psychiatric ward of St. Bartholomew's where both nurses and doctors grew ever more concerned for his sanity. When asleep he murmured of deadly shapes and black sinew, when awake dark flesh from the walls and the air. His babble took fresh form when his eyes stared open, though the drugs he was injected with frequently tainted full cohesion he nevertheless troubled many staff with his vivid and depraved accounts. Morgan found him in a chair in the television room, his wrists bound to it as too were his shins, as he shared this timeless cell devoid of external interference's with patients of similar mental dysfunction, though none quite so intense. Sister Alley had accompanied the policeman to the patient's side, informing him of his ever deteriorating state as they travelled the silent corridors of the hospital, the only sound apart from her voice the echo of their footfalls resounding against the stone walls, and the occasional cry of a patient lost somewhere in its depths.

"Tell me again who did this to you and your wife," Morgan persisted. "Tell me and I will believe you."

It was a bold statement, but it was true.

Jack continued to murmur beneath his breath, syllables that could have been anything, while his eyes dreamed of the house he wanted to have called home again.

"I know where they live," Morgan tried. "I can help you but only if you help me."

Jack's eyelids dropped slightly as if a mist had rolled across his pupils.

"Black shadows," Morgan said to him. "Twisted black shadows. I've... I've seen them."

Jack's head rocked on his shoulders and fell towards the detective as if it would roll off into his lap. His eyes were stony cold but there was a hint of a sparkle in them, glittering like frost.

"Tell me..." Morgan whispered to him. "Tell me your secrets."

Jack's lips parted and a faint breath tumbled from them, its strength barely able to create the words it carried, but it was there and Morgan was close enough to the man's face to catch its frailty in his ear.

"There is a demon..." Jack started.

Another breath.

"...a demon who lives in my house... my home..."

A breath.

"It is black... but not. Veil... but made flesh..."

A tongue emerged to wet his lips.

"Evil..." he said.

"Sick..."

"Diseased..."

Morgan's face was just inches from Jack's pale waxen skin, and he watched as the man's head turned and fell away to the other side, his lids heavy once again in their sockets, the soft murmuring once more on his lips.

"I hide from the shadows, and yet they share my cage. I open myself to embrace oblivion if only they would give it, but they taunt me, and will not kill me. The sound is silent, the view is black. For all the world I am locked inside my own head and my head is the well of darkness."

Jack continued on and on until Morgan could stand no more. He rose to his feet finally and took Sister Alley to one side.

"What will happen to him?"

"He'll stay here like the rest of the patients, until he shows signs of recovery or..."

She did not finish.

"I don't want anyone from outside the hospital to gain access to him until I come back. I don't care who they are. I think I may be able to stop the pain inside his head."

442

"But -"

"He may be in great danger, but I cannot be certain. That's why I don't want anyone to see him until I am sure. Do you understand me?"

"I understand," she replied reluctantly. "No one."


The car slipped silently and unnoticed from the gateway of the guest house at mid-morning and drove just below the speed limits to the outskirts of town where it found the slip road to another motorway and began yet another leg of its journey. They drove all day, mostly in silence, but by late afternoon, Catherine had developed a headache from squinting at the sun and inhaling the road fumes.

"Where are we going?" she asked finally, holding her head as the car past yet another junction board at sixty-eight miles per hour.

"Don't worry," Roker told her. "We're going the right way."

Catherine studied the man beside her. His features were expressionless and he looked straight ahead as always, his eyes occasionally drifting to the rear-view mirror. She turned back to look out her window again, at the pattern that was emerging as they slowly made their way North; the towns of houses and offices were gradually giving way to villages and farms, as concrete became swallowed by grass. Just where the hell were they headed, she wanted to know? This whole journey was ridiculous, and it constantly played on her mind that what she was doing - travelling blindly with a complete stranger - was just plain crazy. But it were the occasional insights into her youth that plucked at her, convincing her that all that he told her was true. Yes, she had seen creatures in the shadows. Yes, she had witnessed things that her memory could only vaguely recall. He had given her explanations for those, offering further insights into her youth that no one could ever have known if it were not the truth. But what was the truth anyway? A bunch of words strung together to explain something? No, it must be more than that, surely. Catherine glanced across at him again, his face fixed permanently on the road ahead. Was this the man of her dreams? Literally speaking. Her whole life suddenly seemed a sham. Who were Mandy and Chrissie and Julie? Were they really her friends? Was any of it real? Would they even miss her now that she'd left on this bizarre journey. It was all so crazy. That was the only word for it. Roker's eyes flicked suddenly to the rear-view mirror. Were they being followed, she suddenly mused? What did it matter? What did any of it matter? Was he aware that she was watching him? She spoke.

"Will you read me one of your poems?" she asked him suddenly.

It took a while for Roker to answer her, the silence of the car penetrating.

"Why?" he wanted to know, looking across at her for a moment, and then back at the road.

"I'd like you to."

"No," he said, coldly.

"Do you mind if I read one?"

He hesitated.

"Can you..." he started, but got no further.

"Can I what?"

"Read them. Read the words, I mean. So that they make sense."

There was an uncertainty in his voice that she

444

couldn't decipher.

"Sometimes," Catherine replied.

"I read the words," Roker said to her, "but I do not feel them. That's wrong, isn't it?"

"What do you mean?"

"You should feel words of love, shouldn't you?"

"Sometimes," Catherine said again. "If spoken by the right person."

"Words should inspire. Words should make you happy, make you think, make you wonder."

"Is that why you read them?" she asked.

"I try," he said, "but I feel nothing."

Catherine said nothing after that, and Roker did not continue. After a few miles, he spoke again.

"Have you... loved?"

"A few times," she replied, a tiny smile encroaching across her lips as she remembered her past.

"A few?"

"Yes."

"Is love not forever then?"

"No," she replied flatly.

The smile went from her lips.

"Have you ever loved?" she asked after a while.

"No."

"Surely there must have been someone."

"No," he said again, his eyes finding her once again. "It is something that I just cannot do."

Roker turned back to the road, and pressed his foot harder on the accelerator. Catherine watched the needle of the speedometer climb from just below seventy and up into the mid-nineties. She could see his fingers grip the wheel more tightly, paling his knuckles, and she even caught the muscles of his jaw swell. His face creased for a few miles, and then the car gradually began to slow. She was glad.

The remainder of the day's journey was accompanied only by the drone of the tyres on the tarmac, and it wasn't until they pulled off the motorway and into the reaches of a small village that Roker spoke again, but it was not about poetry.

"It would be best if we rested here for the night," he said, as the car slowed to a halt outside a bed and breakfast. Catherine nodded her agreement indifferently. The villages and farms had waned, and had given way to a plethora of forests and a horizon of mountains. As Catherine stepped from the car and slammed shut the door behind her, she looked around at the towering pines, and at the gold and scarlet slashes of sunset against the purple-grey mountains, and breathed deeply the fresh crisp breeze that lifted her hair gently. This beautiful land was a long way from the grimy polluted town of her home, and though she was still perplexed as to her journey and the man with whom she shared it, she still missed the faces of her friends. But it was strange, though, that she was happy in her heart and contented for the first time in a long while, maybe for the first time ever, now she had this new world and this new life, and Roker to share it all with.

The so-called sensibilities of her life back home suddenly seemed ludicrous and comical as she looked at Roker against this wondrous new terrain; her job, her rent, the shopping, the weekly clubbing in search of decent men; it was all nonsense compared to this. Roker waited at the gate to the small hotel for her while she stared out at the world, lost in thought. Little could she have known that he would have stayed there all night, and forever if necessary, waiting for her until she was ready to join him. He never questioned her once when finally she joined him at the gate. There was a smile on her face when she passed him that she gladly shared, and happily they entered their night's accommodation, little knowing that it would be their last night alive under God's sky.


When Detective Morgan stepped over the threshold of the house again it was early evening and at the end of his shift. In either hand he held a petrol-can, the contents of which slapped inside as he walked. The tranquil light of the hour flowed past him into the hallway, his shadow diminishing as he stepped further into the building. As he reached the bottom of the stairs, however, his step became more tentative, until by the time his foot went towards the first stair, his body would not move at all.

His eyes fixed hard upon the chasm where the third step had been ripped out, the place where Hoskin had disappeared, the remains of the incident still littering the first and second steps below. Morgan placed the petrol-cans down on the floor beside him, his heart pounding with trepidation inside his chest, as he opened them and began to douse the staircase, hurling the first can down into the chasm when it became empty. He started to panic now as he picked up the second, showering the walls to the left and right, soaking the floors of both the kitchen and the living room, as he retreated hurriedly back through the house. As his heel caught the doorstep he hurled the can back into the gloom of the hallway, and fled, leaping the three steps out into the driveway, back to the relative safety of his car, where he stood and stared up at the house once again.

With a fevered temperament, he slowly withdrew a small whiskey bottle from his pocket, which he had been uncorking frequently throughout the day, and began to force his handkerchief roughly into its neck. Pulling his new cigarette lighter from his coat pocket, he padded slowly back towards the house, holding the thin flame to the rag which readily ignited. Staring into the evil house for the last time, he pulled his hand back as he prepared to hurl the bottle back over the threshold. But as his hand went back, so the gloom behind the windows of the house began to grow darker, swirling and congealing until he could discern nothing inside its inky blackness.

The air itself seemed almost to thicken, and then to ebb and ripple and contort, the whole house appearing to breathe new air into its harsh black lungs. And then, like a dark constructed explosion, that same blackness erupted into a monumental chaos that reached out for him, snatching at the figure with tendril-like talons to clutch his every limb, dragging him helplessly into its heart, and then down into the belly of its shadows.

Morgan tried to struggle but his muscles would not obey him. He tried to scream but his tongue denounced his command. His eyes fought to capture a point of reference in the sheer and utter blackness, but they fell upon nothing but the void. The only sense that served his mind was his smell, and he guessed that he must be near the gaping staircase, for the stench of petrol pricked his sinuses, saturating his skull, and crippling his body with nausea.

He could also feel the small whiskey bottle still in his hands, the flaming rag hot near his hand as it continued to burn lower and lower. He winced with pain as the tentacle-like grip tightened further his flesh, biting into him and knotting his limbs like coarse weathered rope. Then came the voice, a deep rasping growl that echoed not only in the air around him but inside the very reaches of his skull.

"Naive pilgrim," it seethed. "Why do you come here to die?"

Morgan tried to speak, to say something, anything, but no words would form in his stricken throat.

"You are not ready to die yet," the voice continued. "But I will not argue with your decision. You have seen much over time, and although you could have forgotten in time, you chose to pursue it. I've lost patience with such people as you. You will die here today."

Morgan felt the fingers squeeze ever tighter around his body. His ribs began to bend in his chest, his legs beginning to buckle and twist, his skull now heavy and thick. The heat near his hand intensified as though his skin was already burning. He wanted to torch the fucker, burn down its house and all that stood here. But his fingers would not open and release the bottle. His fingers would not save him.

"You cannot destroy things just because you do not understand them, or because you are afraid," it said in him. "From chaos there comes peace, and from peace there comes chaos. Light begets darkness, darkness begets light. Life conjures death, death creates life. You cannot destroy what must always be. Only through one, can we see the need of the other. You know so little of the other, but know that I will teach you. Chaos. Darkness. Death."

The fingers tightened further. A rib snapped inside his chest, bringing intense agony, its splinters puncturing a lung that issued a torrent of blood inside it. He would have choked then if his body been unrestricted enough to convulse. Instead he began to drown helplessly in his own fluids, as even his skull began to crack under such pressure. He felt his blood begin to flood into his throat, forcing itself up into his mouth, its sickly taste coating his tongue like wax before it seeped down between the gaps in his teeth. Still the intense stench of petrol seared into his nostrils, fusing with it the taste of his own blood, create a heady sickness inside him.

As his mind thickened beneath the slow torment, the agony in his burning hand seemed almost to disappear. The thumb of his left hand was virtually numb with pain now, and he could only vaguely feel the glass of the bottle with it. It did however carry one last pulse of energy, and as his heart collapsed and his arteries flooded, the digit snapped against the melted husk of his hand, forcing the bottle out and down towards the solid ground somewhere beneath him. He just had time to hear the glass break, the darkness around him flashing a brilliant white as the resultant furnace torched every timber in the building, before his consciousness went from him altogether.

Jack had warned them before they had even strapped him into his bed that the shadows would take him that night. As the nurses pulled hard at the straps in their buckles and secured his limbs and torso beneath them, he pleaded with them to let him die with some dignity and not like some pathetic lamb left as a shackled sacrifice. He couldn't hide from the shadows, he told them, not ever, not again. There would always be shadows, he knew that, but these demons did not live in the shadows, they were the shadows.

His words of frustrated wisdom fell on stony ground however, as the doctor present heaved a suitably large dose from his syringe and into his bloodstream to silence his babble. Then he turned and left him to it, extinguishing the thin fluorescent tubes above him before closing the door, sealing his cell, and leaving him to face the shadows alone.

The small room was dark but for a thin sliver of pale moonlight that trespassed unknowingly through a gap between the ill-fitting curtains. Its path pierced the cold tiled floor, the long solitary shaft penetrating the black of the room, its soft light greatly outweighed in the balance. Jack studied the slender finger for a while as he craned his head as far as his bonds would allow. The effects of the potent drug in his veins began to swiftly take hold of his senses dulling them to indifference, and he couldn't tell whether it was the drugs or the imminent approach of the shadow demons that darkened the murk inside the room.

He struggled with his failing eyes to keep bearings on the few objects around him, but as the blackness grew slowly to totality he lost track of them altogether. He thought he may have rolled his head from one side to the other to look for any point of reference but even of that he couldn't be certain. He at least presumed that his eyes were still open, but again he couldn't be sure. His fears surfaced rapidly when he felt his flesh being gripped by something far tighter than the straps of the bed. The air in his lungs was suddenly purged as his chest became constricted by the same force that was now coiling itself around his throat. He could feel his drug-tainted blood pumping hard inside his head, numbing his brain and pricking his eyes. And then a strange smell drifted through the black tides towards him, a faint odour at first, but growing ever more pungent, the unmistakable stench of petrol filling his nostrils until his stomach was set to heave. And then, somewhere inside the assaults in his skull, there resounded a deep rasping voice, its tone cold and evil, but carrying a falter of discomfort somewhere within its reaches.

"We meet again, Jack Darwin," it growled, from a place inside his head. "Sadly or otherwise, it makes no difference. You proved a convenience for a while, but now you have proved yourself troublesome and pathetic and you must come to an end."

Jack did not even attempt to struggle. His limbs were weak and aching, and would not have moved even if he had wanted them to. Perhaps he would have even flung his arms wide to embrace the darkness to him, to deliver himself into oblivion more quickly than his dispatcher intended. Whatever his desire, the voice was right, it made no difference. He would die here tonight.

The fingers of darkness tightened rapidly around his already restricted body, crushing bones, reshaping flesh, and turning form to pulp. His blood ran freely from the fissures as they opened up, pouring as unseen silent rivers over the bed and across the cold tiled floor. His mind went quickly enough, however, slipping away silently before the demon could torment him any more.

Catherine lifted the small leather-bound book from the top of the bedside cabinet. Roker lay beside it, his eyes closed, his hands crossed at his chest, and seemed not to notice her taking it. She wasn't even sure if he was sleeping, but she silently flicked through the well-thumbed pages one at a time, scanning each one's homage to a different man's dream. There were no pictures or illustrations to detract from the power and grace of the words, yet the stanzas themselves seemed to bear a different power to that of a simple drawing. The pages almost turned themselves in her hands as though knowledgeable of their course and duty, but they would pause momentarily here and there at certain pages, until they held themselves perpetually at one particular page, its edges soiled and worn, eroded by frequent study.

Catherine looked closer and read the first few lines, and then turned to look at the man whose body lay atop the covers of the bed beside her. She now knew for certain that the anguish he had felt in the car was for his own heart, and for the loss he had never had, yearning for such things that he seemed unable to comprehend. She had enough anguish of her own, for the loves that she'd had and thrown aside ready for another, their potency diluted by the certainty of the next lover to know her embraces. Here was a man who had surely never felt the love of a woman, known the exhilaration of the very first kiss, the moment of losing virginity, or the love that can bond two people together, not only in flesh but also in mind and soul.

Catherine knelt down beside him now, and read aloud to him the words on the worn page he had read but never understood, in his quest to learn the experiences of their devotions. As she spoke, his eyes opened and found her in the half light of the room, and he seemed to understand almost immediately how such simple words mean infinitely more when spoken by another, voiced with passion for the one for which they were penned.

As the words fell from her lips, she looked up at Roker. His eyes were as glazed as hers, and as she continued, the tears within them slipped and washed down over his face, tears of frailty and purity, of innocence and desperation. He did not move as she finished, nor even when she closed the book and laid it back down on the cabinet beside the bed. But as they stared into each others eyes, Catherine reached out her hand, her fingertips to his tears, and took them from his face, gently caressing their paths away. Tentatively she leant forward towards him, her lips parted a little and moistened from the grace of her tongue. Her eyes grew heavier as she neared his face, and as their lips were mere inches apart, a single solitary word rose from his throat and passed between them like a ghost.

"No," he murmured softly.

His hand went to her and hesitantly pushed her back, as if his mind were not sure that such an action was even the correct one. He rolled away from her and off the bed, getting to his feet on the other side before going to the window, keeping his back to her. A second tear appeared on her face, and took the same course as the first.

"I thought..." she started, "I thought that's what you wanted."

"I do," he replied, his voice almost a whisper.

"Then why?" she persisted.

"I... I cannot," he said. "I told you."

"Speak to me," she demanded, rising to her feet. "Tell me why you can't."

Roker turned away from the window and looked

back at her. His features were a mask of torment and despair, and outweighed anything that Catherine had to offer.

"I am an angel," he cried. "And a guardian. Your angel. Your guardian. And I am here to protect you from the shadows."

"Hold me then," she continued.

"I'm your guardian. I can't. It is forbidden."

"Why?"

"Because I will..."

"Because you will what?"

"I will die."

Catherine stared at him, speechless.

"Any physical act of love or passion will dissolve my very existence. It is the law that binds me together. By committing such a love, it would violate and negate my purpose. I can only dream and read of love. I can never touch it."

"You say you can only have a life without love," she said, taking a step towards him, "yet what kind of life can that be?" She reached out her hand and put it to his face. "Which should we choose - a love without life, or a life without love? Neither one can exist without the other, yet your pain tears at its very sinews. Is your life worth more to you than the premise of love, or can love be stronger even in death?"

Roker's eyes strained as if to burst as she went to him and put her hand in his, holding it up to his trembling lips. He shuddered inside as he let it happen, putting his lips to her soft delicate flesh and tasting her. Catherine moved closer to him, wrapping her other arm around his neck as though to draw him to her.

"But what of you?" he whispered. "If I die, it will be

forever. You will succumb to the demons that prey on you. They follow us even now, and they will not stop until they devour you utterly."

"If you say that you love me, I will say I love you. To Hell with the shadows for I care not. If I am destined to die by their terrors then how can I run? If you are destined to die by your own torment then how can you go on living? Take me now and let it consume us both."

Roker lifted his hand and placed his trembling palm upon her breast, their bodies moving closer still so that their harried breaths blew hot upon each others skin. Then with his face to the cascades of her hair, he whispered:

"My heart is dry."

Catherine pressed her lips to his and he let her kiss him. The blackness of the night outside seemed to rage and scream, as if everything known shuddered around them, conjuring a wave of unnatural horrors that howled forth into that night. Its storm shook those it rushed through for the briefest of seconds, the few who were caught by its tumult trying their hardest to turn their collars to it before hurrying home. Alongside the motorway it gathered speed, hurling itself across fields and through forests of trees, its tide of darkness swirling uncontrollable and unstoppable, heading towards its certain destination. On it surged, breaking only at a dense wood that surrounded a small northern valley as it homed in upon a small hotel, whereupon it slowed a little, its journey's end in sight.

Roker knew not whether to draw her to him or to kiss her again, so sweet and soft were her lips upon his, but in the moment of hesitation Catherine reached inside his shirt and slipped it from his shoulders. He watched her at work, and gazed entranced as it floated to the floor, landing in a heap at his feet. He looked back to her and she returned his uncertain gaze with a soft smile. Her hands stayed at his bare chest, her fingers exploring him so gently, and she watched as her head bowed to follow her touch upon him, her lips at his breast. His arms lay redundant at his side as his whole being took to the forbidden pleasure of his ward's attentions. Her tongue tasted him, its touch profound, her teeth bit tenderly upon his flesh, not savage but blissful beyond his knowledge. Her hands played down across his stomach, reaching to discard the remainder of his clothing, and all this he watched in utter fear of the unknown. His whole existence seemed almost to escape right there in a single breath as his loins stirred and groaned at the mercy of her touch. No fear of death or threat of reclamation turned his thoughts from this precious mortal who continued to express such love upon him. He stood before her naked and vulnerable, his arms beside him, his head down, as his mind cascaded with a tempest of thoughts subdued by emotions that he was rapidly trying hard to evolve. He felt maybe embarrassed that he knew not what to do with his limbs, yet this woman seemed concerned only with pleasuring him. Roker watched spellbound as she took hold of the bottom of her sweater, pulling it up and over her head, exposing herself for him to see. He knew not what to do, not even when she pressed her naked flesh against his, and invited him to touch the small mound of dark hair that lay between her legs. A look of desperation, perhaps even fear, flashed across his face as his fingers found the soft flesh that waited there, but Catherine encouraged his violation, this secrecy, and with a smile she urged him back towards the bed with her, where she induced him to enter her fully.

The calm of the small hotel became ravaged as the midnight tornado hurtled itself against it, circling the exterior as it closed in upon its prey. In the depths of passion, Roker's chest seemed to heave more profusely than it should have done, despite such unknown exertions, and his breath seemed to come in extraordinarily drawn out gasps. Even Catherine did not notice his deteriorating condition, not even as the digits of his hands began to crack at the knuckles as she gripped them harder and harder in hers. Not even as his hips began to dissolve and crumble beneath her assault atop them. Roker's will, however, fought the conflict growing inside him, even as the processes he knew would come were underway, as his body began to break up under the laws of his very existence that he had knowingly violated. His love for the woman he had watched over for years, and the power inside him that had battled the resultant war within him, demanded that his flesh be forfeit. And as Catherine's body started to shudder and convulse atop him he felt a new sensation course through him, a sensation as new and as lethal as the one that drove to tear him apart. His loins writhed and his body shook, until he seemed to pump his very being deep inside her, this mortal that he had loved more fully than anything else he had ever known.

He began to lose the vision of his salvation as his eyes dimmed and washed over with blood. He could just make out the beautiful lines of her features through the scarlet veil of blindness, her enchanting eyes half-closed and blissful, her lips parted and heaving, the flush of her skin stark and red, before it faded altogether and she was gone. The memory of her peace and her love was all he took with him before his eyes melted in their sockets and drained back into his skull. His skin followed as it began to fall away from his bone, unravelling like old threads. There was no blood, that had evaporated behind the flesh, now it was only dry matter that crumbled, flesh, bone and man.

Catherine's own fantasies rotted to horrors as she witnessed the destruction of her guardian beneath her. A choked scream clung to the back of her throat as she saw him slowly collapse and crumble into ash, until she was sat astride little more than a thick black mass. She had only half-believed all that Roker had told her, but now she knew that all he had said was true. He had given his life so that he could know her love for one night. He was gone, just as he had said he would be.

The window rattled then in its frame behind her, the pane shuddering with an airborne assault from outside, and she knew that it would soon be her turn too. Through the gap between the curtains the night was black, a blackness she could not discern, and the air seemed to swirl and coil in upon itself like a grim grisly tide. Shapes seemed to move within that tide, forms contorting, knitting, evolving towards their purpose. Her eye became held by its sickening motion, drawn by its hypnotic rhythms, but it all seemed familiar, as though this was exactly what she had witnessed and half-remembered all of her life, and it numbed both her brain and her body now as these horrors now demanded access to her room.

The dark roiling night on the other side of the glass conjured memories and faces in its inky blackness, images from childhood, from adulthood, from decades, from days, and as she crossed the room as if in a trance, she undid the latch and pushed open the window to allow those memories and faces passage into the room. The world around her seemed almost to disappear as soon as the tides lapped at her feet, the grim soup swirling up and around her to engulf her completely. First to go was the small black leather-bound book discarded at the bedside. The waters washed over its cover and spine, its pages turning beneath its touch. The abandoned clothes on the floor traced into its depths and were gone. The grey-black ash left abandoned on the bed seemed to be swallowed so easily by its course that once it was gone she found it hard to remember just what had been there before. Until finally, as her eyes went to the ceiling and to the room's only illumination, the black surge swallowed its brightness completely, before extinguishing it altogether.

Catherine was alone in the dark void. Its calm silence was matched only by the still of the waves, lapping like rhythmical breaths against what she had known as flesh. No more did the night surge or roll. No more did the sounds of the world linger in her ear. She looked about at the totality of the nothingness around her, and soon she began to think. Soon she began to panic. And soon she began to scream. Yet of even doing these things she could not be sure.

If she looked, would she surely be able to see? If she were to think, then surely there would be thoughts in her head. If she were to panic, would not her limbs writhe in desperation, limbs she could not even see? And if she were to scream, would she not hear that voice in her ears and feel their words upon her tongue?

Damien Wreeks sat in his comfy office chair and idly scratched his pencil across the white A3 jotter in front of him. The grey lines were appearing wide and dull after a long morning's doodling, their graphite tracks nonsensical, incompetent, inconsistent.

It was Wednesday and he'd not had a decent idea in weeks. Jannings would be angry. Resting his head on his left hand, Damien's gaze wandered out of the small window beside him. A number of clouds pottered past in the blue summer sky, but none of their shapes managed to snag his imagination, none of them crept into his subconscious to kick start his creativity, and of all the other concrete buildings opposite, nothing interesting was happening behind any of their windows either. He had no ideas and he was being paid to be creative between the hours of nine and five thirty. Something was bound to come into his head soon.

Pushing himself up from his desk, Damien wandered towards the window and gazed down into the street some four floors below. It was difficult to see much of what was going on, but there was precious little to be gleaned from the congested traffic and disgruntled pedestrians. It never gave him any inspiration no matter how frequently he got up and stared down at it all. But it would pass a few seconds while the day ticked by. Perhaps just once it might spark something out of the monotony, a glistening bell from the drone of nothingness.

On the wall behind him were eight designs, each of them printed lavishly in full colour and mounted

461

inside gold-edged frames. They were his best designs, the company's most profitable children's rides, selling thousands of units nation-wide, available to every child in spitting distance, and they were all featured in the glossy catalogues that were sent out to every carnival, arcade and seaside resort in the country. Jannings had increased his salary twice in that time, making it clear that he had no intention of letting him be head-hunted by any of their less scrupulous competitors. Damien had wondered on a number of occasions just how kid's rides could be so profitable, running on just a handful of loose change, but it simply seemed that they were, and that was the end of it. A nagged parent is a poor parent, was one of Jannings' sayings.

His favourite of all the rides that he'd designed was a strange little piece called The Travelling Pig. It basically consisted of a large upright fibreglass pig, dressed as a farming yokel, with a pitchfork in one hand and the handle of his hay-filled wagon in the other. The toddler would sit in a seat inside the wagon which would then rock from side to side while the pig lifted the pitchfork up and down in a six inch loop. It was a simple motorised routine, the programme for the small processor tucked away inside written in just over an hour, but it had brought in profits to the company that had outstripped anything else they had ever produced before. Go figure.

Another design of his, the ride he called The Killer Clown, but officially indexed in the company catalogue as The Magic Circus, consisted of a clown that rolled round and round in a three hundred and sixty degree arc at an incline of about ten degrees, with the child seated upon its back. That, essentially, was the ride, but it too brought in a staggering amount of money.

Damien left his vigil by the window and crossed the room to study these mounted prints more closely, staring at them hard in an attempt to study their inextricable simplicity, trying hard to squeeze out any ounce of influence from them, however paltry. He knew, however, that it would be useless. New designs just appeared inside his head when they wanted to, almost as though he had no control over them, despite the previous one always being better than the last. It almost felt sometimes as though they were not even his own ideas. He'd never had much of an artistic streak at school, (or throughout much of his life at all, come to that), but it had been about a year and a half ago when the first pictures of walking pigs and flying alligators had started to simply appear inside his head. He'd tried to ignore them at first, fearing for his sanity, wondering where such weird and bizarre images could possibly be coming from. But then he began to set them down on paper, hoping that by condemning them to simple pencil lines and rough shading, he might perhaps exorcise them from his mind. But it was in that simple act of drawing, of applying a stubby pencil to an old scrap of paper, that he'd discovered a talent that he'd never known he'd possessed.

A friend had taken one of them and shown it to his employer, one Edward Jannings of EDJ Entertainments Inc. He liked what he saw, hired him directly over the phone, and the rest, as they say, was history. The only problem he'd had on occasion, though, was one that other people might have called writer's block. He drew pictures with a pencil, but he guessed the same criteria applied.

The office clock hanging on the wall became a

463

magnet once again, and Damien couldn't stop his gaze from being attracted to it. It now read twelve minutes past ten, five minutes since last he had looked. Furtively he ducked out the office door and headed swiftly along the corridor towards the vending machines. Perhaps a quick break might help alleviate the drought in his head.

As he was feeding his change slowly into the tall silver slot, an image slipped into his mind with the same ease as the disappearing coins. A dragon. A dragon with big eyes and a tubby yellow body. A cartoon dragon. Damien struggled to keep the image in his mind's eye now that it was there. The vending machine made its clicking selection noise, indicating that it was ready to dispense his chocolate bar, but Damien tried hard to keep his focus inside his head, clenching his eyes against the din of the office around him, but he was already losing the battle. His sight drifted down to where the chocolate bars and the packets of crisps were lined up in long symmetrical racks. He chose one, he couldn't help it, and as he pressed his finger against the flashing light beneath it, the image of the cartoon dragon disappeared in the same instant, back into the bowels of his own confused imagination.

He stood helplessly and watched the chocolate bar drop from its rack and tumble down into the tray at the bottom of the machine. He knew there had been a dragon, but he could no longer picture it. It had been wonderful to look at, like a flower blossoming into full bloom, but he could do no more now than describe it with words - cartoon, tubby, yellow - but they were of no use now. They meant nothing. Whenever he drew these mind-pictures, it was almost as if they drew themselves, his fingers merely tools that would keep the pencil in motion. The sight of the dragon was gone, that much was certain, and his brain was not about to reward him with a second showing. So breathing a frustrated sigh, he stooped to nudge open the metal flap and pick up his chocolate bar, glancing about him as if there might be some new and inexplicable revelation waiting somewhere behind him, before wandering unfulfilled back to his small office.

He took a seat in front of his A3 jotter once again, plucking a fresh pencil from his novelty Wallace and Gromit desk tidy, and began to idly drag its sharp tip across the doodle-filled page hoping that something might come, some fragment of memory that might guide the lines without his conscious input. But nothing happened. After perhaps ten minutes of scrawling badly-proportioned stick figures and awkward-looking caricatures, he slapped the pencil down irritably on his desk and slumped back in his chair.

As he closed his eyes, however, the dragon miraculously reappeared with almost a wink in its large bright eyes. It was big and fat and green, its teeth stubby and round like pebbles, and it loped along with a kind of springy bounce. Then it slumped down into a dumpy sitting position so that it looked almost like an overripe vegetable, an off-colour eggplant or something, and then proceeded to blow fluffy clouds of dull grey smoke out in front of it. No flames or anything, just smoke. His own thoughts drifted alongside it into his head, swirling round the shape of the dragon like fleeting clouds of his own, telling him that kids would love this thing. It was unthreatening. It was charming. It was adorable. A pouch suddenly conjured itself at the front of the dragon's plump belly for the toddlers to sit in, even as he thought this, gaping invitingly. A short spine-covered tail flicked round from behind its back, swishing joyfully like that of a playful dog. And then a fine v-shaped tongue flicked out to taste the smoke on its own breath, the dragon-ride creating itself without any effort from Damien as he just sat there and watched all this from inside his mind.

Then his eyes flickered open to the room, and without any further thought, snatched the pencil back up off his desk and began eagerly to guide it across the pad in front of him. His job was virtually done. He'd seen the dragon be born inside his head, witnessed its life evolve instantaneously, and now all he had to do was watch it being sketched out in front of him. He didn't have to do anything more that that. He never did.

His hand seemed like a foreign object to him. He could no more feel the pencil, or his fingers in which it sat, than he could the cold glass of the window behind him. He sat back and witnessed yet another design tumbling out of his head. Was this how other artists created their work, he wondered to himself? Detaching themselves completely from what they desired and just let it come. It seemed unlikely, but what other explanation was there? They came from inside him, that must be how it worked.

Suddenly the pencil ceased scratching, and the sudden halt of his fingers jerked his attention back to what was happening in front of him. Damien looked down. It seemed the dragon ride was complete.

He sat and stared at it for a few minutes, taking it all in. It looked pretty damn good, everything in its place, everything proportioned adequately, and yet he didn't feel quite comfortable enough to congratulate himself for it. It almost felt as though he were forging someone else's work, stealing their ideas and sneaking them in first to make it look as though they were his.

The more he looked at the sketch of the dragon, however, the more he became settled in the realisation that this was his own work. But then he also began to wonder about the practicalities of having a dragon as a children's ride. You couldn't just draw a dragon and then say, 'There you are, may I have another pay rise please, sir?' It needed mechanical contraptions inside, and a program to run them. That was a skill in itself, and a skill he felt downright more comfortable with.

What could a smoke-blowing dragon do, he asked himself, in a matter-of-fact kind of way? This was only a little kid's ride, not a complex rollercoaster, but it still needed something to attract a young kid's imagination. Perhaps if it was mounted on a short stretch of track and rolled up and down on it? Maybe some kind of mechanism could be installed so that it snorted a safe cloud of smoke too. Kids would love that. Parents too, most likely. Something else to snag that loose change of theirs that Jannings loved so much.

Damien set to work now that the idea had come, and began drawing out detailed plans of mechanisms and counter-mechanisms. In the afternoon he would begin drafting a preliminary computer program that would make it all run.

His brain started to whirr into life now, his thoughts building and building as momentum overtook him, the bonus being that he would at least be able to have something to show Jannings by the end of the week, and show that he was still worth all the money that he was being paid.

Writer's Block? Rubbish. That was just something for the untalented people of the world. He had ideas aplenty inside him. It's just that he couldn't always get his hands on them when he needed them. But at least he knew they were there somewhere, lurking wrapped inside the swirling darkness of his head.

Jannings saw The Puffing Dragon first thing Friday morning and loved it. Another benchmark, he said. Another wallet-opener. Every kid in the country under six would soon be hopping up into its pouch.
All was well once again, Damien mused happily to himself, as he made his way back to his office. All until a report came in approximately four hours later that day, when Jannings suddenly called him back up to his office.

"There's been an accident," Jannings informed him. "One of your rides."

Damien stared at him. What was he talking about?

"The pig ride," he told him. "You know the one I mean."

"The Travelling Pig."

"That's the one. The pitchfork managed to work itself loose somehow. Speared some kid that was sitting in it right through the shoulder."

"Oh my God."

"Exactly," Jannings remarked. "Oh my God. I've already sent an engineer out to the amusement park to check it out. I've told him to call me as soon as he's found the problem. I want you to stay as long as you have to as well, just in case he needs some information from you. You designed it, you fix it."

"Yes, sir. Yes, of course."

Damien's head was reeling. One of his rides had actually hurt a little kid. That eventuality had never been explained to him. Those kids were supposed to have fun, not get hurt.

"How is the child?" he asked tentatively.

"He's not dead, if that's what you mean," Jannings told him, rather bluntly, as if all this was somehow his fault. "The pitchfork went in through the back of his shoulder and out through the other side. It apparently took an ambulance crew over an hour just to separate the kid from your infernal contraption. This is the worst thing that has ever happened to this company, and I trust it will be the last."

Damien stared at him. It took him a few moments to realise that it was a statement directed at him and not a wishful hope.

"You don't think I did this on purpose?"

"Of course not. I just hope for your sake that you followed all the safety procedures. Negligence on our part could cost us a fortune if the parents decide to sue. Not to mention the potential loss of business that bad press might bring."

Damien excused himself for a few minutes and tumbled out into the corridor, stumbling past colleagues, bewildered by his state, on his way to find the nearest vending machine. His throat was suddenly as dry as sand, parched and rasping, and a crawl of sickness had somehow managed to find its way down into the pit of his stomach. A young boy had been seriously hurt on a ride that he had designed. He tried to reason that he hadn't designed it at all, not consciously, because it had simply created itself. But it was a shallow argument, and the sickness of guilt didn't leave him as he leant against the wall and sipped a cupful of water from the cooler.

He slumped into one of the hard plastic seats beside the vending machine and gazed into middle distance. His fingers were trembling now. This was serious. He was reasonably sure that he wouldn't be held personally accountable for the accident, but that still didn't help the way he felt about it. He almost felt like he'd driven that pitchfork through the boy's body himself. He could imagine him now in his mind's eye, prostrate in the fibreglass wagon, a black painted pitchfork impaling his tiny chest, the wide grin on the yokel pig's face, now sickening and evil, all of it rocking from side to side as saccharine music jingled in time to the boy's cries of agony.

Jannings had spoken of checking safety procedures. He hadn't done that, not with any of his designs. They'd all seemed reasonable enough in his head, there'd been no reason to double check them. But now he began to worry about The Puffing Dragon, The Wild Stallion and, God forbid, The Killer Clown. None of them were dangerous in their own right, but then neither was The Travelling Pig. Damien pushed himself swiftly to his feet and hurried back to his office where he could double-check his sketches. The mechanism drawings and program scripts would need some checking too, before it was too late.

It only took a few more days before the second accident happened. Sitting in front of his computer, Damien leapt startled as the phone suddenly rang beside him. Jannings wanted to see him immediately, and Damien left his work in untidy stacks and hurried back up to his office.

"Not another child?" Damien asked hurriedly. That same sickness had crawled into his gut and taken a good hold on his way up to the top floor.

"Luckily no. The engineer that I sent to take a look at the ride managed to get himself speared as well. It's a goddamn nightmare. He told me that he started the ride, bent to check the mechanism, and then the pig just seemed to drive the pitchfork into him. The angle of it wasn't even anywhere near the one that you programmed. Almost as though it had a mind of its own. His words."

Damien fell into a seat opposite him and stared at him. He just couldn't believe it.

"That isn't possible," he murmured under his breath. "The pitchfork had a fixed vertical movement of about six inches. There's just no way for that to alter."

"And yet it did," Jannings said. "Twice. I've got a kid in the hospital, and an engineer following on behind. Now I want you to go down there yourself, with whatever shit you think you need, and just get that damned thing back here and dismantled."

"But what can I do?"

"I don't give a shit what you do, just get it off the park, find out what went wrong, and then scrap it."


It took a little over two hours to reach the amusement park by which time the park owner had removed the ride from public view and placed it inside a grimy warehouse. Damien was taken to it by a park worker and then left to inspect the ride on his own. He wasn't too sure quite what he was supposed to be doing, he was a designer not an engineer, but there was precious little he could say at the moment. He just had to agree to anything Jannings asked of him.

Removing one of the side covers, Damien glanced down at the mechanics inside. To the most part it all looked the same as he had designed it. There'd been a few changes, but nothing major. It was the pitchfork that was the worry, and more importantly, how it had managed to work itself out of the fixed pattern it had been made to run in. He expected to find something broken or out of place, a bolt sheared or a sensor out of line, but everything seemed just fine. He stood back and stared at the pig, its porky red face grinning up at him with neither remorse nor concern for what it had done.

"What were you thinking?" Damien murmured under his breath to it.

The pig's expression remained unaltered, and just stared straight back at him with that fixed fibreglass grin on its face. There was reason for this madness somewhere, he knew, but he was loathe to plug the damn thing back in and find out for himself. There were already two people in the hospital. He didn't want to make it three.

As he started away back towards his car, he heard a low creaking sound behind him. Guessing it to be one of the motors just idly clicking over under the weight of something, he only idly glanced over his shoulder. But when his eyes connected with the pig ride, he stopped in his tracks. The pig had turned its head slightly and was now looking directly at him. Nothing else had changed but this slight turn of its head. The pig's eyes were still wide, its teeth still set in that white painted grin, and its fat trotter remained tightly wrapped around the shaft of its pitchfork. Damien turned slowly to face it, and only now became aware of his heart thumping loudly in his chest.

"What's on your mind?" he found himself saying to it, even as he realised that he was addressing a mere assembly of metal parts and fibreglass. He watched in horror, however, as the creaking came again, only this time it was the pig's lower jaw that groaned open to form its awkward reply.

I.

Grow.

Impatient.

Its voice grated like the gears within its body, hard and grinding, stuttering and metallic. Damien stared perplexed at it, horrified, afraid. The paint around its mouth was already beginning to flake away from the fibreglass beneath as the hard shell creased and contorted to form these syllables. Its head tilted once again, only this time followed by its torso as it tried to straighten its posture into a more upright position.

I.

Need.

To.

Find.

My.

Creator.

Its voice juddered, and lifting its feet clear of the base of the ride, it staggered away from the wagon it had just been grasping until it stood before him, facing him, approximately three feet high, its pitchfork still gripped menacingly in one trotter. It had not left that behind.

"You need to find me?" Damien stammered, bewildered at the sight of this monstrosity. "What do you want with me?"

The plastic pig stared at him for a moment, its painted eyes squinting as it regarded him somewhat curiously as though the question had forced a fatal exception error in the processor of its mind.

Not.

You.

It said finally, its voice clanking, deep cracks opening in its paintwork.

The.

Creator.

Not.

You.

"But I made you," Damien said, with a frown. "You were nothing until I thought of you."

Not.

You.

The pig said again with a furious bellow.

Not.

You.

Not.

You.

It started forward, teetering on two tiny rigid trotters that click-clacked across the cold concrete floor. But its bulk was too unstable to be born up by such tiny feet, and gravity would ultimately have its victory. The Travelling Pig stumbled forward, reaching its pitchfork out towards Damien even as it toppled, as though it was its last attempt to get at him. Damien staggered backwards, the pitchfork missing him by inches, and the pig hit the concrete floor hard. The cracks that had already appeared across its shell widened further beneath the fall. The fibreglass held momentarily, but then the shell split in two. A brief groan rose out of the fractured husk, like the grinding of broken cogs, and then the toppled pig shuddered eerily into silence.

Damien stood in a horrified silence as he gazed down at the pig, waiting for some final gasp of speech, some threat or assault, but it seemed that there would be no further comment or attack from the children's ride that had been made out of fibreglass and steel. Somewhere in the back of his head, in the meetings with Jannings that would surely come, he decided that he would refer to this in the future as The Talking Pig, not The Travelling Pig. His reasoning, however, he would keep to himself for a very long time.

He tried to put as much of the incident out of his head as possible, on the way out of the warehouse, telling himself that it obviously hadn't happened, things like that just didn't, but it was one of the pig's comments that troubled him more than anything else. As he returned back through the busy amusement park to where he had parked his car, he passed flocks of families, the children bawling, the parents stone-faced, as they coined fistfuls of coins into the slots of similar rides; of rockets and cowboys, of cars and monkeys; how many of these rides might suddenly break free from their shackles and raise a weapon against those that rode their backs, with size two shoes jammed in their flanks?

But the pig was different. He had made it real. His mind had made it real. Even though the thing had inferred that he hadn't created it. A thought occurred to him that maybe it was a sub-program added by one of the guys in the production department, adding a voicebox and a set of verbal comments to make it look as though it was speaking. That was it, surely. It had to be. A smile crept into the side of his mouth as he glanced across at a fat woman tugging her purse out of her handbag, a smile of relief, of assured sanity, as she began feeding change into a gleaming silver slot. He decided that he would have a quick ask round when he got back to the office. Just to be on the safe side.

It was only a week after that that Jannings hurled news at him of another accident.

"Another one?" Damien gasped, clutching his head in disbelief.

"You're damn right. And guess what? It's another one of yours."

Damien stared out through his office window at the clouds crawling snail-like across the deep blue sky. This just couldn't be happening.

"Which one?" he asked nervously.

"Your magic circus ride -"

"The clown?"

"Yes, that damned clown. It's injured some girl. Her parents are freaking and demanding the police. I want you there first."

"I'll get right over there."

"Your damn fucking right you will. If this is some other design flaw of yours, you're going to cost me a shit of a lot of money."

Damien was shaking when he finally put the phone down. Jannings had given him the address of one of their biggest customers, an amusement park down on the south coast. His Killer Clown had scared him witless at times himself, that freaky-looking painted face with a grin that could be either hysterical or psychopathic, and now it seemed that it was probably both. He hated clowns, he always had. They'd never seemed funny to him, just a bit twisted with all that make-up and sick insane laughing. He shivered as he thought of how it might have injured that little girl, what weapon it might have gotten hold of, and as he drove out of the car park and out onto the main road, an image of it coming to life in the same way as the pig flashed all too readily into his mind.

He had to negotiate several police cars and ambulances when he finally arrived at Headland Funfair. He approached one of the officers and told him who he was, and was then ushered swiftly towards a huddle of jabbering onlookers, all pointing and pushing each other. He quickly saw the brightly painted face of his clown, saw too its evil grin of white rounded teeth, and thought in that moment that it saw him in return, its black painted eyes glinting eagerly in the bright afternoon sunshine.

Damien stood and gazed down at the ride. The clown stood in its same simple pose, motionless and silent, its arms outstretched, urging the nearest passing kid to leap into its embrace. One such kid had done that, and now she had paid the price. He turned to the policeman who had brought him, and asked him what had happened.

"The mother is saying that the clown grabbed her daughter around the throat and shook her violently. Her father was just over there picking up some candyfloss and says he didn't see anything until he got back to find his wife hunched over her, grappling with the machine to try and get her daughter out. Of course, it sounds like shit, but she's sticking to her story."

"You don't believe the clown could've grabbed her?"

The officer frowned at him. This wasn't the time to be testing him on the subject of living inanimate objects.

Damien Wreeks glanced uneasily at The Killer Clown, its unrelenting grin seeming to mock his scrutiny. Just what could have happened here? These rides weren't supposed to move like that. It was insane to even consider it. The policeman was still staring at him expectantly, he could see him from the corner of his eye. He was sure what the officer expected him to do, but he only leant a little closer to the clown to make it look as though he was inspecting it, just hoping that it looked like he knew what he was doing so that he could just get the hell out of there. He glanced briefly up and down the clown, his eyes finding those of the clown, its gaze holding him momentarily with a sickeningly icy connection of fear.

Look.

At.

Me.

It seemed to say.

Bring.

Me.

My.

Creator.

Or.

I.

Will.

Kill.

Them.

All.

Damien managed a look of defiance, before a shiver

of fear swept over him and his heart drummed a furious beat in his chest. Something was wrong here, very wrong indeed, and it was something a little more dangerous than a prank being pulled by an engineer back at the factory. Something had turned bad, terribly bad, and it seemed as though he was somehow at the centre of it. He was their creator after all, despite what the pig and the clown had insinuated. It was his problem because he had pulled them from the darkness of his head.

He left the amusement park assuring the manager and the police that the ride would be recalled immediately and any insurance monies paid. He breathed a ragged sigh when he finally slammed his car door shut, glad to be sealed up and away from this madness. His eyes found the tangle of police cars and ambulances still taking up most of the car park, and so he picked up his mobile phone and put a quick call through to Jannings, his fingers trembling on the keypad, as he prayed that this second ride would be the last.

It was only as the call went through and began to ring that he remembered the dragon, and the plans that he'd already had approved and put through for its construction.


The phone rang and rang and rang.

No one picked up, not even his secretary. He tried the main switchboard, but even that rang unanswered. The images of the dragon sketched across his A3 jotter flashed into his mind once again - the teeth, the tail, the proposal for a safe puff of smoke. The potential for trouble was insane, as insane as this whole damn business was getting.

The company car park was full when he finally got there, including the silver Mercedes of Mr Jannings parked in front of the blue glass doors. Lights burned in all of the office windows, but he could see no heads bobbing about or owners of the cars going about their business. He hurried through into reception, but the desk there was deserted, and as he made his way swiftly up to his office he passed not one single person on his route. Where the hell was everyone? Surely they weren't all in the same meeting somewhere. Unless it was the dragon. He shook his head furiously almost immediately, cursing his own stupidity. That was crazy.

He stuck his head briefly round his office door, just to be sure, but the room was empty. No dragon, no fire, no notice of any urgent meeting, nothing. He continued on, up to the top floor and Jannings' office. That too was deserted, and it was then that Damien began to grow even more uneasy. This was not right at all. To have the rides malfunction and attack the kids that rode them was one thing, but to now have the offices devoid of all staff, well, that was simply ludicrous. It just couldn't happen.

He started back along the corridor, one hand held against his head, kneading his temple, penetrating the uncertain thoughts that continued to swirl in the darkness there. The words of The Talking Pig rose up out of the murk, echoing those of The Killer Clown. They wanted their master, their creator, and that man was not him. But if he had created them, why was he not their creator?

And then a thought occurred.

If not him, then who?

He had always had that nagging guilt that the thoughts that had made these things had not been his own. But if they were not his own, then to whom did they belong?

And then, as if to somehow answer that question, a dark swirling shadow rose up across the white painted office wall from the end of the corridor. It washed across the desks, it washed across the chairs, and then the creature that cast that unnatural shadow turned the corner and lifted its twisted malformed head in Damien's direction. He was the last of the humans in its new lair, he now suddenly knew, and he watched helplessly as it snorted an angry gust of fiery intent from its fibreglass nostrils at him, two curls of non-toxic generated smoke rising fiercely towards the rows of spiked metal ceiling extinguishers even as Damien gazed up at them.

The jets of water spurted down with almost uncanny readiness, dousing the desks and the chairs and the two combatants facing each other. Damien stood for a few moments half-expecting the dragon to stagger or shudder or topple awkwardly to one side. But it did not. It simply stood beneath the downpour and let out another snort of fire towards him.

It curled angrily through the air, and it was only as Damien took a hesitant step back away from it that this unnatural monster spoke. He knew these manufactured machines should not have been able to do so, and yet its voice came hoarse and crackling, like the fire that guttered at the back of its throat.

I.

Seek.

My.

Creator.

It said.

The.

One.

That.

Gave.

Me.

Substance.

That.

Gave.

Me.

Life.

"I... I don't know," Damien stammered, the water from the sprinkler system snaking his sodden hair down into his eyes, blurring his sight, forcing him to blink hard through it to see any attack that might come.

Everyone.

Answered.

The.

Same.

And.

Everyone.

Burned.

The.

Same.

Damien stared helplessly at this thing. This just couldn't be happening.

"But you came from my head -"

No.

Not.

From.

Your.

Head.

From.

Your.
Hand.
Tell.
Me.
The.
Name.
Of.
My.
Creator.
And.
I.
Will.
Be.
Gone.

Damien stared at its fibreglass shell, its body moulded into the shape of a cartoon dragon, snorting colourful clouds of billowing smoke, growling its intentions to kill him. It just wasn't possible, that's all he could keep telling himself. He'd drawn this thing out of his head, seen its designs go down to the workshops, and yet here it was, threatening his very life.

And then something happened, something weird deep inside the darkness of his head. It wasn't one of his own thoughts, but a mingling of ideas rising to the surface like bubbles in a beer glass; or rather a glass of discoloured rot.

Me, said one.

Servant, said another.

And then a plethora of thought bubbles.

I am the one.

Kill the little children.

I will have their souls.

The rush of these last two seemed to snag

something inside his head, and Damien lurched sideways and had to catch hold of one of the chairs in order to keep himself upright.

Take me now and we will be gone.

It took Damien a few moments to realise that this comment was directed not to himself, but to the dragon, and when he glanced back up in its direction, saw it approaching quickly with something close to satisfaction on its distorted manufactured face.

With his eyes clenched shut against the inevitable, Damien stood frozen as the monster bore down on him, clutching his skull in its cold hard claws before starting swiftly to squeeze. Then those thoughts came again, only louder and more insistent now that they seemed closer to the surface, closer to freedom. Damien loosed a shriek of pain as he felt something crack inside his head, or maybe it was even his head itself. But soon the world around him became slippery, elusive, and he felt himself tumble out of the office and into some eerie dark nothingness.

A headache like the worst hangover ever greeted his hesitant eyes when they at last flickered open. The office was deserted, just as it had been the previous afternoon, and he simply gazed up through a haze of pain at the ceiling tiles, glad to at least be still alive.

The light was crisp and bright and he guessed the time to be a few hours before 9.00am, and this was confirmed a short while afterward when the first of the cleaners entered the building and began clattering about. It would be soon, he started thinking, when they would find him, sprawled across the floor of an empty office building, unable to move, unable to cry out. Then they would call an ambulance for him, and then when he was better he would tell the police all about the creature that had lurked inside his head that wanted to kill the little children. They would stop it, whatever it was. They would make sure that it wouldn't be able to hurt any more kids, not like the kid with pig, and the kid with the clown.

His eyes drifted awkwardly through the myriad of swirling agonised shapes to the doorway. Was that one of the cleaners now? There was a shape there, something dark, and it looked like it was carrying a mop or a broom. It was difficult to discern much through the soup ebbing through his head, but then it began to grow closer, and vaguely clearer. At last he had been found, that's all he could think, even though he had failed to notice that the approaching cleaner's feet had made no sound across the tiled floor. It seemed only strange now, distantly out of the ordinary, not quite right. And then the mop seemed to rise up, almost above the cleaner's head, and all he could do was frown at the reason for this to be happening. His lips parted to question the cleaner, to say that it was help that he needed, a doctor. And then a voice came, half in front of him, half inside of him.

Worry not about the little children, it said to him. They will be safe with me.

And then the shaft that he had thought had been a mop descended rapidly and knocked the last of his senses out of his skull. The last thing he heard, before his snatches of life slipped away completely, was the sound of the first of the cleaners through the door, as she screamed and screamed and screamed, at the sight of all the bodies littering the reception floor.

It had been crazy to even think of starting the trip, but she had, and Billy had gotten worse. Her parents had wanted the two of them for Christmas, but not like this, not with Billy's flu still hanging grimly on like a battered flyweight in the tenth round.

The snow had been coming down in thick droves over the course of the week, but the house was cold and uncomfortable, even with Jack still staying behind (Jack hated her parents, hated Christmas too if the truth be known), and the air was thick with the stench of sickness. She'd wanted Billy out of it and into her warm parent's home in Penzance, and yet here she was, stranded in a hotel room just outside Exeter, with Billy's forehead ablaze with a renewed fever.

Katie perched on the window ledge and gazed out across the car park, at the heavy flurries of snow lit up bright against the black night's sky by the hotel's streetlamps, and consequently at the ever-building drifts. It was December 22nd, two days before Christmas Eve, and she'd done a stupid and selfish thing.

She glanced back across at Billy. He was sleeping, his forehead wrinkled slightly from the fever, the covers pulled up tight below his chin. She was scared, that was the truth of it. He was six years old and he'd had a bad case of flu, and in her haste to be with her parents for Christmas she'd dragged him out into the freezing December cold before he was ready, and now she feared the worse.

Suppose the flu had snatched him back?

Suppose he'd gotten pneumonia?

Jesus, what a thing to think. Why did she have to think that?

Her eyes dropped down to Elvis lying down on the deep red carpet. He was a collie cross that had wandered into her garden during the summer and had simply decided to stay. The dog had shown no malice or desire to steal food, and had wanted nothing more than to stay with her. With no collar she'd had little choice, and she'd not wanted to take him to the nearest dog shelter either. So he'd stayed, and after a bath and a new collar, she'd named him Elvis; and if on that day anyone had asked her why she had called him Elvis, she would not have had an answer for them.

Her watch read ten thirty. It had taken her the best part of four hours to navigate her way slowly along a hundred miles of intermittently-lit motorway. There had been little in the way of other traffic, most other drivers having no doubt listened to the frequent pleas from radio traffic reports to stay home and wait for better weather. But she'd not listened, had she? No, all she could think of was getting out of the cold house and arriving in Penzance in time for Christmas Eve.

And to get away from Jack, of course. She'd married him before she'd reached twenty, thrilled by his anger, exhilarated by his dangerousness. That thrill had not lasted long, however, and she often lived in fear of his temper. When Billy was born things mellowed a little, and she hoped that having a boy might bring out some good in him. But the older Billy got, the less Jack would spend time with him. And the bruises first began to appear when Billy was four.

Katie got up from the window ledge, sniffing back the grief dragged up by her recollections, took up the hand towel and ice-box she'd filled with cold water, and went back through into the bathroom to freshen it. She ran the cold tap for a while as she stared at her reflection in the small vanity mirror above the sink. Her eyes were ringed deep and dark, and her hair looked like it needed a damn good wash. She was tired, from the drive and from the worry. Elvis yawned and half-whimpered out in the main room, distracting her from her thoughts, and she bent to fill the blue plastic ice-box.

Billy was awake when she went back to his bed. A heavy sweat had broken on his brow, and his whole face was flushed a deep scarlet.

"I don't feel good, mummy," he said, a hand appearing from beneath the covers to press against his glistening forehead.

"I know, honey," Katie told him, squeezing out the cold hand towel and holding it delicately against his skin.

"You said I was getting better."

Katie tried her best to smile, but she knew she'd made him worse by dragging him out into the snow.

"Are you hungry?" she asked him. "Do you want any soup?"

Billy shook his head, and then coughed involuntarily.

Please God don't let it be pneumonia, Katie thought insanely inside her head. Elvis half-whimpered again from the carpet behind them, and Billy's gaze flickered in his direction.

"What's wrong with Elvis?" he wanted to know. "Is he sick too?"

"I think he just wants to go out."

"But it's cold out."

"It's a shame he can't use a human toilet like us

488

isn't it?" Katie said to him with a smile.

Billy smiled back and she was glad.

"It's a shame we can't just give him a key so that he could let himself back in, isn't it?" she went on. "Then I wouldn't have to leave you at all."

Billy didn't know whether to smile at this or not. A grin came first but then his forehead knotted. But before he could voice his concerns about being left on his own in a strange hotel room, Katie reassured him quickly.

"It'll only be for a few minutes, just so he can have a wee and stretch his legs. And the door'll be locked and I'm the only one with the key."

Billy still seemed a little unsure of this, but he knew that Elvis needed a wee and so he relented.

"Take as long as Elvis needs," Billy said at last. "I'll be okay."

Katie leant over and kissed him gently on his cheek, before pushing herself to her feet and turning towards the black and white collie still lying on the carpet.

As she took a step towards him, however, his ears pricked and his eyes rolled up towards her, and before she had even reached for the lead hanging over the arm of the chair, he'd sat up eagerly with his tail wagging furiously. For a stray he was pretty damn well behaved, she thought, and the only quirk she'd found in him so far was that he liked to carry his own lead. Once she clipped it around his collar, he'd leap up to take it in his mouth, and wouldn't let go until he was bored with it. She could even let him carry it all himself because he rarely strayed from her heel, and it amused her to watch him trot just ahead of her, effectively walking himself.

It was bitterly cold outside as she stepped through the hotel's main entrance and out into the car park. The freezing wind carried a severe freight of thick snow on its back that seemed to have worsened in the couple of hours she'd been inside with Billy. But she pulled the collar of her heavy jacket up around her neck regardless, as she headed out towards a steep back of snow-covered grass that led up towards a copse of trees. It was out of main view of most of the hotel, so hopefully nobody would be seeing Elvis take his last shit of the day.

Katie stood huddled with her hands thrust deep into the pockets of her jacket, her head scrunched down into her collar, eyes trying to penetrate the dizzying blur of snow as it came thicker and thicker out of the cavernous winter's sky. Elvis was busying himself sniffing at the drifts of snow at the bases of the trees, his lead now dragging behind him. It would dry out, Katie thought distantly, and she didn't need to be holding onto a cold wet lead now, thank you.

She glanced back towards the hotel and tried to locate their room. Less than a tenth of the windows were lit. Obviously most people had more sense than to attempt a journey in this foul snowstorm, but she still had problems placing it. It was a room on the first floor anyway, she'd insisted on that. She'd always been scared of sleeping on the ground floor, whether it was in a house or a hotel. From the time of being a kid she'd always feared it, always imagined someone lurking on the other side of the glass, just waiting to smash the pane and reach in. A storey up and you were safe. They'd have to break their way in and climb a set of stairs; you had time on the first floor, time and a wooden door.

Her thoughts went back to Jack, and how he was probably still sitting slumped in his armchair drinking beer and watching television. She always got Billy to play quietly upstairs in his room rather than downstairs in the living room, anything to try and keep Jack calm. But sometimes it was just the slightest thing - spilled food on the kitchen floor, toys left on the stairs, the bathroom door left too far open, the bathroom door left too far closed. She couldn't bare the sounds his huge hands made on Billy's body, and she had to force her own hands hard over her ears to stop it, and she'd cry and cry before she had the strength to go in and comfort Billy. But what could she do? Jack had struck her enough times too to let her know not to cross him. No, all it took was resolve on their part to try not to upset him too much. Things would get better, she thought as she studied the soft blanket of snow on the bank, soon they'd be back to how things were when they were first married.

She looked back for Elvis but he'd left the trees and was nowhere in sight. She called his name lightly, expecting him to poke his head through the tall grass at the edge of the copse that missed the mowers, but he remained hidden. Taking a step nearer the trees, she called his name again, and this time the darkness inside the trees seemed almost to reach for her, sucking her towards its hollow void. She found herself drawing a sharp shallow breath, chastening herself immediately for being so foolish; the dark had spooked her, that's all. From the corner of her eye she noticed a movement, something dark against the darkness and awkwardly shaped. She felt her heart skip inside her chest once again, but as her sight focussed clearly on the shape of Elvis emerging sniffing from the trees a dozen or more yards further along, she breathed a long breath of relief and went quickly to him.

"Crazy dog," she muttered under her breath, more to have some kind of sound in the deafening silence of the snowstorm than anything else, and she put a hand to his head, ruffling his ears. His fur was cold and running wet, and she retracted her hand quickly back into her pocket, all melted snow and dog hair.

The bank was slippery on the way back down, and Elvis skipped ahead of her all the way back into the hotel foyer. The old man at the front desk was sitting reading a magazine as she passed. He lifted his eyes for the briefest of moments, she saw him from the corner of her eye, but he said nothing to her, and Katie entered the lift and walked the corridor to her door without passing another living soul.

Billy was mercifully asleep, and Katie hung her wet jacket over the top of the bathroom door before lying on top of the bed next to him. She stared at him for a while, at his wrinkled forehead, at the shallow rise and fall of his chest beneath the covers. She hoped it wasn't pneumonia, hoped to God that it wasn't. Just a touch of cold gotten back onto his chest, that was all. She'd see what he was like in the morning, and try and finish the trip down to Penzance.

But what about the roads?

Shit, she'd forgotten about them. She'd just been stood out in the middle of a blizzard and it hadn't occurred to her how it would be laying on the roads.

Shit, she thought again. She didn't want to stay in the hotel one night, let alone two. Maybe in the morning it would be clearer. By lunchtime certainly.

Katie reached across and took up the remote control from the cabinet beside the bed, pressing the

TV on and running down the volume before the picture appeared. An old Paul Newman film was playing on Channel Four, a young Paul Newman too, in a sailor suit. She flicked over to ITV, a newscaster was talking silently, no one she recognised, regional news, a picture of a young man in the box behind his head. She carried on to BBC2, a drama in a squalid neighbourhood, young people shouting, that was all she needed. BBC1 offered something similar, but a forensic doctor at a morgue.

Katie went back to ITV and touched the volume up a few notches, so she could just make out the newscaster. She glanced back at Billy as he fidgeted beside her, but he stayed sleeping. The words third murder this month suddenly caught her attention, and she shot her attention back to the TV.

The picture of the young man had changed to a photograph of a body hanging from a tree at the edge of a field, as policemen in yellow jackets huddled around it. Katie took the volume up another notch, listening intently as the newscaster went on:

"Mr and Mrs Hughsey have urged anyone to come forward if they have any information about who could have done this to their son. The third victim, Aaron Hughsey, hung from a tree less than two miles from Exeter town centre, was found dead this morning with no clue as to his death other than a hand-written note pinned to his coat; a note which read only burglar. Police have no evidence to confirm this allegation, nor to the notes attached to the two previous victims, both hanged in identical situations, notes written in red ink which were previously thought to have been blood, child molester and thief."

Katie could feel herself shaking. There was a mass

murderer here in Exeter. She didn't know about the others, but this last murder had taken place just two miles from the town centre, and this hotel was right on the outskirts of town itself.

Her eye went slowly to the door, to the single brass handle. There was a lock on it that she hadn't turned, and suddenly her heart was thumping madly. She pushed herself off the bed and stepped steadily across the room to the door. The hotel was deathly silent. Hardly anyone checked in on a night like this. Silent. Deathly. She reached out and clicked the lock over. Was it locked, she thought crazily? She panicked and grabbed the handle just to be sure. It wouldn't turn. Thank God, it was locked.

She turned on her heel, the motion dizzying her momentarily, and she reeled wildly, her heart skipping. Elvis lay on the carpet just in front of her, looking round at her, his eyes wide, wondering why she was so flustered. But all she could do was stare down at him. She couldn't even summon a smile for him, not now. The TV had given her the frights, and she fumbled for the off button on the front of the set with her eyes closed so that she wouldn't see the screen again by accident.

With the television off, the room seemed even more silent that it had been before. Nothing moved or made a sound in the rest of the hotel, and with the double-glazing, she could hear nothing outside either. But even if she were to risk opening a window just to hear the outside world, and risk a freezing draft hurrying her boy deeper towards pneumonia, the thick snow outside would only smother that noise anyway; smother the sounds of the ropeman crunching across freshly-laid snow towards her door.

She shuddered hard. Why did she have to think that shit?

Katie hugged herself as tightly as she could, and stepped briskly across the room to the bed, slipping quickly beneath the covers next to her son. She could sleep fully clothed, she thought to herself. Quicker to run. Quicker in the morning. She closed her eyes, but her head was spinning, rotating madly with images of Aaron Hughsey hanging from a tree branch like a suit of clothes hanging in a wardrobe. Even on the edges of sleep she shuddered, and it would be a sleep that would offer her no rest for the remainder of the night.

She woke with daylight filtering in through the thin curtains, a weak light that bathed the room with a soft watery luminescence. Her eyes ached as they rotated in their sockets, taking in the unfamiliar objects of the hotel room, and the left hand side of her body groaned with a dull pain as she rolled over to glance at the radio-alarm on the cabinet beside the bed. The keen red digits read quarter past seven.

She put a hand to her forehead and found it was hot and damp with a clammy sweat. It was then that she remembered that she hadn't undressed, and as she slid her legs out from beneath the covers, felt her jeans clinging to her legs, and her t-shirt to the small of her back.

Elvis's nose appeared in the space between her hands as she sat bent over the edge of the bed. His tail was thumping the carpet loudly, his tongue lolling long and pink. She put a hand over the top of his head and then got up, pushing past him as she stumbled into the bathroom.

Her face looked wrinkled in the small vanity mirror, her hair a state, but she pushed her jeans and knickers down and sat on the toilet to pee. Her head hurt, and through the dizzying haze of a headache she hoped a shower might repel, she remembered the news on the TV the previous night. It didn't seem quite so bad now that morning had come, but three murders just a few miles away from them was scary.

Rolling a few sheets of toilet paper around her hand, she wiped herself dry and then got up, hoisting her knickers and jeans up before flushing the toilet and going back into the main room. Billy was still asleep, she was glad to see, and easing the curtains open a crack, she peered out to see what hope the morning might bring. The answer was none.

Her heart sank as she saw the heavy drifts of snow banked against the handful of cars in the car park. From her vantage point, she could make out only two sets of footprints leading out into the deep snow, both going to cars, but only one attempting to clear their car of the heavy weight of snow that covered it. It was certain that they weren't going anywhere for a while and had given up.

She let the curtain drop and turned to watch Billy sleep. His tiny frame barely moved beneath the covers, but at least the wrinkled expression had gone from his face. Perhaps he just needed a good night's sleep in a warm bed to bring him round. When he woke he'd be fine, she just knew it.

Elvis was at her feet again, his lead in his mouth, and with Billy still asleep she relented and crossed the room to pick up her jacket from the top of the bathroom door. As soon as she opened the door Elvis was out and bounding down the corridor, his lead still in his mouth and swinging from side to side like a thrashing snake.

When she got to the foyer, the same old man from the previous night was still on duty. He looked up at her as she passed, a strange narrow-eyed expression on his face that disturbed her a little. She was going to say Good Morning to him, but decided not to and said nothing, and he said nothing, and so she fixed her gaze straight ahead of her as she walked right on out through the main entrance and into the early light.

Once outside, however, she chastened herself for being so mistrusting. She had a dog in the hotel after all, and even though he was on a lead, he was carrying it himself so it probably didn't count; no wonder he'd given her a funny look. It had been the same man who had said it was okay to have the dog in the hotel in the first place and had booked her the room, so if he'd had a problem with dogs he should have said then. But then he'd even offered to look in on Billy if she wanted to go out, but she didn't want to go anywhere, only to take Elvis out so that he could take a whizz. She knew it was cruel not to give Elvis a longer walk, but she didn't want to leave Billy on his own any longer than she had too, and Elvis got plenty of walks at home anyway; he'd deal with it for a few days, she was sure. But she found that the more she walked the clearer her head became, of aches and of thoughts. The crisp clean air seemed to rejuvenate her, and the horror of the previous night's news just couldn't take hold of her like it had. She tried to force the fear to return, repeating over and over in her head that three murders had taken place just a few miles from where she was now, as if to dismiss them was to clear the murderer of his unspeakable crimes. But the sun was breaking through the cloud cover now, turning the day into something wonderful, and horror just had no business being there at that moment.

So she walked briskly, Elvis trotting on up ahead, as she made her way through the car park and up the other end of the bank towards the far end of the trees. Maybe the sun would start to melt the snow after all, she thought hopefully to herself, and when she got back to the room, Billy would be better and they could have their breakfast early before setting back off onto the road to her parent's home.

Their walk took them all the way along the ridge beside the hotel, Elvis disappearing intermittently between the trees, down across a playing field, along a semi-sheltered path where hardly any snow had gathered, and back around the other side of the hotel. She took a breath as she made her way back in through the main entrance, but the old man was no longer on reception. In his place was a young girl in a crisp new uniform. She even wore a name badge on her lapel, but Katie was too far away to read it. She did, however, receive a cheery greeting from the girl, and even Elvis got a smile, so as she got into the lift and rode it to the first floor, she was in pleasant spirits as she walked down the corridor and stepped into the room. Billy was awake, she was glad to see, and sitting on the edge of the bed. But as she entered and said Good Morning to him, he continued to stare straight ahead of him at the wall, as if he hadn't heard her or even seen her enter the room.

Her fingers were trembling as she dropped her jacket onto the floor. She crossed the room quickly, and knelt down in front of him, taking hold of his hand as she looked up into his face. But he flinched from the touch and she could see that his face was white and wet with tears.

"What's wrong?" she wanted desperately to know, but he just stared straight ahead at the wall, his hands knotted in his lap.

"Tell me," she persisted. "Did you have a bad dream? Did you worry that I wasn't here?"

But Billy just continued to stare.

"I've just been out with Elvis. Look, he's pleased to see you."

She tried to direct his attention to the dog that was just inches from his clasped hands, but he just wouldn't see it. Eventually Katie pursed her lips and left him for a while. He'd come round sooner or later, she thought to herself. It must've been hard, waking up in a strange room and her not being there, and not answering him if he'd called for her. She looked at the clock on the bedside cabinet now and saw that she'd been gone nearly three quarters of an hour. That was stupid. She should have known he'd worry. Especially with him still being sick.

"Do you want any breakfast?" she asked him, but he stayed where he was, perched on the edge of the bed. "I could get you some orange juice, or some cereal."

But he wouldn't have it. She wanted to turn on the television to take his mind off her leaving him, but she remembered the images of the hanged man in the field and thought against it. She didn't want to see that again herself, and Billy sure as hell didn't need to see it. But there might be cartoons on, she reasoned, and he had to do something while she showered instead of worry.

So she took up the remote and pressed the TV

button, but nothing happened, and she remembered that she'd turned the television off at the set. She went to it now and turned it on, flicking swiftly through the channels when the screen flickered on in case there were any new developments in the news. Thankfully there was only one news station on, and it was national news, something about a banking crisis in Europe. She found cartoons readily enough though, and she left it playing in front of him as she went through into the bathroom to shower. She needed a soak, and she hoped that a few minutes of bright moving colours might swing him out of his mood. She wanted him cheery today, just as she wanted the growing sun to continue to burn its way through the hazy clouds in the sky outside, and melt all that goddamned snow away.

The sun disappeared mid-morning, and the heavy grey snow clouds bullied the overcast sky about four o'clock and laid its burden evenly across the country. There was no wind to blow it into drifts like it had the previous day, but it came thick and it settled swiftly.

Katie cursed from the window sill as she sat and stared helplessly out at it. The hope had gone, replaced by the dreaded certainty that they would be spending another night in the hotel, the night before Christmas Eve. She so didn't want Billy spending his Christmas in a hotel room. But even if they could get to the car and navigate their way along treacherous roads to Penzance, he was still not fully well, and exposing him to the freezing cold outside could still tip him into something bad, if he wasn't there already. And so she watched the snow fall, and watched it settle upon the tops of the few cars still left in the car park, watched it settle upon the leaves of the trees at the top of the bank, watched it settle upon the road that wound its way back up towards the motorway, the road they had come in upon.

Billy finished most of his chicken soup that the hotel kitchen had made for him and went to sleep shortly afterwards at about five thirty. Katie watched him for a while, feeling sure that the worst of whatever had taken a grip on him had gone, and decided to watch the TV for a while. There was nothing much worth watching, idle dramas and ridiculous soaps, and she gazed absently out through the window while it droned, her mind just wandering, not really able to concentrate on much at all. At six, the soaps finished and the news stations fired up. She gave the international stories casual attention, the European monetary crisis, troubles in the Middle East, a bomb scare at Heathrow, but as soon as the regional news began the hairs at the back of her neck prickled, and a nervousness crawled swiftly across her skin.

She prayed that the ropeman had been arrested, or at the very least been named and a face put to him. But the items meandered, the story of the hangman wouldn't come, and she found herself getting more and more anxious, her palms sweating, her mouth running dry. Until the dreaded image in the box behind the newscaster's head appeared, a body hanging from a tree, only this time there were buildings in the background. This latest murder had not taken place in a quiet farmer's field. This was in a small park near a parade of shops. A murder in full view of everyone.

Katie barely heard the report, so intent was she on

the pictures that followed. The ropeman had come out of the secluded areas and out into the open, stringing his last victim up in full view of at least two dozen houses, maybe more. The reporter at the scene was stood in front of the death tree, the body obviously now removed, but the part of the rope that had been attached to the overhanging branch was still mostly there from where it had been cut by police, and to see that still twitching in the breeze knotted her stomach like a corpse's fist.

Then the reporter mentioned the note, the murderer's signature, the scrap of paper written with red ink that had been pinned to the dead man's shirt. Abuser of animals, was all it had said.

Katie clasped her hand to her mouth as if she was going to cry out, and shot Billy a glance lying next to her in bed. A man was dead, but a sick bastard that tortured defenceless animals - maybe dogs like Elvis. Was that a crime - an eye for an eye? Jesus, she didn't know now, and she ran both her hands raggedly through her hair, before snatching up the remote control and turning the television sharply off.

She pushed herself to her feet and paced the room with her hands over her mouth. Where the hell was she, she wanted to know? Four murders within a handful of miles of where they were staying. This was insane.

Outside the world was darkening once more. Night was coming and along with it all the horrors that hid in the shadows. She wrapped her arms around herself as she gazed out at the vague shape of her car still parked down below in the car park, the cloak of snow still covering it, still concealing her escape. Thoughts nagged inside her head - she could make a break for it, perhaps the snow was slush now, perhaps the ice that had frozen beneath it wasn't ice at all, perhaps the grit lorries had done their job - but she knew that to risk anything was crazy. Better to be stranded in a warm hotel room than in a car ditched at the side of a road in the middle of nowhere.

Her eyes tracked across the freshly-laid snow, across the car park and to the trees at the top of the bank. Someone was standing there, at the front of the trees where Elvis had taken his first whizz. Her blood ran cold as she saw it was a man, his hands thrust deep into his long heavy coat, his face turned up towards her. His features were all cast by deep shadow, but she could feel the sharpness of his gaze like a knife held against her skin.

She froze; she couldn't move away from this exchange, couldn't even back away a single step into the safety of the room. He just stood there and stared up at her, not moving, nothing. And then she jumped as Billy spoke behind her, just a murmur after waking, a single enquiry:

"Mummy?"

She wanted to turn her head to look at him, but her eyes refused to break the connection between herself and the man still standing amongst the trees. But then she tore herself fully round and found Billy sitting upright in bed, the covers heaped at his lap, his forehead knotted.

"What are looking at?" he asked.

"Nothing, honey," Katie lied. He didn't need to know that she'd been spooked by someone standing out in the snow. That was all it was though, wasn't it? Just someone standing out in the snow?

"Can we go to granma's yet? I don't want to stay here anymore."

"We can't go yet, Billy. The snow's still too deep. It's too dangerous."

Billy pursed his lips, his forehead wrinkling again, and then he slumped back into his pillow and gazed up at the ceiling. Katie thought that tears were close. She didn't want him to miss Christmas, her mum had everything set up for them both - stockings over the fireplace, a huge turkey fully dressed, home-made mince pies - and she didn't want them to miss it all by being stuck here, and being frightened by passers-by outside.

At ten o'clock Elvis began pacing. She couldn't help it, but Katie went back to the window to look out. The world was black apart from the lamplights in the car park and the blankets of white that their reach illuminated. She was looking up at the top of the bank, to the place where the man had stood watching her, but there was no sign of him now, as she knew there wouldn't be. But still her eyes tracked along the ridge of trees in case he should still be hiding there.

Behind her Elvis began to whimper, and she turned to see him turning in circles by the door.

"Alright," she relented, going to him. His tongue hung pinkly from his mouth as he stared up at her with huge bright eyes. Katie looked around for his lead but it wasn't hanging over the arm of the chair or lying anywhere on the floor.

"Where's your lead?" she asked him, moving a couple of her bags away from the skirting board. But Elvis just began to circle by the door again. Katie had a quick look near the wardrobe, and even stuck her head into the bathroom, but there was no sign of it. But then she reasoned that he was pretty good off the lead anyway and there was no real danger for him out in the car park, so she let it be and opened the door for him.

But he leapt up at her regardless, wanting his lead, wanting to carry it along the corridor to the lift. But Katie didn't have it, she must have dropped it somewhere, so she pushed him out of the way, closed the door behind them, and continued on down the corridor, Elvis still jumping excitedly up at her all the way.

The old man was back in the foyer as she stepped out of the lift. He was watering the tall ferns from a green plastic can and he glanced up at her as the lift chimed. He had a smile for her this time, and his eyes tracked her all the way across the lobby until she was outside. She preferred his welcome this time, but his lengthy scrutiny made her feel cold, even before the chill wind from outside had found her skin.

The image of his smiling face hung in her head as she crunched through the deep snow, of his thin lips and his eyes that stared and stared. They seemed to watch all of her at once, those eyes, but not as though he was mentally undressing her, but like something else entirely. Perhaps he still had a problem with the dog, perhaps more so now that she'd lost the lead, and perhaps he was wondering just what sort of person would lose their own dog's lead. She had no idea, and so much did it occupy her thoughts that she looked up startled to find herself in front of the bank that ran up towards the darkened mass of trees.

Elvis had already bounded through the snow almost to the top, which made slowing her pace difficult. She didn't want to admit that she'd been scared, didn't want anyone to see that fear or even see her behave differently as a result of that fear. So she climbed, one foot after the other, lifting her boots high over the deep blanket of snow to where Elvis now stood looking back for her.

But there was no man waiting for her, no stranger with shadowed features, no maniac with a noose. There was just a suffocating silence caused by the snow broken only by the rustling of the leaves as the cold December wind blew through the trees.

Katie hugged herself as she walked, to keep the cold out as much as to feel a touch against herself. Jack had hardly touched her with any affection for the last few years, and to feel something, even if it was her own touch, brought some comfort and reassurance.

But then something caught her eye, something white and fluttering amongst the darkness of the trees that was not snow. Something small blustered beneath the grip of the wind, something pinned against the bark of one of the trees, a scrap of paper.

Katie went to it with trembling fingers, glancing round in case should anyone see her, and tugged the note from its place. It was a single sheet of paper folded in half. Across it was written in rough red writing, four words that shook her inside: photographer of naked children.

She nearly dropped the note, so crazily did her head spin. And she thought she would fall into the snow and freeze. What the hell did it mean? Who the hell had written it? Was it for her? Was it some sick trick? But then she knew. In a sickening heartbeat she suddenly understood.

Her head spun back towards the hotel, her eyes searching panicking now for the room in which Billy now lay sleeping. Her mind conjured those same images of the old man in the foyer, of his thin lips, of his wandering eyes, of his hands that slipped across the smooth green plastic of his watering can like the buttocks of a small boy. Her stomach knotted with sickness, twisting and contorting as though someone had gotten in there and had begun to punch it apart with their fists. Her thoughts blackened and slipped inside her head, and the world seemed to tilt a few degrees, catching her off-balance as she stood on the bank beneath the trees. Then she began to run, down the slope in a kind of sliding gallop, the hard ground slick beneath her weight, her heels scrabbling madly. She stumbled and slipped frequently, but she had to get back to the room, had to get back to get Billy.

The foyer was empty when she reached it, and she ran to the lift with tears streaming down her cheeks. Elvis yapped behind her, but she ignored him as she hammered the button to make the doors open. And then she hurried inside and hammered the first floor button until the doors slid closed.

Her chest was burning as she stumbled out into the corridor, her breath barely able to reach her lungs, so horribly did they ache. But she forced her legs to carry her along the corridor to the door, legs that didn't feel as if they were even hers, praying that Billy would still be inside and asleep, still undisturbed and oblivious to the horrors that the world might want to bring him.

But as the door came in sight, she almost collapsed to see that it stood partially ajar. She fell against it as she stumbled through, and felt her stomach turn itself over as she saw the old man standing over the bed, a camera held up to his face with one hand, his other holding Billy's pyjama bottoms down around his knees.

Katie screamed with a force that she didn't know she even possessed, and felt herself rush towards him with a fury that erupted from her fists that had clenched into white knuckles. She saw the old man turn his face towards her to see her coming, saw the lusty gaze in his eyes, saw his thin lips slick with saliva, but then the following moments flashed by in such a daze that she could barely separate the briefest of images.

The old man's camera flew from his face in a slowly-turning arc, striking the wall on the far side before the flash bulb cracked and broke away. In the midst of a rain of blood from an opening wound to his cheek, she saw those eyes wander over her again. There was a reflection of her child in those eyes - a reflection of a hundred different children - a picture of his bare skin, his exposed groin, and she felt her fingernails break as she gouged at his face and throat.

But then there was a dull thud somewhere inside her head, and blackness pounded everything into nonsense. And then all she could see were heels as the world tilted a second time. She'd hit the ground, that's all she could think as she lay there, as a heavy drum thumped madly against the inside of her skull. Her limbs would not obey her, they refused to bear her up, and all she could do was lay there and stare at the now vacant doorway. He'd gotten away, her fury told her, he was gone.

The thumping inside her head went on, but Katie slowly managed to haul herself back to her feet, unconsciousness always threatening, and crawled across the bed to look down at Billy. He had pulled his pyjamas back up over himself, and now lay in a curled up ball sobbing quietly. She went to him, her own body wracked with grief, but he recoiled from her touch, recoiling away from her to the other side of the bed.

Katie staggered to the window, staring out into the black night as tears ran down her face. Her hands shook with fear and rage, with desperation and with helplessness, and the man who had done all this to them had run away, gone for good, never to return.

But then her eyes went back to the place where the man had stood. There was motion there, she saw, two men struggling, and she watched with horror as one of them suddenly soared upwards. He was on a length of rope, his legs kicking out wildly as the other man stepped casually back to view his work, and Katie watched as he thrashed his legs to try and find the ground once more. But there would be no purchase for him, no saving of his life, and she watched as the ropeman watched, as his life was jerked out of him, until death eventually claimed him and he hung still.


The lights from the police cars lit the room with flashes of blue within half an hour, but Katie didn't leave the room. She didn't need to see the body close up to know that it was the old man from the reception desk that had been cut down. She was glad that he was dead, glad that the ropeman had caught him and had done to him what she could not. Instead, she remained in her room and held Billy in her arms as they rocked slowly back and forth. They both cried too, both sobbed until no more would come, but it would be another day before they could leave the hotel and the horrors that the room still held.

When the snows melted enough for her to dig her car out and make it out onto the main road, she found that the grit lorries had done their job. They made their way slowly onto the A-roads towards Penzance, which were clear enough for them to do a steady forty, and they eventually arrived at her parent's house mid-afternoon on Christmas Day.

It wasn't a happy break, but it was a break away from Jack and the house, and with her parents doting on Billy, it gave Katie a while to get to grips with what had happened, not just over the past few days, but over life at home too.

She didn't tell her parents about what had happened in the hotel, but she did make a few decisions in the week that they stayed. Once she and Billy returned home and were back beneath Jack's roof, she began to think about leaving him and taking Billy away somewhere safe.

It was just after nine o'clock on the 6th of January when Katie put Billy to bed. After tucking him in tight and kissing his forehead gently, she went to the window to draw the curtains. But as her fingers grasped the fabric, her eyes caught the figure of a man standing amongst the trees at the far end of the garden. She froze, her heart suddenly hammering afresh, as they stood and stared at one another. She knew him immediately, even without seeing his features - she didn't need to see a face. What did he want? Why had he followed her?

She glanced quickly over her shoulder to make sure Billy was not watching, and then turned back, but the man had gone, vanished from the space beneath the trees. Slowly she drew the curtains across, and stepped quietly back across the room before slipping silently out, pressing the door closed after her.

She went downstairs with a thousand thoughts whirling in her head; what did it mean, why had he come back for her, where had he gone? Jack was in the living room watching TV, another beer in his hand. He said nothing as she came in, didn't even look up, and she stood and looked at him for a few moments, but not for too long. He didn't like scrutiny, or the fact that someone might be having secret thoughts about him. It was crazy to slip out, she knew, but she went out into the kitchen and stepped quietly out through the back door, out into the night and down to the far end of the garden.

It was bitterly cold and she had not put a coat on, and she hugged herself hard as she walked amongst the trees looking for him. It was dark, unutterably dark, but she somehow managed to stifle a scream as she virtually walked straight into him as he swung from one of the branches.

She knew it was him immediately and not another victim, and she staggered back against one of the other trees with both hands over her mouth as she stood and stared up at him. It was impossible to make out his face, so dark was it beneath the trees, and she was glad that she would never see it. But then she saw the small cloth bag that hung from his belt, and the scrap of paper that he had pinned to it. Her hands were shaking with both cold and terror, but she knew that this was meant for her.

She took a step forward, her trembling fingers reaching for the string that bound it to him, and tugged the knot loose. It slipped readily into her other hand, and she fell away from him before examining it. She had to go back a short way into the partial light thrown into the garden from the street, but as she unfolded the scrap of paper, she saw that upon it was written just a single word, written in the same rough red ink, murderer.

Had this been his final act, she thought to herself? Had the guilt been too strong for him, taking out of society those that did not deserve to be a part of it, taking himself out along with them?

She felt a pang of sadness for him, for the passing of someone who had chosen to make a stand. And then she eased open the small cloth bag, and took out the notepaper on which he wrote his labels, along with the red pen whose ink had looked like blood. Had he passed his things on to her in the hope that she would continue what he had started? Did he know about Jack? Jesus, what had he seen?

But there was something else at the bottom of the bag. She reached in, feeling what felt like leather inside. Her breath froze in her throat. It was Elvis' lead. Had the ropeman taken it that first night, or had he merely found it? She knew she would never find out, but then she saw another note folded in half and pinned to the brown leather. With numb fingers she tugged it away, opened it wide, and saw that upon it was written four words, abuser of my child.

Katie swallowed hard as she stared at it.

Did he deserve death? Did Billy deserve vengeance? Her thoughts wanted to spin, she could feel their agitation inside her head, but she didn't want to initiate that - where might that lead, what actions might her own hands be capable of? But then her eyes lifted from the scrap of paper in her hand and flickered back towards the house, finding the living room window with the undrawn curtains, and finding the shape of her husband still sitting watching television as he took another sip from his beer can.

Where might such thinking lead, she couldn't help her own mind ask, as she remembered the bruises that appeared across Billy's fragile body? And what actions might her own hands be capable of, tightening the strong leather lead around his neck and watching him jerk at the end of it? Did he deserve death? Did Billy deserve vengeance?

It was a cold day, colder than it had been, and the wind was blowing in hard from the North. It was afternoon too, about three o'clock, and quiet, the sort of eerie suburban quiet that deadens the air when most folks are at work during the daytime. But the leafy cul-de-sac had seemed more so, silent and deserted, and that had been the main reason for them choosing it. In and out, relatively quickly, and taking anything light that was of any real value with only a few extra minutes to have a brief nose round. It was the few people with all the money that was the problem. The masses just got by, while the poor sad wretches like them who had to scrape a living off the streets, they were the ones that needed it the most. The window had been half-open when they'd got there, so it didn't take much to simply lift the latch and clamber inside. This was going to be a cinch.

"Look at all this shit," Casper gasped, climbing in through the window after his friend and gazing about the living room they'd been delivered into. "We could get a few quid for this lot."

He heard Adie sniggering from the corner of the room and turned to see him playing with something he'd found on the mantelpiece.

"Look," he said, holding up the lipstick for him to see. "A chick's house. Let's see what else she's got."

Casper watched as Adie left the room in search of God knows what, and went to follow, but stopped as he caught sight of a book lying on the floor. Dropped, presumably, from the armchair, he would not even have given it a second look except for the scarlet stain smeared across its cover. He stepped towards it, stooping to take a closer look. There were a number of little drops of red, and a number of them had been smudged together. He frowned as he stood up again, and noticed a line of the scarlet drops trailing beside the armchair that he had not seen before. He was sure it was blood, but he had never seen so much of it in one place like this before, except in films. He stepped back away from the chair, and then retreated out of the room altogether, pursuing Adie in his eager search for bounty.

Casper trotted into the kitchen, stopping briefly at the refrigerator to feed his hunger and fill up on what he could find - some salmon, a couple of rolls, an unhealthy dose of mayonnaise - before hurrying into the dining room across the hall. This too was empty, and cautiously he climbed the stairs to a strained and muffled sound coming from one of the bedrooms. Casting his head round one of the doors, he discovered Adie perched on the edge of a bed and holding a white bra up to his chest. He looked up as Casper entered, a mischievous grin spreading rapidly across his face.

"Look what I found," he said, snatching up a fistful of other silk underwear he had already pulled out from one of the drawers.

"We shouldn't be doing this," Casper murmured, looking uneasily around the room. "This isn't right, going through people's stuff."

"What's your problem?" Adie snapped, hurling the bra to the floor. "It's just some bitch's stuff. What do you care?"

Casper turned and stared at him. He was anxious, perhaps even a little scared.

"I found some blood downstairs."

"So?"

"So perhaps she's hurt herself," Casper explained. "Or maybe even died."

"Cool," Adie grinned once more, staring off into space, dreaming of the macabre possibilities. "Maybe the body's round here somewhere, decayed and rotting."

Casper stared at him, his nose curled with distaste.

"You're sick, you know that?"

Adie grinned at the comment. He kind of liked the sound of that.

"Look what else I found," he said, holding up a pack of cards. "It was hidden at the back of the drawer where she thought no one would find it."

"What is it?"

"Looks like a bunch of tarot cards or something," Adie explained, handing over the deck of pictured cards. "Cool skeletons and stuff. I'll stick 'em up on the wall when we get back."

A crackling sound came then from somewhere off the landing behind them before Casper could even take a look at the cards, and they both turned their heads startled. It sounded like branches breaking, or wood cracking and splintering, and yet it seemed so out of place to come from inside a house. It was very close by, almost as though it had come from one of the other upstairs rooms, and the two thieves stared at each other with a sudden alarm.

"What was that?" Casper hissed to his accomplice.

"Perhaps it's the woman," Adie replied. "Perhaps she's come back."

"Let's get out of here."

"Let's take a look first," Adie countered, and was off the bed and creeping eagerly towards the door, that grin of his once more wrapped mischievously about his face.

Casper followed behind him uneasily. His hands were shaking, and his skin had suddenly got cold and clammy. He knew they shouldn't be doing this, breaking into people's houses and going through their stuff, but there was no money to be found on the street, and these people with their big houses seemed to have plenty. But it was this looking at the owners that was new, and it was starting to creep him out. Adie was already a few steps ahead of him, and Casper could see him peering into a second bedroom. Then another crackling sound came, like breaking timber, but off to their left and from the bathroom. Adie grinned over his shoulder, and whispered something about checking her out in the tub. Casper hissed at him to come back, but Adie was already at the door, and pushing it gently open.

Casper was at his back now, his heart thumping like crazy, trying to peer round him as they both entered the small bathroom together. There was indeed a figure in the room, kneeling down in front of the bath, and hunched over the side. But it was not the silk-clad lady that they'd hoped to find, but a man dressed all in black. He looked round suddenly as he heard their footsteps on the cold linoleum. His eyes were wide and bullish, the pupils set inside them sharp and piercing like tiny pinpricks, and his lips and chin ran with blood as he gorged himself on the corpse lying twisted in the bath. Here was the real owner of the house, lying dead in the bathtub, being slowly devoured by this hideous and unnatural creature.

Their eyes locked for a handful of terrifying seconds, blood running down the throat and neck of the man that was not a man as he returned their shuddering stare. Then he seemed to be on his feet with chilling speed and coming after them, spiny tentacle-like fingers clawing out from beneath his robes, eager to clasp them and rip away their flesh. Casper stumbled backwards away from this clammy reaching grasp, knocking Adie to the floor as he fell back sprawling through the open doorway. He caught a brief glimpse of Adie trying to get to his feet, his fingers clawing the air for the door handle, but then he caught sight of the man dressed in black once more, looming over his friend's body and reaching for him in turn. Casper scrambled to his feet as a scream slipped freely from the back of his throat, and he found himself stumbling headlong for the stairs as he ran for his life. His blood was pounding hard and loud in his ears as he tumbled down the last few stairs and spilled out into the hallway, and it wasn't until he was outside in the street once more with the cool breeze of the day on his skin that he realised that Adie was no longer behind him.

He stood in the middle of the cul-de-sac, his chest heaving with panic, as he gazed back up at the placid and silent facade of the peaceful suburban house. Nothing moved. Nothing screamed. No curtains twitched. And there was no sound but the ruffling of the wind through the leaves of the tree-lined boulevard behind him. The front door still stood ajar, swinging gently beneath the weight of the breeze, but of Adie and the creature in black, there was no sign, and no hint of pursuit.

What should he do, Casper thought desperately? Return for his friend? Call the police? What if that thing was still in there? Of course it was in there, where else would it be? It was probably feasting on Adie's body right now, sinking those terrible teeth deep into his legs and throat. Casper backed away a step, fearful of the creature dressed all in black, his imagination conjuring the memory of its ghastly face, its jaws and throat awash with the blood of the woman. Just what sort of creature would eat human flesh? Especially a creature that seemed less human than not, but still clever enough to look like one. Perhaps it had been human once, he tried to reason, and something had happened... Casper shook such horrible thoughts away. Whatever it was, it was real, and Adie was still trapped inside with it.

The wind gusted suddenly along the cul-de-sac, lifting his hair as he continued to stare up at the cold and silent house. It was no different to any other house on the street, just a normal everyday suburban house, and yet it petrified him now simply to look up at it. He took a breath, a breath of false courage, and took a step back towards the house. He's dead, was the only thought that kept sparking in his head. Adie's dead. Why risk your own life for a dead man? Casper tried to shake the fearful notion away, as well as the bloody image that came with it, of Adie lying on his back with his chest and stomach opened up to the creature that was even now feeding upon him. He reached the front gate, still flung back against the neatly cropped hedge. It was perhaps only ten or fifteen yards to the front door from here, he could see part of the inside through the narrow gap, quiet, motionless and deathly still. He wanted to call out his friend's name, or throw something through the breach simply to disturb that horrible silence, but as soon as he thought to open his mouth or stoop to pick up a stone, that same terrible sound came from inside, of crackling branches and breaking bones.

It made something in his chest stutter, and his feeble body shudder, and a cry of panic suddenly tumbled out of his stricken throat as he stumbled helplessly back down the pathway away from the house. His legs buckled and turned to rubber as he felt himself fall backwards, catching himself only partially on the gate. The black iron spikes pierced his skin and sent dull ragged pains throughout his arm and hand. But it was enough to at least keep him upright, enough to allow him to turn and flee, and to run as hard as he could away from the house, with tears that streaked his eyes and baffled his escape.

As he reached the main road, however, the suddenness of the traffic and the proximity of the real world startled him, and he stumbled wildly across the pavement. Several pedestrians veered out of his way in order to avoid his ragged route, fearful of this dangerous youth. But he looked back only once, a half-glance shot quickly over his shoulder as he made his way along the pavement. There was nothing there to see, of course, and yet it must have been his imagination that conjured those same sounds of branches breaking on the air behind him.

Only once he was back in the squalid warehouse they called home did Casper stop running. Sweating profusely and breathing hard, he hauled himself up the ladder to the top floor loft to gaze out over the city. How was everyone going about their everyday business - shopping, working, collecting their kids - when there was a monster at work in a house amongst them? How could that be? How could that happen? It just made no sense. The same vivid image came back to him to dispel the logic of all that he knew, of the blood and the teeth, and that same terrible sound of cracking that permeated his mud-thick thoughts. Was Adie still there, he wondered as he gazed up at the darkening sky, or had he managed somehow to escape? Yes, that made sense. Adie must have managed to escape out back. That was why they hadn't met up out the front. That made sense. It had to. His hopes were shallow, very shallow, but he knew that it was all he had.

Casper turned away from the windowless opening, and as he trudged back towards his mattress lying on the grimy floor at the back of the loft, he remembered the stinging ache that still seared through in his arm. With his back against the cold concrete wall, he pulled off his jacket, which was torn across the sleeve, and turned his arm to inspect the damage. The wounds - there were three puncture marks and some ragged grazing - were bloody and flecked with black paint and rust from the gate. It looked quite bad and now that he poked it with his finger, it stung like hell. He flinched at the pain and decided to leave it be. There was nothing he could do but let it get better on its own. Pulling his jacket back on he sat and stared into middle distance, thinking about the house they had dared to break into, while his arm throbbed incessantly, nagging him with its dull coarse agony.

The law was not the only thing they should have feared from their burglaries, it seemed. Just what was that thing, he wanted to know? And how did it come to even be alive? Something was digging into his side, distracting him, and he reached absently into his jacket pocket. It was the pack of cards that Adie had found in the woman's bedroom. He had forgotten that he'd taken it, and he pulled out the deck and held it up in front of him.

The packet was not much to look at. Square, dull, uninteresting. Tugging open the flap at the top, Casper eased out the cards and began to look at them, one after the other. Yes, they were cool, some of them, but the sight of them couldn't help raise his spirits with the thought of his friend lying dead somewhere in that house. He shuffled them distantly as he stared back out through the windowless opening in the far wall. A great grey wall of heavy cloud was rolling swiftly in from the North. Even colder weather was coming. Great. What else could go wrong?

With his thoughts rattling around inside his head, Casper felt his hands shuffle the cards once again. But then he stopped as he went to shuffle them a third time as he heard a footstep echo up from the cold depths of the derelict building below. Was it even a footstep, he thought? Of course, what else could it have been. Perhaps it was Adie, come back to the warehouse just minutes after him. Casper sat up a little and strained his ears against the chill winds that blustered in through the many breaches of the empty building. No more footsteps followed the first. Not, at least, until he got to his feet and went to the doorway leading to the ladder. Then the footstep came once more, only more loudly, and close by. Casper spun on his heel, searching the shadows for the intruder already inside the building, and caught sight of a dark figure standing in front of the open window behind him. It was silhouetted against the bruised sky, but still illuminated sufficiently so that Casper could catch the vague shapes of its face. A chill ran across his body as his eyes deciphered the forms.

This was not Adie.

This was the monster from the cold suburban house.

Its skin glistened with a sickly yellow-white pallor, its eyes sunk deep into its skull and ringed with dark circles. The skin of its lips and chin was still stained from the blood of its human meal, its teeth chattering intermittently like the rickety ticking of an insect scuttling across a cold hard floor. Casper stood for a few moments just staring at this creature, this unnatural beast that ate human flesh. How had it gotten into the loft? There was only one door and he was stood in it. So just how had it managed to get behind him? The creature's eyes were dark and almost gone inside its head, but from just those two dark cavernous sockets, Casper could see the intent, the intent of butchery. You will die now, those cruel eyes seemed to say, and my chattering teeth will know your flesh and devour it swiftly.

A cold wind blustered through the loft then, chilling Casper as he watched this thing stare back at him from the mask of its human body. Once again he felt the weight of the cards in his hand, and as he remembered that he still had hold of them, he felt the creature's gaze go to them also. Was this what it wanted, Casper thought? Was this why it had followed him all the way back from the house? It seemed ludicrous, and yet he was certain now that its attention was fixed firmly upon the deck. For some reason, Casper felt himself slide the first card from the top of the deck, and as he did so, he saw the creature's brow shift slightly, and heard too its teeth clatter to a halt. So there they stood, for what seemed like an age, as Casper offered the top card forward, the monster seemingly fearful at the sight of it. Then what followed, and Casper would never be sure of what did follow, was simply not to be believed. But happen it did, and it was to save his very life.

Casper pulled that top card, the card that the creature had seemed so terrified of, and held it out towards it. On its surface was a symbol, a symbol of fire, and as Casper turned it out towards the creature, so the card began to shake with a fury of its own. Fire came from that card, a ball of flame so hot and furious that it leapt from his hand to engulf the creature entirely. Casper faltered as he witnessed the scene, almost as though he was a spectator looking in upon the room, and watched horrified as the beast dressed all in black covered its head with its arms, as the flames leapt up and burned it like a raging living candle. Stumbling back through the open doorway, Casper forced the cards back into his jacket pocket as he hurled himself back down the ladder as the din of crackling bones and chattering teeth harried his back. Once out in the open air again, he ran like an athlete, as hard as he could, back across the waste ground, the way he had come only minutes before. He had to find Adie, that was the only thought now raging through his head. He was the only person he knew in this cruel dark city, and he only hoped that he would still be at the house and alive.

He met the same stares from the people on the streets that he'd seen as he'd fled the house the first time. Perhaps they were fearful of the intentions of this lad, hurling himself through town. Perhaps he was dangerous, or perhaps it was his hard breathing, his wide fearful eyes, or maybe even the words he heard himself jabbering as he ran. Can't be dead, he was stammering, grinding bones, drinking blood. He can't be.

He eventually found his way back to the corner where the trees grew bright and abundant, their limbs bowing low against the cold Northerly wind that gusted through the cul-de-sac. Was there snow promised somewhere in those dark burgeoning clouds, or numbing rain that would come in driving sheets to chill him if he lasted unprotected until nightfall?

The leaves in the tree-lined cul-de-sac rustled and blustered beneath the ever-strengthening wind as he hurried beneath their billowing canopies. So normal, so suburban, and yet hiding a den of murder and bloodshed beneath a façade of mock-Tudor and landscaped gardens.

And then there it was. The house. Tucked away in a corner, and set back a little way from the road behind a low green neatly-cropped hedge. Casper stumbled to a ragged pace as he approached the small black iron gate, a gate that still probably carried scraps of his own blood on its spikes like trophies. The front door still stood ajar, inviting him inside, taunting him and daring him to go through. He went anyway, his false courage once more on his breath, to stand upon the threshold, gazing deep into the hallway now darkened by the decaying day.

The house was silent as the world continued to bluster outside. There were no sounds, no cries, no footsteps. With his pulse thumping rapidly around his body, he forced himself forward for the sake of his friend. The stairs went up to his right, and even as he slowly began to ascend, he kept a fearful eye on the door to the living room, the room where he had first noticed those droplets of blood.

On the landing, he could see that all the doors that ran off from it stood ajar. The bathroom was just yards away, he could be there in less than three strides, and yet something held him back. Suppose Adie was in there, he thought, slumped inside the bath beside the dead owner of the house. What if he too had been devoured by the creature, drained of blood, his arms and legs broken. The creature was back at the warehouse, dead, there was nothing to be feared from that thing now. Only what lay on the other side of the bathroom door mattered now, but his fear of seeing Adie's face battered and cracked open kept him from entering.

Casper's hands were shaking as he held tightly onto the banister at the top of the stairs. What was he to do? The bodies would be found sooner or later, by neighbours first surely, and then by the police. If he was seen here with them, he would surely be their first suspect. And a young man living rough and desperate on the street? Who would care about him enough to object? Especially with his record anyway. Slowly he turned back and began to descend, away from the bathroom door, and away from his friend that was probably lying dead behind it.

In the downstairs hallway, he paused for a moment, and then stepped dismally into the living room. Why he did this he had no idea, perhaps for one final look, perhaps to check to see if those droplets of blood had been wiped away. He stood gazing down at the book still lying on the carpet beside the armchair. The scarlet drops remained untouched. But then the sound of shallow breathing caught his attention from the corner of the room behind him, and he turned quickly, so quickly in fact that he lost his balance and toppled awkwardly to the floor. Why had he not checked the room first? That was stupid. He had simply stepped inside and looked for the book. But he looked round now, though, and his eyes settled quickly on the darkened figure stood hidden amongst the unearthly shadows, a tall figure, cloaked by darkness, and his eyes, although cloaked by that same unearthly darkness, seemed fixed intently upon him.

"Good afternoon," was all the stranger uttered, the simplicity of the welcome disturbing, given the circumstances.

Casper stared at him, uncertain of what to do, and stammered the same unnerving welcome in reply.

"Something has gone on here, has it not?" the stranger continued, to which Casper could only offer a feeble nod of his head. Was this the police? Here, so soon? The stranger took a step forward, the first movement Casper had seen him make, and he now came into the grey light coming in through the living room window. He was certainly not the ugly creature he might have expected, a grim brother of the monster he had left to burn back at the warehouse, and yet nor did he seem like a policeman. He was human, this stranger, at least human looking, and his skin was unblemished, almost perfect and radiant beneath the dull light of the late afternoon. His hair was dark and burnished, his forehead smooth beneath it, and his smile was convincing now that it came upon his thin lips.

"You have something for me, I believe," the stranger said, the smile fixed like a mask of forced pleasantry. "I would like to have it back. Then we can depart on pleasant terms."

"Who are you?" Casper managed to utter,

scrabbling to his feet but needing the support of the armchair to keep himself upright.

"My name is Anameus," the stranger replied. "I have some property that I would like to reclaim. It's upon your person, if I'm not mistaken. I will just take it, if you please, and then I'll be on my way."

Casper stared at him, uncertain of what to say, but knowing suddenly that it was the pack of cards of which he spoke. What else could it be? His creature had been sent, no doubt, to reclaim it from the woman, and he and Adie had stumbled upon its work at the wrong time, unwittingly stealing the cards out from under this man's nose once again. Was that all Adie's death was? Bad timing? If they had chosen the house next door, might he even be alive still? Casper looked up as the man who had called himself Anameus took another step towards him. It was certain that he was growing impatient, perhaps even considering his brutal murder as well. Would he even allow him to live once he'd handed over the cards? Should he even hand over the cards at all, he wondered suddenly? There was something powerful in that small deck that he could still feel nudging his ribs through the lining of his jacket, that much was indeed certain. Could it be that simple to just hand over power like that?

"You delay," Anameus commented. "Why is that?" Casper stared at him, uncertain of what to do, and ran a shaking tongue over his dry lips.

"Give me back what is mine," the man continued. "That is only fair."

A movement in the shadows from across the room caught his attention, and Casper turned in its direction. A second figure loomed there, previously unseen, another minion of this man. It was getting dangerous, this dealing with whatever forces stood before him. He knew he was nothing to them, a mere harmless human, and yet he felt that the deck of cards in his pocket could at least offer him some kind of protection. He could sense the second figure itching to be unleashed from the shadows that held him, and sensed too the ominous intent of Anameus, restraining himself from simply taking back his property with violence. Casper wanted to burn him with the same fire that he'd burned the other, but until he managed to discover just what he'd done, they were simply printed cards with pictures on them. Adie himself had thumbed through the cards in the woman's bedroom, and no fire had slipped from their surfaces. So what, then, had he done differently to conjure those deadly and destructive flames?

"Return my property," Anameus said more forcefully now, as another creature appeared from the hall to fill the doorway. This looked like the first, its eyes sunk deep and hollow, its teeth ticking with the eagerness to devour. His escape was sealed, and his eyes searched the room desperately now for another route. He didn't want to relinquish what he had found so quickly, and his eyes settled upon the living room window that thankfully still stood open. The creature at the door made a step into the room, and the shadows shifted as he felt the presence of more beings, unearthly and looming out of the darkness towards him. He ran then, darting away from their needle-like touch, evading their sickening grasp, and hurled himself out through the open window and back into the daylight.

He landed heavily, and found a mouthful of gritty dirt in his teeth as he fell into the flower border.

Hauling himself to his feet as he stumbled forward, he threw himself back down the path and out through the gate. He glanced over his shoulder only once as headed back along the road, and did he even see right, because he thought he saw Anameus standing at the open window, his eyes fixed intently upon him, and a smile of admiration spreading casually across his face?

He had nowhere else to go, that was the cruel honesty, and he wandered for an hour or more through the dark city streets as the blinding wind berated him in freezing gusts. It numbed every part of his body, and he tried to keep it at his back as he walked, but junctions seemed to harry him from all directions, and no respite could be found. With his hands thrust deep into the pockets of his jacket, he kept his fingers clasped tightly around the magical deck of cards. He needed somewhere to get out of the cold and try to learn their secrets, and what wouldn't he give to be able to conjure that fire again, if only to keep himself warm for the night.

A bar was open up ahead, its glittering light spilling out across the pavement, and Casper crossed the street swiftly towards it. He had a few coins on him, not enough for a meal, but perhaps enough for a shot, and he guessed that his body could do with alcohol inside it more than it could food. He entered a heaving smoky atmosphere, blissful after the cold night outside, and wondered only briefly if it was safe here as his entrance caused a number of furtive glances in his direction. His clothes were torn and dirty, he knew that, and he hoped that they only stared at him for being homeless, and not as some kind of enemy, even if he might have stolen from one of their homes some previous night.

He ordered a whiskey and took it to the back of the

room, to a ill-lit booth in the corner. He sipped it slowly to make it last before pulling the cards from his pocket, taking them out one by one and laying them face up in front of him. The whiskey entered his system more rapidly that he'd expected, warming his throat and stomach, but drawing a haze of tiredness down over his eyes. He forced himself to concentrate, to stare at the cards and look for any connections between them, to find any reasons for magic. Here was the skeleton Adie had spoken of, and here the fire card, its edges singed and blackened from its recent use. Here was one with lightning sparking down from a cloud, and here a blade, glinting and new. These cards could be weapons perhaps, their pictures denoting their powerful force. But then there were others that didn't seem to follow. One of a stone tower, another of an ocean. One of a maiden in a long white gown, another of a two-headed dog. What could be the point of these other cards? He took another sip of the warming whiskey as he wondered just who might have made them.

He tried to think back to what had happened in the loft, why fire come from the fire card, and why he had been able to incinerate the creature that had hunted him down with it. The whiskey had started to deaden his body all over now, drawing a veil of fatigue over his thoughts and ideas. Perhaps a shot had not been wise after all. But at least the chill of the night outside had all but left him. He tried to focus once again. What had happened earlier in the loft?

He had shuffled the deck, he remembered that, but so what? Then he had heard the creature downstairs. Had he shuffled the deck a second time? He wasn't sure. Yes, he had, because that's when he had gotten up and found the creature standing behind him. He had drawn the first card on the top, that had been the fire card, and the magic had done the rest. Was that it? It seemed ridiculous.

His mind was racing uncontrollably from both the insanity and the whiskey, and he collected up the cards and pushed them back together once again into a deck. He neatened the pack and then proceeded to shuffle them. He stared at them, nervously, and then slowly shuffled them once more. His hands were trembling as he slowly drew the top card out away from him, pointing it towards the bar. His eyes flinched as the card began to shake in his hand, and he only had time to see the picture on the top before the lightning bolt burst out from the card, its crackling white stream obliterating the side of the bar in a shuddering shower of wood shards and broken glass.

The explosion was sudden and devastating, and for a while the bar stood rattled in both silence and shock. Broken bottles tinkled across the floor, glasses smashing as they continued to roll from shattered shelving. Casper sat and gaped at the effect of the lightning card, as the rest of the customers in the establishment began to stumble forward with ragged cries and gasps of disbelief. Casper barely heard their suspicions or their shuddering moans of relief, not even as he picked up his stuff and staggered past them and back out into the night. Some may have said it had been a freak thunderstorm, others a terrorist attack, perhaps even chancing a guess at an exploding beer barrel. All ludicrous theories, but none more so than the truth. The cards were powerful, and vengeful, and he now knew the secret to unleashing that power. Oh, how he was going to deal those cards out one by one, drawing them face up with each and every terrible death to the man who had killed his one and only friend in the world. Oh yes, Anameus, you would pay for that.

The freezing wind numbed his face as he stormed back through the city streets, back the way he had come, the heat of revenge warming his bones nearly as much as the whiskey had done. He would have that revenge, he repeatedly told himself as he marched, and he would climb those stairs and learn the truth about who had laid inside that bathtub. Would the owner of the house continue to lie alone, or would she be joined in the bath of her own blood by Adie? If any of those shrouded monsters were lying in wait for him, or even attempted to stop of control him, he would have them too, burned, blackened or dismembered, whatever death the cards chose for them.

As Casper reached the corner of the street, he stopped to glance to his left and right, checking the traffic that was intermittent at this hour. A string of cars passed from his right, driving swiftly by in the cold darkness. His eyes, however, picked out the shape of a figure huddled on the other side of the road a little further up. There were still a few people out on the streets, it was not that late, but there was something noticeable in the motionless stance of this figure, something not right. Casper stared at it without trying to be seen to be staring, but it just stood there, this thing, almost like a solid black smudge, with no movement and no discernible features. It dawned upon him slowly that this was one of Anameus' creatures, stood waiting and watching, perhaps even for his return. Shit, he thought. His surprise attack ended before it had begun. A shiver coursed through him as he wondered if there were any more of its kind about, come to watch and follow him. Casper glanced along the road in the other direction, searching the shadows desperately for some other sign. He looked hard, gazing into the darkest of all the doorways and overhangs, and he found them here too.

Another of the dark creatures lurked motionless inside an empty bus shelter, only its head and shoulders visible as it gazed back at him. A third figure stood hunched beneath a line of trees, their limbs and overhanging branches disguising its twisted frame. He continued to search, both to his left and right, and even behind him, but could find no more. But because he could not see them, it did not necessarily mean that they were not there to be seen.

He started forward now, his pulse skittering inside his body, as he made his way deliberately across the road. Cars still came, from the left and the right, and people still walked the streets in either direction, and yet they all seemed ignorant of the unnatural creatures that walked beside them, sharing their space, lurking amongst them. There are monsters, Casper wanted to shout out to each and every one of them. Look around you and you will see them.

But as he thought this he quickened his pace, and thought too about how regular people with their regular lives and their regular jobs would listen to a homeless man telling them of how he could see demons and monsters, especially with the stench of whiskey on his breath. His loneliness came down upon him more heavily then that it ever had. He was alone. There was no one for him to turn to. Not now. Not with Adie dead.

His eyes caught those of a couple hurrying home, and he saw in that returned gaze exactly what they would think of anything he might say. It chilled him. Perhaps more than the freezing wind. Perhaps more than the creatures following him. It echoed his own thoughts that he was alone. He would have no help tonight, or any other night. This was a solitary battle.

He realised that he'd wandered further away from the house than he'd expected, and now found that he had to double back a good part of the way. A short cut through an alleyway would afford him a long trek back along the main road, but he knew, even before he reached it, that it would be tantamount to suicide. His grip tightened on the deck of cards in his pocket. He had the power with him. What did he have to fear from these things? Only Anameus might give him a fight. These other things were just conjured beasts, lap dogs that would topple like felled trees. There would be no resistance from such things. He would kill them all, and scatter their broken bones like ash. Then the entrance to the unlit alleyway suddenly loomed into view, and with a forced breath, he stepped into its blackest depths.

The cold northerly wind hammered through the narrow thoroughfare, blustering with raging gusts. It was a struggle merely to stand upright against the howl it was throwing at him. His eyes streamed into blindness against it, as he tried to penetrate the almost total darkness, but he would be able to see nothing. He persevered, telling himself that this would save him time. He had to get back to the house before word reached Anameus of his intent. A sudden gust knocked him sideways, almost sending him to the foul litter-strewn ground. His hands went out to steady himself against the rough wooden boards that made up the alley, the wind seeming to be growing worse. He glanced back behind him, his mind almost made up to return to the main road and take the long way round, but through his blinded sight he could make out that the entrance to the alleyway was no longer empty. The darkness of two shrouded creatures filled it, blocking the light from the streetlamps behind them, and as he stood and stared at them, slowly they began to approach.

The decision had been made, the creatures were after him, and he forced himself onward once more on his ragged journey. As he looked up, however, so he came face to face with yet more of Anameus' army. They blocked his route just yards ahead from him, their needle-like hands already reaching for him out of the darkness. Casper staggered to a halt, a cry of alarm already in his throat, as one of them caught hold of his jacket and dragged him into their fold. He was screaming now, yelling for them to let him go, but then he suddenly felt another constricting grasp, tugging at his ankle, and then another tearing at the front of his jeans.

His hand snatched out the deck of cards, and in the pitch blackness he struggled to pull them from the packet, his shaking fingers fumbling with them as the hands of the undead creatures pushed and pulled him, their clammy grasp upon him growing ever stronger as their tentacle-like claws sought to tear him apart. He had to do this right, he knew, or he would feel the needle-teeth of their terrible jaws, chattering blindly in the darkness of the alleyway.

Casper felt himself shuffle the deck, the cards slipping awkwardly between his fingers. He managed to keep a hold of them, and even to shuffle them a second time, but as his right hand told hold of the edge of the top card, his teeth suddenly grinning with the eagerness to destroy these foul creatures, a blow came out of the night, swift and unseen, and sent the entire deck flying.

A breath froze in his throat as the touch of the cards left his grasp. He knew in that instant that he no longer possessed that power, and that his death must soon be imminent. The choking hold that the creatures had kept upon him left his flesh the very moment after, as they sought to recover their master's cards from the dark and filthy ground.

Casper staggered back away from them, his hands clasping his head and throat as the weight of what had happened sank into him. He had possessed magic, vast and powerful magic, and now he had lost it. He gazed down at the incoherent shapes fussing and chattering at his feet, rummaging through the dark grim matter for the cards that still lay there. A thought came that he should try to reclaim at least a few of them, but he realised that he had at least managed to retain his life. Would they even leave him to breathe after they had found the cards? He had no idea, and even as he turned to look for the two that had entered the alleyway behind him, he could see the entrance clear once more.

The dilemma heightened inside him, to stay to find a handful of cards at the expense of his life, or to leave swiftly before the monsters looked up to take out the throat that they had been choking only moments before. It was a question that seemed not to be easily answered, but he took a final look down at their surging forms still busy amongst the muck, before he turned and headed quickly away.

The remainder of the night passed without further incident. He returned to the loft, and slept only briefly beneath blankets that could not keep out the freezing cold. The charred husk of the first monster probably still stood where it had fallen, he had not looked for it amongst the tangled shadows, and for once he was glad that there was no electricity in the disused building to light the rooms.

As dawn broke, he left quickly to find somewhere new to stay, another building, another city, it didn't matter. His stomach ached from a hunger that had not been sated since the previous day, but he knew that he was unlikely to find anything just lying around waiting to be eaten. Adie was surely dead, he had to at least admit that. This city was bad, corrupt by monsters that nobody else had seen. But he had seen them, and he had been beaten by them. How could he have thought that he could win? He had held power for a matter of hours, and felt the strength and potential within himself for only a fraction of his life before it had been taken away. He had been arrogant to think that he could have defeated things that had moved unnoticed for countless years, perhaps even lived amongst mankind forever, how did he know? He looked at himself as he trekked back over the waste ground. What was he now? Just what he had always been. A homeless man with nothing to call his own. He was a ghost.

Casper made his way out towards the old town, keeping his back to the district that had claimed his friend's life. He knew a short cut out to a truck stop near the motorway where he would be able to pick up a lift to somewhere far away. He didn't know where, and didn't much care, just as long as it was far away from this place.

The old town was quiet at dawn, just a handful of cars and delivery drivers passing through the cold gloomy streets. His stomach knotted again as he crossed a junction, that same Northerly wind gusting icily across its expanse, and he put a hand to it as if to let it know that nothing was coming anytime soon. He passed a row of terraced houses, some with their curtains drawn, others with concealing nets, and wondered if it would be wise to break into one swiftly, if only to put something in his belly before continuing on his way out of the city.

Passing a quiet road he slowed his pace a little to glance down its length. Plenty of money here, he thought to himself, even in this part of town, but not so much that the owners deemed burglar alarms necessary. But then something caught his eye, a brief glimpse of something dark and awkward slipping neatly through the shadows between two houses. It came and went so suddenly that Casper could barely grasp what it was. And then the wind suddenly gusted, lifting the heavy canopies of the trees that lined the road, and carrying that same dreadful sound of chattering teeth and breaking bones that he had heard before. Casper staggered back away from it, a shudder creeping back across his spine, and hurried quickly on in the direction of the truck stop and the motorway.

# The Hikers

Back home in Kent this had seemed like a good idea, the two of them camping out in the Welsh hills for the weekend, just like they used to do many years ago. Frankie was driving, his mate Bob beside him, while Frankie's wife and two kids huddled in the back, making smug comments about how the weather seemed to be deteriorating. Frankie tried his best to ignore them, but Bob had begun leaning forward and looking up at the looming dark clouds towards which they were heading, and voiced his own concerns. It had been years since they'd done this, and with Callie wanting to visit her sister in Gloucester it seemed like the perfect solution. But as the terrain became mountainous and they reached their drop-off point, the small village of Colm, the rain had already begun.

A cold wind blustered through the steep valley as Frankie and Bob climbed out of the car, whipping the cold rain hard into their faces. Callie climbed out of the back and hurried round to the driver's side, quickly pulling the door shut after her. Bob was complaining even as he hung back at the rear of the car as Frankie began to unload, explaining how ridiculous this all was, and that they should probably come back some other time when the weather was more clement.

Above them the clouds were loaded, purple black with a glowering weight of rain, but Frankie had made it clear that it was nothing the two of them couldn't handle. They were here for one night, for Christ's sake, what was a bit of rain?

The car pulled away with a cheer from the kids, and Bob watched it go with a long face.

"Take the fucking tent, will you," Frankie yelled at him, thrusting the rucksack hard into Bob's chest. Bob took it, but didn't sling it round onto his back until Callie had turned the corner and disappeared from sight. She wasn't coming back again until five o'clock the following day.

The hiking trail led out of the village and up a steep incline towards a ridge in the hills. Sheer bluffs hung out over their heads as they climbed, and despite the rain that gusted into their faces, the view was spectacular. At the top of the ridge they rested for a few minutes, looking back at their ascent and at the small village of Colm nestled below. The valley floor stretched for as far as they could see, the mountains rising slate-black up to the clouds. Mist shrouded much of the upper slopes, making it difficult to see, but despite the heavy rain Frankie suspected that Bob was glad he had come.

They pushed on, over the ridge and down into another valley, following a black shingle path that meandered a winding route along the side of the mountain. There were few trees, but an almost permanent carpet of dense shrub, tall grasses and what looked like gorse bushes. It was bleak and cold, and on this side of the ridge the wind came down harder, whistling through the undergrowth and battering them with turbulent gusts. Frankie expected Bob to argue the benefits of turning round and waiting out the weekend in a pub or a guesthouse with every gust that harried them, but it surprised him that no complaint came; it seemed as though Bob had resigned himself to the weekend's camping now that he was out of the car, and walked behind him in silence.

At a junction in the path, Frankie pulled his

ordnance survey map from the deep front pocket of his jacket and attempted to study it as the wind tried to whip it out of his hands. Bob stood huddled beside him, not even attempting to offer an opinion or insight, but willing just to follow Frankie wherever he said they should be headed. Frankie looked up from the map to one of the three routes that led down towards a long lake, and pointed down towards it with his thick-gloved hand, yelling over the storm as he did so. Bob just stared at him over the high collar of his jacket that rose up over his nose, and waited until Frankie had pushed the map back into his pocket and started away, before moving to follow him.

The gorse bushes grew thicker for a way, and encroached in places along the path. Their stiff branches were lined with hard sharp spines that snagged at their waterproofs that blustered in the wind like sheets on a line. They couldn't have meandered from the black shingle path even if they'd wanted to, but to lose the path in this weather would have made trouble for them that they didn't need.

At a turn in the path, and nestled amongst taller scrub, they came upon a ramshackle outbuilding that maybe had once been a shepherd's barn. There were boards missing in the walls and slates missing from the roof, but it offered them a hour's shelter while they rested and ate.

"I vote we stay here," Bob said, as he opened a box that contained sandwiches. "We could pitch the tent in here and be doubly warm."

"We haven't even walked two miles yet."

"We're not going to find anything else like this."

"We're not stopping here."

"Look out there, Frankie. We're not going to be able

to pitch a tent in that."

"We're not stopping here," he said again. "I didn't come all this way just to stay in an old barn. What's the matter with you anyway? It's not as though you're not properly dressed for all this."

Bob scowled at him as he started on one of the sandwiches.

"This weather's bullshit," he said as he munched, bits of sandwich flying out of his mouth. "I didn't think it was going to be like this."

"It's fucking rain," Frankie exclaimed. "If there were rocks falling out of the sky then I'd agree with you. But it's only water. You'll dry out."

Packed up once again, they both headed back out into the foul weather. The clouds were still loaded but the rain had let up considerably, and the wind seemed not as harsh as it had been earlier.

The day seemed more accepting of the two hikers as they continued along the shingle path beside the lake, the sky brightening, darts of sunlight glinting off the rippling surface of the black water. The air smelled sweet and fresh, and Frankie for one was glad to breathe it in. When the rain stopped altogether, he was glad to pull the hood of his jacket back and take off his beanie, glad to let the air get to his head that had been sweating inside his waterproof clothing. He glanced round to see Bob do likewise, and was happy that Bob was finally letting up, and thought that he might even get some conversation out of him.

They followed the lake path around the slope of the mountain, and as they rounded the corner, saw the lake expand into a huge expanse of water. What they had thought was the lake was just an estuary. What they now saw was the huge body of water that Frankie had missed on the map as the wind had fought to rip it from his hands. They both stood there for a moment gazing out across the vast flat surface of the lake, jagged black mountains circumscribing it as they rose high into the low heavy sky. Frankie pulled his map back out of his pocket and traced the line of the path they had taken from Colm. This was White Angel Lake.

"Doesn't look very white or filled with angels to me," Bob said, reading the map over Frankie's shoulder.

Frankie gazed back out over the dark surface of the water.

"Maybe when the wind picks up, the angels are the white peaks that are whipped off the surface."

"Maybe," Bob murmured, and followed Frankie's gaze.

Further around the lake, they came upon a man busy at a small boat moored up at the edge of the water. He was wearing a heavy coat and rain hat, and as they approached, saw that he was working with nets at the bottom of his boat.

"Are you catching many fish?" Frankie called out to him in greeting, as the path made its way within yards of where he was moored.

The old man looked up, his face carved deeply with wrinkles. He eyed them both as if they weren't real, as if they were mad to be walking out here in this weather.

"Aye, when you can find them," he said eventually, his voice deep and gruff. He was a heavy-set man, a barrel-like torso hidden away beneath his dark coat. "What are you two boys doing out here so far from home?"

Frankie saw Bob smirk at the comment. They were both on their way to forty, and probably compared to the old-timer in the boat they were boys. The fisherman saw their humour and stood upright, dropping his nets to the floor.

"I'll call you boys because being out here means you're too foolish to know better."

Frankie and Bob exchanged bemused glances, Bob already beginning to shuffle away. Frankie lingered however.

"Why do they call this White Angel Lake?" he asked.

The old fisherman stared at him, and for a moment Frankie didn't think he was going to answer him at all.

"There are no angels here," he said sternly to them.

"So why -"

"Boys!" the old man yelled at them, pointing his finger at them.

"Come on," Bob said to Frankie, taking hold of his sleeve to coax him away. "We should be going."

"There used to be wyrms here," the old man shouted after them as they began away. "White wyrms that lived in the lake."

"He's fucking lost it," Bob whispered to Frankie as he turned to look back.

"Everyone thinks they're dead," he continued to bellow. "But there may still be some, just waiting to breed. Go home, boys, before they eat you up."

"Crazy fucking cunt," Bob went on, sniggering as they followed the black shingle path away from the old fisherman. Frankie wanted to believe him, but there was something about the old man's words that wouldn't shift out of his head. In his mind he could see white worms sticking their heads out of the water, and the locals seeing them and thinking they were angels, naming the lake after the weird indigenous creatures. He glanced across the surface of the water, even as Bob continued to pull on his jacket, coaxing him along, keeping their pace up, but there were no heads poking out of the water, white or otherwise. But as the mad old fisherman had said, they were dead now, all gone. And he should know if he fishes this vast stretch of water.

Rain started to drop again as the sky darkened, heavy black clouds rolling in from the mountains, sending cascades of mist down the upper slopes towards them. The downpour started not long after, water literally falling out of the sky, flooding the path ahead of them like a river. The day grew darker and darker, until Frankie checked his watch and was surprised to find that it was not yet five o'clock. The sky was unchanged in all directions, just a solid mass of smudged purple-black, and it was clear that this time the weather would not let up.

They followed the shingle path around another slope of the mountain, but there was nowhere useful to pitch the tent. Gorse bushes and dense shrub still lined the lower slopes, and they were forced to continue on through the heavy rain.

The lake path continued uninterrupted around a series of bluffs, their vertical jagged heights shielding much of the wind and rain as it blustered down off the slopes above them. They stopped for a moment, huddled together beneath the sheer jagged rock, and discussed their options. Frankie retrieved the ordnance survey map again and studied what they might find ahead, and then looked along the lake path. Finally he looked back at Bob.

"I don't think we're going to find anything better," Frankie said to him.

Bob looked up at the jagged face of the bluff.

"What if it falls down on us?"

Frankie gazed up at it now.

"I don't think that's going anywhere."

He was not as convincing as Bob would have hoped for, and they could both see the huge boulders that had fallen away from it over time, although neither of them drew attention to that.

"It's either here or somewhere more out in the open where we'll be more exposed."

Bob looked back up at the bluffs.

"I've fucking had enough," he yelled at him, and swung the rucksack up and off his back.

It was easier to pitch the tent than they'd thought it would be, but it still took time. The bluffs shielded a lot of the wind and rain, but by no means all of it, and by they time they had everything stashed away inside, they were both dry from the rain, but soaked with sweat.

Frankie changed out of his waterproofs and clothes and put on the clean set he had brought with him. Bob was still trying to even out the shingle beneath the ground sheet, manoeuvring his sleeping bag over the least sharpest stones.

"Why didn't you bring your air-bed?" Frankie said to him, bemused by his actions.

"Because I'm not a fucking genius like you," Bob retorted, casting him a livid glance over his shoulder.

"Why don't you do it later?"

"In the fucking dark?"

"If you don't change out of those wet clothes, you'll have more to worry about than rocks in your back."

Bob shot him another look, but it was clear that he knew Frankie was right. He fumbled about with the ground sheet for a few more minutes, just to make his point, and then clambered backwards out of the sleeping area to where he could slip off his sweater and leggings. His socks, too, were wet, but whether that was from sweat or cheap hiking boots he didn't know. Once he was redressed and both warm and dry, he sat down opposite Frankie and took the mug of hot tea he was offering.

With the stove lit and its heat fighting the draughts that found their way inside the tent, they were both happier than they had been. Night was already setting in, darkening the already black clouds outside. Rain still pattered across the surface of the tent, the sides billowing against the onslaught of the wind, but they were more secluded than they might otherwise have been, out in the unprotected open, and they were both content with their lot.

They ate their evening meal of two steaks and beans with white crusty bread, and after a lakeside trek in the cold and wet, to have that hand-cooked over the naked blue flame of a gas-fired camping stove was the best meal they could have dreamed of. In a restaurant they might have sent it back, but in a canvas tent in the middle of a rainstorm, it was bliss.

The pattering of rain ceased a while after that, yet the sides still blustered with the wind gusting through the valley. Frankie settled back on one arm, half-dozing with an after-dinner glow, while Bob ventured outside for a cigarette. The wind was fresh, and smelt damp, and fog hung across the lake like the heavy clouds that still hung atop the mountains. Bob lit his cigarette as he stood just outside the tent, hugging his arms around himself; he was wearing a thick woollen jumper but the cold was still getting in. The end of the cigarette burned orange like the embers of a fire as the wind blew across it and snatched the smoke away. There was little comfort to be had from it, but Bob remained outside the tent until he had finished it, and flicked the butt out into the lake when it was done, the wind carrying it away in an arc where it landed in the inky black water several yards away.

Bob crawled back inside the tent and found Frankie asleep. He watched him for a moment, the man who had been his friend for as long as he could remember, with his mouth hanging open, sucking air in noisily. Bob crawled over to his rucksack and opened one of the side pockets and pulled out a half bottle of brandy. Cracking the seal, he took a mouthful as he sat cross-legged, making himself comfortable with his spare clothes under him, before taking another mouthful. The liquor warmed him instantly, heat flooding through his throat and stomach. He closed his eyes with bliss, taking another quick swig before replacing the cap, and then settling back in a similar pose to Frankie beside him.

His head was starting to swim, and he let it wander as he listened to the sound of the wind gusting against the sides of the tent. Everything outside, apart from the wind against the tent, was silent, and as he lay there now warm and dry, he realised that this had been a good idea after all. Frankie had been right to want to get away from it all; it had been too long since they had last done this.

Bob lifted his head, undid the bottle, took another mouthful, replaced the cap, swallowed, and then lay back again. Heat coursed through him anew, burning his insides with a welcome fire. He was happy now, glad to be out of the wet and the cold, and glad that he had that steak and beans inside him.

Outside the tent, he heard the slap of water, as though someone had dropped a rock into the lake. Instinctively he lifted his head and stared at the flap of the tent that was still zipped shut, straining his ears in case it came again. He wondered if the fisherman had come back this way, and what he had heard was one of his oars dipping into the water. But it was dark. The old sod would have been home by now. He reasoned, finally, that it was probably one of the rocks above them that had tumbled off the edge of one of the bluffs into the lake. The sound hadn't been that loud so it would be fairly safe to assume that it was just a small rock. He glanced across at Frankie but he was still asleep. It hadn't even been loud enough to wake him, so it can't have been that bad. Not until it came again. Bob sat up this time, ears straining once again for any other sounds. The sides of the tent were now motionless, the wind gone, but it was still difficult to discern anything outside. There were no footsteps on the shingle path, or any rocks tumbling onto the ground around them, but he couldn't make out any other sounds coming from the lake either.

Slowly he pushed himself onto all fours and crawled towards the zip, tugging it back and staring out into the darkness. From the light inside the tent he could only see a handful of yards ahead, and he ducked back to retrieve the lantern, taking it with him as he crawled out into the night. Holding the light out in front of him, he checked the path in both directions but there was nothing there.

And then he stepped closer to the edge of the lake,

staring out into the foggy murk. The water was blacker than the sky above it, and only the fog was illuminated by the feeble light emanating from the lantern, sucking the light away from it, making it useless to see any kind of distance. Bob wanted to call out to see if it was the old fisherman still making his way home, but he probably wouldn't reply anyway, and he'd be able to see the light before he even heard his voice. Boys, he'd called them, the cheeky old duffer.

Bob started back for the tent when he heard the third splash of water, only this time it was close-by in the water just off to his right. He held the lantern out in the direction of the noise and saw the circles from the disturbance still rippling outward, but there was no sign of just what had made them. It was obvious, however, that it hadn't been made by one of the fisherman's oars. Bob stood there for a few minutes just watching the surface of the lake. But the sound never came again, and nor could he detect any motion beneath the black surface of the water either. As he stood there with the fog seeming to press against him, he eventually had to return to the tent, the coldness of the night overpowering the warmth he had managed to find earlier. He crawled back inside the tent, cursing as he shivered from the chill that had found his skin. The gas-fired stove was still lit, keeping the edge off the inside of the tent, but he picked up the brandy bottle and took a couple more sips.

"I hope you'll be keeping some of that for others to enjoy."

Bob looked up to find Frankie awake and watching him.

"It's this fucking cold," Bob muttered, taking a long sip before handing the bottle over. "It gets in when you least expect it."

Frankie examined the contents of the bottle.

"You been on this for a while?" he asked.

Bob shook his head.

"It's the cold, man."

Frankie tipped the bottle and took a mouthful, swallowing it slowly before handing it back.

"We've got the night and tomorrow to get through," he said, "so take it easy on that stuff, okay?"

"That's it until later, Frankie, I promise," Bob assured him, and slipped the bottle back in the side pocket of his rucksack.

As the warmth of the brandy began to course through his body again, Bob stretched out on his sleeping bag, glad that he had flattened out the sharper of the stones earlier. Now he just relaxed, slipping his boots off and stretching out his legs, as Frankie began talking about the route they'd take the following day. There was another pathway that joined the lakeside path about a mile and a half further on, Frankie explained, reading the directions from his ordnance survey map that would take them up to a ridge overlooking the entire valley. It would be a steep climb when their legs were the freshest, and then in the afternoon they would descend all the way back down another trail right into the heart of Colm. Bob was only half-listening. With his legs already aching from the day's hike, and the brandy seeping out through his body, sleep was tugging him quickly away from Frankie's trip. With his eyes closed and his sleeping bag nestling his tired limbs, he drifted quickly away from it all, and did not wake until much later, when he found the entire tent enveloped in a silent and clammy darkness.

"Frankie?"

There was no reply. Bob reached over to Frankie's sleeping bag but it was empty. He sat upright and called his name again, but he was not in the tent. Bob scrambled onto all fours and ran his hands over the ground sheet, searching for the lantern, but he couldn't find it. He did find his jacket, however, and managed to pull it on in the confined space, scrambling out of the tent, the flap still unzipped.

Outside was utter blackness, but he saw the light cast upwards by the lantern shining like a beacon out of the reeds fifty yards along the path. Bob ran as hard as he could towards it, shouting Frankie's name, but there was no response, no reply to his screaming calls. The lantern was in the water, nestled by the reeds, and Bob went down on one knee to fish it out. The lake was ice-cold and chilled his skin, but he lifted the lantern out and held it up, hoping to cast some sort of light in which to find Frankie. But the fog had rolled in thicker during the night, stealing any vision other than the ghostly white luminescence, and he could make out no sign of his friend in either direction along the path.

Then something moved in the water just in front of him. He caught sight of something pale reflected below the surface, rippling with the current of its movement. It seemed to rise quickly, a gaping maw opening to scream, until it broke the surface and came shrieking towards him. Bob staggered backwards, screaming his own cry of terror, and tumbled backwards onto the hard shingle path, the lantern slipping from his hand and skipping out of his reach. The light went out, sending everything back once more into maddening blackness. Bob sent sharp shards of rock flying as he flailed to find the lantern, pain coming to his fingers as the sound of ragged breath came at his back. He continued to scream as the lantern refused to be found, his knees hurting on the jagged ground as he fought to find it. The world was a blur of night, a nonsense of black on black, as all the while something began to claw its way out of the lake. Then his hands found something circular and plastic, and he fumbled with the switch until the lantern illuminated the path once again. He could see his hands were soiled, but with blood or muck he couldn't tell. Bob half-turned as he tried to find his feet, his hands shaking violently as he tried to illuminate what was thrashing around in the shallows of the lake, hoping to God that he wouldn't. Then another cry rose up, half strangled by water and weed.

"Bob," it was Frankie's voice. "Fucking help me, Bob. Help me."

Bob stood there shaking, his eyes still unable to make out the shape of his friend. But then he saw a hand rise up out of the water as if to snatch hold of a life preserver, clasping at thin air. Bob lurched towards him then, setting the lantern down safely on the wet grass before grasping hold of Frankie's sodden clothes and hauling him back, out of the water and onto the wet shingle of the path.

"What the fuck happened?" Bob was crying. "What were you doing in the lake?"

But Frankie had hold of him, his hands wrapped tightly around his waist, sobbing into his chest. He was mumbling, crying words into his body that Bob couldn't make out. Bob put his hand on Frankie's head, his hair soaked and thick with slippery weed, and tried to comfort him, even as his own heart hammered in his chest.

"You're out now, buddy," he said to him, his eyes still searching the rippling black surface of the lake. Fog still hung over its surface like a thick blanket, dense white in the pale glow from the lantern still sitting beside them. Even if anything was out there looking back at them he wouldn't have seen it.

Bob tried to get them both to their feet, picking up the lantern with one hand and manoeuvring them back along the path towards the tent. They were miles from anywhere, no one really knew where they were, and he was fucked if they were going to wait out the rest of the night in a tiny fucking tent with God knows what lurking outside.

But Frankie was soaking wet and freezing. He had to change out of his clothes, but that meant turning their backs to the lake. Hiding inside a tent, they wouldn't see what was coming. Frankie was mumbling again, something about angels, but he had no time for that now. He kept the lantern held out in front of him, trying to pick his way through the dense fog that seemed to growing thicker with each passing second, as though it wanted them to be cut off in the desolate mountains.

They were only a handful of yards from the tent before they saw the domed shape of the canvas, and Bob helped Frankie down onto his knees and coaxed him inside. He didn't know what state he had to be in for hypothermia to set in, but he was sure that Frankie couldn't be far off. Bob glanced behind him before he followed Frankie inside, but so thick was the fog that something could've been standing ten yards away and he wouldn't have seen it.

The sides of the tent had remained motionless once

the fog had rolled in and the wind had disappeared completely, leaving everything eerily silent, but then something suddenly whacked hard against it like a huge fucking hand and Bob dropped the lantern to the ground, screaming as he stumbled backwards away from it. A deep moaning sound followed from the other side of the canvas, like some demented zombie risen from the grave. Frankie had collapsed onto the ground, Bob could see him shivering hard. He was on his own. Alone with whatever was outside.

Bob lurched towards his rucksack, tugging everything out as he searched for his knife. It was a multi-purpose knife, with a four-inch blade on the bottom and a cerated edge like a saw blade on the top. He sat with it held out in front of him, his hands shaking like they were hammering in a nail.

He sat there for what seemed like an hour, listening for the moaning to come again, or for something else to attack the tent, but nothing else happened. He glanced down at Frankie, but his eyes were clenched shut, his teeth visible through thin pale lips and chattering. He knew he had to somehow get him out of there and at least back to Colm or he wouldn't survive at all.

Slowly he edged forward, the knife still extended in front of him, and tried to peer out through the narrow slit in the opening. But with the lantern still behind him illuminating the inside of the tent, he could make out nothing but blackness and the slowly drifting fog outside. He put his head outside and looked in all directions, his vision swirling as he struggled to make sense of the darkness, but there didn't seem to be anything out there anymore. He reached back in, took hold of the lantern, and stepped back out into the night, swinging it around him as he searched more thoroughly. Whatever it was that had been out there had gone.

He turned to go back into the tent, but something huge and white suddenly loomed out of the fog. Bob screamed as he staggered backwards, but the creature came slickly after him. It was wet and slimy, and reflected the light from the lantern. Its body was like a giant rectangle of slime, seven feet tall, a vertical antenna flapping at each corner; but there was no head, no eyes staring down at him, no mouth opening wide as if to devour him. Bob's heel caught amongst the shingle and his balance lurched. He tried to keep it, but as he turned, he fell sprawling, and landed hard on the ground, his senses reeling. The wyrm tumbled after him, its weight immense as it slithered across his body. He felt fluids secreted onto his skin, soaking through his clothes, burning like acid, and he realised that it was trying to dissolve him - it needed no mouth! He clasped his knife tightly in his hand and drove it as hard as he could into the spongy mass of its pale body. There was no resilience like flesh, but instead it seemed to absorb both the knife and his hand. He screamed again as the acid burned like fire, searing his hand, his chest, his neck. Bob pulled out the knife and plunged it into the wyrm again and again, but it seemed to have no effect, he could inflict no pain. The creature was huge, probably two feet taller than he was, and weighing probably twice as much. He tried to wriggle free but it had him fast, its fluids gluing him to both itself and the ground. His knife was surely in its innards, if it had any, but it seemed to make no difference. Then, as the wyrm slithered further up his body and up and over his head, he felt the sticky burning fluids across his face, seeping into his nostrils and mouth and throat as they forced their way in. All he could see was the white of its slug-like mass as it absorbed him, until his eyes burned away and were consumed like the rest of his body.

Come morning, with the fog lifted and a gentle breeze drifting across the lower slopes of the mountain, a group of hikers were making their away along the lakeside path when they came upon an old man packing away camping equipment near the edge of the water. He looked up at them as they approached, his face gnarled and creased with a heavy wrinkles.

"Did you get a good night's sleep here last night?" one of the hikers called, by way of a greeting.

"Aye, when the wind drops away," he said eventually, his voice deep and gruff. He was a heavy-set man, a barrel-like torso hidden away beneath his dark coat. It seemed strange that he should have such modern camping equipment, and a two-man tent at that. "What are you boys doing out here so far from home?"

The old man saw the hikers smirk to themselves for they were far from being boys. No matter, he thought, as he looked them up and down. They had fine clothes and backpacks; maybe this time there would be something left intact enough to fetch a decent price.

It's become the time and place to meet, an hour before midnight at the small hillock between the ring road and Peacock Farm. Henry is already here as I crest the rise, I can see his silhouette between the thinning trees. It's a short climb up the slope, not much to look at from the bottom, but it gets hold of my breath just the same.

"Is that you, Ted?" comes his voice out of the darkness.

"Aye, it's me," I call back.

It's January and cold, a hard dry cold that makes my breath visible in front of me, delicate clouds of white ether illuminated by the brightness of the moon. The long frost-covered grass, glistening silver by the same light, crunches beneath my boots, and where the grass has been nibbled away by rabbits or worn down by other walkers' boots, the mud beneath has turned as solid as concrete. It is a wonderful night though, nevertheless, and quiet. The motorway is less than four miles away, but its drone is muted almost to silence by the surrounding trees, and leaves the dark side of the hillock a silent shadowed void.

I step through the gap between the trees and come out on the side where we sit. Henry is in his usual spot, lying back in his fold-up picnic chair, wearing his thick winter coat with a blanket over his knees. He glances over as I set up my own fold-up chair, and then we both stare up at the sky. There is a feeling of unity in us doing this together, like a club that watches a secret part of the world while the rest of our kind sleeps.

"You've not missed much," Henry says plainly,

snorting back a wad of phlegm as a show of indifference to the night's paltry offering.

I make a murmur of acknowledgement before setting my bag down on the ground between us. The flask of coffee will be gratefully received in half an hour or so when the first of the cold finds its way in. And there are sandwiches too. We'll be here for a few hours or more. Each time I sit out here I think of something else to bring next time. Last week my cheeks went numb; I haven't worn it here but my balaclava is ready in the bag.

Settling into my chair, I lean back and take in the view of the heavens. The map of the stars is breathtaking, it always is, but on this side of the hillock, with the trees behind us and shielding a lot of residual light from the town, the sky becomes darker, which makes the stars glow brighter.

It's staggering to see just how much there is up there, given a sky as clear as this, and I want to say so to Henry, but that's not the way things are done. We need to stare in silence for a while, concentrate on patterns, examine constellations, in case something is amiss, some light in a different place to where it was the time before. That's how this works.

I believe UFO watching is big in America, people travelling for miles to reported abduction sites. I'm fairly new to it myself so I kind of take things as they come. I can't for the life of me remember what first started our initial conversation on UFO's, but it resulted in Henry and I coming out into the fields at night more and more to sit and watch the skies. I haven't seen a UFO yet, although I have seen a couple of shooting stars - meteorites burning up in our atmosphere, Henry tells me - but you never know.

"That light's moving," Henry says quietly, but with no real urgency.

I try to see where he's looking but it isn't clear. I want to ask him whereabouts in the sky but I don't. Finally he points vaguely upwards, nodding his head too.

"Not real quick, but you can see that it's moving."

I see something now, a single faint light, and Henry is right, it is moving, but not quickly.

"See that red light flashing next to the main one?" he goes on.

I murmur something vague.

"That means it's a satellite."

Henry's got a lot of books about what's up there, what roams around the atmosphere between our sky and space. Not just UFO books either. He showed me around his study a few months back and there's almost two whole bookshelves dedicated to this stuff. Astrology, physics, astro-physics, books about NASA, biographies of astronauts, you name it. I nodded quite a lot that afternoon, I can tell you. Personally I just like being out here. I don't expect ET to go skimming across the sky strapped to a kid's bike, and I don't expect Henry does either, but we meet here twice a week and sit and watch just the same.

I think that constellation of three stars up there is Orion. I like the name; it suits it somehow. I remember Henry telling me some stuff about Orion, about how it was quite important in Ancient Egypt. The pyramids at Giza are built in the same almost-straight line, and there's a narrow channel that runs from a tomb deep inside one of them right the way through hundreds of feet of stone, and guess what it points at? Yep, the constellation of Orion. That kind of stuff creeps me out, but in a good way. I've got a feeling that the Sphinx points to something as well, but don't quote me on that. I didn't get that from Henry but from a documentary on TV, so perhaps that's why I can't recall it exactly. I do remember this guy with a laptop trying to map the heaven's back to Ancient Egypt to see what they would have seen in the sky, and basically the Sphinx was looking out towards something, perhaps something to do with Leo, I don't know; in other words, it's not just pointing in one direction for no reason - it's got a purpose. Creepy.

My nose is already starting to get cold, my cheeks too, but it's too early to break out the coffee or the balaclava. I look over at Henry and see that he's still looking up. I do likewise, and lose myself in the map of stars once more, the romance of the glittering heavens washing swiftly over me, and I let it take me.

"I'd love to go up there," I say, without realising what I'm saying or that I'm even saying it aloud.

"Be nice, wouldn't it?" Henry replies.

His response surprises me. I'd not expected him to share such a whimsical fantasy.

"I heard that when they start commercial flights up into space," I continue, "a single ticket's gonna to set you back about twenty thousand pounds."

"Probably be nearer to forty," Henry says assuredly. "Those rockets aren't cheap to run, you know."

"Still, I'd sell my house if it would mean going up there, seeing space up close, without the clouds or city lights getting in the way."

"I'd be right there next to you," Henry says with a smile. Then adds with a sudden grin: "I went to one of those IMAX cinemas when I was in Australia, the ones with the panoramic domed screen. They had one of their special cameras on-board one of the shuttle flights and basically filmed space all around you. I sat and gazed around like a kid in a sweet superstore. I'd never experienced anything like that before. The film didn't last long, though, and the next showing was not for another four hours. But I waited, and I saw it again."

"Forty grand would be a good price to pay to be up there for real."

Henry nodded sagely, murmuring his approval.

"I'd go on the first shuttle too, just in case there were problems and they scrapped the whole idea."

Henry laughs at this. It's good here when the mood is right.

"Like in the movies," I go on. "Things go wrong all the time. Something explodes; there's no way back."

"And you'd want to be on a crate that had problems like that?"

"Sure," I say, without really thinking this through. "I'd say my goodbyes to people down here before leaving, you know, just in case something did go wrong, but to die up there would be wonderful."

"And you wouldn't care about not coming back?"

I turn and see that he's looking at me like I'm crazy. I guess I was kind of hoping that he'd be right there with me on this, to die where you long to be, rather than in a dank hospital bed lying in a pool of your own urine. There were some good things to be said about old age, but dodgy bladders wasn't one of them. A blaze of glory every time.

"What I mean is," I try to explain to a still bemused Henry, "if something happened like the landing gear didn't work any more, or the engines had died, I'd rather stay in space and die than try to return and burn up in the atmosphere. Spend my last few days gazing at the depths of space whilst finishing off the in-flight snacks, you know?"

Henry says nothing for a while after this, and we stare up at the sky in silence, watching the stars glimmer brightly. I hope he understands what I was trying to say, because I don't think I explained it well, and that his silence means that he is thinking about it.

The cold is starting to creep through my boots and into my feet. My thoughts wander to the flask of coffee in my bag, but I don't want to move; not yet. I'm glad that there's no wind tonight, otherwise I would have been frozen within minutes, and sitting out in a dark field when you're cold to the bone does not make this fun.

I find The Plough and look at each of the stars that make up the constellation. It's the biggest constellation I know, and I stare at it for a while. Something nagged at me the first time I saw this again on one of my meetings with Henry, and it took me a while to realise what the problem was. I'm sure, but not deadly certain, that when I was young The Plough was horizontal, and now it's vertical, it's handle pointing straight down to the ground. This sight kind of fits in with what the guy with the laptop on TV was intimating, that the heavens rotate and change over time - from our perspective, that is, what with us living on a swivelling planet - but I'm not about to pin that fact on a dodgy childhood memory either. The other nagging thought, and this one's a doozy, is that the middle two stars are significantly dimmer than I recall. Again, I'm basing this on an old memory, but if that's true, and those two stars are dimmer, does that mean that those two stars are dying? And if so, taking into account the speed of light, have they already burned out and all I can see now is a ghost of their former selves?

Sitting in fields looking up at the night's sky can hurt your head at times, but it's a good kind of hurt. It makes me feel like I'm performing some kind of workout for the mind, get the grey cells hurdling or pole-vaulting or whatever. I glance across at Henry again but he's not looking at The Plough. He's busy scanning the entire sky now in slow steady sweeps, his head rolling from side to side like windscreen wipers set on real slow. I'm not sure if he's humouring me by having me here, or whether it's better than sitting here on your own, but he knows so much more than I do. He says it's a UFO thing, coming here, but I'm not convinced. He doesn't say much when we're out here, but when he does it seems like he just likes to sit here just as much as I do. I'd love to prompt him about the two dying stars in The Plough, but I'm not sure how to start. I can't point out something that to astrologers might be bloody obvious - did you know that star is dimmer than it used to be? Of course, you idiot, doesn't everyone?

I glance at my watch furtively and see that I've only been here twenty minutes. Not time for the coffee yet. "Henry?" I ask suddenly, my voice loud and breaking the tranquillity of the darkness around us. "Do you think that each of those stars is a sun with it's own system of planets revolving round them like ours?"

This sounds a bit lame, sounded better in my head, but it makes me think about how lonely our planet must be in space.

"That's a nice idea," Henry says, "and one that's been hypothesised frequently."

"So someone could be sitting in a field on a planet revolving around that star," I continue, pointing to the brightest one above us, "wondering about life on planets revolving around our sun?"

"And how far would they have evolved too?"

It's almost a science fiction comment from Henry, and it catches me off guard for a moment. I didn't think he was a science fiction kind of a guy, not where stars and space was concerned. I love to let my imagination drift when I'm out here, so I test him.

"If you had a telescope that could see right down onto the surface of another planet, what would like to see?"

"What do you mean?" he asks, turning to look sideways at me.

"Would you like to see versions of us, two guys in a field looking back with their own telescope? Or medieval knights roaming the land? Cities or interstellar war? What?"

Henry puffs out his cheeks and rolls back in his chair with a wonderful contemplation. To see this takes a huge weight off me, releasing a whole torrent of thoughts and whimsy that I hope I can now unleash upon him.

"Aliens would be interesting to see," he says. "To know that something else is out there. Something different from us."

It's an expected response.

"And what if you saw a 1920's New York? Something mundane."

Henry glances across at me again, with a look that says I might have gone too far too soon. It seems he doesn't care much for parallel universes, or benign gods seeding planets at will. Comes from having that many books in his study, I guess. Or not watching Star Trek.

Personally, I could think this stuff up all night, sitting here just staring up at the stars, gazing up at a sky that's seen millions of years of history, itself been looked at in wonder for as long as there have been creatures with eyes on this planet or any other.

Take any period in history and surely everyone will have gazed up at the night's sky with wonder. It's the stuff of dreams and imagination. What are these pinpricks of light that come back to us every time it gets dark? We tell ourselves now that we know what they are, but we know nothing more than the Ancient Greeks or the wide-eyed natives of the primal rainforest. We say they're suns belonging to other solar systems, but that's just the best guess going, the same as any other period in history. I can pick any one of those stars and imagine a series of planets circling it, imagine a habitable land on each of them, imagine people riding horses, farming, listening to a town square proclamation. In much the same way, I can imagine myself hundreds of years ago, camping out beneath a clear night's sky, a day's ride from Camelot or wherever, staring up with bountiful wonder. That's the real beauty of me coming here to sit with Henry.

I glance across and find Henry looking at me with an odd expression on his face, as though he's thought of something worth sharing but unsure whether I'm worthy of it; either that or he's just discovered a chunk of meat between two molars. It turns out to be the former, and he opens his mouth to speak.

"Do you know Albert?" he asks me slowly.

"The old guy from the garage?"

"That's him," Henry says, his eyes now eerily

focussed. "He was walking his labrador over near Bill Hill a few years back, late, the dog's last whizz of the night, and he saw something up in the sky."

"Lights?" I offer. I'm not sure what the outcome of this is going to be but I'm pretty sure where it's going.

"Lights at first," Henry says, lowering his voice a little, but heaven knows there's nobody within ear shot of us, not at this hour or with this cold. "There was one single bright light hovering over the tops of the houses, and as he stood and watched, it slowly blinked out. I remember him telling me how quickly his heart began racing at this, but that was only the start. That single bright light blinked back on again, forty feet above those rooftops, and it was big. Then a second one blinked on, quite some distance away, and just hovered there like the first."

"And neither of them moved?"

"Just hovered."

Henry runs the back of his hand across his nose as if to emphasise the enormity of this, his eyes still utterly focussed.

"Those two lights stayed on for about five minutes, without moving an inch, before they finally blinked out altogether."

"And that was all he saw?"

"That was all he saw."

As far as UFO encounters go, it doesn't seem much to me, but Henry is adamant about the seriousness of this sighting. As I picture those lights in my head, all I can think of are those huge spotlights that police helicopters have suspended beneath them. Perhaps they were targeting a criminal somewhere beneath them. I want to offer this, but I don't want to take anything away from Albert's story. And besides, the more I think about it, the more it seems unlikely that two police helicopters would remain motionless for five whole minutes.

"My father," Henry says suddenly, jolting me out of my thoughts with a start, "saw something too. He'll tell you now that it was a dream, or that he never saw anything at all, but I remember him telling me about it, and I know abductees have had their memories washed."

I've heard of aliens 'stealing time', as a documentary I'd seen had called it, but I'm sceptical about the whole issue. There are plenty of things I could say about it, plenty of things I could offer into the conversation, but I'm going to leave this one alone.

"Do you know anything about an alien craft that's shaped like a V, red lights flashing along each of its undersides?"

I shake my head. I know of saucers and pods and the Roswell weather balloon, but a V is something new.

"It was well documented a couple of years ago," he informs me a little testily, as if I know nothing about this stuff, which to be fair is mostly true. "The whole of the west coast of America saw it, thousands of sightings in the space of two nights."

I shrug and shake my head again. I haven't seen it.

Henry purses his lips with disdain, and again that expression comes over his face, as though perhaps I might not be the right person for him to share this with. And yet he relents, perhaps realising that I'm the only one he can share this with, and continues with the story about his father.

"He told me that he woke one night," he says, "because he needed to take a leak. Now, he always sleeps with the curtains open so that he can wake with the dawn. But as he passes the window, he sees this V shape of flashing red lights. He told me about how he watched it for a while, even as this craft approached the house across the lawn. But when he told me, his account was vivid. He told me how many lights there were, how big the damn craft was, how long it waited outside the window for. And I'll tell you, I was more than a little bit scared about how real it sounded. But when I asked him about it a few days later, he looked puzzled, and said that it had happened months before. He was vague about what he had seen, and wouldn't dwell on the subject. A month later and he denied the whole thing; never saw it, doesn't know what I'm talking about. I tell you, I remember because I know what he told me, and if what they say is true, and that these things do rob you of your memories, then that's proof right there. I remember. He doesn't."

I'm not totally convinced, but the hairs on the back of my neck are standing up, so make of that what you will. Henry turns away finally and glances uneasily back up at the sky. I follow his gaze, and find myself looking at the stars a little differently. Are they all stars? Are any of them red? The sky is just as it was before, but there's a feeling of unease now that wasn't there before. I half look back at Henry sitting there in his old canvas folding chair. Is this why he comes out here twice a week, hoping to perhaps catch a glimpse of something that his father inadvertently saw because of a full bladder one night?

I return to the stars myself now, and try to forget about Albert's sighting over Bill Hill, or Henry's father's view through his bedroom window, and try instead to remember the fantasies that I'd grown in my own head before this conversation started.

I'm not a UFO kind of guy, but I'm not going to tell Henry that, because I like him, and it's as good an excuse as any to sit here in a field like a fool and watch the open sky. Maybe I'll see something later, maybe I won't, but I can't help thinking that perhaps my secret dreams and whimsy have been tainted forever. Some part of me has changed, and I don't know whether that's for the better or not.

# Notes

When I was bought my first Stephen King collection of short stories (I believe it was Nightmares and Dreamscapes) I loved everything in it. But I found something wonderful at the back, a section called notes. It was basically just some inside information about the stories within the collection - how and why they came to be written, amusing anecdotes about them, you get the picture - and I don't know whether it was the writer in me, or the reader in me, but I loved all that. It was kind of like a personal one on one, just the author and the reader, and to discover a few insights into the stories I'd just read was astonishing. So basically what follows here is a similar kind of thing.

The stories in this collection are taken over a span of about seven years; some I think are good, and some I think are exceptional. A few of them I really love, but I won't name them here. Not everything that I've written has been included, because a lot of it was not fit for human consumption, and those are the ones that will probably never see the light of day. And for good reason.

If these notes are your cup of tea, then I hope you get as much out of them as I did out of Nightmares and Dreamscapes. If not, then it doesn't matter because you've already read the stories you bought the book for. I just thought I'd throw this bit in as a little something extra.

### The Business Of Fear

Okay, the lead story and the title of the book: I'm sure this kind of thing happens to a lot of professional writers, although probably never to this extreme. The thought must surely occur, at least, and because of the nature of horror it must be both conscious and sought after, anticipating the ramifications of playing with people's minds. Now I'll try my hardest to scare you, to make you see things moving in the darkness that perhaps you wouldn't ordinarily have seen. To take that one step, or many steps, further is to step into Kingsley Steven's shoes. The result of that is to pay the price for being too good.

### Bad Kitty

A lot of people have told me how they've looked at their beloved pets differently after reading this story, so this has got to be one of my favourite stories just for that. Cats just do their own damn thing, and then can turn on you when they feel like it. Have you ever been stroking one on your lap only to have it sink its needle-like claws into the meat of your leg for no good reason? Strange creatures, cats, and a staple horror icon.

### The Garages

Yes, this is my street, with a couple of changes here and a dash of fiction there, and of course no murders as far as I know, although we do have our share of oddballs as any street does. This is a real short short story and I love it for that. There's no character definition here and no plot development of any kind. It's a simple short piece that's meant to unnerve you and quickly. It's homely but close to the bone and features just another normal-looking guy in another normal-looking street.

## Otherworld
This story began life as a novel, but hit a dead end part way through. I think it still works as a story in its own right, and I like it a lot, which is why it has been included here.

## What Came In The Floodwater
One of those 'under the bed' chillers that crawls beneath your skin and stays there. Maybe not one of the most original storylines, but classic horror fiction, I think. If it gets you checking around your bedroom before you put out the light, or wondering what that sound really is up in the attic, then I'm satisfied.

## The Man Beneath The Carpet
This was a friend's recurring childhood nightmare, and with the exception of a few embellishments here and there, it's pretty much just as she used to dream it. She told me how it was irrational, to be scared by a dream of seeing someone or something moving about beneath her carpet, but we know, dear reader, that rationality never halts terror, especially at night when we are at our most vulnerable. Pure horror story fodder. Thank you Catherine.

## The Ghost Behind Me
An odd one this, and I'll leave it to your imagination whether this is really about a malevolent ghost or just a blot on a guy's retina. If you turn your head real quick, you can sometimes see a shape just beyond your vision, something that almost dares you to see it. Is

that a spirit or just a distortion of your own sight. And what would happen if you thought the former and then began to almost see it more and more?

## Man In A Red Suit
A grisly Christmas tale and one I particularly like, if only for the fact that there's a glistening red suit - I mean, come on, this is a horror story, why else would it be red?

## Nine Forty Two
Why should stories have rational or explained endings? Weirdness happens because it does. Does this story need an explanation, because I'm sorry to tell you that I don't have one for you? We've all experienced some kind of strange phenomena in our lives that we can't explain, and perhaps deep down we don't want it resolved in case it becomes just some other mundane occurrence in our lives. This is a tale of the paranormal, and I like it because it captures just one guy who's passing through in what is obviously a timeless mystery.

## Angel Of The Secret Fires
I wrote this story a long time ago, but having reread it for this collection, I discovered a wonderful simplicity that I've somehow lost from my later writing. There's something about it that sings to me, and for that reason I wanted it here in printed form. Its imagery sits very vividly in my head, and the influence of angels and demons upon our simple mortal lives is one that is not going to go away.

## Desires, Dreams And Deals

Another old story, this one, but one that I think belongs in this collection too. It's a classic tale of selling one's soul, and I love the torturer's side of it too.

## Coachman's Drive

This is one of two horror stories in this book that have nothing to do with the other demons and monsters that inhabit the other stories, but have everything to do with the monstrous nature of man. Ropeman is the other. There's little to be said about these two stories, other than they just kind of wrote themselves. I don't think there's anything more horrifying or sickening to the decent hearted than what some individuals can think of to do to other people, especially to kids. Our imaginations are all susceptible to what might be lurking in the darkness waiting to get us, but to have it reduced to the level of what the man in the next house, or the next room, might do to us, can be frightening in a whole other way.

## Afraid Of The Dark

I like this story for the shadow creatures, but I openly accept that the accuracy of the medical side of things may let it down somewhat. I'm extraordinarily lazy when it comes to research and accurate details, which is why I stay clear of it as much as possible. I prefer to deal with regular people in regular settings. This story could have been written in a hospital ward from the consultant doctor's point of view, and I could have spent weeks researching current medical practice and ways of working. But I don't write technical manuals, and I would never compromise the human element or the regular Joe for jargon. However, I'd rather leave it out than be wrong.

## The Devil Owns A Xerox

I know my way extensively around photocopiers, I've been running them for years, but to write about them was weird. Write what you know - that's the usual advice for writers - and so I did. I'm not sure how well it works as a story in its own right, but as an exercise, I think it works okay.

## Passion

This one's a doozy. I've had people get sexually excited by reading this on a train and having to put it away for being too erotic; I've had people telling me their emotions were twisted from being turned on and then being repulsed (which is exactly my intention); and I've had people say how much they love vampire stories. To this last comment I've said, "Hang on, who said he was a vampire? I never said he was a vampire," and they've looked at me quizzically. To this day I still sit on the fence. Just because he drinks blood and bites and devours flesh, does not necessarily make him a vampire. I'll leave it to you to make your own decision.

## You Know They Got A Hell Of A Band

This was the title of one of Stephen King's stories, and although the title inspired this story almost immediately in its entirety, my version has virtually no connection to his, but has got everything to do with rock music and how it drags me right back to my youth. You see, I was that bass player and I loved playing up on that stage, and how many musicians have desired to play for all eternity? If you've never done it, you probably can't get the vibe I tried to get across. If you have been there as I have, and are perhaps still part of a band, then I hope it comes across. Jeanette told me this story was obvious in how it progressed, and maybe it is, but I still like it if only for the fact that a lot of my memories have been included within it.

## Swinley Forest

This is one of the places where we walk our dogs, and I've seen these wigwams made of sticks, and let me tell you, they can be scary at times.

## The Black Woods

I think we've all driven through unlit wooded stretches at night, and perhaps we've all thought we've seen faces looking back at us. Just thinking about it now and writing this down has broken gooseflesh over my body. I used to live out in the country and I always seemed to be driving through it at night, but luckily I never had the misfortune to break down at night. I'm not sure how I would have coped, walking those last few miles alone in the dark.

## Chaos Of Calm

Too short to be a novella, this one, and although one of my first attempts at a book, I think it still has some good things happening. I've included it here because it's kind of like a milestone for me, a progression from where I started to where I am now.

## Kiddies Rides

There's something spooky about those funfair rides that kids are invited to climb up into, something not right about their fixed grins and wide staring eyes. Maybe next time you come across them, or maybe hoist your own kids up into them, you'll see what I mean. Perhaps you already have and now steer clear of them.

Ropeman
The second 'real life' horror story. A lot of it plays like a film in my head - the snow that's an unsurpassable obstacle, the image of the hangman's victims that cannot be evaded - so it is very much a visual story for me. There is some light relief from the weight of the child pornographer, but the dog is also an important plot developer.

The Card Player
This started out as a couple of entirely separate ideas that sat in a pile for a number of years, before finally being dug out and incarnated as the story that they were both meant to be. I liked both nuggets - which were basically just scene fragments and a bit of dialogue - but I had no idea what to do with them. For years they sat around as nothing but fragments, until one day I tried to work on them again, and then it all came together very quickly. I love writing when that happens. It's kind of like an explosion that takes a long time to write down, but which seems like it's continually sparking and travelling outwards.

The Hikers
This was a culmination of a vivid dream - the white wyrms - and Jeanette's brother-in-law's disastrous weekend camping trip. The two came together seamlessly and the whole story was written in its entirety, pretty much as you see it here, in a single day.

The UFO Watchers
This probably doesn't belong in a horror collection, and I wouldn't say that it's science fiction either, but it's mostly how I feel when I take my dogs out for their last

walk across the open fields every night. I get taken over by a wonderful serenity, surrounded by both peace and nature, and walking beneath clear starlit skies is sometimes too exhilarating to describe. I've tried to capture something of how I feel in the story, and the title is ambiguous because it has nothing really to do with UFO's at all. The story, originally, was going to be about a group of men who just met up and talked about things, the subjects of which weren't important; it was just about male bonding, about getting out of the house, about just sitting in a field and talking. There was never meant to be any UFO's. However, having said that, I have seen some unexplained lights in the sky. Now I'm sure nobody can walk around a field close to midnight every night and not see something. I'm not going to say what or where or when, but let's just say that they put the chills up me, and we'll leave it at that.


Okay, so that's the first collection done. I hope you enjoyed it, because I know I did.

Take care of yourself until we meet again, and remember to check the lock on the back door, check the glint in your neighbour's eye, and more importantly, check the abyss of darkness that lurks under your bed before you go to sleep at night. And carry something heavy too, because you never know just what might be hiding in there.


Paul Stuart Kemp
England, 17th February 2003

# The Unholy

## Paul Stuart Kemp

In an old forester's cottage in rural southern England, Irene and Michael Rider, a young married couple, decide one night to 'play the ouija'. What they invite into their new home begins to take its toll not only on their lives, but also on the lives of those around them, and the lives of their, as yet, unborn children.

Trapped in a world in which they no longer have choices, they struggle to raise the idyllic family of which they've always dreamed.

The birds in the trees are watching them, waiting for some eternal event, but the ancient evil that sits behind their eyes has time on its hands, time enough to wait forever.

Paul Stuart Kemp is one of England's darkest writers. The Unholy takes the reader into his darkest world yet; a place of demonic possession, of nightmarish visions and creatures, and the destruction of an entire family. But only at the heart of this world can true values be found: the resilience of love, the sanctity of marriage, and what it means to be human.

ISBN 0 9538215 4 4

# Bloodgod

## Paul Stuart Kemp

An archaeological expedition to a desert region uncovers both an ancient temple with strange hieroglyphics as well as an old man with a story to tell. Merricah speaks of a creature that decimated most of two tribes, and relays the whereabouts of a magical box that contains the Master of Kar'mi'shah. He has remained in isolation inside the buried temple for hundreds of years, waiting for the tribes to return, and for someone to release his Master.

Jenner Hoard is a thief recently released from prison. Montague, his benefactor, does not want him to quit working for him, and already has two lucrative jobs lined up for an anonymous customer, a deal involving the Blood Of The Ancients, and the theft of a mysterious box from an apartment building in London.

Times have never been more desperate for the vampire community living in the darkest depths of London. Alexia is one such vampire who has a brutal encounter with The Howler of Westminster after a butchered corpse is found floating in the Thames.

Human vampire hunters, known as Skulkers, have become more skillful and connected over the years, and find easy prey in those demons who are too careless about their actions. Join Alexia as she struggles to survive in a dark and foreboding world, where even demons suffer anguish, and in death there is still a fight.

ISBN 0 9538215 2 8

# Eden

## Paul Stuart Kemp

There is a gateway to paradise, and it exists in the most unlikely of places, the very heart of London. If someone owns it, it can be bought. If no one owns it, it can be claimed. The race is on to hold possession of the eighth wonder of the known world, and the name of that eighth wonder shall be called Eden.

Jenner Hoard is now a prophet for what few vampires remain in London, guiding those that would not open his throat towards the gateway that would lead them home. Catherine Calleh, the most vicious of all vampires, is forced to endure the mortal world she loathes as she searches for her dead husband now risen from the grave. Her journey between worlds will not be without suffering and loss, but only at its end will she learn the truth about love, hate and devotion, as well as the responsibility of existence itself.

Paul Stuart Kemp is one of England's darkest writers. Eden is the long awaited sequel to his best-selling novel Bloodgod, and continues the reader's descent into the dark underworld of the vampire gods of Kar'mi'shah.

ISBN 0 9538215 6 0

# Ascension

## Paul Stuart Kemp

Hampton, England 1172: After witnessing the death of her family in a frenzied witch-drowning ritual, Gaia, an eight year old girl, flees for her life. Alone and afraid, she stumbles upon a magical young boy who takes her on a journey to meet Calista, a spirit capable of harnessing both dreams and time, with promises of so much more.

Makara, Kenya 2589: There are desperate times at the end of the human race. Kiala is a man living at one of the last stations on Earth, a planet where all life has been eradicated by snow and ice. With his future hinted at, could he hold the key to preserving what little life remains, and if so, why is Calista intent on stopping him?

London, England 1994: When Carly Maddison's fiance is suddenly abducted under very strange circumstances and her fleeing brother is accused of his demise, she finds herself trapped in the depths of a dark and secret world. Her love for them both draws her deeper into that world, and if she is to discover both its rules and, ultimately, its solution, then she must face the past as well as the future, in order to learn truths that she would previously have thought unimaginable.

Witchcraft, alien abduction, ritual murders; all unfathomable mysteries, all with a human heart. Paul Stuart Kemp's science fiction horror fantasy takes the reader on an extraordinary journey, where such mysteries are found to be sown into the human soul, unable to be removed, and unable to be revoked.

ISBN 0 9538215 0 1